Dorian Mode is best known as one of Australia's leading jazz musicians. Born in Sydney in 1966, he was schooled in the Eastern Suburbs and sat for a degree in Composition at the Sydney Conservatorium of Music. He was eventually signed to EMI and released *Rebirth of the Cool*. The album was nominated for best jazz composition later that year.

After suffering a nervous breakdown, he lost his record contract, and was unable to compose music. He floated from job to job until he found himself writing copy for advertisements and brochures 'for insignificant products and services no one really wanted or needed'. Sadly, he was adept at it. He discovered he could write.

Dorian eventually returned to music, signing to ABC Records and releasing *A Café of Broken Dreams*, which received critical acclaim. He also started writing his first novel.

He has recently written an autobiographical screenplay (currently in production) based on his time at the Conservatorium, entitled *The Mozart Maulers*. Its director calls it 'a laugh-out-loud comedy that is Australia's answer to the *Full Monty*'.

This is his first novel.

The CD *A Café in Venice* is available at Dorian's web site or at all leading record stores.

Dorian's web site is www.dorianmode.com

A CAFÉ IN VENICE
Dorian Mode

PENGUIN BOOKS

Penguin Books Australia Ltd
487 Maroondah Highway, PO Box 257
Ringwood, Victoria 3134, Australia
Penguin Books Ltd
Harmondsworth, Middlesex, England
Penguin Putnam Inc.
375 Hudson Street, New York, New York 10014, USA
Penguin Books Canada Limited
10 Alcorn Avenue, Toronto, Ontario, Canada M4V 3B2
Penguin Books (NZ) Ltd
Cnr Rosedale and Airborne Roads, Albany, Auckland, New Zealand
Penguin Books (South Africa) (Pty) Ltd
5 Watkins Street, Denver Ext 4, 2094, South Africa
Penguin Books India (P) Ltd
11. Community Centre, Panchsheel Park, New Delhi 110 017, India

First published by Penguin Books Australia Ltd 2001

10 9 8 7 6 5 4 3 2 1
Copyright © Dorian Mode 2001

The moral right of the author has been asserted.

All rights reserved. Without limiting the rights under copyright reserved above, no part of this publication may be reproduced, stored in or introduced into a retrieval system, or transmitted, in any form or by any means (electronic, mechanical, photocopying, recording or otherwise), without the prior written permission of both the copyright owner and the above publisher of this book.

Designed by Susannah Low, Penguin Design Studio
Cover photograph (café) by Roman Cerny
Cover photograph (piano) by Getty Images
Digital imaging by Susannah Low and Ben Evison
Typeset in 10/14 Sabon by Midland Typesetters, Maryborough, Victoria
Printed and bound in Australia by McPherson's Printing Group, Maryborough, Victoria

This is a work of fiction. Names, characters, places, and incidents either are the products of the author's imagination or are used fictitiously. The author points out with great respect that the indigenous stories contained in this novel are not intended to be exact replicas of the original tales.

National Library of Australia
Cataloguing-in-Publication data:

Mode, Dorian.
A café in Venice

ISBN 0 14 100319 7.

I. Title.
A823.4

This project has been assisted by the Commonwealth Government through the Australia Council, its arts funding and advisory body.

www.penguin.com.au

ACKNOWLEDGEMENTS

I would like to thank Mushroom Music for permission to reproduce my lyrics in this novel.

I would especially like to thank my publisher, Julie Gibbs, for her belief in my talent and her fabulous sense of humour; my editor, Heather Cam, for her witty, erudite guidance; and assistant editor, Sophie Ambrose, for her much-valued suggestions.

For Lydia, the truth in my life

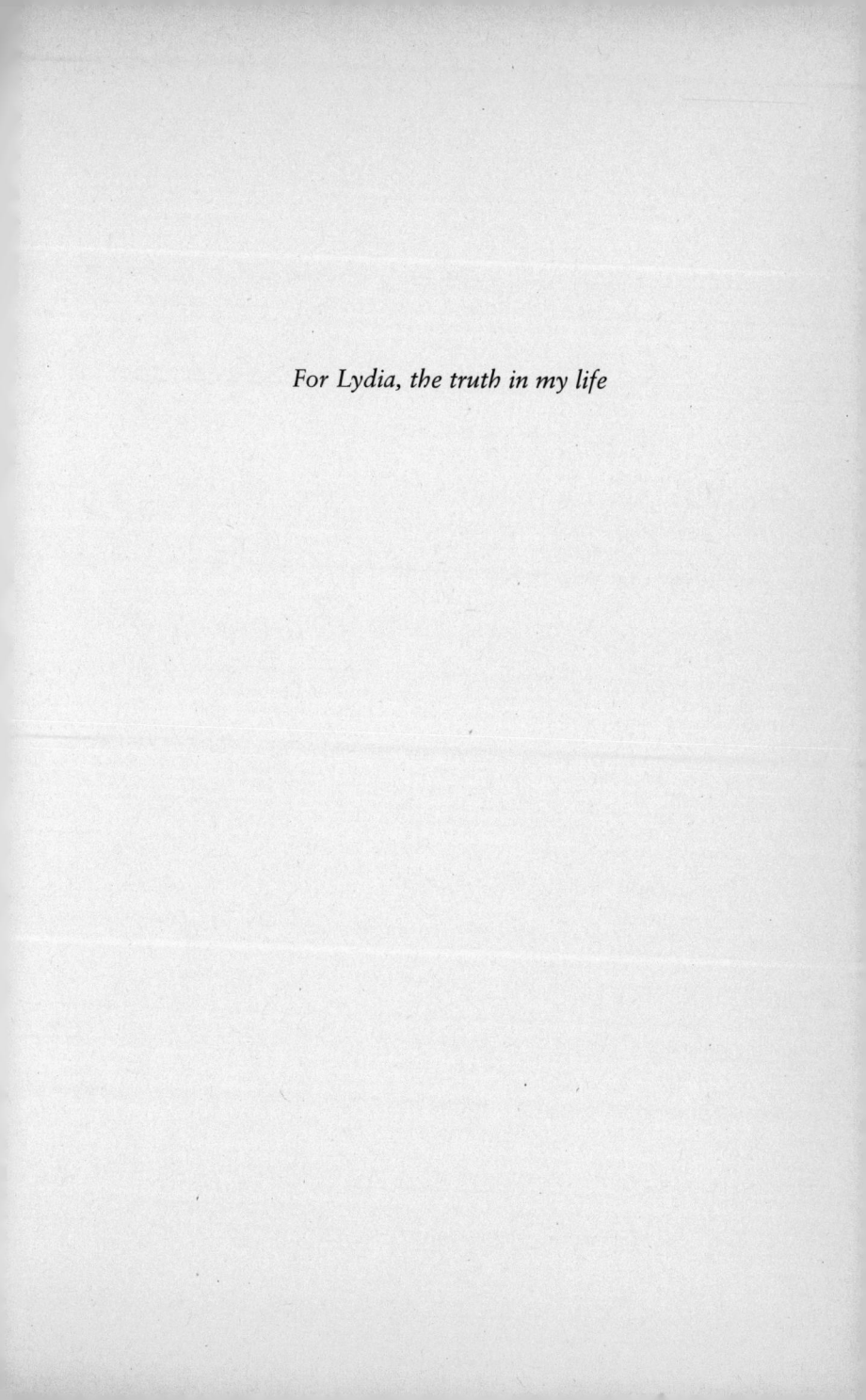

PART

ONE

THE PHONE CALL FROM DREAMTIME

∽

THE IDEA OF A MAJOR label offering me a recording contract was so far removed from my imagination that having a foursome with Elle MacPherson, Liz Hurley and a bowl of ricotta cheese seemed more of a possibility.

Let's face it, why would one of the 'majors' offer a local jazz musician a record deal? Besides, I was a mess. I carried around so many bottles of pills that if I ran for the bus, people around me would spontaneously break into the lambada. So when I received a phone call one sleepy afternoon to meet with Felix Smedly, the head of A&R for Delta Records, for a 'cup of coffee', it was met with a mixture of excitement, trepidation and relays to the toilet. I had actually met the record executive at a party once. He was disguised as a human being. Smedly was famous for leading musicians up the garden path and leaving them knee-deep in horse shit. He once spent over $50 000 in demos on a fledgling band without ever actually signing them. Finally, on a whim, he demanded that the singer have a nose job in order for the band to 'make it in Europe'. (Continent of small noses apparently.) His lackey dragged the poor girl down to the clinic, but she baulked at the last minute. He punted the hapless band the following day. Hard to believe? True story.

I told myself rationally that this 'meeting' was probably nothing. An ego session. I was quite aware that Smedly often got off on the fact that when he spoke, a thousand tongues were enthusiastically inserted into his anal passage. So naturally I was keen that nobody should know of this meeting in case it turned out to be a waste of time. After all, Smedly had merely intimated that he wanted to have a 'cup of coffee' with me, no more. What I didn't know at the time was that what Smedly usually meant by a 'cup of coffee' was: I'm half interested in talking to you, let's find out how far *your* tongue will extend up my ass. And make no mistake about it, I was prepared to jam it right up there. Although I was hoping he'd offer me a glass of wine first.

Smedly didn't actually make the call. His assistant made the initial contact. It was fortuitous because, thinking it was a practical joke, I was my usual, weird, flippant self. Most people find me funny. Mainly people on long-term medication. However, Smedly's deadpan assistant was less than amused. Eventually I explained to her that I thought it had been a friend playing a joke and she understood. The appointment was set for Monday morning and I was left wondering why the hell they wanted to see me. I had a theory.

My girlfriend Jenny had recently hustled a full-page review on me in the weekend paper. The headline ran: 'The new cool'. The editorial was flattering. For a jazz musician, I was a little different at the time. My music was deliberately simple. While other jazz musicians were writing songs using the Lydian concept or polyrhythms, or around the tri-tone substitutions, I was writing songs about people who worked on fishing trawlers or girls who worked in dress shops. The audiences connected with my music, but the 'jazz mafia' was less than impressed. I hated elitism in the arts and they hated me. And they weren't shy about telling me that a bevy of other musicians deserved the editorial more than I did. And they were probably right. But they didn't have a girlfriend who worked at the *Herald*. It certainly was a coup. Jenny pulled serious strings to get Humphrey Duddle (the paper's leading music critic) down to the gig. So that's why I got the call from Delta, I reasoned.

Later that afternoon, I mulled things over. I put on a Bill Evans record and pondered. I listened to the long shhhhh of the brushes against the snare drum. The smell of my poky flat was an aromatic blend of dirty laundry and dirty laundry. Perhaps it was time to do the laundry. I went to make a cup of coffee. I checked the cupboard. A cockroach darted out. I soaked it in a white cloud of bug spray and shut the cupboard.

Shit. No coffee.

I dropped my foot on the pedal of the kitchen bin. It reluctantly revealed its contents like a toddler with a mouthful of stolen sweets. Sitting on top of the week's refuse was the old coffee filter and its remains. I looked around. Why did I do this? It didn't make any sense, I lived alone. Perhaps it was out of guilt and loathing for what I was about to do. Perhaps it was a moment of bourgeois pretense. Perhaps it was that crick in my neck from driving. Yes, it was the crick in my neck from driving. I rolled my neck and picked up the soggy filter and, after removing a spiralling mandarin peel from the centre, defiantly placed the dregs into the machine. I started going over the telephone conversation in my mind again. I felt excited and paced about. Before long, some beige water dribbled into the pot.

I looked around the apartment and sighed. A single, damp room with a cramped kitchen and a leaking toilet that hissed continuously in A flat. The sort of apartment oily real-estate agents called a 'bachelor apartment'. What they mean is: if you brought a woman home, the relationship would end. Not the kind of pad a famous recording artist would live in. There I go again. I promised myself I wouldn't do that. It's probably nothing. Put the damn call out of your head! The record hissed to a finish.

My piano listed against the mould-green wall. The rickety, yellow and ebony keys drew a bag-lady smile. A tired aspidistra drooped on top. Its brown-edged, psoriatic leaves were being eaten by some parasite, but it looked pleased. In an act of resignation it decided that being eaten alive was better than living in my apartment and listening to my tedious compositions. Beneath the plant was an athenaeum of manuscript paper containing scrappy, half-baked ideas.

I dragged my cup over to the piano and played a chord I thought I'd heard on the Bill Evans record. My ear never failed me. It was the wrong chord. I held the notes. They resonated through the sour apartment. I plucked some lyrics from the top of the piano that I'd been working on. A vignette about two people who meet on Oxford Street, and break up on Oxford Street. I decided to call the song 'Oxford Street'.

We accidentally met on Taylor Square,
Both trying to be charming yet debonair,
The Mardis Gras was humming out of tune,
As we gently kissed beneath a wanton moon . . .

Not bad, I thought. Perhaps I'll record it with Delta. There I go again. Stop! I couldn't resist running through the phone call again. Maybe they just want me to play a little piano on some pop star's album. Maybe I should ring the Musician's Union to find out what sort of bread I should ask for. I don't want to get hustled. I looked around for the *Yellow Pages*. Unable to find it, I wandered over to the mirror and looked at my moth-eaten face. It left a lot to be desired. It didn't look like the face of a thirty-something on the verge of stardom. More a forty-something after hearing about the death of his labrador. I stood back a little so the acne scars would move out of immediate focus. My liquid brown eyes looked tired in the scaly glass.

'We'd like to see you for a cup of coffee, Mr Shoesmith . . . hmmm,' I told the mirror. I flicked my limp, black hair.

I started to get excited about the phone call again. I couldn't help it. I thought about calling Jenny with the news. Then changed my mind. I guess I should tell you about Jenny.

Jenny Harris is a competent journalist in her early thirties. She writes for the business section of the *Herald*, but occasionally scribes the odd review of some unimportant gig or other. She much prefers the latter, but has a vast knowledge of the world collectively known as 'big business' and her editor, recognising this gift, is reluctant to remove her from that section entirely. So he throws her the odd bone in the way of a concert ticket for the purpose of review. As you've guessed, this is where Jenny and I first met.

Jenny is an ambitious person and becomes quite frustrated with my lacklustre efforts to further my own career. Especially as we have talked of marriage and a family. I have great ideas about my career. I was always good at talking over a short black about what I was going to do, but never good at actually doing anything about it. She is always on at me, saying things like: you're throwing your life away, think about your future, practise positive thinking, etc. I wouldn't mind but I wish she'd wait until we finished making love.

I played a minor ninth chord on the piano and reflected on our last conversation. We had met at a favourite café just around from her office.

'These days, if you haven't made it by the time you're in your thirties, you can kiss your career goodbye, Gordon,' she said through a frothy cappuccino. 'Are you listening to me, Gordon, or have you popped off into your imagination, again?'

'Yes, yes, I'm listening.' There were those words again: 'make it'. I looked around at the waiter. He was wearing a pair of those aqua blue sunglasses that people wear indoors these days in case they open the fridge and suddenly become blinded for life. Had *he* 'made it'? He seemed pretty happy: burning focaccia and making coffee that was so strong it made you instantly crap yourself, and if you asked for a weaker one he could look at you like you came from Dubbo. Perhaps he was doing an Arts degree and was planning to 'make it' in the near future? By virtue of my staring, he flopped over to our table in his Italian sandals.

'Everything cool, folks?'

We nodded.

'Why does everybody have to make it?' I asked her.

'It's called *making* something of your life, Gordon. It's what we were put on earth to do. Move forward with our lives.'

'You sound like your old man when you talk like that.'

She remained silent.

'What do you want me to do, Jen?'

'What about those jingles you did for Dad's agency? They were so funny!'

'My uncle wrote those.'

'You wrote them, Gordon.'

'I hated doing that and you know it.'

'You were good at it.'

'That's why.'

She shook her head and sighed.

'I'm happy just being a musician, Jen. I'm happy with who I am and what I've got. And with who I've got and what I am. And vice versa.'

'You're nobody and achieved nothing. Kick back, enjoy it.'

'You should write Hallmark cards.'

I tried to reason with Jenny that afternoon that, for me, creating art for the sole purpose of financial advancement betrayed the muse. Jenny, being the craftsman rather than the artist, struggled with this quixotic credo from time to time.

'Picasso – not that I'm putting myself in his class – could have painted pretty bowls of fruit all his life. Where would the world be if its artists took the easy road' – I made quote marks – 'and "gave em what they want"?' (I hated people who made quote marks in the air, so why did I do that?)

She sipped her latte and frowned, leaving a ruby print on the glass. 'Don't get precious, darling. I'm not saying you should sell out. All I'm saying is you should think about your future sometimes, that's all. We've been together for five years and nothing's changed. I mean, are you going to live in that horrid little bed-sit and drive a cab for the rest of your life?'

Ouch. This was a low blow. I remained silent as I 'rubbed my testicles'. I hated being jolted into reality without prior written consent. I felt depressed. I tried not to think about the apartment (okay, okay the bed-sit) and the 'real job'.

Prince's pop classic 'Sign o' the Times' bounced across the polished wooden floors of the café. I tried to sniff out the 'jazz' in it. The phrasing. The syncopation. I thought of a myriad of jazz harmonic possibilities. Anything but reality.

'Earth to Gordon. Earth calling Gordon . . .'

'Oh . . . sorry, Jen. Go on.'

'Oh . . . I don't know. You should think about where your life is heading.'

'Why?'

'You know I think you're talented. I just want the best for you, Gordon. That's all.'

We sat for a while in silence.

'We talked about a family one day, remember?' she said.

'You want me to write jingles, is that it?'

'No. But . . .'

'Do we have to run this number again, Jen? Let's drop it, eh?'

'All I'm saying is —'

'I hate people who start sentences with: "All I'm saying is".' I grinned.

'Okay. Basically —'

'*Or* "basically". I hate people that start sentences with: "Basically". In fact, someone once said to me "Basically, all I'm saying is . . ." and I attacked him with a piece of par-boiled fettuccine.'

'Will you shut up for five minutes.' She laughed, her plump

breasts shimmying beneath her lycra top. 'All I'm saying is that . . . basically –'

I pulled a silly face.

'Arggg . . .' she flashed her sea-green eyes, 'for you to be happy, perhaps you might have to compromise.'

'Jen. I'm not writing any more goddamn jingles. So where's the compromise?'

I picked up the bill and we took a stroll up Oxford Street in silence.

⌢

Jenny was a talented writer and extremely focused on her career. They say we're fascinated by that which most eludes us. Jenny was no exception. Art defied all reason in her book – yet she was intrigued by it. And therefore, enamoured with artists. Her boyfriends had been a succession of shabby painters, drunken poets and deadbeat bohemians. (So I fitted in nicely.) Yet her own milieu was the very antithesis of this ethos. Although Jenny had great skill and flair as a writer, each article was another rung on her ladder of success. Perhaps her upbringing helped shape this belief somewhat. I'll fill you in.

To couch it endearingly, Jenny's father was a smug, rich bastard. He worked hard at it. He was on the board of fifteen different companies. He drove a Rolls and made sizeable donations to any politician that leaned to the right. In fact, ambitious ministers were seen outside his house standing on one leg holding a heavy bag. All in all, Harris was the living embodiment of the existential tenet that you can't be something without pretending to be it.

Needless to say, Harris was an ambitious man, who paid through the teeth to send his only child to the best schools. When Jenny went on to the leading university in the country, he seemed pleased with his gilt-edged investment. He was always probing her about 'career news'.

Jenny's father thought a lot of me. He thought about me in the same way a haemophiliac thinks about razor blades. He informed Jenny that I was a 'quasi-intellectual loafer' (which was fairly accurate if you left the 'intellectual' and 'quasi' part out of it), a layabout and a sponger. He declared that I had a philosophy and theory for every shortcoming and disappointment in my miserable life without taking any responsibility for it. (This was also fairly accurate.)

He was always quoting gleaming-toothed, motivational speakers like Anthony Robbins *ad nauseam*. I remembered the last time we met. Her father was a bit tipsy. The old boy had drunk one too many ports after dinner. I noticed he kept burping up Calais. Jenny was in the kitchen with her mother and, God forbid, I was stuck with him on my own. After cutting the air with a machete, he finally spoke. His large nose pointed at the moon.

'Well, what are you going to do with your life, son?' he asked as he downed another glass of purple liquid.

I looked down at my cheap, worn shoes and thought.

I finally said, 'I'm certainly not going to eat shit from you for the rest of my life, Daddy dearest.' But it came out something like: 'I haven't really thought about it, Mr Harris.'

Jenny's mother crept into the room to find a job to do – like cleaning an empty ashtray – in order to eavesdrop on the pre-planned assault.

He turned to me. 'You can't just dream your life away, boy. No future in driving a cab.'

It always came back to the cab.

'Have you got any Scotch, Mr Harris?' I asked, sending for reinforcements.

'There's some Chivas behind the bar, son,' he gestured lazily, almost spilling the vintage port on his silk shirt.

I poured myself a tall glass of rust-coloured spirit. I looked around the room. This was the 'rumpus' room. So if you needed to do a little rumpusing, this was the place. The walls were a mosaic of Australian painters – Nolan, Lindsay, Boyd, etc. He had bought carelessly. The paintings were a dull selection. However, this was insignificant when compared to their value. Harris would never say, 'Look at the way the light is reflected in this one'. Or 'What do you think he's trying to say here?' But 'How much do you think this one set me back? My dealer tells me that this Nolan's doubled in price since I bought it.'

I leaned against the bowling-green-sized snooker table, sipping my Scotch. There was a rip in the cloth where some inebriated jazz musician had stuck a cue through it attempting a jump-shot. Harris never had it repaired. This was too easy. It would mean, in time, the culprit would be able to forget about the nefarious oversight. Harris would line up the white ball, lean over his cigar, sighing. 'This snooker table was handmade in Scotland, you know'.

I gulped some whisky with a sneaky valium. Mrs Harris left the room.

'Pace yourself lad, pace yourself.'

'Sorry.' I picked up Jenny's graduation photo and looked at it.

He noticed and beamed. 'Proud moment. Graduated with honours, you know.'

I feigned an impressed look. I knew she graduated with honours as he told me almost every goddamn time I came over.

'What about doing some more of those advertising jingles?' he said. 'You seem to have a flair for that sort of thing.'

'Yes, but last time I fired it I was rescued by a passing trawler netting postmodernists.'

'*What* happened?'

'They came across a school of abstract expressionists and sold us all for $4.50 a kilo.'

'I don't follow.'

'Don't worry. It's my imagination.'

'I see.'

'That and the drugs,' I mumbled into my glass.

'Not an easy thing to do, jingles,' he persisted. 'What about that one you did for our ad agency? That was excellent! Mexican sauce or something?'

'I'm afraid it's just not my gig, Mr Harris.' I gestured to look at my watch. I didn't own a watch but noticed a new freckle. 'I really should be pushing off.' I looked around despairingly for Jenny. Her old man sighed and shook his head. He walked over to the mahogany drinks cabinet and poured another drink.

'We paid you well enough for that ad, didn't we? Well, didn't we? Hmmm?'

'Hum . . . what . . . oh . . . yeah, sure.'

'Well . . .?'

I sighed. 'I just don't feel my future lies in writing stuff like: *I feel like nicey, spicy, salsa, feel like nicey, spicy, salsa*!' I sang the last phrase at my silver-headed host.

'But everyone remembers it!'

'Exactly.' I spilt a little Scotch on the carpet.

'Careful. That Axminster's $350 per square metre.

'Sorry.'

'Fay! Cloth!'

Mrs Harris ran through the door just as the last syllable escaped from Harris's thin lips. She tutted as she scrubbed in tight, jittering movements.

'Well, I don't mind saying that Mrs Harris and I were quite chuffed when we saw it on TV. Weren't we Fay?' Fay nodded and scrubbed like Lady Macbeth. 'One of my board members was also rather impressed. He has a small agency in North Sydney. Wants to talk to you about a job.'

'Really?'

'It pays $50 000 per annum.'

'How many annums would I be allowed to produce in a year?'

Harris rolled his eyes at his wife. She bustled out.

So that's what this is all about, I thought. A day gig. I thought momentarily about giving up music and becoming a 'wage slave'. Working in an office day in, day out. I turned the colour of marine algae.

Harris removed a long, fat cigar from a wooden box. He unwrapped some cellophane and lit it. It smelt pleasant. Like a burning turd. He puffed and followed a plume of smoke to the ceiling.

'Cubans,' he said.

'Yes, I heard them chattering in the box. Something about: "José, next time we use the fricken life raft".'

'$150 each,' he gloated.

This made sense because cigars always looked to me like somebody smoking a rolled-up wad of cash, anyway. I feigned an impressed look.

'You don't *seriously* think you're going to make a million dollars playing that jazz lark do you?' he puffed.

'Jazz lark'? What's he mean by fucking 'jazz lark'? I thought. I helped myself to another glass of courage. 'So, if you don't make a million dollars, you've failed in life, is that what you're saying, Mr Harris?'

Jenny's mother slinked into the room to empty an ashtray with a lone olive pit in it. She walked out again like someone having to make a trip to the bathroom in the middle of an opera.

'I think a lot of "normal" people would equate money with success, yes,' he said. 'Perhaps not in the university canteen, but after they had finished their studies, shaved off their beards and grown up, I think they would be endeavouring to make something of their lives, yes.'

This was either addressed to me or Allen Ginsberg. I guessed me. I thought for a moment as I studied the ice cubes at the end of my glass. I looked around at the 'gallery-bank'.

'So are you saying that Van Gogh and Mozart were losers

because they died penniless, Mr Harris?'

'Van Gogh blew his brains out, didn't he? Do you deem his a successful life?'

'Is that how you would sum it up?'

Harris took a swig of port. 'That's the bottom line.' (He used to dine out on that phrase.) 'Anyway, I'm sure a lot of fathers would say the same thing if you were contemplating some sort of future with *their* daughter,' he said with a paternal tenderness and the subtlety of a proctologist with Parkinson's disease.

Unbeknownst to Harris, this was always an effective parry. I always felt that if *I* was a father, I wouldn't want *my* daughter to go out with a deadbeat like myself. Harris wasn't a bad guy. After all, he was only looking out for his daughter's best interests. He loved her. You couldn't blame him for that, I guess.

Harris downed another port. Lisbon. He placed his lips, fish-like, around the cigar. His diamond ring glinted in the light of the chandelier.

'Set yourself some goals, lad. Have some direction.' He looked to the heavens and blew a cloud of olive smoke. 'Someone once said: *Dream lofty dreams, and as you dream, so shall you become. Your vision is the promise of what you shall one day be; your ideal is the prophecy of what you shall at last unveil.*'

'I have one also,' I cleared my throat. '*When you're smiling, the world smiles too. When you open up your heart, the world belongs to you. Just dream amidst the daffodils with a smile across your face, and feel the blessed happiness of the entire human race.*'

'Tennyson?'

'No, Pol Pot, 1972.'

He shook his head and mumbled something unkind into his glass that could have been either 'I quit' or 'fuckwit'. I wasn't sure. Anyway, it didn't really matter. We both knew the score.

George Harris was the ultimate pragmatist. He saw things in all colours: black *and* white. He measured a man by the cut of his suit, plus the car he drove, divided by the distance his house was from the harbour. These were his iron-clad parameters. Unfortunately, his swag of inspirational quotes and clichés performed miracles in the boardrooms of corporate Australia, where the lines of commerce and plutocracy are drawn clearly in the sand. But Harris's quotes were limp-wristed in the enigmatic lopsided world of Art. I studied the silk-suited patriarch for a moment. I suddenly remembered that Harris liked to claim he was a Christian. I gathered my troops.

'Was Jesus Christ a failure because he didn't have a Gold American Express card?'

Now Harris knew this was a direct dig. 'Weak argument,' he mumbled into his glass.

'Frequent flyer points would have been handy at the resurrection.'

Harris looked down the end of his large nose at me. He wasn't impressed.

'So was Christ a failure because he died penniless?' I persisted.

'No, but he wasn't sleeping with my daughter, either.'

Ouch. I downed the last of my Scotch and spat an ice cube back into the glass with a loud kerplunk. Jenny bustled into the room after being artfully distracted by her mother in the kitchen for long enough. She stole an apologetic look at me and I volleyed with a furious glance.

'Dad, we have to go. I have an editorial to write tonight.' She looked away because her father could always tell when she was lying, or had she just noticed that the new curtains from Paris had arrived?

Harris beamed. 'That's what I'm talking about, lad. Diligence. Get some of that into you, son. Sprinkle it on your cornflakes.'

'Makes your hair fall out and die of heart failure at 45.'

He shot a deadpan expression at me.

We made a speedy exit. As we pulled out of the palatial driveway lined with bowing willows, I posed a few subtle questions.

'How long do I have to go on being lectured to by that pompous fucking arsehole?'

'I'm sorry, Gordon, Mum cornered me in the kitchen,' she said, pulling nervously at the neck of her cashmere sweater. She stuck her hand through the passenger window and waved at her parents.

'Jesus, it's my life. Do I have to put up with the same middle-class sermon every time we visit, Jen?'

'What does that mean? And am I too middle-class for you?'

Attack was always the first form of defence with Jenny. I remained silent.

'Anyway, I didn't know anything about it,' she added.

(Yeah, right.) 'My life's *my* business, Jenny.'

'They're just worried about me, Gordon. That's all.'

'I think they're more worried about *me*, actually.'

'I hate people who finish sentences with the word "actually",' she grinned.

We looked at each other and exploded with laughter.

⌢

The percolator spat and hissed. I poured myself another cup of coffee as I thought about that evening with Jenny's parents. I wandered over to the piano and picked some more notes at random.

If I did score a record deal, old man Harris would have to chomp on the proverbial turd sandwich, I smiled to myself. And Jenny would be over the moon. Maybe I should call her. What if it's nothing, I chided myself. Ahh, what the hell.

I raced over to the window and picked up the phone, paused, and put it down again. Perhaps I was setting myself up for a big fall, I thought. I was just so excited. I *never* had good news. This was the most exciting thing I had to tell her since the grape-like lump on my arse turned out not to be a tumour but a haemorrhoid.

I picked up the phone and dialled the number before putting the receiver down, yet again. I picked up my Milo-strength coffee and gazed out the window.

My flat was located in the back streets of Sydney's Darlinghurst. The charming view was a dingy alley, littered with broken bottles and used syringes. It was what oily real-estate agents call a 'city aspect'. I swigged some coffee and peered through the sooty glass. I mulled over the phone call again as I leaned against the window in sagging white underpants. A slither of pink sunlight caught my pock-marked face. I had always dreamt of making a record. I dreamt in spades. In shiploads. Now it was about to actually happen. There I go again. Stop!

As I looked out the window, an old woman with a bad back hobbled down the alley. She was carrying a heavy bag. I don't know why but it made me think about my sister, Julia, washing dishes and serving baked beans and runny eggs and cups of muddy tea in some squalid café. *She* chased the dream. And to what end? At least she had one, I suppose.

She never took the safe road. But was it worth it? To end up in depressing little cafés in London's East End, constantly bullied by Pakistani owners. I imagined her counting pennies for the gas heater in the bedroom with a gloved hand, asking herself, was it really cold enough to light?

Julia had moved to London to become a painter, but in twenty years had had only one exhibition in some insignificant gallery in the unfashionable end of Soho. The last time I saw a photo of her she looked terrible. Wan, heavy-eyed with hunched shoulders, yet bravely optimistic, as always. What would she have ended up like if she were still living in Sylvania. In a 'safe' job? Would she have been any happier? I asked myself.

Sylvania was a depressing place to grow up. My parents had been killed in a car accident when I was five and my sister and I were brought up by my aunt and uncle. They were typical

Australian folk of their generation. You know, they needed a satellite navigation system to find their emotions. My sister, being the older sibling, moved out of home when she was eighteen. She couldn't get away from Sylvania fast enough. I was very close to her and it broke my heart when she eventually moved to London. She was so full of life and colour that living in that grey house without her became unbearable. When she still lived in Sydney, on weekends, she would often collect me and take me to the theatre or art galleries or museums. On those days she would talk about the arts as if it were a kind of spiritual nirvana. She always chided me to practise the piano and compose music and write stories.

'One day we'll be famous, Gordon, and all of our loneliness and despair will be captured in our work. All of this will one day make sense, you'll see. It's our karma' (a popular word in the seventies).

I could remember the day she told me she was leaving for London. Australia was not the place for artists in those days. She had to go. It was simply a matter of when. However, this is the rationalisation of a thirty-four-year-old, writing this now. At the time, her departure burned in my heart like a hot coal.

We had been to the movies that day. She loved the movies. She sometimes saw three movies in one day. This became tiring running between theatres at intermission.

As we waited for her bus in front of the Paragon Milk Bar, she broke the news about leaving. I was fourteen. I can still smell the vinegar on fat chips.

'Please don't go, Julia.'

She answered in her typically dramatic fashion. 'I have to, little man! I can't live in this provincial outpost any more. I want to be inspired. Visit castles. See the works of great painters. See the great museums of the world!'

'But I need you. I need you here. You're all I've got. I feel so alone when you're not around. Alone in that horrible house.'

'I have to follow *destiny*.' Julia loved that word.

'It will only lead to *inevitability*.'

'So be it.'

'I'm told you can't get a bus from there.'

'I'm sorry, Gordon. But I have to do this. For me. Anyway, I only see you one or two weekends a month.'

'That's not my fault.'

'Here's my bus.' She pecked me on the cheek and tears glazed her eyes. 'Look after yourself, little man,' she choked.

She squeezed her head through a back window. 'I'll remember to write!'

She never did remember. (Not until years later, anyway.)

As I stood in the black exhaust, a clap of thunder startled me. I watched the bus disappear down Fig Tree Avenue. And I watched Julia disappear from my childhood. As I ran for home, the rain washed away the sticky tears.

It was more depressing than ever to walk into the dark-bricked, Federation, semi-detached house that afternoon. The word 'skylight' wasn't in the lexicon of Australians in the 1970s. The hallway was dark even at midday with a searchlight pointed at the front door. As I groped the floral wallpaper to my bedroom, my aunt, pearl necklace, cardigan and blue rinse, was waiting with a razor-sharp comment. Her wintry eyes narrowed as she smiled, 'Leaving again, is she? Where to this time? Some workshop in New Guinea, is it? She doesn't care about *you*. When will you understand? She only cares about *herself*.'

I ignored her and threw myself on my bed, drying the tears on my ABBA pillowcase – staining Agnetha's breasts. My aunt stood in the doorway and folded her wrinkly arms. A smile dragged at the corners of her mouth. At least I think it was a smile. My aunt was one of those people who had the kind of smile that was both smile and sneer at the same time.

My aunt was what people in Sylvania called 'a cold fish'. Although she loved 'the poor orphaned children', she stopped short of actually showing us. Maybe she just found it hard to express it. She was not a demonstrative person. She grew up in a farming town in Queensland where people hugged each other by telegram. Like most of her Anglophile neighbours in suburban Sydney in the seventies, her religion was a benevolent blend of Protestantism, Malcolm Fraser and the Ku Klux Klan. Don't think badly of her. My aunt was a good person, really. She stuck by us. She was even capable of random acts of kindness. She'd bake you treats for after school. Or she'd buy you that shirt you wanted. At times, you didn't know whether to poison her tea or give her a box of chocolates. (To this day we still have no idea how the poison got into the chocolates.)

My aunt was a little old for teenage children, the generation gap outsizing the Grand Canyon. Taking her husband's niece and nephew in her golden years had been a secret burden. She had been looking forward to a life of playing bowls, tending to her azaleas and writing to her local MP about the lack of family programming on television. She never openly said she didn't want 'the children'. She didn't have to. A true Celtic martyr, she just made everyone around her miserable instead. However, there was a contributing factor.

My uncle thought everything was fine at home. Mainly because he never *came* home. Like most blokes at the time, if he wasn't working late, away on business trips, or at meetings, he was at the club till all hours. This aggravated the situation at home as my aunt was not the most mature person in the world. She would instantly take it out on us. It was unbearable – especially when Julia was still living with us. It would usually start around dinnertime.

'Julia, that's not how you hold a fork!' she would snap.

I would feel the acid in my stomach ripple.

'You look like your slobby uncle when you do that,' my aunt would say, adjusting her lacquered helmet of lavender hair, and peeking at the clock, watching another dinner go cold as my uncle chased that elusive final schooner at the club.

'Do you have to chew like a cow, Julia? Terribly bovine, dear. Young men don't find cows very attractive, you know.'

'Even lonely cowboys?' I asked.

'Be quiet, Gordon.'

'I'm not interested in men. I'm going in for lesbianism,' Julia would say. Red rag to a bull.

This is the moment when my aunt would become slightly hysterical. It was on a scale somewhere between Elizabeth Taylor forced to take a bus to the Academy Awards and Madonna having beetroot soup spilled down her white dress at Spago's.

'Don't speak to me like that, you little pig! I've brought you up like my own daughter and this is the thanks I get.' The sound of dishes crashing in the sink. 'I'm the only one stupid enough to look after you two ungrateful children. No one else will do it. I'm lumbered with it.'

This was part of our self-esteem program.

The best thing that ever happened was when I discovered the piano. A rollicking blues would drown out the sound of warfare quite effectively. Although sometimes it made the whole thing seem like a scene from a Woody Allen film. Sometimes it didn't work. So I'd just run away. I was always running away. Away from the fights. Away from the colourless suburban streets of Sylvania.

The place I would usually run to was my grandmother's listing fibro house in Granville. Aside from my uncle and aunt, she was my only living relative, and when she used to hold me in those fleshy arm of hers I'd feel safe and warm. She'd wipe away the tears and give me what every grandmother gives their grandchildren who are sad: sugar. My grandmother loved giving me sugar. Even the toothpaste had sugar in it. I'd have so much sugar that by the afternoon, I'd be collapsed on the floor shaking, and speaking in 'tongues'.

My grandmother was the mother I never had. She loved television.

I'd sit on her lap and we'd watch old Marx Bros movies. She loved the surreal comic genius of Groucho Marx. A big woman, she'd laugh and her whole body would ripple in waves. I remember that as if it was yesterday. Like everyone else in my life around that time, she left me. She died.

⌢

That phone call made me think a lot that afternoon. Question a lot of things. I felt as if I was beginning a new chapter in my life. It was exciting, but at the same time terrifying. But was it worth it? I couldn't help wondering if I was like a salmon swimming upstream, who on completion of the exhausting journey, finds absolutely zip! Most of the other fish are content to simply float around the ocean and excrete those noodle-type turds all day. What makes the salmon so different? Maybe the artist is a kind of human salmon. But that would only explain Jeff Koons. Anyway, I was prepared to keep looking for whatever the hell it was I was looking for.

I finally decided that life was like a day at the beach. You made a pattern in the sand with a piece of driftwood, only to discover that, by the end of the day, the tide had quietly washed it away. Some were lucky enough to carve something in the rock at the cliff face, but that was arduous and fraught with danger and ridicule. I at least wanted to head for the rocks. The beach was too crowded. And besides, I looked like shit in bathers.

PIANO ACCORDIONS ARE SEX MACHINES

∽

THE AIR WAS FAT with car horns as I waited outside Jenny's office. I felt excited and stressed at the same time. Beneath a mullet-coloured sky, I rehearsed my story with an invisible understudy. I was apprehensive about telling Jenny about Delta but I simply couldn't contain myself any longer. Finding it hard to relax, I felt my stomach purl with acid.

I asked for the time . . . again. Ten to six. Any time now, I thought. The newspaper employees spilled onto the street in a blur of tweedy colour. With a harassed expression, I tried to pick Jenny from the torrent of workers.

I rehearsed the story again. I talk with my hands a lot, so I must have looked strange. Through a sepia blanket of exhaust, I saw her.

'JEN!'

Jenny waved like a castaway. I skipped across the street to meet her – artfully toreadoring a taxi.

'So what's this exciting news you've got for me?' she asked.

I placed my hand on the small of her shapely back, guiding her through the throng of flesh. 'Let's get something to eat. You hungry?'

'Ravenous. Oh, listen, sorry I'm late, but Charlie kept me back with an idea for a story.'

'I guessed as much.'

Jenny always walked briskly – as if she were on her way to meet a headmaster who had slapped her child. I was always asking her to slow down and we used to argue like seagulls whenever we walked together.

She screwed up her brow and looked at me. 'How have you been sleeping?'

'I had that dream again.'

'The same one?'

'Yeah, I'm sitting at the end of a long table. I'm about five years old. My parents and relatives are all there. They're wearing those paper party hats. My sister holds a long black feather. She wants me to take it.'

'That's weird. You okay now, though?'

Jenny would usually start the conversation with 'How have you been sleeping?' whenever we met. This was her polite way of saying, 'Have they commited you yet or are the pills still holding you together?' She was always asking about the attacks. You see, I suffered from crippling anxiety attacks which I used to fight off with a drawerful of pretty coloured tranquillisers.

'Do you feel like Italian?' she asked

'Yes! Why don't we go to Maria's?'

Her eyes beamed. 'That's expensive, isn't it?'

'Ah, what's money when you have a girlfriend with an expense account.'

'Gordon, I simply can't wait. You've got to tell me the news right now. Right this instant.'

'Jen, you've waited five years for this little news item, another ten minutes won't kill you,' I smiled.

'Come on. Don't be a bugger.' She punched me softly on the arm.

I got up. 'I will. Soon. Let's eat.'

Then she flung out an arm, nearly breaking my nose. 'TAXI!'

Maria's was always crowded and this underpinned the restaurant's unique ambience. It sat tucked away in a back street in little Italy in East Sydney. It made you feel that you had to be 'in the know' to dine there. And being seen in the place just added to your own innate hipness.

The smell of garlic and fresh basil assaulted our senses as we waited to be seated, sharpening our appetites. I folded my awkward frame into a chair. We ate some crusty bread. Glossy-haired waiters raced past with steaming bowls of pasta to the clinking of cutlery and the rumbling surf of conversation. Maria sauntered over for a chat – as was her custom.

I should tell you about Maria.

Maria was your typical matriarchal Italian. Big-bosomed, a shouting, singing voice, black hair with silver threads, five-o'clock shadow. Oh, yes. Did I mention Maria was a drag queen? In fact, Maria was the ugliest drag queen you ever saw. Not that it mattered, we all loved her. She never made you feel anything but welcome.

'Gordon, Jenny. I missed'a you lately. Where you bin?' she asked in the gravelly voice of a wrestler. 'Ow you music bin comin along?'

I tried to make myself seem important. 'I . . . um . . . I've been doing some gigs out of town . . . jazz festivals . . . you know how it is, Maria.'

Jenny took control.

'He's been flat out. He can't keep up with demand. Everyone wants to hear him perform.'

'You musician leed'a such excitin lives,' Maria boomed with a glint in her eye. 'What you lak to eat, tonight?'

Although Jenny's deadpan delivery would have fooled the Gestapo, Maria knew that I was broke most of the time. I was always broke. If I wasn't broke, I was penniless. And if I wasn't penniless, I was insolvent. Sometimes I just didn't have money.

'You sing'a for your supper tonight. Any time you sing'a few song, I no charge,' Maria whispered. She kissed me, her stubble scratching my forehead.

I stuck out my bony chest. 'Thanks Maria, that's awfully sweet of you, but I'm okay. Money's not a problem tonight.' Which meant Jenny was paying. (Told you I was a bum.)

In true renaissance fashion, Maria would often ask a painter to paint a picture for the restaurant or a poet to recite some tedious poetry in order to slip the fledgling artist a free bowl of pasta, at the same time investing in the artist's self-esteem. As you can imagine, these impromptu soirées made the restaurant a very fashionable place at which to eat. The diners almost came to demand an artistic aperitif on each occasion. (I should point out that Maria was not unaware of this, but it was not her prime motivation.)

It wasn't long before the food arrived. The woody smell of pasta crept up our nostrils.

'So what's the news, Gordon? I won't enjoy my meal if you don't tell me *this* instant,' said Jenny.

I felt immediate stress. To calm myself, I took a Tai Chi breath.

'Promise me you won't get too excited because it's probably nothing. You know, these things always –'

'Okay . . . okay,' she said.

'Promise me?'

'Okay, okay. I promise. Now what's the scoop?'

'You sound like a journalist when you say that.'

'Stop stalling, Gordon.'

'It's probably nothing . . . but . . . Delta's A&R manager – he's the guy who signs new talent – well, his secretary actually, asked me to come in for a meeting.' My eyes flashed, I couldn't help myself. Damn!

'Wow, I can't believe it. That's incredible!' She jumped out of her seat and promptly sat down again. 'That means they're going to offer you a deal!'

'Now . . . now, just hang on a minute, Jenny. It could be nothing. In fact, it's probably just –'

'Gordon, you don't understand. I sent Delta your demo tape the other week! They would have got it a couple of days before the editorial came out. I timed it that way.'

'You're kidding?'

'Well, someone had to get things moving for you, you big doofus.'

I felt a lump in my throat.

'Are you all right, Gordon?'

I couldn't speak.

'Say something.'

I still felt the lump in my throat. It was the scampi. I was choking. Maria rushed over and tried the Heimlich Manoeuvre but got it confused with the Heinrich Manoeuvre and had me beaten around the head with a copy of *Mein Kampf*.

I finally spat out the scampi. The diners resumed their meals.

'You . . . you did that for me?' I quivered.

Jenny nodded, unable to say anything. She looked like she was going to cry.

'But they must get a thousand tapes a week,' I said, my voice cracking on the last word.

'So why have they suddenly called you out of the blue?'

At that moment I realised just how much Jenny loved me. How much she really believed in me. If nothing had come of it, she wouldn't have told me and I would have been none the wiser. There was no hidden agenda. No relationship point-scoring. The only motive was love. I was never really sure of her motives at times. She was so slick. So competent. I asked myself time and time again what she saw in me. Did she really love me? She told me in bed she loved me, but people will say anything in bed. People will agree to having The Spice Girls' interpretation of *La Boheme* played at their funeral, while you're making love to them. Yet in that one, selfless gesture, I knew just how unconditionally she loved me. I suddenly felt intoxicated with love. A real love that I had not felt for anyone in my life. Before I knew what I was saying I heard myself say: 'Jenny . . . if I get this deal . . . will you marry me?'

She was in shock, but played it cool as usual. 'Marry a complete lunatic?'

'No, me. You've never even met Pauline Hanson.'

'I was talking about the lunatic sitting across from me.'

I turned around. 'Yes, but look at the way he holds that fork. He'll kill again.'

'Be serious. You. Gordon B. Shoesmith,' she said through a white-toothed smile.

A lunatic? I never thought of myself as a lunatic in the *real* sense of the word 'lunatic'. As in someone who eats sand. Or someone who beats up old ladies. Or someone who votes for the Democrats and expects them to get in. Jenny leaned over and kissed me.

'Yes,' she said.

We ate our meal with good appetite. The wine felt warm in our bellies. I looked around with the expression you have on your face after having too much good food and wine. Maria's was a queer place. With the student paintings and crude sculptures around the room, it felt like we were eating in the Art School cafeteria in Sicily.

Maria sauntered over, waving a hairy finger. 'You two'a cheeky lovebird look very happy tonight.'

'Gordon's just been offered a record contract with Delta Records! And not only that, he's asked me to *marry* him! Can you imagine this lump ever marrying *anyone*?'

Maria touched my cheek affectionately. 'You can have it removed with'a laser surgery.'

'Maria, this means we're engaged!' Jenny said.

'This'a call for a drink,' Maria boomed. The happy Italian raced over with a bottle of her best and poured us all a generous glass. We drank and chatted garrulously. It is rare to find an Italian without a romantic heart, and Maria was no exception. She was so excited by the good tidings that she drank a little more than a lady in charge of a busy restaurant should. A little later she stumbled out of the kitchen with a pearly-white piano accordion strapped to her hairy neck. She asked me to sing.

I gulped some wine for courage and turned to Jenny. 'In the Bible it says that when you arrive in heaven, they hand you a harp. And when you arrive in hell, they hand you a piano accordion.'

Jenny laughed.

Maria was an accomplished musician and her repertoire mainly consisted of French and Italian folk songs, a few choppy arias and the odd jazz standard. But when she put away the bassoon, she was the worst piano accordionist you ever heard.

I don't care what anyone says, after a few glasses of grainy red, the sound of a piano accordion has to be the most romantic sound in the world. Whether it's a balmy summer's evening on the Isle of Capri, a candle-lit Parisian café on the Champs Elysée, or a prison cell in Alabama with a twenty-five-stone cell-mate in pink lipstick called 'Puppy', it seldom fails to strike a romantic chord. After all, melody is melody whatever the instrument. Shakespeare once wrote, with a little Elizabethan exaggeration:

The man that hath no music in himself, nor is not moved with concord of sweet sounds, is fit for treason, stratagems, and spoils, the motions of his spirit are as dull as night, and his affections dark as Erebus: Let no such man be trusted . . .

(But this was possibly before the piano accordion came on the scene.)

'Gentleman and lady. You are about'a to hear one of the finest'a musician in all of Australia – who, I might'a add, has just bin offered a big'a record dill. So you all very lucky tonight.' Maria turned to me, a little glassy-eyed from the grape juice, 'What'a you want to sing, darlin?' She knew I sang mostly Gershwin or Porter.

'You choose,' I said.

'Can you sing "Night & Day"?'

'Yes, but after about three-thirty I feel tired. Do you know an old song by Gershwin called "Our Love is Here to Stay"?' I asked. 'It's Jenny's favourite.'

She hummed a couple of notes. 'Yes, yes I think'a I do. Is that the one that goes like'a this.' Maria played a couple of notes with some inappropriate chords.

'Yeah, yeah, that's it. The "William Tell Overture".'

I sang for Jenny who sat with her chin resting on her arms on the table, propping up a wide, inebriated grin.

The room erupted with applause and Jenny beamed with pride. Maria proudly gazed around the room with a look in her eyes as much as to say: 'Table 5 needs more parmesan'. I sat down with Jenny as Maria continued to play. As the gentle melodies trickled out of the old squeeze-box, Jenny snuggled up to me. 'You sang beautifully,' she whispered.

'What a record deal can do for your confidence, eh?' I generously flashed her Amex and ordered coffee. She peered at me through a curtain of long lashes.

'Well, you deserve this, darling,' she said. I could smell the wine on her breath. 'You were meant to have this record contract.'

'It's funny. Play sport and you're a God in this country. Run ten metres with a piece of pigskin and you're fulfilling your destiny. Write some poetry or paint a picture or something and you're a self-indulgent wart on the arse of society. Funny, isn't it?' I said, sounding tediously philosophical.

'Hmmm . . .' She rubbed her nose against my cheek. She wasn't listening, but I went on with my point, anyway. In case she missed it.

'It's hard for you to understand, Jen, because you work within a corporate framework. I don't have that kind of structure. You don't walk out of the Conservatorium of Music or Art School, look in the classifieds and find: "Wanted. Artist. Must be willing to travel the world, bore people in cafés and suffer from mood swings, $250 p.a.+".'

Downing a short black, I sneaked another glass of our host's wine, furtively glancing at her. She was still playing as if she were opening for The Three Terrors. 'You don't lie awake till four in the morning wondering whether you've made the right choices. Society allows you to be the person you want to be. You're a journalist,' I said, boring her further.

'And a damn good one at that!' she slurred.

'Yes. A *damn* good one. It's your career. But when people ask you what you do for a living and you tell them you're a *musician*, without fail they ask you what you do for a "real job". Then you spill your guts and tell them you sometimes . . . drive a cab.' I sighed. 'You can always tell what they're thinking: another loser. They're thinking, just another dreamer. If he had any real talent, I would have heard of him. Elton John doesn't drive a cab.' I lifted my glass. 'Let's face it, Jen: *money* equals *talent* to most people. Just ask your father. He could lecture on the subject in thirty-seven different universities across Europe. I can see him now at a lectern in Munich pointing to a giant slide of my head.' I slurped down some more wine.

'He doesn't understand, Gordon. He's from a different generation. He still talks about the Depression.'

'Jenny, the problem is, they forget about all the artists and scientists and philosophers who struggled for years without recognition. Some of them never receiving any kudos till long after they were dead. What this record deal means to me, Jen, is some kind of recognition. It sends a message to the world that someone thinks I'm worthwhile enough to invest in. Invest their hard-earned cash. That what I have to say is vaguely significant. That I'm not just kidding myself with blind ego.'

Jenny flashed her eyes at me to go. She was only half-listening to my laborious rhetoric anyway. Maria waved goodbye as she continued to play to the smiling diners. We jumped a cab to Jenny's flat.

Jenny lived alone in a neat apartment in the café-society side of the lower North Shore. Her father had purchased it because his daughter needed a flat in the 'right' suburb and it was a shrewd investment. She opened the door. I smelled potpourri and perfume.

I glanced around. As always, it was neat as a pin. It was one of those sought-after Art Deco flats that had been gutted and completely renovated so it no longer resembled an Art Deco flat. Her bookcase was an archive of journalism and biographies. She really loved biographies – especially on artists and musicians and writers. I picked up a biography of Orwell. I loved his work, but what was he thinking with that moustache? It looks like he's had a big night on the Black Sambucca. He thought it was fashionably proletarian, I suppose. On the bright lemon walls hung a series of lithographs by Whiteley. They were quite wonderful. Unlike her father, Jen could pick art. The flat was open-plan. This meant I could chat with her while she was in the kitchen. Her kitchen was an aircraft-hangar of stainless steel. It flared with neon as she hit the switch and made coffee. She had every modern appliance known to man. She even had a machine to juice pineapples.

I sprawled on her designer sofa. It was a pebble beach of tapestry cushions. (What is it with women and cushions? They always seem to be buying, lay-bying, or on the look-out for cushions.) She had picked up most of these in Europe. They almost seemed too nice to stick your bum on.

Jen leaned over my shoulder and kissed me. She looked into my eyes and gave me a sexy smile. Eventually she disappeared into the bedroom. I helped myself to an imported beer in the fridge. Some exotic Scandinavian brew called '*Schitt*'. Holding open the fridge door, I played out a scene in a tavern in Denmark:

'Waiter, this beer tastes like shit!'

'Yes sir, brewed right here in Denmark.'

Jenny poked her head out of the bedroom.

'Who *are* you talking to, Gordon?

'Sorry.'

I draped an arm on the cold stainless-steel door of her fridge.

I loved Jenny's fridge. It was a veritable Aladdin's cave of gastronomic treats. Paté, overpriced stinky cheeses, Italian sausage, smoked salmon, grilled eggplant. It was certainly a stark contrast to the week-old pizza and ubiquitous rotten tomato that lived in my fridge.

'You know, Jen . . . hmmm . . . yum . . . this record deal is going to change my entire life,' I mumbled through a mouthful of chicken. 'It's going to –'

I turned around to find Jenny wearing nothing but a G-string and a smile. I dropped the chicken on the slate floor. I looked at Jenny. She had a flawless body. My eyes gazed down to the G-string. I've seen dental floss thicker than that, I thought.

She took my hands and placed them on her warm, plump breasts. Beneath my fridge-chilled hands her nipples stood to attention. I kissed her softly on the neck. Her breath grew heavy. I smelt the wine, fruity on her breath. Her hair smelled of peaches. She unbuttoned my shirt and kissed my thumping chest. My tongue found her ear. It was the most perfect ear I had ever tongued. Her cheeks turned sanguine and burned against my cheek. Her hot breath was rapid. We stood, pressed against the kitchen bench.

'Oh, Gordon!' she moaned.

'Oh, Jenny,' I replied.

'Oh, Gordon!' she moaned.

'Jenny?'

'Yes?' she moaned.

'What if Delta called the wrong Gordon Shoesmith? It happens.'

'Oh . . . shut up and screw me!' she panted, throwing me onto the cold slate floor of the kitchen.

DWLIDLY DOO
BEE DEE BOP
AND OTHER DREAMS

∽

'BULLSHIT!'

'Straight up, man.'

The old man fingered his long white beard and peered at me through wonky eyes. 'Delta Records, eh?'

'Delta Records,' I nodded.

Chuck McCall shook his scabrous face as he rolled a trumpet-shaped joint, good eye on the reefer, the other on Pluto. With a spent match, the seventy-five-year-old jazz singer pushed in the escaping green flakes with the concentration of a prize-winning chemist. He lit it and took a deep, pleasing drag.

'Delta Records. Well, how about that,' he said, smoke trickling through broken teeth.

The sound of Charlie Parker drifted through the cramped Housing Commission flat. I tapped my toe inside my shoe. Chuck cocked his head to catch an unfamiliar lick before blowing a cloud of honey-coloured smoke at the bare bulb that dangled above. He passed the smoldering reefer to me with the deference of an Olympic torch-bearer. I shook my head.

'Thanks, I don't smoke.' (He would always forget.) I didn't smoke dope because it induced anxiety attacks of mammoth proportions.

He shrugged and pulled some acrid smoke into his lungs. Seeds crackling, fuse-like. He blew it out again. I studied him through the fug of smoke.

Chuck didn't look well at all, I thought. Perhaps drinking whisky and smoking dope every day since 1947 somehow contributed to this. With his bulbous belly and long white beard, Chuck looked like Santa Claus after a heavy week on the booze. He was kind of losing the plot lately too. A doctor told him he was in an advanced stage of Alzheimer's, but he forgot all about it as soon as he left the surgery. He was happy. My mentor stared at me through liver-yellow eyes.

'So is jazz cool again or something, man?' he wheezed, holding the smoke as long as it took to achieve the desired effect.

'Must be. Last time it was *in* was 1958, then 1962, then a late afternoon in August in '87. It was out again by seven-thirty.'

The old bebopper gave a bassey chuckle.

I looked around the kitchen. Piles of dishes listed in the sink and I could smell stale egg. Peeking through the door to the lounge room, I could see cairns of records leaning against the wall. The sofa was a seventies lime-green vinyl affair with a blanket concealing a crossword of slashes and rips. Curling posters of black jazz musicians flapped on the wall in the draft. He had a plastic-wood coffee table with a broken leg. He had gaffa-taped it, but it always collapsed when someone put anything heavier than a petal on it. I sighed. Is this all you ended up with after a lifetime of dedication to your art? Suddenly, I saw myself at seventy. Living in a damp pension flat. Reading old reviews of myself. Playing old tapes of myself. Telling young neophytes that I should have recorded when I was in my prime. It sent a chill through me. I thought about the job again. Fifty grand a year was a lot of bread.

'Got any gigs?' he asked.

'Nothing. You?' I said.

He smiled that salt-and-pepper smile of his and shook his head.

'It's a joke, isn't it?'

'Yeah. I can remember when everyone had a gig, man,' he said in a swinging rhythm. 'Before videos and home-delivered pizzas and that fuckin Internet and whatnot. When people went out to hear music, man. When people dug you for what you did with your sound. Early fifties was a great time for me. The streets of Sydney crackled with atmosphere. Jazz spilled out onto the streets from the nightclubs like a fuckin carnival.' He clenched the joint between the tip of his index finger and thumb and took a lingering drag. 'Yeeeeeaaah. A carnival, man. The whole of the Cross would be a blur of sound and colour. Men in broad-shouldered suits with flashy ties. And all them fancy, wide-brimmed hats. And the women ... man ... they were like giant butterflies. They used to wear beautiful dresses that would catch in the breeze like a smile. Silk stockings and high-heeled satin shoes. Yeah, I can remember them satin shoes, man. That's when I met Ava. She wore them shoes,' he said, blowing out a stream of smoke at the ceiling. He passed me the reefer. I shook my head.

'Who?'

'The big love of my life, man. Ava.'

'Who's Ava?'

'Ava Gardner.'

'What? Are you trying to tell me that you had an affair with Ava Gardner?'

'I am, dear boy. She was out here in '59 making *On the Beach* with Gregory Peck. She came to hear me sing in a little nightclub in Melbourne. I was singing and playing the drums in them days. She was still with Sinatra so I was kind of nervous about making love to her.'

'Chuck, is this on the level?'

'Absolutely.'

I tried to picture Chuck as a young man with the lavender-eyed screen goddess. He pulled out a yellowing newspaper clipping. The headline ran: 'Film star's steamy affair with local jazz musician'.

'Wow. That's some heavy shit. What happened?'

'She went back to old Blue Eyes in the end.'

I looked around. 'What, she gave up all this?'

'Sinatra was the man.'

'Jesus, Chuck, if Sinatra ever found out about you and Ava, they would have been calling you old "No Eyes". So what did you do?'

'She left the country and I just got on with my life. Kept playing all this exciting new music.'

'Is that when you first heard bebop?'

'Oh, that was a long time before.' He folded up the clipping and put it back in a canister. 'It used to be called "Rebop" back then,' he said over his shoulder. 'People called it "bebop" much later. I first heard Parker and Diz in '48 at the 2KY auditorium. Or was it '47 . . . now I met Bob in '46 . . . no it was definitely '48.' (What is it with old people and minutiae?) 'Some DJ had brought these new records back from New York . . . or was it Chicago . . . no, New York. And man! What a mother-fucker! It just blew me away. Those lines were like nothing anybody had ever heard before. So fast. Crazy, baby.' He passed the weed. 'Crazy!'

'Thanks, I don't smoke.'

'Oh.'

'It'll never be the same, Chuck. Those were the halcyon days, man. I'll never know what it was really like.'

'I know. It's a shame. You would have been in your time, man. Not like now,' he sighed. 'My only regret about those days is that I didn't record. We weren't really given the opportunity to record. I should have gone to New York. I would have liked you and other young cats to hear my scatting when it was really firing. It was strong, man. Strong as a fuckin ox,' Chuck coughed.

'Are you still planning to get to New York?'

His eyes flashed. 'Look at this.' He grabbed something from a tin canister. 'What do think of *that*?' It was an airline ticket.

I sat dumbfounded.

New York is to the modern jazz musician what Paris was to the artist at the turn of last century. Chuck had talked about going to New York for so long, and hanging out with Max Roach (and all his other jazz-musician friends whom he had met in Australia over the last fifty years), that I had dismissed it. We all had dreams. New York was his.

He pointed to the ticket. 'It's open-ended.'

'What does that mean?'

'It means, my dear boy, that I can go whenever I'm ready. As soon as my next twelve pension cheques clear the bank, I'm off!'

'Good for you, Chuck.'

He placed the ticket back into the canister. Fagan-like. 'Hey, did you read what that prick Duddle wrote about me last month, man?' he said. 'Called me a musical parody! What's he fuckin mean by that?'

'Who cares what he thinks? You're the most original singer that I've ever heard in my life. No one sings bop like you, man. No one scats like you. You have what they *all* want: originality.'

'Yeah, if you only wrote the reviews, Gordon.'

'I think it was Arthur Conan Doyle who wrote: "Mediocrity recognises nothing higher than itself, but talent instantly recognises genius",' I said with a little self-adulation.

'Doyle. Didn't he play drums with Sonny Rollins in '58?'

'I think so. No one can do what you can do, Chuck. You learned all of Parker's solos over forty years ago. You can sing every one of his compositions from "Ornithology" to "Barbados". Most *horn* players would struggle with that, man.'

He stroked his beard sagely. 'True.'

'Why don't you try and record now?' I asked, trying to cheer him up.

'No one's interested. Too fuckin old, they reckon.'

'What about that tape on the radio program? Couldn't you re-release that?'

'Not the same. Not like making a record, man. New arrangements. New tunes and shit. I want to record with Max Roach. In New York!'

This last sentence was uttered at such a volume that my fillings rattled slightly. As a result of singing for over fifty years, Chuck's voice could crack a brick. He took another toke of the reefer while I looked out the window. I thought about the phone call again. I turned to him. 'So what about Delta? What if they start telling me what songs I should record and shit like that?'

Chuck remained silent for what seemed an eternity. Eventually the guru spoke, 'Life's like a shit sandwich: the more bread you have, the less shit you have to eat. You don't have a lot of bread, Gordon, so you might have to eat a little shit.' He passed me the reefer.

'No thanks. I don't smoke.'

'Oh.' He took a tug on the smoke.

'Christ. What time is it?' I asked.

'I don't know, I don't own a watch.'

None of us owned a goddamn watch. 'Can I ring for the time? I'm supposed to meet someone.'

⌒

I sat in the empty café. A waiter read a newspaper in the corner. Rain wept against the front window as I thought about Chuck and his Big Appled dream. I was happy for him. I imagined him bouncing through customs at La Guardia. Bottles of tequila and cartons of duty-free Camels under his arm.

Brian strode in and interrupted my thoughts. It was great to see him again. I couldn't wait to tell him about Delta. Good tidings kick-start a conversation nicely – or so I thought. That day I learned that it's bad form to show someone who has just returned from the bankruptcy court a winning lottery ticket.

'You look less than excited about the news,' I said, sipping a latte.

'No, mate. It's great . . . I'm really happy for you,' he said with a cardboard smile while studying the cafe's laminated menu.

'Brian, you're a rock musician. You don't understand. I mean, jazz musicians never get offered –'

'Just watch those guys, mate. Especially the A&R blokes. They're the ones with the dorsal fins poking out the back of their suits.'

'Versace, eh? Was there no limit to his genius?'

'What I'm trying to tell you is that the recording industry is full of sharks.'

'I've heard they're like that.'

'You heard right.'

'So, Bisho, what was it really like being signed to a major? I figured you were the best person to ask.'

He laughed cynically as he continued studying the menu.

Brian Bishop was a brilliant rock singer/songwriter. Tall, blond, Rugby-nosed, square-jawed, with a chest girls caress in deodorant commercials, he was the quintessential Aussie bloke. Girls flocked around him like fish to berley. He didn't have the usual Auschwitz complexion that we all had. He looked more like a surfer than a musician.

Brian had been very popular in the eighties. You had to literally fight to get into one of his gigs. His talent was obvious to even the most hardened Philistine. He had 'star' written all over him. (In hindsight, this publicity stunt was a little over the top.)

We met when I got a call to play some piano for him one night. Someone had let him down at the last minute. We hit it off straight-away. Although our musical styles were different, our ethos was the same. I also found him a refreshing change from the young jazz musicians I used to hang with who seemed to be under the misapprehension that being a boring, arrogant arsehole was somehow synonymous with being cool. Brian was cool because he didn't try to be. This came through in his music. He was a writer more than a musician. His spartan music served merely to augment the poignant vignettes he penned about love and life on the streets of Sydney. He inspired a whole bevy of artists in the ilk of Paul Kelly *et al* (including yours truly).

'So you want to know what it's really like, eh? What happens when you walk through those "Golden Doors"? The same doors that a million other dreamers have walked through and have never been heard of again?'

'I know all about Scientology. What about the record business?'

'Waiter! Do you sell alcohol?'

'No, this is a café, sir,' the waiter whined, without looking up from his paper. 'We sell *coffee*.'

'Pity, cause my mate's gonna need some before we leave.'

Brian had spoken about the record business before, but now that *I* was about to walk through those doors, Brian decided to give me the real dope on the 'majors' and his desperate attempt to realise *his* dream. It was not what I wanted to hear at the time. That afternoon I was made to feel the full pain of my friend's anguish with every snigger, every profanity, every caustic jibe.

Delta Records was one of several major recording companies operating in Australia. Like most multinational entertainment corporations, it mainly profited by forcing its stable of international artists upon the spoon-fed Australian public. A choking smog of performers ranging from Madonna to The Spice Girls suffocated the airwaves. The 'majors' would throw obscene budgets at the acts to concoct a prefabricated musical cheeseburger which then required very little hype to achieve chart success in Australia. Australian sales were merely cream for the majors. Any commitment to developing Australian talent was minor. As in television, film and all the arts, the perpetuation of Australian culture is of little value pitted against the sweet smell of the greenback.

Brian decided to make an album after a critic wrote a glowing review of one of his gigs, suggesting he should record. But, despite his obvious talent, he couldn't get a look-in with the majors. It wasn't until he independently released the single, *Susan's Kiss*, and it raced up their own charts that the impregnable door of the majors creaked open.

He signed a lucrative contract, and it must be said that the record company threw bucket-loads of cash at Brian. The sort of cash his miserable royalties would never recoup in a lifetime. Every time he was picked up in a hire car, taken to lunch, every time they flew him interstate, put him up in a motel, unbeknownst to him, he was paying for it. The bill ran high. Very high. While (on paper) they made a profit on their ninety per cent immediately, Brian would have to wait until a certain red-haired Queensland political leader moved into the Nuremberg Memorial Retirement Village before he'd see any of the cash. In the end, money being no object, they sent him to L.A. to record. Why, I don't know.

It was a fine record, but for some enigmatic reason that is the wonderful world of art, the album stiffed. And the musical intelligentsia of Sydney proclaimed with righteous indignation that Brian was now 'too commercial' (why, I don't know, he recorded exactly the same songs that he always played live) and had sold his arse to a major. Basically, he was 'out' and someone else was 'in'. The record company dropkicked him out the door and the fickle public stopped coming to his gigs. In the space of eight months, Brian Bishop went from fledgling superstar to local cab driver.

Brian had always wanted to make another album. But, in his eagerness to sign, he had failed to read the small print. Now he discovered that he was not released from the contract until the record company had recouped its entire investment outlaid to record and promote his album.

Roughly seven years later, Brian had somehow negotiated his way out of the deal and started the heartbreaking task of knocking on doors for a *new* deal. Sadly, Brian Bishop had about as much chance of getting a gig with a major as Ahmed Mohammed the Magnificent Magician had of getting the gig for

Salman Rushdie Junior's tenth birthday party.

On that drizzly afternoon he told me that the lowest, most frustrating rejection came from the assistants of the A&R managers. He called it the Worthless Shit Department, because the whole demoralising exercise was surely designed to make you feel like a worthless shit. Most of these assistants were fresh out of school: glorified gophers with a laminated business card. If you were lucky enough to penetrate the steely defences of the receptionists, you were immediately put through to someone called 'Kylie'. Even if you asked to speak directly with the person whom you knew to be the A&R manager (the only person authorised to make a decision about your future), the receptionist would ignore you anyway.

'Putting you through' – the last word, severed by muzak. You'd hang on the phone long enough to have grown a beard and, just as you were about to hang up, you'd hear a pubescent voice squeeze a pimple and whine, 'Kylie Perkins, A&R.'

Brian would lumber through the usual spiel and try to get an appointment with the real A&R manager. She would cut him off and instruct him to send off his demo marked: 'Attention Kylie Perkins, A&R Manager.' (She would give herself a promotion.)

After sending his demo, he would painfully chase the assistant up a few weeks later to 'get some feedback'. If she didn't simply brush him off over the phone, she would summon him to her 'office'. This office was usually a glorified cupboard in the bowels of the record company. She would proceed to lecture him – *ad nausem* – on why his sound was not right for the marketplace at this point in time. That his music wasn't really 'us'. And, of course, she'd politely point out that she should know as it was her job to 'sniff out talent'. Brian confessed that he sometimes felt like saying, 'Is this judgment based on your *entire* ten years of hanging out with your friends at the mall, or the two months you've been working with the record company since you left school?'

Brian just felt that he could skip the lecture on what a loser he was from someone whose idea of cutting-edge music was Dannii Minogue's tribute to Lou Reed.

He told me that on one particular occasion, he *finally* managed to get a 'real' appointment. He was waiting nervously outside the office when he heard the A&R Manager bark at his secretary.

'Brian *Bishop*? Oh, Christ, not that burnt-out old has-been. Piss him off! Just give him the usual spiel.'

'Shhh . . . he's just outside,' the secretary hissed.

'How the fuck did he get this far?' he said in a screamed whisper.

'You agreed to see him.'

'Well, you let him in here, sweetheart, you can piss him off, okay?'

The secretary, sporting the usual T-shirt with the company's latest overseas band on it, slithered out of the office. She looked down her nose at Brian with false bravado.

'I'm sorry, he's too busy to see you now. Our roster's full at the moment, anyway. Leave your demo and we'll get back to you.'

Brian smiled and motioned to leave.

With a sudden pang of conscience she added, 'I'm sorry, Brian, he thought you were someone else.'

Brian said that when he got home he actually felt like killing himself. He said he felt like throwing a rope around the light fitting and jumping off the sofa weighed down by a box of his unsold records. I laughed uncomfortably.

☹

I left Brian and took a long walk in the spitting rain. The sky was colourless and the sun was a pale yellow against it. So that was Brian chasing his dream, eh? Was it really worth all the pain and humiliation? Brian had trained as a primary school teacher. Wouldn't that have been easier? Suddenly Harris's job loomed in my mind. I thought of a cosy office. A smiling receptionist talking to me about sporting results that she had no interest in. A sign above the coffee machine announcing: *You don't have to be mad to work here, but it helps*. A little yellow sticker on my phone asking: 'Can you chip in for Barry's leaving gift? We've decided on a putting-iron.' Yes, after seeing Brian, the office was a comforting thought.

I popped a couple of antidepressants and kept walking. Unfortunately, they were sleeping pills and I fell asleep standing in line for a movie ticket. The movie was *The English Patient*, so I told people I'd seen it.

ASSAULT AND BATTERY
WITH DISCO BARBIE

∽

EDDIE 'THE GREEK' artfully combed the few lonely strands of blue hair across his moist scalp before making a note in a dog-eared ledger. He blew his large red nose. He was listening to a greyhound race at the same time. He loved the dish-lickers and hit Wentworth Park religiously on Monday nights. He usually punted on wobbly trifectas. Sometimes he threw a tip my way, but the mongrel usually ran the *other* way.

The smell of pizza tickled my nostrils as I cleaned the car. I felt depressed after the meeting with Brian. So driving that evening filled me with absolute dread. This was reality. I hated the job with a passion. I always told myself that it was temporary till a steady gig in some classy nightclub came my way, but I'd been driving for Eddie for five long years.

'Don't take all night cleaning that fuckin thing. I need you outa here in ten minutes,' bellowed Eddie, without looking up, studying a sauce-stained form guide.

'Keep your wig on, man.'

'Hmmm. Nice little pooch running in the fifth tonight.'

'Put a couple of bucks on the nose for me, will you, Eddie? I'm so hot at the moment I'm smokin,' I said, wiping sour-cream dollops of bird shit from the windscreen.

'Listen pal, you still owe me a lobster from last time,' he said, leaning through the window frame of his office.

'Since when did I owe you $20?'

'Golden Boy. Remember?'

'When?'

'Dapto. In the seventh. Last Thursday.'

'Oh, yeah. That's right. And the mutt's still running. I was crazy to throw money at that fleabag. It couldn't outrun a fat man.'

I pumped some petrol into the car. Eddie took an overly large bite of a greasy steak sandwich. Brown sauce dribbled onto his trousers, much to his annoyance.

'I don't fuckin train em, I just punt em. Don't ask me for no more tips then, will ya,' Eddie bellowed with a mouthful of sandwich. 'Why are you feelin so hot then? You tell me.'

'Are you sitting down?'

'Yeah . . . yeah . . . how do ya think I got these fuckin haemorrhoids.'

'Having sex with donkeys in Cyprus?'

'Sitting in this office and organising you pricks all night, that's how.'

Eddie walked over to a filing cabinet and grabbed a calculator. He pulled his baggy green pants over his globular belly. They slid down again. 'So tell me the big news,' he mumbled, punching numbers with a fat index finger.

I plopped myself on the bonnet of the car.

'Delta Records asked me to come in and talk about a record contract!' I couldn't help myself.

'Is that good?' he asked, circling three numbers on the form guide.

'Are you listening to me or what?'

Eddie looked up.

'I *said* . . . I'm going to be offered a record contract, man.'

'That's fantastic,' he said, scratching his balls.

'I see you're thrilled.'

'Hey, what about your job here?'

'Oh, I'll have to give up my star-studded career as a driver in order to settle for international celebrity. Yeah, it's a tough decision. Perhaps I should consult a tarot-card reader.'

'So . . . Lady Luck smiles on our little muso, eh?'

'I told you I was hot, man.'

'You might just be.'

'What's that mutt paying, anyway?' I asked.

'Five to one. If you don't mind me asking, why does a record company want to sign you, anyway?'

'Because, my dear boss, when not working for you, I have been in training to be the next Frank Sinatra.'

'Yeah?'

'Yeah. I've even had people killed.'

'Well, in the meantime, Old Brown Eyes, your first job is 12 Walker Street, Redfern.'

'Right.'

He handed me six hot cardboard boxes.

I screeched out of the garage, which never failed to irritate Eddie, but that night he just sniggered. I adjusted the mirror and some confetti fell out of my sleeve.

I told everybody that I drove a cab because that's what Robert De Niro did in *Taxi Driver*. Or at least that's what I think he did. Perhaps it was a limo. Anyway, driving a cab was a kind of cool job. I *did* drive for Eddie. However, I delivered pizzas. Oh, and did I mention that I was dressed as a clown? (Yeah, go on, laugh! But you try driving a manual car in size 17 shoes!)

Funny Pizza was the only job I could seem to hold down. Mainly because they couldn't find anyone else to work there. The tips were great though. And at least they gave you a car that was yours to keep. The downside was that it had a giant red nose on the bonnet, a tiny hat and green wig across the roof. It was awkward on dates. Mostly it sat parked in my alley. Jenny kept asking about it, but

I denied all knowledge of it. She would say, 'Surely you must have seen *someone* get into it'. I would shrug my shoulders, and sweat slightly.

Eddie took care of organising deliveries while his brother Stavros made the pizzas. Originally their father made the pizzas. The old man would tell me in that wheezy Cypriot voice that it was not the Italians but the Greeks who made the first pizza. I said no, that was the discus and has led to confusion at every Olympics ever since. I liked the old man. We got on. He died peacefully in his sleep one night when a truck careened off the highway and drove through his front bedroom. However, the old man must have been right about the enterprising Greeks because Funny Pizza made the best pizzas in Sydney.

Though Eddie didn't deliver any more, he still wore full make-up. 'Team spirit' he liked to call it. This was impractical at times since Eddie used to sweat a lot. As you can imagine, we delivered to kids' parties from time to time. One day we were swamped with orders, so Eddie decided to help with the deliveries. It was a stinking hot day. Exhausted, Eddie pulled up to a house for the day's final delivery. He pressed the doorbell. A little girl in a pink fairy costume answered. She became hysterical and started screaming. You see, Eddie's make-up had run so far down his face he looked like a serial killer with food. The girl was calmed but the father eventually sued Funny Pizza. (The lawsuit seemed a little over the top. After a couple of months of therapy, she was fine, but Eddie never delivered again.)

I pulled up at a house in Redfern – my first delivery for the evening. It was a rough neighbourhood. It had that rotting vegetable smell that rundown neighbourhoods have. Every second streetlight was broken, and cannibalised cars encrusted with cinnamon-brown rust were dotted along the street. There must have been a council clean-up, as a pyre of junk sat on the footpath outside each dilapidated terrace. They all seemed to be the same piles of crap. The ubiquitous gutless sofa. A broken toaster. A television with the back hanging off. A record player. Bags of grass clippings (you weren't supposed to do that) that had been ripped open by someone thinking it was clothing. Records – the Dumpster Collection: *Barry Crocker: Get Funky*; *Kamahl: The Sri Lanka Years*; *Jim Neighbours Sings Songs of Praise*; *Classic Hits '76*; *Kenny Ball and His Jazz Men Play Thelonius Monk*.

Balancing the delivery, I picked through the junk of Number 12.

'Make sure you clean it up this time,' a voice snapped from behind the door. The TV flashed blue behind him.

I kneed open the gate.

'What do you want?' he asked.

'I have your pizza.'

The door opened wider and a guy, tattoos and muscles, snatched the pizza. 'Thanks.' He slammed the door. But he hadn't counted on my size 17 shoes.

'What about paying me, man?'

'What for?'

'What for? This *is* Walker Street, right?'

'Yeah.'

'Number 12, right?'

'No. This is Number 10. You want Malcolm. Next door. Now fuck off.'

It was going to be one of those nights. Back to base.

I eventually came back to Number 12.

'You're twenty minutes late,' Number 12 reprimanded.

'We've been busy. Sorry. Um . . . now . . . you ordered a Funny Marinara, two Garlic Feet and a Coke. That's $16.60. And, oh, have a funny evening,' I sighed.

'You're late. I want my joke.'

Oh, crap.

I forgot to tell you about that. You see, if it's not delivered in seventeen minutes or less, you get a free joke. If you can't make the customer laugh, the food is free. Eddie's 'great' idea. With five pizzas in the car going cold, I needed a quick joke.

'Um . . . er . . .' I couldn't think of one.

'Come on, get on with it, for Christ sake! My food's going cold!'

'Um, okay, okay, I'm thinking . . . um . . . two bishops and a nun walk into a strip club –'

'Heard it.'

'Oh. Eh . . . an elephant sits at a bar . . .'

'I've heard that one, too. You guys are crap.'

'Oh . . . eh . . . a Chinese waiter went to see an optometrist.'

'I'm listening . . .'

'Um . . . he sat this Chinese waiter in the chair and studied his eyes. The optometrist said: "I see the problem. You have a cataract." The waiter said: "No, I drive a Rincon Continetal."'

He smirked.

'You laughed, so pay me, man.'

'I didn't. I grimaced.'

'Look buddy, a grimace is still considered "being amused".'

'No, it's not.'

I sighed. 'Okay, how about a magic trick?'

'Okay, make it quick. If I'm not impressed you can piss off.'

'Give me the twenty bucks for a second.' He handed me the money. 'Now close your eyes. There's twenty bucks here, right? Feel it.'

'Right.'

I hopped in the car and floored it.

'WHAT KIND OF MAGIC TRICK DO YOU CALL THAT?' he screamed from the end of the street.

'A FUCKING GOOD ONE. THANKS FOR THE TIP!' I honked the horn. It played the 'Big Top' theme.

It was a slow night and rain fell on the streets in a meditative 6/8 rhythm. I'd been delivering for a couple of hours in the choppy city streets and taken forty-three dollars in tips. (Not bad, eh? See, you laughed at me before.) Anyway, I was content. But hot in the clown make-up. I looked in the rear-view mirror. I straightened my round, red nose. Clown pride, Eddie called it. I listened to a tape of Art Pepper and fantasised about my impending life of fame and fortune as a jazz musician. Most of the customers were subdued that night due to the rain. This suited me because I didn't feel like doing any clowning unless absolutely necessary. I merely wanted to dream. Dream about walking into a record store and finding my CD in the jazz section. Dream about turning on the radio and catching one of my tunes by chance. Dream about running over to Chuck's place with the first copy and writing something sentimental on the cover. As I waited for a light to change, I thought, this record deal will change everything for me. No more delivering pizzas in large shoes. This is the break I've been waiting for all my life, my karma, as Julia would say.

The rain lulled. The metronome of the window wipers started to stutter against the dry windscreen. I wound down the window. The air smelled fresh and moist. The city looked alluring after the downpour. All the filth and soot had been washed away and the streets shined like a new pair of shoes. I drove into the city and suddenly spotted a trumpet player I knew. He was cool. I had worked with him a lot. He was chatting with a very good-looking blond guy who could have just stepped off a catwalk.

'Steve!' I yelled.

They gave me an odd look. Steve tilted his head and screwed up his face.

Oh. Jesus. I forgot. I was *dressed as a clown*!

He crossed the street.

'Do I know you, buddy?' he said.

'No.' I sped off.

I drove around the streets for a while, deep in thought. I was feeling low. Funny Pizza was a humiliating job really. Jazz musicians simply didn't dress up as clowns.

Next delivery was a kids' party. Eddie had a special 'party pack', where the sap doing the delivery stayed and did some lame clowning for the kids for five minutes. It was mainly aimed at parents who were too cheap to hire a real clown, but wanted the other kids to tell their parents that little Freddy had a clown at his party. The money was good, so I was usually happy to get the job. It was pretty easy. The kids were usually busy stuffing their faces and I would do a couple of crappy tricks and slip out in a cloud of confetti. Tonight, I was tired and feeling low. It had not been a good night. By the time I got there, the tranquillisers had started to take effect. (This was bad, I know. I have no one to blame but myself for the following.)

I'd got there a little later than expected and the parents were annoyed. The seven-year-olds were wild with excitement so the parents soon cooled down in that nothing-must-spoil-their-boy's-big-day kind of way. They left me alone in the kitchen with the kids, handing out pieces of pizza. (I could have sworn I saw the parents running out of the house and down the street.) The party had been going since midday and the kids were wired with sugar. A Mardi Gras of sweets and cakes and fluorescent-coloured drinks stretched across the entire house. The kids had that twitchy, sugar-crazed look on their faces. Some were jumping around me, others were filling up water pistols and squirting me. But something happened that never happened before. They didn't eat the pizzas. Birthday Boy, dressed in a Ninja costume, spoke, 'Come on. Do something!'

'Oh, um, okay, let's all settle down and sing a song –'

'This isn't karaoke, pal. We want to see magic.' The other kids started chanting 'Ma–gic, ma–gic'.

I proceeded to go through some lame trick, but they weren't buying it. Birthday Boy started getting nasty. 'How long have been doing this?' he said.

Ignoring him, I turned to a little girl dressed as Posh Spice who was popping Smarties and trembling. 'Okay, what about a funny story, Posh?' I slurred.

'This is crap!' Birthday Boy said.

It had been a cold night and it was too warm in the house. I started to nod off a little.

Birthday Boy jumped up and turned to the others. 'Look! Now, he's falling asleep!'

'No, I'm not. Hang on, wait until Mr Clown has a drink of water.' I splashed some water on my face and then remembered my make-up. Shit, what was I doing here? I'm about to become a major recording star and I'm dressed as a clown, babysitting. I waited for the water to wake me up. It didn't work. I was exhausted. I was also being squirted up the crack with a Super-Soaker. I had to get out of there. Fast. I turned to the kids.

'Um . . . now for my ultimate trick. Close your eyes and count to ten. Now, no peeking.' I crept out of the kitchen, backwards. I ran for the door. It was deadlocked. In my delirium, I frantically jiggled the lock, tugging at the door. I heard a horrible sound: stampeding seven-year-olds. I turned, terrified, as Birthday Boy said in a slow, low voice: 'Get him.'

They lunged at me, knocking me to the floor. I must have passed out because the rest is sketchy. I can remember Birthday Boy straddling me and hitting me up the balls with plastic nunchakus, while his friend, dressed as Robo-Cop, drenched me with the Super-Soaker. I vaguely recall one kid using my spine as a trampoline and a little ribbon-haired girl who smelled of strawberries batting me over the head with Disco Barbie.

After coming to in casualty, I checked myself out and drove over to Eddie's. I handed in my resignation. Being a clown was getting too dangerous in this city. He was cool about it, actually. So now, jobless, I really sweated on this meeting with Delta.

In my regular clothes again, I wandered into an all-night café for a cup of coffee. My nose had stopped bleeding by this stage, but I still had little flags of tissue stuck up my nostrils. I bought a newspaper but threw it away – too much on my mind to read. I ran the telephone conversation through my mind again. I tried to recall the exact tone in the secretary's voice, analysing each inflection.

'Felix will look forward to meeting with you then . . .'

I caught myself mouthing the words in the reflection of the window. In the glass, I could still see the indents in my forehead where the kids had driven into me with Ken's Campervan. I dunked my donut. Half of it fell into the coffee.

'Great! What a night.'

I fished it out with a teaspoon like an angler netting a dead trout. I swallowed it. It felt slimy as it slid down the back of my throat.

I wonder what I should wear to this powwow tomorrow? I asked myself. Maybe I should get my watch out of the hockshop. Mustn't be late for the meeting.

I looked out the window and onto the glassy road. Cars wooshed past at random intervals, their ghosts trailing them in windows opposite. A prostitute staggered up the street in platform shoes. It looked as though she had two office blocks strapped to her feet. She had that junkie shuffle that they all have. She walked with mouth open, showing only the whites of her eyes, knees buckling slightly with each step. Her mascara spider-webbed across her face in the drizzle. Her tights were teardrops of ladders. She came in and asked me if I wanted a fuck and if not, could she have a cigarette. I told her I didn't smoke and, despite her glamorous offer, I didn't want to have sex with her. She staggered out with a wearied snarl on her face. I watched her as I drank my coffee. I wondered what her dreams were? Did she still have any? I hummed a melody I'd been working on. It was around eleven. I usually did my best work at this time. Soon I'd be at home quietly tinkling on the piano, with my accompanist, Mrs Bloomsbury, banging her mop on the ceiling in a muffled voice saying she was calling the police. I pulled out a few crumpled notes to pay.

Looking up, I noticed an old Koori trying to hail a cab. His grey matted hair looked like a giant bird's nest. He stood as still as a flamingo, arm outstretched, as one empty cab after another splashed by. If you were black, you had about as much chance of hailing a cab as hitching a ride from a bus full of Hare Krishnas while eating a hamburger in a T-shirt saying: '*Bad Karma*'.

The hooker asked the old Koori for cigarettes. He ignored her. She persisted. He reached into his moth-eaten, grey overcoat and gave her a small, polished stone. She threw it at him, swore and wobbled off. I studied his indignant, proud face. It reminded me of one of those carved Easter Island heads that stared into the endless Pacific. Another five cabs swished past him. Suddenly, he looked over at me. It was uncomfortable. It was as if he knew I was surveying the whole racist vignette from the sanctuary of the café. I hung my head. He resumed his search for the cab.

'Thanks, Tony!' I threw some change on the counter and walked out into the slushy street. It started to rain again. He stared at me.

'Can I hail a cab for you?' I asked.

He remained silent.

I felt my face. 'Oh, I was beaten up by a gang of seven-year-olds. You've got to watch kids, they can turn.'

Silence.

He walked up to me. 'What you looking for, boy?'

'Nothing.'

'Everybody looking for something in this life. What *you* looking for, boy?'

'Oh, the usual.'

'What?'

'You know, a super model, a record contract, and, oh . . . the meaning of life.'

'The meaning of life?' He pulled out a long black feather. 'Take it.'

I took it, but it was snatched by the wind. We watched it sabre and parry down the street, till it disappeared from sight.

He shook his head. 'You have a long journey ahead, boy.' On that note, he walked off into the drizzle.

I stood there, dumbfounded. Tony beckoned me back into the coffee shop.

'Don't worry about old Bill Starlight. He does that from time to time. He's always giving stuff to people. Stones. Little things carved from wood. Most people just toss em away. Thinks he's a spirit man. He is, but only if it's one hundred per cent proof.'

'Likes a drink, eh?'

'Yeah. Drinks all day and then harasses people all night. He's harmless though. One night I saw him point a little bone at some Abo kid and he died on the spot.'

I was freaked out. 'You're kidding!'

'I'm kidding. Get some sleep, Gordon. You look terrible.'

⌒

At home, I disgorged my pockets onto the table. Glancing at the phone, I thought of the call again.

What do they see in me, for Christ's sake? I guess it's the article. Maybe the tape. Maybe both. But why? Delta aren't interested in jazz. Jazz doesn't sell, I told myself. I started to think about the old Koori. In my mind's eye I watched the feather disappear down the street. What was *that* all about? Spooky.

The pills started to numb my brain. I downed them with vodka, which made them work faster. The beating had shaken me. I just couldn't cope with a major anxiety attack at the moment. If I got out of control I could wind up in St Vincent's for a few days and miss the whole meeting, I thought. Voices inside my head started doing vocal exercises. I *had* to do something about calming down. Quickly. I needed to see Dr Goldstein.

I stuffed some notes into my polished-worn suede coat and walked out into the night. I walked so quickly that if I'd been competing in the Olympic walk, I'd be shown the red card. I weaved through serpentine alleyways and around the back streets of the Cross. Then up New South Head Road and past Edgecliff station.

Panting, I eventually arrived at the elegant Deco-style apartment building in Double Bay. I wasn't sure if he'd still be awake. I breathed a sigh of relief when I saw the light on.

Dr Goldstein had asked me *not* to call him outside office hours. But, fortunately, he never mentioned anything about dropping around his house at 11.30 at night.

Dr Goldstein was my twelfth shrink. The last one – Dr Fields – said my need to see him was starting to border on the obsessive. He had some fancy medical term for it. Oh, that's right: 'stalking'.

Dr Goldstein was an irritable man. He never lightened up and showed his vulnerable side. I never saw him smile. Even on his birthday. Once during my session, his secretary brought in a birthday cake in the shape of a straitjacket. Expressionless, he blew out the candles and mumbled something about a diet. Dr Goldstein was the sort of guy who was always right. He always had to win. Therefore, he was short on real friends. I knew he played golf every Thursday with his medico cronies. If losing, he was the sort of person who'd suggest to the leading player that perhaps they had a psychological hang-up of some kind. He would ask the urologist on the putting green why he washed his hands all the time. Or why the neurologist, heading for the bunker with his wedge, seemed to be complaining of headaches lately. If the gynecologist lined up the ball on the tee on the eighteenth for a winning drive, I bet he would point out that he was playing very aggressively, and does it have something to do with his deep-seated hatred of women?

I gingerly buzzed his apartment. Nervous, I hopped from one foot to the other. I felt *slightly* concerned that Dr Goldstein would not like me doing this, but, after all, he did say, any time I needed to talk to him, just contact his secretary.

'Who is it?' a deadpan voice asked through the squawk of the intercom.

'Um, it's . . . er . . . one of your patients.'

'Gordon, these are not office hours.' I heard voices and the clinking of glasses.

'How did you know it was me?'

'Gordon, you've called me at home three times this week already.'

'I just need to talk to you for five minutes, that's all.'

'I've told you before, you'll have to call the office in the morning, Gordon.'

'I can't wait that long. It's urgent.'

'Then drop into St Vincent's and see a locum.'

'Give me five minutes and I'll be gone.'

'No.'

'Pleeeeeeease?'

'*Five* minutes, Gordon. That's all.'

'Thanks. Buzz me up.'

'I can't. I'm having a dinner party. You have four and a half minutes.'

'What? Talk out here? In the street?'

'Yes.'

'Can I lie down?'

'Who is it, Geoffrey?' A tipsy woman asked in the background.

'Just one of my patients, Margaret. Tell them I won't be long,' he whispered.

'It's not that "Gordon" again is it?' she whispered.

'Be a pet and make me a martini, will you?' he said.

'Was that your wife?'

'Yes.'

'Nice lady.'

'You have three minutes.'

'Right, well, where shall I start? Well . . . when I was six years old my . . .'

'Let's cut to the chase. What's happened tonight? You sound upset.'

'Well, I was beaten up tonight.'

'Oh, God. By whom? Are you injured?'

'AARRGHH, FUCK! . . .'

'My God! What's happened? Are they following you? Gordon . . . HELLO . . .'

'No, no. I'm lying across your doorway and one of your neighbours was stepping over me with a bag of groceries. A can of beans fell on my head . . . yes, yes, here you are . . . they're full of salt you know . . . no I can't hold the door open for you, lady! I'm in THERAPY HERE IF YOU HAVEN'T NOTICED!'

'Gordon, who on earth beat you up?'

'A seven-year-old ninja.'

Click.

'Hello . . . hello? Dr Goldstein . . .?' I kept buzzing. 'Dr Goldstein?'

He answered. 'I can't see you on Wednesdays any more, Gordon.'

'Why, are you playing golf?'

SLIM CHANCE AND HIS OTHER COWBOY FRIENDS

∽

I WOKE UP FEELING DISORIENTED. I'd had the dream again. But this time the old Koori had joined the merry cast of players. In the dream he is wearing a paper party hat. He passes the feather to me across the table.

I got up. My head felt like a concrete block. My stomach felt like it was filled with green paint. Apart from that, I felt fine. I had been so anxious the previous night that I'd taken too many pills. I vomited them up all night. They sat in pink and blue puddles around the apartment. But, hey, this was a new sensation. I got through a whole night without drugs! I was proud of myself. I walked into the bathroom and looked into the mirror. My eyes were black moons. I threw some water on my face. It felt like gravel. I took my hands out of the pot plant and washed them. I must move that freaken pot one day. I keep doing that. I looked in the mirror again. I studied my lime complexion. Wouldn't make the cover of *Vogue*, I thought. I suddenly remembered the meeting. Shit! I ran to the phone to call for the time. A yellow post-it note clung to the receiver.

You have no more excuses for being late. Love Jen XXX

Jenny had got my watch out of hock and had had my suit pressed, ready for the meeting. It hung in a plastic membrane on the door.

She must've dropped it in last night, I reasoned. What a doll. I strapped the watch to my wrist.

'About four hours sleep, oh well, better than nothing, I suppose.'

I rubbed my forehead. What a terrible night. I'll have to tell Dr Goldstein on Wednesday.

I staggered into the kitchen. The morning sun crept in behind me. I opened the cupboard and grabbed a packet of coffee. Another cockroach darted out and I hit it with a tea towel. I shut the door and peeled open a fresh pack of coffee. I took a pleasing whiff before shovelling it into the percolator. Before long, some ebony syrup trickled into the pot. I downed it and felt almost human again. Wincing as I opened the fridge door, I undertook the breakfast assault. I found a rotten tomato and a slice of three-day-old pizza. It was the pizza, I decided. I picked it up. It's got bacon in it. That's kind of breakfasty, I thought. I took a bite and washed it down with some coffee. The phone rang.

'Hello?' I said through a mouthful of pizza.

'Good morning, is that Gordon Shoesmith?'

Suddenly my blood ran cold. Was this the record company cancelling the appointment? Of course it was! Oh, what a fool I'd been to think they'd be interested in me all this time. What an idiot, I chided myself. They must have found out who I really was. That I had no gigs. No fans. No future. No life. And that I was on long-term medication.

'Hello, Gordon, this is George Harris.'

'Oh . . . um . . . hi, Mr Harris.' I swallowed the mouthful of pizza in one gulp. My shoulders dropped.

Jenny's father had *never* called before. I found myself unconsciously cleaning the table as he spoke.

'Is Jenny all right?' I asked, trying to sound alert.

'Yes . . . yes . . . the reason I'm calling . . . is . . . well . . . I just want to wish you luck today, young man. Jenny's told us all about the big news and I just wanted to say congratulations and jolly good luck.'

'Ahemm.' I wrestled with some phlegm before clearing my throat. 'Thanks very much, Mr Harris.'

'Jenny's conveyed to us on many occasions over the years that you possess considerable talent and . . . well . . . I suppose this confirms it.' I could hear the pain in his voice. 'And I'd . . . um . . . also like to say, er . . .' I felt Mrs Harris prodding her husband in the back with a manicured fingernail. '. . . that Mrs Harris . . . what? . . . oh . . . er . . . Fay . . . and I would like to officially welcome you into the family. What? Oh, and we're . . . proud to have you as our future son-in-law.' This last sentence was said through clenched teeth.

'Thanks, Mr Harris. I'm sure we'll be seeing a lot more of each other now. Probably every second weekend. I'm looking forward to sailing with you and dining at your club and stuff.'

'Looking forward to it,' Harris said flatly. 'Now, don't rush into anything. Make sure you don't sign anything without talking to a solicitor.'

'We won't be getting married straightaway, Mr Harris.'

Harris burst into nervous guffaws. 'No, I mean at the meeting. You know how unscrupulous those record companies are.'

I detected a sentiment I had not heard before. 'Thanks for the advice, Mr Harris.'

'I have the name and number of a solicitor for you,' he said with chairman-of-the-board aplomb. 'His name is Philip Bard. 15–25 King Street, Sydney. His number –'

'Slow down. Slow down, Mr Harris. Is that Philip with one "l" or two.'

'One.'

'So . . . hang on . . . Philip with one "l".'

'Yes. His number is 9223 8476.'

'9223 8426?'

'No, 8476.'

'Got it. 8476.'

'Right.'

'Now, did you say King Street or Kent Street?'

'For God's sake. 15–25 *King* Street, Sydney. Have you got it?' he asked irritably.

'Perhaps I better get a pen and write this down.'

I looked for a pen, but couldn't find one so I used one of Jenny's over-priced lipsticks.

'Are you there?'

'Yeah.'

'Philip Bard. 15–25 *King* Street. 9223 8476.'

'Got it.'

'He's a friend of mine who's a solicitor for various celebrities. He's expecting your call.'

(Oh, I'm a celebrity now.)

'I've told him he'd make more money as a corporate lawyer, but he likes dealing with arty types,' he added.

(Hmmm. I'm an arty type, too.)

'Call him before signing ANYTHING. Make sure you mention my name,' he stressed.

'Thanks. I will, Mr Harris.'

'Eh . . . call me George, Gordon.'

I put the phone down and shook my head. The telephone call started to make me think about the meeting with increasing alarm.

Now I've dropped myself right in it, I thought. The reality is that even if the meeting goes well, I've got a snowflake's chance in hell of getting a record deal – a slim chance at best. I looked at my watch. Six hours to go.

I took a calming breath and wandered over to the piano with my coffee. Taking an index finger, I laconically pegged out one of my melodies – as if to give me a shot of confidence for the interview. It's a pretty tune, I thought. Needs work though. The phone rang.

'Hello.'

'Hi, Gordon,' my uncle said.

'Oh, hi.'

'I just rang to wish you luck.'

'Thanks.'

'Whacha wearing?' he asked.

'Black suit. Gold watch.'

'I thought you pawned that?'

'Jenny got it out.'

'You don't deserve that girl.'

'So she keeps telling me.'

'Is the suit clean?'

'Yeah, she had it cleaned too.'

'She got his suit cleaned, Helen,' he hollered to my aunt in the background. 'She's a gem that girl. Oh well, you should look quite smart then.'

'Maybe it's too formal. What if he's in T-shirt and jeans?'

'Then he'll know he's dealing with a person who takes himself seriously, won't he?' my uncle quipped with 1950s logic.

'Obviously you've never gone as Carmen Miranda to a fancy-dress party that was changed to normal-dress at the last minute.'

'Did that happen to you?'

'Yeah. I wouldn't have minded so much, but people kept picking fruit off my head on the dance floor.'

'Anyway, good luck today, Gordon.'

'Thanks, Dad.' (I've called him that all my life. Made it easy at school meetings and things.)

⌒

I wandered over to the stereo and picked out a record. *Round Midnight*. I plucked a flea of dust from the stylus before playing it. The room was now white with sunlight. I listened as Miles blew frail notes across the room.

I moved to the window and gazed out. My brain was now beginning to join the rest of my body. A wino lay prostrate across the doorway of the building opposite. A couple of 'God's helpers' from the Salvation Army were asking him to come with them, get cleaned up and sing hymns about virgins. The old drunk was waving his arms about, trying to tell them something of importance. I opened the window to find out what it was. Like all the windows in the apartment, the sashcord was broken, so I had to jam a stick in the frame. A heady aroma of urine and smog raped my nostrils.

'Ffthhuck orfth,' yelled the toothless old reprobate, spitting crimson sherry over his shirt.

Having spent the night in a comparable position, I instantly sided with the black-footed vagrant. They pleaded with him for another five minutes. He threatened them with a bottle, pouring the rest of the spirit over him. He was like Bacchus in a cheap suit with no teeth. After a few more minutes, I watched the disciples of lemonade shake their heads, and eventually disappear down the alley with thoughts of Jesus in their pious hearts.

I wonder where *your* family is, old man? I asked myself. What was your dream?

I closed the window. A large black parrot smacked against the glass, startling me. It perched on the ledge, twitching and looking askance at me the way birds do. Its long black tail feathers looked as though they were dipped in red paint.

I'd never seen a bird like this in the city before. I reasoned that it must have been someone's pet that had escaped. Maybe it was worth money. A reward. It continued to stare sideways at me. I opened the window. It flapped off. I watched it. Black against the lemon sky. I sat down and listened to the record.

Man, I wish I had Philly Joe Jones in *my* rhythm section. What a feel! That cat swings like a clock. I realised that the record had stopped. I was listening to the clock. I put on a new record. Bloody vinyl.

The phone rang. I panicked. I turned down the music. What if it was the record company cancelling the appointment? Oh, God. Maybe I shouldn't answer it. Just front up. They can't do this to me. Not on the day of the appointment. These people are sadists. I won't answer it. Just turn up! It stopped ringing. I sighed. It rang again. I fretted. I didn't answer it. It stopped. I sighed again. It rang again. Shit! I picked it up.

'Hello,' I said slowly.

'Why didn't you answer the phone?' It was Jen.

'I was in the toilet.'

'Anyway, you're up,' Jenny said flatly.

'Yes.'

'How you feeling?'

'Stressed. I think I'm going to screw it up.'

'Don't be negative, Gordon. Life's a self-fulfilling prophecy, you know. Did you get the watch?'

'Oh, I forgot. Thanks so much for doing that. That was sweet.'

'I love you, that's all.'

There was a pause. I was supposed to say it back.

'It back,' I said.

'Cheers,' she said dryly.

'You're good to me, Jen.'

'I know. You don't deserve me,' she said.

'So everyone tells me.'

'You were out last night.'

'Yeah. Had a blow with some guys.'

'Liar.'

'No flies on you, lady.'

'You didn't call poor Dr Goldstein at home again?'

'No, I didn't *telephone* Dr Goldstein.'

'Good.'

'Some people called to wish me luck today.'

'Who?'

'Well, my uncle and, oh, I told you the other day my sister called from London telling me it was my karma, etc. That she knew this would happen eventually, etc. Go in really positive, etc.'

'Yes, yes, yes. You told me all that. Who else called?'

'Are you sitting down?'

'I'm at work, I always sit down.'

'Your father.'

'You're *kidding*!'

'Nope.' I tucked the phone under my chin and changed the record.

'What did he say?'

'Good luck today . . . welcome to the family blah blah blah . . . call me George etc.'

'Wow!'

'My thoughts exactly. I haven't had much sleep,' I said, rubbing a bloodshot eye.

'I didn't think you would. Today's been on your mind.'

'I know. I'm nervous. I hope I don't blow it because I'm tired.'

'Don't be melodramatic.'

I laughed because I was always being melodramatic.

I could hear the whispering of keyboards in the background. 'Anyway, I just wanted to –'

'I know, I know . . . wish me luck.'

'Anyway, make sure you stay focused today. Don't say the wrong thing.'

'Okay.'

'Call me as soon as you leave the meeting. Don't forget.'

'Okay.'

'Ciao.' Jenny liked to say 'ciao'. It made her feel urbane.

'Later.' I liked to say 'later' because that's how Miles finished his autobiography. It made me feel cool.

Quite sad, really.

I threw myself on the bed and dozed.

Despite my shortcomings, Jenny loved me. There was a part of her that wanted to mother me. The other part wanted to strangle me. Sometimes she just wanted to strangle me in a motherly way. I don't think she knew exactly why she was in love with me. She knew she could do better. Friends and family were always politely letting her know. They were always trying to set her up with some polished, cocktail-drinking executive who drove an imported car and referred to his old lady as 'mother'. Were her friends all blind? Those executive types just didn't do it for her. They weren't vulnerable enough. Weren't human enough. She needed to feel in control. And with me, she was. I was simply hopeless.

⌢

I looked at myself in the mirror for the eighteenth time. My shirt had a cigarette burn on it. I studied the sultana-looking mark in the mirror.

The jacket will cover it as long as I don't lean hard to the left, I thought. Putting the jacket on, I practised a guarded handshake that wouldn't expose the burn.

I walked over to the record player and turned it up. Coltrane peppered the apartment with squealing notes. I continued to dress. I looked at my shoes. They were scuffed and sorry. I spat on them and wiped them on the backs of my suit trousers with schoolboy logic. Buttoning the freshly pressed jacket, I grabbed my keys, a few dollars and slammed the door.

The Funny Pizza car sat in the alleyway. Eddie had felt so bad about the beating that he gave me the car. As the car was a 1973 Datsun 180B, I would have preferred cash. Pools of acid gurgled in my stomach as I placed the key in the lock. I turned the engine over. Would you believe it? No start.

'Fuck.'

I slumped over the steering wheel.

It's the rain! I thought. I dowsed the carburetor with some

WD40 that I kept in the glove box (does anyone ever actually *keep* gloves in a glove box apart from thieves and serial killers) and got back in. I turned the engine over a few more times. It coughed like a war veteran, blew a puff of smoke and started.

I made my way over to Delta Records in thick traffic. The sound of barking horns and whining brakes were an echo of my thoughts. I felt nervous in the extreme. I rehearsed my opening statement with the rear-end of the car in front.

'Thanks for your time, Mr Smedly. Nice office. Is that a picture of your kids, Mr Smedly? They have your eyes. Call you Felix? Why certainly. Well, "Old Feel", it's like this . . .'

At last, I arrived at the corporate Taj Mahal that was Delta Records. I trembled up the steps to the main office. I stood gawking at the building's cathedral-like dimensions. The building was a monochrome of black marble. I stood anxiously at the large tinted glass doors. A sign in massive titanium letters shouted: 'Delta Records'. I nervously hopped from one foot to another. This was the music world's version of a lowly monk being summoned to the Vatican. After a great deal of pacing and puffing outside, I finally found the required intestinal fortitude to enter.

Three frosty receptionists in spatula-applied make-up sat behind an enormous granite reception desk. They were all sporting identical black T-shirts with some rock band or other on them. The switchboard lit up like a Christmas tree as the women juggled calls in a choir of nasal tones. I could smell the chemical potpourri of their collective perfume. The reception area was so large, twenty-foot palm trees mushroomed overhead. I felt at any moment their green fingers would reach down, grab me by the throat, and throw me out. I watched as a current of couriers in tight shorts and sneakers, holding clipboards, collecting or dropping off parcels, rushed past. One asked me to sign for something. I did. I stood anxiously for ten sheepish minutes before one of the receptionists addressed me in a deadpan voice.

'Yeees. Can I help yooou over there?'

'Um . . . my name's Gordon. I'm here to see . . . Felix Smedly,' I choked. Strangely, a queer feeling came over me as I repeated Smedly's name in my head. Where have I heard his name before? Must be at that party – when I met him, years ago. No, it feels like somewhere else. But where?

The receptionist irritably flicked through an appointment book. 'I'm sorry. I see no appointment.'

I panicked. Could I have got the day wrong? Had they changed their mind and I missed the call? I have no answering machine. It's possible.

'I believe I do have one. Could you check again?' I asked, dry-mouthed.

'Mr Shoeshine is it?' she said through a manufactured smile.

'Shoesmith.'

'You're twenty minutes early, Mr Shoesmith.'

'Eh . . . I wasn't sure of the traffic.'

'Take a seat and I'll have someone pop down to collect you. Can I have someone park your car?'

'Yes. No! I mean . . . er . . . I came by bus.'

'Wasn't that you who stepped out of that clown car?'

'No.'

'Oh. Coffee?'

'Thanks.'

'Cappuccino, latte, short black . . .?'

Wow, it's a regular coffee shop. 'I'm easy. Whatever,' I said.

'What will it be?'

I threw a limp wrist. 'Ah, something simple. Um, I'll have . . . eh . . . a latte, half-caf, half decaf, half skim, half regular, one and a half sugars. I prefer a mug if you have one. Oh, actually, do you have Equal?'

I noticed her smile turn to a snarl. She returned with a coffee and a small chocolate. It sat like a gold nugget on the rim of a plate-sized saucer. I sat and was swallowed by a fat leather lounge. The coffee table was out of arm's reach so I had to hold the cup and saucer with my feet slightly in the air. Unless you were Michael Jordon or on growth hormones it was impossible to drink the coffee in a 'cool way'. After about fifteen minutes a young girl appeared wearing the ubiquitous black T-shirt. She greeted me in cordial tones.

'Gordon Shoesmith?'

'Ah, yes.' I was pretending to read some industry rag. I struggled from the sticky sofa and shook her hand – trying not to show the cigarette burn.

'I spoke with you on the phone the other day. Come through,' she said.

She ushered me through a side entrance. Then I was led through a maze of corridors and doorways. I noticed giant posters of the same band that was on the T-shirts. The poster showed various members of a band called 'Screaming Arthritis' riding motorbikes with large-breasted, bikini-clad girls on the back. The girls were grabbing the band members' crotches as they rode. It was tastefully done, mind you.

'How come the band wear leather and the girls only wear a bikini?' I asked, trying to make conversation.

'Oh, that's what the band wanted for the photo.'

'I know what I'd rather be wearing coming off a motorbike at two hundred k's an hour.'

She laughed uncomfortably.

Trailing her hound-like through dimly lit corridors, I spotted various gold and platinum records of renowned musicians. They were mounted along the walls like the heads of big game. Employees darted in and out of cubicles, cockroach-like. They all wore the same black T-shirt. I heard the pounding drone of heavy metal music in the background. A door must have opened because the aural stench wafted across the office.

'You're all dressed up,' she said, breaking silence.

I pulled at my collar. 'I guess I am.' I knew I shouldn't have worn the fucking suit. I looked around. 'Looks like it's . . .' I pretended to study her T-shirt, 'Screaming Arthritis awareness week'.

'Yeah. They go off!'

'I believe you mean *gone* off.'

'That was them you heard coming from Johnno's office. What do you think? Do you have it?'

'My aunt has it.'

'Cool lady!'

'I hear celery extract is good for it.'

'We're promoting their new single at the moment.'

'You don't say.'

'Do you like heavy metal?'

'Mainly in new cars.'

'Hang on a sec.' She darted into a storeroom and returned with a CD. 'Have a listen to it. You'll love it!'

'Well, you never know. I thought I'd never like masturbation till I tried it.'

She laughed uncomfortably. Again.

Dumb move, I said to myself. Keep your fat mouth shut, Gordon.

I just couldn't help myself. Grown men jumping around in lycra jumpsuits in a cloud of dry-iced smoke was a little hard for me to take seriously. I went once when I was a kid and I've never been to a Christmas pantomime since.

We continued in silence.

Finally we arrived at Smedly's office. I could hear rap music thumping against the door. She knocked timidly. I was again trying to remember why Smedly's name seemed so familiar. She knocked louder.

'Do you like rap music?' she asked enthusiastically.

'Yeah, but they keep misspelling it.'

'Huh?'

'You know. Rap. With a silent "C".'

'Enter,' a voice barked from behind the door.

We walked in.

Smedly waved the girl away and directed me towards a diminutive chair. 'Take a seat. Won't be long. I've got London on the phone.'

I sat in a chair that was designed to make you feel insignificant. It was probably fashioned by some pretentious Italian artist named 'Nono' or something, who had a write-up in *Vogue* that particular month. My nose hovered inches above the desk as Smedly bigshotted over the phone. I waited nervously.

The A&R man's dull face glanced over at me between limp phrases such as 'kick his arse' and 'I made that little turd what he is today'. (I later found out that Smedly had never 'made' anyone, but the law of averages was simply charitable on occasion.) Smedly had never met a jazz musician before. He was curious. Someone had told him that jazz was now 'cool'. He wanted to find out why. I remember him laughing – telling the caller that some fool had turned up for a meeting in a clown car.

Artistic people were an enigma to Smedly. Being in the position to manipulate their miserable lives would be the closest he would ever come to being one of them. With a bit of luck, after he used them up, he could dissect the carcasses and extract the residue of their souls, drink it, and be transformed into someone with some semblance of a personality. Others just drink light beer.

After what seemed like an eternity, Smedly hung up and addressed me. He threw his freckly arms behind his balding head. He leant back and plopped a pair of pointy cowboy boots on the rambling desk. I peered around them.

'Jazz, eh?' he said.

I couldn't help thinking how ridiculous a balding forty-five-year-old looks in dreadlocks, an Astro Boy T-shirt and high-heeled cowboy boots. (Really, balding people should avoid dreadlocks.)

The rest of his clothes were an uncoordinated hotchpotch of what he deemed to be the latest fashions.

'Got a lot of gigs at the moment?' he asked.

'Too many,' I lied.

'So I hear, so I hear. In demand, eh? That's the vibe on the street about you.'

There's a *vibe* on the street about me?

'Oh, by the way, we may get interrupted. A guy's calling from New York at four.'

'That must hurt his voice.'

'So we may get interrupted,' he added.

I shrugged my tense shoulders. 'That's cool.'

'Cool, yeah, cool!' replied Smedly. 'Very cool!' (He seemed to really like that word as that afternoon everything was 'cool', 'totally cool', 'extremely cool', or 'a tad brisk'.) 'Now, why did I want to see you?' he mumbled to himself. He flicked through some papers. There was nothing in the papers, but it made him look like an executive and not the ex-manager from a failed punk band that was being sued for embezzling the band's money.

I felt my stomach tighten. In a split second I saw myself collect a Grammy and thank Jenny and Chuck in my acceptance speech.

'Yes, I remember. I need to find some cool jazz musicians for David Hasslehoff's new album. He'll be down-under next month. He's huge in Germany.'

I felt my stomach drop fifty floors. So this was what the meeting was all about.

The phone rang again. This time it was 'LA' on the phone. LA? Now, why did that sound familiar? *Now* I knew where I'd heard this guy's name before! This was Brian's old A&R manager! The guy that sold him down the river. The guy that destroyed Brian's career! In my self-absorbed coma I'd completely forgotten.

Smedly finished the call and eventually pulled out charts and babbled on about '*Baywatch Down-under*' and 'demographics' and 'fan bases versus merchandising' but very little about music. I wasn't really listening, anyway. I was in a daze. To be perfectly honest, I struggled to stop a tear from splattering onto Smedly's goddamn designer chair. Anyway, I wouldn't give him the satisfaction. A musician weeping in his office would no doubt induce an instant hard-on for the balding record executive. There was no record contract. No deal. No dream. Nothing. As I sat there in his office I felt utterly worthless. (The 'worthless shit' tag, as Brian would say.) I started to get angry with myself for thinking Delta would even offer me a deal in the first place – and in a funny kind of way this helped pull me together a little.

'So what do you think?' Smedly finally asked.

I sat there in a daze. I fantasised about a record contract and how exciting it would be to hold a CD in my hand. A CD with *my* name on it. I even had a title: *The Cool School* by Gordon Shoesmith.

'Brian Bishop used to talk a lot about you,' I said softly.

'I didn't know you knew Brian?' Smedly smiled nervously, pulling at the collar of his T-shirt. 'How's the old rocker going?'

'Made cabbie of the month last week.'

'Fantastic.'

Arsehole, I said to myself.

'I discovered him, you know,' he nodded.

I chuckled. 'Is that right?'

Now was my chance to tell this prick where to go. I imagined relaying the episode to Brian over coffee. There'd be a lot of laughter. I'd exaggerate things of course. I'd tell Brian that Smedly offered me an incredible deal, but when I remembered who he was, I told him to stick it up his arse. My friends counted when it came right down to it, I'd tell him.

'So what do you think, Gordon?'

'What do *I* think, Smedly, old boy . . .?'

Now was my chance to let him have it. I'll tell him that he has the fashion sense of George W. Bush in drag. I'll tell him he has the charm of Pauline Hanson in a Chinese restaurant. Better still, I'll tell him Brian asked me to give you this, and then give him the finger. Brian would love that. He'd laugh and laugh. The word 'integrity' will be thrown around the café no doubt. Suddenly the phone rang.

'Your manager's outside. I didn't know you had management, Gordon.'

Neither did I. I sat open-mouthed. Jenny bustled into the room.

'Sorry, I'm late, Gordon. I had Phil from Sony on the phone again. He heard that I was on my way here and wouldn't get off the phone. I've got the contract in my briefcase. Can you go and grab us a couple of coffees, Gordon? I'd like to talk with Felix alone.' She hustled me out the door.

NEW KID ON THE BLOCK CHORDS

∞

WHEN I WALKED into The Cellar that night, I felt like I was walking on air. Only a handful of Australian musicians were signed to a major and I was one of them – and I played jazz! I sat at the bar and ordered a drink. Danny was behind the bar. He was a fine piano player, who would sometimes sit-in between orders and play for me if I sang out front. I sipped a beer. Sitting at the bar, I scanned the black-and-white photos of the various musicians that played there. I noticed mine. Since my record contract, it had been moved to a more prominent position. Yes, life was sweet. Betty sat on a stool by the door. She raised an eyebrow to say hello. She must have been in a good mood to give me such a reaction.

The Cellar was my favorite jazz club in Sydney. It was a cramped basement beneath a department store in the heart of the city and it was tricky to find if you weren't 'in the know'. As you'd descend the stairs into the darkened cavern, you'd smell that familiar smell: cigarette smoke and mould. It was the shabbiest club in Australia, but had a *fabulous* atmosphere. The piano was unique. It had the subtle sound that could only come from an instrument that had been dropped down a flight of stairs, thrown into a swimming pool, left in the sun for days, and then used as a makeshift stage for the show 'Tap Dogs'. The Cellar's concealed lighting was state-of-the-art. You usually played beneath a couple of bare bulbs. The microphones were shot, the PA was cactus – the monitors pointed across the stage so there was a constant ring at twelve decibels that sounded like someone continuously dragging a fingernail down a blackboard, and the power points were iffy. The audience were so jammed together that often someone would have to walk across the stage – mid song – in order to get to the toilet. The food was ordinary, but it was a true jazz club. In every sense of the word. I loved the place. My uncle used to take me there as a teenager (being a 'restaurant' it was the only jazz club I could get in to) to listen to fabulous Australian jazz luminaries like Merv Atchison, Charlie Munro, Errol Buddle and Julian Lee. My uncle used to get drunk and enthusiastically talk about a sax player or trombonist as if he had descended from Mount Olympus to play for us that night. Whether this was true or not, I knew then, from that early age, that I wanted to be a jazz musician.

'Hey, man, I heard the album the other day. Congrats, man,' said Danny.

'Thanks, man.'

'How on earth did you pull it off?' he said, cleaning a glass. 'I mean Delta Records – crazy.'

'Talent knows no boundaries, Danny,' I said with a wry smile.

He chuckled. 'Right. So you on for a blow tonight? You know, Chuck's not on till late.'

'Yeah, he asked me to sit in. You going to have a blow yourself?'

'We'll see how busy it gets. Mr Levinsky's in tonight,' he whispered.

Mr Levinsky was the owner. He was about seventy-two. By late evening, about ninety-three. He was a real character though, who donned a black beret and drove an old '65 Lambretta. (How he didn't kill himself was a mystery to all of us.) He worked hard for a man of his years. He used to like me and would often give me a free beer at the end of my gig. This was unusual, as he was a parsimonious man who was always griping that he didn't make enough money to keep the club going. But somehow he had for over twenty years. His many sons and daughters helped run the place. They were nice kids who were doing university degrees and thought of the place as a means to make occasional pocket money while helping out the old man.

On the door sat Betty. Betty was in her mid-fifties and must have been quite a looker in her day. Through her tobacco face twinkled two beautiful sapphire-blue eyes. You had to work hard to see them though. She wore those enormous glasses that older people seem to wear under the misapprehension that the greater the circumference of the glass, the greater the amplification of vision. This hypothesis only applies in high-powered telescopes and glass-bottom boats. Therefore her glasses looked like two tinted passenger windows from a jumbo jet. Betty booked the bands for Mr Levinsky and sat there all night drinking gin and tonics and chain-smoking cigarettes. She was a lovely lady once you broke down the steely defences. She always gave me a gig if I nagged her enough. Like most people who booked music, she was not a popular person as there were never enough dates to go around – she was really in a no-win situation.

Chuck went on – finally. He was always late. In all the time I knew him he never turned up to a gig on time. Sometimes I would collect him on the way to a gig and he'd be sitting at the kitchen table in his underwear lighting up a big spliff and telling me to 'chill baby'.

I was meeting Jenny that night. We were to talk about the plans for the wedding. I wanted to go to New York to get married. For two reasons. One, I didn't want to listen to her mother crying in the church as she walked up the isle: '[*sob*] . . . if she'd only [*sniff*] . . . given Douglas a chance . . . [*sob*] . . .' And two, I thought she might like New York and think about staying for a while. The current plan was to get married in a heritage mansion at Watson's Bay. Her mother had it all planned. God, it was a cast of thousands. The Sandersons had to come because Old Man Sanderson was a board member. The Palmers must get an invite as they had invited Harris to *their* daughter's wedding. The Penfolds were old friends from sailing. And the Jamiesons were seen at every society wedding in the eastern suburbs. Anyway, I think you get the picture.

Jenny appeared at the stairs like a Homeric nymph. She descended in her miniskirt, bare legs flashing white with each step. Betty let her in without paying. I was keen to point out that my photo had moved ten inches higher since the album came out. After nonchalantly nodding to my photo and saying, 'Oh, God, they even have my photo up here. I must have them take it down', we found a seat. We placed our coats over the chairs, grabbed a wooden tray and went and lined up at the servery for our food. We stood in a hot line looking at the white skull-capped man doling out something that was either Lasagna or Beef Wellington. Standing in line with my greasy tray, I realised The Cellar was kind of like Long Bay Gaol with live music.

'I'll just have the soup, thanks,' I said.

Jen quixotically asked to see the specials.

'On the board,' White Cap grunted.

'But . . . that's just what you have right here, isn't it?'

'Make it easy for you,' he mumbled in a thick Slavic accent.

'I'll have the soup', she said.

We sat down and chatted about our day. She was working on a story about big business and pollution and had found a multinational corporation that had been dumping waste in a Third World country. She had ambushed the MD about it during a conjecturable interview about 'Executives Having Bigger Sex Drives'. I gingerly broached the topic of New York.

'Gordon, for the final time. I'm not living in that rat's nest.'

'I think you'd really like it there. They *like* Aussies over there,' I ventured timorously.

'Gordon. My family is here. My friends are here. My job is here. And I find Americans loud and tedious. Is that clear enough for you?'

'That's resorting to a racial stereotype. You're a snob, Jen.'

'Then I'm a snob – who lives in *Sydney*.'

'What about New Jersey? They have a casino?'

Ignoring me, she checked her eyebrows in a shell-shaped compact.

She'd never liked the idea of living in New York. She said she was not prepared to live like a rat in a box just so I could play in smelly jazz clubs. Fair enough, I suppose. She said she was prepared to go on a holiday in the future. But this was no good. I couldn't pick up a gig walking through customs. I needed to live there. Become part of the scene. Blow with guys. Be around. Walk through Harlem and try to get mugged by guys who might know someone in a band. I needed to live there for a year at least. Simple as that.

Then *he* walked in. Betty jumped up from her stool and greeted him like a visiting earl. I'd never seen her so animated since the cigarette company offered to sponsor the place.

The twenty-year-old Adonis then sat at the bar and chatted with Mr Levinsky. It was the guy I'd seen with Steve the night I was beaten up by those kids. Jenny placed a stealthy eye on him as she checked her teeth for green specks of coriander in the compact. I could see him clearly in the light from the bar. He was beautiful. Tanned, with curly, honey-coloured hair, thick lips and a square jaw. He had a smile that would ripen fruit. In his white linen suit he leaned against the bar with the lassitude of landed gentry. At the time, I honestly thought he had popped down from the department store in the middle of a fashion show or something.

My thoughts were interrupted when Chuck hit the stage like a volcano. He sang Cole Porter's 'What Is This Thing Called Love?' then scatted Todd Dameron's 'Hothouse' over the classic standard. As he scatted, becoming red in the face, his fingers moved as if playing an imaginary saxophone. With his fez sitting squatly on his head, the audience cheered and applauded to the tinkling of glasses and snapping of cigarette lighters.

Later that evening, he asked me to sit in.

'Ladies and Gents of the hippest kind, please welcome to the stage, Delta Records' new international recording artist, Gordon B. Shoesmith.'

The crowd eagerly applauded in the way Australian audiences applaud anyone in the arts who has been acknowledged by someone outside their own country.

Chuck and I sang 'How High the Moon' and scatted Charlie Parker's 'Ornithology' over it. (We had jammed on it in Chuck's kitchen a hundred times.) We then blew over the changes for a while, scatting wildly.

Suddenly, Adonis jumped onto the stage. This was unusual, as he wasn't invited. (Musicians simply don't do that.) This guy must be very drunk or supremely confident, I thought at the time. Chuck looked at Hank, the one-legged piano player who was smoking a fat cigar. The piano player gave the nod that Adonis was 'cool'. He'd heard him blow before. The new boy grabbed the mike, regardless. The bass player and the drummer softly played a pedal over a 'two-five' as Adonis scatted crisply. Hank hobbled to the bar for a brandy and I sat at the piano. I was eager to check out what he had. I tinkled lightly as Chuck addressed the apprehensive audience.

'Will you also welcome to the stage,' he turned to Adonis, 'what's your name, man?' Adonis whispered in the old man's ear. 'Put your hands together and really dig, Mr Finius Thistlehorne.'

The crowd politely applauded as Finius turned to me, clicking his long fingers, speeding up the tempo on 'How High the Moon'. He scatted like a machine gun. I struggled slightly with the tempo. It was full steam ahead. Finius was nothing short of sensational. Then he scatted over Coltrane's 'Giant Steps'. (The Mount Everest of tunes for any jazz musician.) He made it look easy. Hank sat back at the piano and I got up and grabbed the other mike and scatted. Finius and I traded fours. Chuck stood back in awe and gaped. It was a shoot-out at the OK Corral. He sprayed me with lines, licks, quotes and funky notes. I returned fire with riffs, scales and modes that I never dreamed I could sing. Then Finius pulled out the big guns. He took it inside, outside, changing his voice, injecting humour, scatting in head voice, making his voice sound like other instruments, other singers, till I was writhing on the floor in a pool of blood. Then I looked up and saw him. Smedly. He was standing at the back and had seen the whole damn thing. I waved at him, but he pretended not to see me.

I slinked off the stage to the bar and ordered a double something. I looked at Jenny, who had her eyes riveted to Finius's full mouth. He noticed and started singing directly at her. She clung to every note. He was awesome. I looked over at Chuck. He had a look on his face as though an elephant had just put its foot through his kitchen window. I wandered over to our table, suddenly feeling like yesterday's news.

'This guy is sen-*sational*!' Jenny yelled over the music without looking at me.

'A little too cocky, if you ask me.'

'Talent knows no boundaries, Gordon.'

'Thanks,' I said.

'Cheer up. It's not the end of the world, at least he doesn't play the piano.'

Then came the end of the world. Nodding to Hank, Finius leapt onto the piano and played like an Oscar Peterson on amphetamines. His right hand was a blur of notes equal to his singing. His chords and voicings were daring, yet tasteful. All in all, the goddamn kid was amazing.

This was a real shock. I mean, there had always been better singers than me before. Better piano players, too. But locally, there were no legit singers who could sing and play the piano and put it all together like I could. Who could really swing. Make the music dance. Until one Finius Thistlehorne.

He jumped triumphantly off the stage – for a minute I thought the salivating Smedly was going to catch him in his arms. Smedly placed a sweaty arm around him and they chatted seriously in the corner, occasionally glancing over to me. Smedly was wearing a white T-shirt with 'DARE' written across it, a pair of brown, plaid, flared trousers (that were back in – or so his twenty-year-old assistant had told him) and a pair of NASA-sized white Nikes.

Jenny riffled through her handbag for a notepad. 'I *must* do a review on him. What was his name again?'

This was too much. Now she wants to do a fucking review on him! I cursed and slipped her notepad and pen into my pocket and went to the toilet to splash some water on my face. This was either a bad dream or I'd died and woken up in a neverending Liberal Party conference with live music. Holding my breath at the urinal, I pulled the chain that never worked. I washed my hands and looked into the mirror. I looked old and haggard. My eyes were dark. My hair was grey and my back was hunched. God, I looked terrible. Hang on, I realised I had been looking at Mr Levinsky in the mirror.

'Not bad this boy, eh?' the old man said, washing his hands.

I nodded and sighed, 'Yes, Mr Levinsky. Not bad at all.'

When I did find my own sad reflection, my face looked tired, my skin pocky, and I could see that I needed a haircut, a shave, a new suit and a facelift. In fact, Mr Levinsky looked better then I did. When I walked out, Jenny was talking with Finius. She was all smiles and boobs, leaning over in a chesty hunch the way girls do to give them more cleavage. He had one foot on my chair and was smiling that smile of his that could instantly make you give him all your money to invest in a prawn farm in Indonesia. That was enough for me. I left. On my way out, I noticed that the 10×8 he had given Betty was placed above mine. Eclipsed.

I walked out onto the city street. Blinking caterpillars of traffic inched foward as people darted in and out of them to get from one side of the street to another. Street cleaners in beeping yellow machines swept the gutters in opposite directions. I could smell the petrol in the air as I walked with no place to go. Groups of laughing teenagers shouldered me as I stood on the footpath in a daze. I felt like crying and screaming at the same time. My hands were shaking.

The pills took a while to take hold. I tried not to vomit from stress and fear and panic. Since signing to Delta, I had been down to one therapy session a week. But after this setback . . .

I was wandering along Castlereagh Street when, as luck would have it, I spotted Dr Goldstein. He was having dinner with a blonde perched in the front window of one of those minimalist restaurants. You know the type, everything is chrome with stark lighting and, if you ask for salt, there's a fifteen-minute discussion with management as to whether salt and pepper shakers would upset the feng shui of the room. I gingerly tapped the glass. Dr Goldstein waved a limp hand, smiled politely, and then continued talking to his dinner date as if I weren't there. Can you believe it? I took the notebook from my jacket and tore a piece of paper out and wrote. I held it up to the glass.

I NEED TO SEE YOU!!!

He had a look on his face like I'd just scratched his new Mercedes with my belt buckle. He scribbled on a napkin. He had neat handwriting for a medico, actually. He held it up to the glass.

CALL THE OFFICE IN THE MORNING!

JUST 5 MINS!

NO. GOODBYE GORDON.

I started to panic. I frantically scribbled.

ISN'T THAT YOUR SECERATARY? The woman flushed.

SECR*E*TARY. OK 5 MINS.

I AM HAVING AN ANXI . . . my pencil broke.

He asked the hovering waiter for another bottle of champagne.

LEARN TO LIKE YOURSELF. THIS IS ALL ABOUT SELF-WORTH.

HUH?

The minimalist waiter returned (did he sneer at me?), cradling the champagne bottle like a newborn child. As it was cheap sparkling wine, it seemed an affectation for a tip. The waiter was wearing a black T-shirt with the word 'FOOD' written across it in white letters. He looked down his nose at me, then turned to Goldstein and mouthed 'police'. To his credit, Goldstein rolled his eyes and shook his head, dismissing the waiter.

MY $65 MEAL IS NOW COLD.

I peered at the oversized white plate with the quail that lay pornographically in purple sauce.

$65 FOR THAT? THEY'RE ROBBING YOU.

GOODBYE GORDON. SESSION OVER.

⌢

It was ages before Chuck got home. He was still on a high from the gig. He found me on his doorstep with my face buried in my hands.

'You okay, Gordon? You look like shit, man.' He patted for his keys. As usual, he couldn't find them. I knew the ritual. He reefed through his bags and pockets for ten minutes. In the end, I had to climb in through an upstairs window to let him in. I almost fell and broke my goddamn neck.

He threw his stuff down in the kitchen and eventually lit up a large joint. He blew some copper-coloured smoke across the room and stared at me in silence, sensing I was stressed.

'Nice crowd tonight,' he said, nodding sagely. 'I pressed Betty for another date, but she gave me the usual spiel about checking the diary and all that kind of bullshit. Hey, what about that young cat, Finigan?'

'Finius.'

'Riiight. Man, I sure felt old tonight. Felt like I was kidding myself up there,' he said, watching me carefully. 'So many new young cats on the scene.'

'You? *You* felt like a joke? Jesus, I felt like that, too! I felt like I died a death up there. I mean, the little prick scats like Ella Fitzgerald, sings like Stevie Wonder, plays the goddamn piano like Keith Jarrett, he's younger, better looking . . . Jesus, he's probably hung like a donkey, too!'

Chuck took a long drag of the bowed joint and let out that tuba chuckle of his. 'Gordon, I've been blowing for over fifty years. There's always some new kid on the block. Keeps you on your toes, man.'

I sighed.

'Bit like being a pro boxer', he added, trying to hold the smoke in. 'There's always some young punk waiting to take your title.'

'Chuck, that guy totally blew me off the stage tonight. No question.'

'Who gives a fuck?' he said through a billow of smoke. 'You do your shit, he does his shit. At the end of the day it's all music.'

'Chuck, I never thought I'd hear myself saying this, but I *have* to be the best. I want my shit to be the best shit. I want people to say: that guy's shit is the ultimate shit around. I want to make it at the highest level. I want to *make it*.'

There was a sepulchral silence as the words echoed in the kitchen beneath the canopy of smoke. Well, I finally said it. 'I want to make it.' Since signing to Delta I had enjoyed the heady feeling of success. I had always looked down my nose at Jenny for being ambitious. Told her how terribly middle-class she was. Was I any different? Let's be honest, I was as hungry for success as Jenny or even – God forbid – Old Man Harris was for that matter. Now I had heard its siren call.

'There's only one thing you can do, Gordon.'

'Tell me what it is and I'll do it. Whatever it takes.'

He flashed a wide-eyed smile. 'Do what *I'm* going to do. Go to New York, man.' He pulled out his ticket from the canister and placed it on the table like an art dealer with a DaVinci sketch. 'If you can make it in New York, Finigan will never be a problem again. Let's be honest, jazz is about who you've worked with. Who you've blown with. You cut it with those cats, you've made it forever. That is if you *really* want to make it.'

'I want to make it, Chuck. Yes, I *have* to get to New York.'

'I'll see you there, baby. We'll hang together.'

'Oh, wait on, Chuck, what about Jenny? She wouldn't live there in a million years.'

'No problem.'

'Yeah?'

'Easy. Just leave her. Split.'

This was hard to contemplate. Only a few hours ago Jenny and I were arguing over the wedding cake.

'But I love her, Chuck. She's my soulmate. We're getting married, for Christ's sake!'

'What's more important to you, man. Your chick or your music?'

I sighed and buried my face in my hands.

Chuck did something he had never done before. He chuckled and rubbed my head. I guess it was his way of saying, Cheer up, you silly bugger, life ain't that serious.

He made me a cup of tea and we talked and played records until four in the morning. Chuck partied like no other septuagenarian alive.

MY GURU IN THE ARMANI LOINCLOTH

∞

I STARED AT THE BLANK computer screen. The office was quiet. The only sound was the hum of the computer and the rustling of two copulating cockroaches who shall remain nameless. I needed to come up with some copy before six-thirty in order to catch a seven o'clock movie with Jenny. I picked up the packet of Super Sponges. There was nothing particularly 'super' about them, but market research had identified that consumers picked up the product 86 per cent more times with the word 'super' slapped on the packaging.

What can you say about a sponge that hasn't already been said? I asked myself. I tried not to think about *The Cool School*.

It had been over two years since the record came out. There wasn't a day when I didn't think about it. The 'what ifs'. The 'should'ves'. The 'maybes'.

Harris's solicitor turned out to be quite a find. While Smedly made assurances that he would stick to me like 'shit to a blanket' and that he saw me as a 'long-term proposition', my solicitor knew Smedly's reputation only too well. He shrewdly convinced him to sign a three-record deal with no option. In other words, if the first album didn't do as well as expected, the second or third would capitalise on the earlier releases. Therefore, they were contractually obliged to release three albums, but it was a waste of time in the end. When Smedly heard Finius perform at The Cellar that night, he decided I was 'out' and Finius was 'in'. Six months after the release of my album, two days before Christmas, Smedly posted back my 'iron-clad' contract in little pieces. He was nice enough to include a handwritten explanation.

Shoesmith,
You're canned.
Try and sue us and we'll crush you like an ant.
Merry Christmas.
Smedly
P.S. Thanks for the tie.

I was shattered. This was more than a record deal, this was my dream. Delta's heartlessness even shocked my wily solicitor. My legal man's final exacerbated comments to Delta's Managing Director were: 'You know Bob, we *are* talking about a human being, not a can of *dog food*.'

In the end my lawyer gave me some shrewd advice: change your name to PAL Meaty Chunks and get on with your life. You see, I didn't have the funds to fight a corporation like Delta, and they knew it. Thus I learned another lesson: the law only helps you if you have money. Jenny had me quickly signed to a smaller label – Hip Records – and I released a second album. As luck would have it, their distribution was taken over by Delta two weeks after the release and the album received no publicity or distribution. In the end, I asked Philip, my lawyer, how long they could keep doing this to me with my pants on. I was left wondering what the whole experience was meant to tell me. What conclusion was I meant to draw from it all?

Naturally, with my dream in tatters, my life began to disintegrate. I became very dark. If people thought I was cynical before, I now made the writers of *South Park* look like they worked for Disney. I even stopped playing the piano. To get through each day, I swallowed a confectionery store of pills – I took so many pills that, if I leaned hard to the left, I fell over.

On the strength of that awful jingle I wrote, Harris talked a colleague into giving me a job in a small advertising agency in North Sydney. I initially refused the offer. I already had a daily appointment with the ceiling of my bedroom. Harris insisted I take the job. The idea began as an oak seed at the wedding. (Yes, despite my paranoia about Jenny and Adonis Thistlehorne, we had not thrown each other aside. We were hitched.)

Jenny's old man laid on the kind of ceremony for his daughter that made the King of Jordan's son's wedding look like it was held in McDonalds. At the reception, he whispered that if things didn't work out with the 'jazz lark', the job was always waiting. With a belly full of champers, and my new CD getting strong reviews, with Faustian aplomb I agreed. But it became a vulture on my shoulder. At the time, I dismissed it. I was a rising recording star. On the way up. He was quiet. But when I came crashing down, he was like the cat that ate the fucking canary.

At his house one evening, at my lowest ebb, he demanded I give up the 'jazz lark' and face responsibility. In a smiling delirium, I replied, 'Is that North?' He simply glared at me, arms folded. There was no fight left in me. And he knew it. Jenny said nothing. I knew she agreed. I needed a change. The time had come. I said to Jenny out of the blue one day, 'I'm too lazy to work, too nervous to steal, think I'll try advertising.'

Although I had penned the odd piece of music for ads in the past, this was different. I was a full-time copywriter, writing press ads, flyers and brochures for insignificant services and products that no one really wanted. And what was even more depressing, I was good at it. The creative director of the agency became my new mentor.

Julian Charmers was a true lateral thinker and possessed one of the most creative brains I had ever come across. Advertising being the precinct of the young, Julian kept his age a secret. But I guessed he must be in his early seventies. He was originally an art director (creative directors usually start off as art directors or copywriters) and over the years had won numerous awards for his work. In his youth, before he joined the advertising industry, he had been a successful painter. The fact that Julian had walked away from the art world and into the corporate world with no regrets had a great influence on me. He no longer painted, and told me that the art world was full of 'try-hards' and 'soft cocks'. And that he hadn't picked up a brush since he joined the business over thirty years ago. What's more, he couldn't be happier. Julian told me that I was born to write ads. I remember my first week at the agency. He was scurrying around the office in his forest-green Gucci slippers demanding to find the person responsible for changing a new campaign. One of the suits had pointed him towards my office.

I was reading the paper with my feet on the desk when he flung open the door. I nearly crapped myself when he walked in.

'Oh, sorry Julian.' I dropped my feet off the desk. 'Bad circulation. I need to have my feet above my pelvis each day otherwise I get corns.'

'Did *you* write this?' he said, holding a piece of paper in front of me.

I read it and handed it back and cringed. 'Um . . . yeah.'

He paced excitedly around my office. 'Gordon, I have to tell you, you're writing is on the cutting edge.'

'Oh, sorry. I'll try and write more in the centre of the page next time.'

'No, I mean why did you decide to throw out hours of creative strategy and change the byline to this?'

I looked at it. 'Because it was trying to be funny. But it wasn't. It was just being cute. People in advertising think they're being funny all the time. But, at the end of the day, all they're being is lame. Twee. I mean, how many times have we seen a fat Italian in a chef's hat with a spoon of spaghetti sauce say the same thing? It's a perpetual cliché.'

He broke into a wide smile. 'Yes, you're absolutely right. I can see this is the start of a beautiful friendship, Gordon. What are you doing for lunch?'

'Just these pills.'

That afternoon, over a bottle of Grange Hermitage and much laughter, he told me I had a first-class mind. I agreed, but confessed I had a second-class body and this made it difficult when flying. He informed me that if I were prepared to listen, he would teach me all there was to know about the world of advertising. I can't tell you why he was so keen to take me under his wing. Perhaps because I was so unimpressed with the business he determined to convert me. Maybe he saw something of his former self in me. Something that set me apart from the others. He spoke of the other creatives as pencil-pushers and philistines, but referred to himself as an artist. It's true, he was very different. He was brilliant. Everyone knew that he could have run a more 'high-powered' agency, but that meant he would have had to actually *work* instead of sucking expensive wine all day at his favourite bistro. The clients absolutely adored him, so the owner of the agency let him run his own race. The owner couldn't care less about the business as long as it made him money – and he could make par on the eighteenth.

Julian was always immaculately attired, if not bordering on dandyism. Italian suits, shirts imported from Saville Row, London, and shoes handmade in Barcelona. He had lashings of style and aplomb and a boozy-cheeked opinion on every subject from life on Mars to Maoist China.

Over dinner one night in his rambling house in Vaucluse, I poured myself another glass of burgundy and looked around the house. It was exquisitely decorated. His wife, who had died some years earlier, had been an interior designer and had renovated mansions across the eastern suburbs for the sort of people with more money than taste. I stood against the window. The dining room had 180-degree views of the ocean. Moonlight poured in and glinted in rainbows on the crystal chandelier that was reputedly designed by Chagall. The house was a veritable museum of modern painting and sculpture. He had so many fine pieces that when he used to open the house to the public to raise money for some charity or other, the director of the Sydney Art Gallery would hide behind the Modigliani with his chablis and caviar-on-a-wafer, in tears.

I placed my glass on the attenuated backside of the Henry Moore that stood before the window – the reclining nude looked like a gigantic stick of twisted marzipan. I stood gawking at the Matisse. His use of light was breathtaking. It was as if the artist had discarded paint and dipped his brush directly into the sun. He had many paintings by Matisse and I wondered how he could afford them all. He said they were a gift from the artist himself. I walked into the library. You had to have money to have a library, I thought, as I picked up a leather-bound Dickens first edition. The only library most people can afford is the wicker basket beside the bog – and that's stuffed with old *National Geographics* and toilet rolls. I moved back into the dining room. Julian grasped a glass of Moët, little finger pointing to Venus.

'Advertising is the Impressionism of today,' he declared. 'We are the true artists of our time.'

Jenny scoffed.

'You may sneer, darling, but *our* images have shaped our century as much as the images of El Greco and Da Vinci shaped *theirs*,' he said.

Jenny remained silent.

'Ironic, isn't it. Years ago, young men and women used their creative powers to convey high truths or poetry. Now they use those gifts to dream up five-word slogans. They've abandoned their squalid garrets and rusting bicycles for five-star penthouses and BMW convertibles.' He raised his glass. 'And let us toast their enterprise!'

Jenny refused to raise her glass.

'Oh, Jenny darling, don't exclude yourself from that little club.

You're an associated member, my dear. It's our journalist friends who are the ultimate image-makers.' He twirled his orbiting Daliesque moustache.

I listened, monk-like.

Jenny raised a plucked eyebrow. 'Is that right, Julian?' she said.

'Perception is reality, darling. The press know that better than anyone. They've crucified more people than the Romans ever did. Image is truth.' The ad man paused to guzzle some bubbly. 'Let's look at Gordon's old business. Music. Take that singer for instance, what's his name . . . eh . . . George Michael. George was in the closet for years. He was constantly hounded by gay groups trying to "out" him. Eventually, he was caught with his pants down in a public toilet in LA. It was a publicity disaster for him. The spin-doctors decided to turn the tables on the salivating press. They made it into a gay issue. George had finally "come out", they said. They even made a video of him dressed as a policeman in the toilet arresting himself. Brilliant! Now, anyone who attacks George Michael is attacking him for being gay. Inspired!'

Jenny broke into a laughing frown.

'What brand of cigarette do you smoke, Jenny?'

'I don't smoke.'

'What about you, Gordon?'

I shook my head and shrugged my shoulders.

'God, what is it with young people today? We spent years convincing them to smoke. Now, they can't be bothered. There was a time when you'd hear a group of young people coughing and wheezing up the street and you'd feel like a success. It'd put a smile on your face.'

Jenny was about to explode but I gave her the he's-winding-you-up look.

Julian removed a fag from a gold case and lit it. 'Take my brand, for example. What images do you see when you think of Dunhill? Class? Elitism? Privilege? Polo ponies? Private clubs? Exclusivity?

That's why I smoke them rather than, say, Marlboro, for example.'

'Perhaps you simply don't like the taste of Marlboro,' she said.

'If it was only that simple, darling.'

'Again, when you think of Marlboro cigarettes, you think of steely cowboys on horses and crackling campfires and endless prairies. Am I correct?'

'I guess so.'

'But did you know that Marlboro used to be marketed as a lady's cigarette?'

She put her glass down. 'Rubbish.'

'Hard to believe, isn't it? In fact the packaging hasn't changed that much over the years. Still red and white. Initially they had red filter-tips so a lady's lipstick wouldn't be left on the butt. After the war, when lipstick stains on cigarette butts became less of a taboo, sales declined. A radical change in the marketing strategy was needed. Thus the "Marlboro Man" was born,' he said in a silly, deep voice. 'The tobacco is exactly the same, my dear. The only difference is the image in your mind. This alters the taste.' He turned to me. 'Remember Gordon, *perception* is *reality*.'

I nodded sophomorically.

'That may be true in advertising and pop music, Julian, but not in art,' Jenny said.

'Is that right, madam?' Julian refilled her glass, grinning like a Cheshire cat. 'Where would Picasso be without publicity? Publicity created the man. Picasso said, "A picture lives only through the one who looks at it. And what they see is the legend surrounding the picture." It's the image of Picasso you see when you look at his painting, not the "art". He knew this himself. He was the world's *greatest* publicist.'

Jenny slammed her glass. 'But he was a great artist!'

'So your image of him tells you,' he smiled.

'Rubbish!'

'Think of Hemingway: bullfights. Byron: swimming across great lakes. Our little friend Van Gogh: trouble wearing sunglasses. Nothing more than image distorting your perception of the work.'

'You're a very cynical old man,' she grinned, through the end of her wineglass.

His eyes flashed across the antique dining table as he wrestled with a stubborn cork. He loved shocking people with his cynical opinions. Jenny would always take the bait.

Julian and Jenny argued and debated and flirted with each other that evening as I sat in silence, digesting my new master's words. He went on to tell Jenny that giving up music was the smartest thing I'd done. Copywriting was my true gift. He reiterated that the arts were for misguided fools and it was good to see me use my creative talents in the 'real world'. The world of money.

Jenny reluctantly agreed. Convinced that advertising was a fill-in job until my music career was relaunched, she felt apprehensive about Julian and his artistic credo of cash. Something wasn't right. She had begun to notice a change in me. A change that left her feeling confused and depressed. I was becoming the sort of person that she never dated. I was turning into, God forbid, an 'executive'. (I even had a mobile phone and a laptop.) The lengthy discourses we used to have about spirituality and art into the wee hours I now sabred with snide remarks and pointy jibes. Another strange development was that I got on well with her father. (*I* even thought that one was weird.) Now that I had a 'decent job' and a Rolex and designer suit, Harris invited me to the golf club and the yacht club on a regular basis. Jenny told me she thought I was turning into him more and more every day. To which I was amazed to hear myself reply, 'I wish I had his capital'.

⌒

I wound the venetians to extinguish the tangerine slits of afternoon light. I opened the packet and placed the limp, pink sponge on the table and peered at it. I leant back in my chair, picked up the sponge and held it, arm outstretched. As usual, Julian went into his office, closed the venetians and locked the door. He always did this at this time of the day. Matt came in chewing a pencil, 'Got a line for me, Tolstoy?'

'Not yet. Let me see those roughs again.'

Matt pulled out the sketches. 'Just write anything and let's go. I've got a hot date tonight,' he said.

'Write anything? Are you serious? This is a new account.'

'You know what I mean. I don't want to be here again at midnight ordering Chinese and talking about market research and product placement,' he said.

'What about if we spoke Chinese and ate market research with product placement?'

'I don't want to work back tonight, Gordon. That's all.'

'Me either. I'm meeting Jen for a movie, but if we have a deadline . . .'

We were interrupted by the crackle of the intercom. 'How's it coming?' Julian said, with the casualness of Mephistopheles asking Faust for a bacon and egg sandwich.

'Nearly there,' we said in a discordant duo.

'Excellent.' Click.

'Look, I know Julian's counting on us, but . . . just write anything and let's go,' he said.

'You go. I'll handle it on my own.'

He blew me a kiss. 'Cheers. You're a pal.'

'Remember me in your memoirs.'

Matt Stevens was a talented cartoonist in his mid-twenties. He hated advertising, but it paid the rent. He had a cult comic book that was his labour of love, and Julian allowed him to work on it after-hours – as long as he could make dry comments about the plots etc. Julian was forever giving him a hard time, saying that if he'd channel more of his creativity into his advertising career, he'd be a better art director. 'Matthew, in a few years, you'll have a family. You'll have a mortgage. You'll need money. Your values will change. This is a young man's business. Make hay while the sun shines, my boy.'

He told Matt that people don't give a toss about art in this country. Only sport. If he wanted notoriety he should buy himself a cricket bat. I agreed. I used to tell Matt about my sister in London. Struggling in a damp bed-sit in the East End. Painting by the gas heater. I even showed him her long, dramatic letters imploring me to leave advertising and return to music. I sometimes showed them to Julian and we'd laugh unkindly.

I knocked the coffee over the desk.

'Jesus Christ!' I tried to mop up the coffee with the Super Sponge. It wasn't very effective.

'This product sucks! It's a piece of crap! It wouldn't wipe the sweat off a fat man in a sauna.' I grabbed some paper towel. 'That's IT!'

I frantically tapped at the keys. 'Yeah, I'll use a graffiti-style font. Shit, where's Matt when I need him ... *"This product really Sux! That's right! The new Super Sponge from Parry's will out-suck any other sponge, or your money back".*'

The agency always offered money back for FMCG's (fast-moving consumer goods), because few people ever returned a product worth less than a couple of stamps.

I buzzed Julian's office. The sound of Vivaldi trickled through the speaker.

'Yes?' he said irritably.

'What *do* you do in that office, Julian?'

'Pay your wages. What is it, dear boy?'

'I think I've got it!'

'I never doubted you wouldn't, Gordon.'

It wasn't long before he bounded into my office. I showed him the idea. A slow smile stretched across his face, forcing his eccentric moustache to arc, pincer-like.

'Excellent,' he said slowly. 'Gordon, you remind me of myself at your age.'

'Really?'

'Yes. Only shorter and uglier and with a different face. But believe me, you could be working at Saatchi's in twelve months. I outsourced this to three leading copywriters. In two and a half months, they came up with nothing but clichés. You've nailed it in two and a half hours.' He placed a paternal arm around my shoulder. 'Let's go to Pasquale's and have a shiraz to celebrate.'

'I can't. I'm meeting Jenny.'

'Shame. They do fabulous lobster bisque.'

'Thanks, but I'll take a raincheck.'

⌢

I called Jenny and met her for cocktails at our usual place: the Dugout Bar on Oxford Street. The aural neurosis that is collectively known as 'dance music' hammered our ears as we chatted. Dance music always sounded to me like three car alarms going off simultaneously. We were forced to yell over the music.

'Late again,' she shouted.

'Working for a living does that to you. How was your day?' I shouted back.

'Threw up again after you left this morning. I must still have that bug.'

'Greg had that last week. Asian flu.'

'Asian flu?'

'Yeah, apparently you sneeze a lot and have an overwhelming desire to gamble at a casino. You smell nice. What is it?'

'Passion, by Chanel,' she shouted.

It was hot and I unbuttoned my silk shirt. 'Passion. I love that. They're real copywriter buzz words.'

'What?' she hollered.

'You know. A buzz word. Flavours your perception of the product. Of the smell even.'

'I'd wear it whatever it was called,' she said.

'Crap.'

'I would.'

'Even if it was called "Old Fish" or "Compound H2O40"?'

She threw her pretty ski-jump nose in the air, 'Yes.'

'Liar,' I grinned.

'New shirt? Expensive?'

'Cheap. On sale. $250. Hey, you know what Julian said to me today?'

'What?'

'He said I could work at Saatchi's if I wanted to.'

'Yeah?' she said, studying her eyeliner in a compact.

'Yeah. I must admit, I *am* very good at it.'

'Good at what?' she shouted.

'Copywriting. I'm like the Dostoevsky of bullshit.'

Jenny smiled and looked around, glancing at the young barman's arse.

'Yeah, and get this. He's going to give me the Renco Tools account. That means more money. And free tools. Do you need a band saw?'

'That means more hours, too, I suppose.'

I shrugged my shoulders.

She looked around at the yapping crowd and then repainted her lips with scarlet. In her low-cut, red, velvet dress, Jenny looked stunning. The music stopped for a few merciful minutes. 'How's Matt going?' she asked, stealing another glance at the barman's arse.

'I'm not happy with him at the moment.'

'What do you mean' – she made quote marks in the air – '"You're not happy with him"?'

I frowned, 'I think he has a bad attitude.'

'You *what*?'

'Yeah, I've got to talk to Julian about it. He cares more about that bloody comic book than the campaigns.'

Jenny shook her head, 'You've changed.'

'It's what you all wanted, isn't it?' I said softly.

She remained silent.

'Come on. What if your photographer wasn't giving you the right shots?' I said.

'It wouldn't be my problem. It would be my editor's problem. Let Julian sort it out,' she said, answering a call on her vibrating mobile.

I nodded, 'Yeah, I guess you're right.'

⌒

It was Saturday afternoon and the office was empty. I needed to catch up on some work. I called Jenny, but she wasn't answering the phone. I turned on the Mac and looked for a space to place my coffee. I could smell stale cigarette smoke in the office. You weren't supposed to smoke in the building. I wondered if it was Julian. I'd always suspected him of having a sneaky fag when he closed the blinds and locked the doors every afternoon. Everyone in the agency had a theory. One of the suits, an account-executive (a euphemism for 'a salesman'), insisted that he was watching freaky porno movies. Tina, from production, said she could smell hash in his office from time to time. I didn't really care either way, but it *was* very mysterious. After all, if it were all so innocent, why would he shut the blinds and bolt the door?

I opened the door to Julian's office. I peeked in the champagne bucket (that he used as a wastepaper bin) for incriminating butts. Nothing. There was no evidence to suggest that he smoked dope or read kinky mags or did anything out of the ordinary. So what was he doing locking the doors every afternoon? Curiosity got the better of me and I found myself trying to open his desk drawer. It was locked. I looked around the office. It reeked of money and good taste (albeit a tad eccentric).

'Nothing but the best for our Julian,' I said to myself. I sat on his executive chair. It was made entirely of snakeskin. I swivelled around with my feet in the air like a five-year-old. I got up and noticed the cabinet of awards that flashed gold in the sunlight. I plucked one off the shelf and presented it to myself. 'And the winner is Gordon . . .'

As I grasped its hefty base, I felt a tiny key blue-tacked in a hollow beneath. Extracting it, I tried the desk and, sure enough, felt the lock yield with a gentle click. I drew open weighty mahogany drawers. My jaw dropped.

I found hundreds of metallic packets of empty medication. I spilled them fish-like onto the desk. I read them in disbelief: *Prozac*.

⌒

In the bottom drawer were some browning newspaper clippings: 'Menzies to meet our Queen', 'More troops heading for Korea'. And then:

Promising young Sydney artist takes out Archibald Prize

Julian Charmers becomes the youngest recipient of the prestigious award and has a bright future ahead of him. He leaves for Paris next month to study with Matisse.

And beneath them was a stack of paintings and sketches. The harbour at sunset. The city skyline. The Opera House. Ferries. Yachts. Birds. The Harbour Bridge. A couple of them were still damp. I was blown away – they were extraordinary. It was kind of Picasso meets Pollock meets Degas. I looked again at the packets of Prozac sprawled across the polished mahogany desk, flashing silver in the sunlight.

I felt betrayed. I recalled all the boozy lectures about art being the moil of romantic fools. About him not picking up a brush for thirty years. About him naming his farting dachshund 'Art'. I thought about not playing the piano for so long. I thought about *The Cool School*.

I remembered my dreams of becoming a world-class jazz musician. I felt like crying, vomiting and smashing the place up simultaneously.

I took an unfinished painting to the window and tried to pick out familiar landmarks. Yes, these were recent paintings. Among the watercolours, I found a small work in oil. The canvas was hard and brittle. It seemed much older than the others. I studied it in the sunlight. It was a portrait of a woman in a Parisian cafe.

'The old man was quite fond of that one,' a voice said softly. Julian stood in the doorway in a pair of paint-dotted Calvin Klein track pants, smoking a cigarette. 'Even offered to buy it.'

'Matisse?'

'Yes.'

I picked up the Prozac. 'What's all this shit?'

'I've been on that, or the equivalent, for over twenty years, Gordon.' He looked at me and smirked. 'Anyway, people in glass houses and all that . . .'

'So what about all the "art is bullshit" trip, Julian?'

He remained silent.

'What happened in Paris?' I croaked.

He took a drag of the cigarette. 'She happened.' He pointed to the painting. 'She fell pregnant. Matisse died. I was broke. We came home and I had to get a "real job" – as the family put it.'

'Couldn't you have sold your paintings?' I asked, holding back a river of emotion. 'You won the Archibald, for Christ's sake.'

'When I came back, the art world decided that I was "up myself". A tall poppy to be cut down. I became depressed. I needed money. I found advertising. Or should I say, it found me.'

'So, this is how people like you survive. Convince others to abandon their dreams so you feel justified in abandoning yours?'

He remained silent. Puffing on the Dunhill and staring at me.

'You know, Julian, if it was bent pornos or something I could forgive you, but watercolours . . . it's disgusting!'

He chuckled.

'I'm leaving.'

'What for? I admit I lied. But don't be a fool, Gordon. Your future is here.'

I walked over to the window. I rested my head against the glass. I looked out.

Seagulls wheeled. Yachts cut inverted Vs across the glassy surface of the harbour. Ferries bobbed at their jetties. And the Harbour Bridge painted latticed shadows on the green water. I heard the faint note of a ship's horn. I chuckled to myself. I'd been working at the agency all that time and had never even noticed the view. I was so busy writing about sponges and ball bearings and tinned peas that I'd forgotten to look out the window. And dream. As I did at school. When they'd talked of 'careers' and 'responsibilities' and the 'workforce'.

I spoke with my back to Julian. 'You know it's funny, I was going to talk to you about Matt's attitude. Can you fucking believe that? His *attitude*.' I shook my head.

'Good. So what's the problem?'

I pulled out my company mobile and threw it on the desk. It bounced onto the floor. 'I don't like the sort of person I've become, Julian.'

'Gordon, I feel like you're looking to me for answers that I don't possess.'

'Problem is, I need answers, Julian.'

☙

The glass doors hissed open as I walked out of the building and into the sunshine. For some reason I started to think about Chuck. I hadn't seen him for over six months – not since he'd got out of the nursing home.

I started my black Saab Turbo. The motor purred like a fat tabby. The reflections of buildings oozed across the polished paintwork as I made my way to Chuck's place. I double-parked and knocked on the door. A frail voice answered.

'Yes, who is it?' A pale eyeball attached itself to the peephole.

'Chuck? Is that you?'

'No.'

'I'm looking for Chuck,' I said.

A wizened old lady opened the door and peered through the chain. The smell of mothballs crept out from behind her.

'Who?'

'Chuck McCall.'

She closed the door and opened it again without the chain.

'Oh, you must mean the old man who lived here before.'

'Doesn't he live here any more?'

'No.'

'Do you have a forwarding address?'

She held my hand. It felt like a gloved skeleton. 'I'm sorry lovey, he died.'

I dropped my keys.

'Your name wouldn't be Gordon, would it?'

'Yes,' I choked.

'I'm told he left this for you.' The old woman came back with some music. 'This was all he had of any value, they said. Apparently he told his niece that you were to have it.'

I opened the brown paper packaging as two hot tears splashed onto Chuck's compositions. He had told me that he composed but I had never heard any of his work. They looked like contrafacts: bebop melodies written over the 'changes' of standards. Some had lyrics. Some didn't. There was also an envelope. Inside was an open-ended airline ticket to New York in my name. There was also a note in Chuck's wavery writing. It read:

Never give up.

I stumbled into the car and buried my face in my hands. Then, my face sticky with tears and snot, I drove. I needed a double something, so I headed for the Dug-out Bar.

Squeezing through the afternoon throng, I ordered a drink. Downing it, I ordered another, and that's when I saw them. He was kissing her on the mouth. Long and passionately.

I walked up and threw my drink over him. Finius just laughed in my face. Jenny sat open-mouthed with an expression that was a mixture of outrage and shame. I walked out. I got in the car and drove. In the rear-view mirror I saw her running out of the bar after me.

⌒

All I can remember is driving. Away from the city. I just kept driving and driving and driving. Beyond the city limits. Into nowhere. On and on. Endlessly into one blurred horizon after another. I passed an endless grey monochrome of bush. Hours turned into days and days dissolved into weeks. I drove deeper into the outback. Into the vast empty void that is middle Australia. The dead heart of the continent. I only stopped when absolutely necessary. A bite to eat. Some coffee. Petrol. I had very little sleep. I drove deeper and deeper. Occasionally I'd pull to the side of the highway and nod off until a truck would boom past and wake me in a panic. I travelled the highways and dusty, gun-barrel roads of brain-numbing monotony. I can recall struggling to keep awake at the wheel at times. On that dream-like journey, Chuck scatted at me and Julian toasted me with chardonnay.

Eventually, after driving for days in a state of trauma and confusion – also known as South Australia – I found myself on a long highway. It seemed to have no end. After many hours, I saw a lone figure on the horizon. Standing in the middle of the road. I tooted the horn. The charcoal statuette stood motionless, pitted against the steel of the moonlight. I flashed my headlights. He still wouldn't move. I flashed again and rubbed my cherry eyes. At that stage,

I wasn't quite sure if I was dreaming or driving. As the silhouette stood rigid in the centre of the road, my car sped towards him. I was now only metres away from the eerie figure. I slammed my foot on the brake and pulled hard on the steering wheel.

PART
TWO

THE UNBEARABLE LIGHTNESS OF LIGHT BULBS

JOE WADDLED, walrus-like, over to the front window of the café. He stood at the nicotined glass. Peering over a pair of 1970s Elvis-style sunglasses, he looked into the saffron-coloured desert.

I must clean these fucking windows one day or the moon will start looking like a giant lemon, he thought. He pushed the glasses back onto his fat nose. Adjusting his towering quiff, he looked at his blanched reflection. Did he really look like Elvis? *He* thought so. He was obsessed with 'The King'. He'd actually once sung 'Viva Las Vegas' for him in the late '80s. The fact that Elvis died in '79 was unfortunate.

A groan from the back room.

I wonder who he is? That's an expensive car he's totalled. Probably some Jew from the city, he thought. Jews drive flashy cars.

Joe hated Jews. He thought of Hitler as merely misunderstood.

Moaning again, calling out her name.

I wonder who she is, this girl he keeps calling for?

He pulled out a fresh pack of Camels from the storeroom. He always smoked Camels. They reminded him of home. He looked around for a match. Unable to find one, he lit a fag from the stove, singeing the hair on his shrubbery of eyebrow. It smelt like burning

Vegemite. He sat on the front step of the café and gazed into the desert. He felt lonely of late. He was forever sitting on that front step, smoking cigarettes and wondering what the hell he was doing with his life. In the middle of nowhere. Was it time to leave? Time to go home? Or was this as good as it ever gets? Anywhere? He had dreams once. Was he too afraid to realise them?

He seldom even thought about women these days. It had been a long time between shags. The last time he remembered being inside a woman was travelling through the birth canal. He'd been talking to himself of late, too. Just out of the blue. He didn't quite know why. Probably the piss. A shiny black crow made a mocking sound as it flew past. 'Haaaaarr.'

He *must* be a Jew. What was the name on the licence? Shoesmith. That's a Jew's name, for sure. There's only one way to find out, he thought.

⌢

'WHAT ARE YOU FUCKING DOING, YOU PERVERT?' I clutched at my trousers, accidentally whacking my attacker in the face, knocking his sunglasses onto the floor. I felt his chunky hands around my neck, banging my head against the wooden frame of the bed head. The guy was as strong as an ox.

'Get out, you stinking Jew!'

'What?' I choked.

'I *knew* you were a Jew. And look, you're circumcised!'

'So was [*gag*] half my class at [*cough*] St Mary's, you fucking lunatic!'

His hands loosened.

I took the gasping breath of a drowning man.

'You're not Jewish?'

I rubbed my throat. 'I'm circumcised, not keen on pork, and buy wholesale, but that's it.'

'Sorry, my fren.'

'Just how many dicks have you seen, Elvis?' (Calling him Elvis was a compliment, I was to discover.)

'None.'

'Not even at the urinal – to compare notes?'

'I'm no faggot.'

'Oh, why would I think THAT!'

'Rest, my fren. I'm very sorry. A thousand apologies. My café is yours.'

I heard the sour strains of someone crooning 'Suspicious Minds' in the next room before passing out.

⌒

A strip of mango sunlight reached my eyelids. I squinted.

'Jesus Christ, who ran over me?' I said, rubbing my head. I nursed a minor headache that felt like an elephant balancing on my skull.

'Ahhh . . . you finally wake, my fren,' boomed a voice from the other room.

I looked up from the squeaking camp bed. Streamers of chipped paint dangled from the ceiling above. A single bulb, dotted with specks of black ink that were years of baked fly shit, drooped overhead. It ached to look at it. I looked down at my clothes. They were covered in dry rivers of dark blood. I felt my purple torso. It hurt to touch. I could smell bacon.

'Want some breakfast?' the voice boomed from the next room.

'Um . . . where the hell am I, man?'

'You are in number one café in world, my fren.'

'I hope you have a certificate.'

'You feel okay?'

'You were the one checking out my dick, right?' I squinted.

'Sorry, my fren. It was simple mistake.'

'Yeah, right. Don't mention it. Could happen to anyone.'

'You seem groggy, my fren? Flying doctor says you be a bit sore and sorry for few day, but you okay.'

I squinted through watering retinas. The beefy man, dressed in a rhinestone-studded, satin jumpsuit, walked in and switched off the light and pulled the blind. Elvis stood in a halo of sunlight.

I panicked. Was I dead? Were all those bumper stickers right? Was Jesus *really* Elvis? I noticed in paintings of the crucifixion that Jesus sometimes curled his lip. But then you would too if you were nailed to a plank and people kept pestering you with asinine questions.

'Jesus, what shall we do with John? He's very depressed about all this,' a disciple asks Jesus on the cross.

'Jesus, will you return in our lifetime? Tell us. We must know,' another asks.

'Jesus, I know it's wrong to covet thy neighbour's ass. But have you seen Mrs Needleman in a pair of slacks?' a third asks.

'Jesus, you are silent. Are you praying? Why aren't you answering us?' Disciple #1 asks, tugging him on the bleeding toe.

An exhausted Jesus replies, 'I'm being CRUCIFIED HERE IF YOU HAVEN'T NOTICED. Couldn't you work it out for yourselves today, for My Sake? And . . .'

'Quiet! He's trying to say something else! Yes, Jesus, what is it? Speak to us,' Disciple #2 says. The disciples lean in. A hush falls over Calvary.

Jesus leans over, groggy with pain. 'John, I need you to do one thing. Could you ask Joseph to bring some aspirin? It's in the bathroom cupboard. At the very back. Behind the myrrh.'

☾

Elvis felt my forehead. His fat fingers felt clammy.

'You sure you feel okay, my fren?'

'Yes.'

'Do you remember anything about accident?'

'The last thing I remember . . . is . . . driving and . . . running over some kid or something. Shit! Did I kill him? Is he all right?'

'The only person you kill is one dopey kangaroo, my fren.'

'No, man, you're wrong. It was a little Koori kid or something. He was standing in the middle of the goddamn highway.'

Elvis laughed. A bellowing, yellowy-brown laugh. 'Tell me, my fren. How long you drive without slip?'

'A couple of days, I guess. Two . . . three, maybe.'

'When you drive without slip on highway for long time, you start to fall aslip at wheel, yet you still wake. Understan? Also, my fren, when roo is caught in your headlight, he is stunned and cannot move. That is how them shooters kill the busteds. You know. A spotlight.' He aimed an imaginary rifle. 'POW! Good night, sweetheart.'

The word 'pow' resonated through the caverns of my skull.

'So, when I pull you out of car, guess what I find on the road?' he said. 'Dead kangaroo.'

'So where's my car?'

'Where you left it.'

'Good, cause I gotta split. I'm trying to catch a plane from Perth to New York.'

He gave a bellowing laugh. 'That car, she no go nowhere, my fren. She's rooted. You must of rolled in her bout ten, fifteen time maybe. You lucky to be alive, my fren.'

This was a problem. I thought for a while and sighed. 'Well . . . er . . . thanks for pulling me out, man.'

'You're welcome. Now, how bout breakfast, cause you bin aslip now for three day.'

'Really? Okay. Well, maybe something light.'

I got up and stumbled into the 'dining area'. Sitting at a laminated counter, the King placed a napkin on the table as I looked around.

Aside from sporadic pockets of sunlight, the café was dark and gloomy. It had a damp, rancid smell about it. In its original faded, 1950s state, it reminded me of an old car that had been run into the ground and held together with pieces of wire. There were some grimy laminated tables, with sweaty vinyl chairs. The tables had bakelite numbers on them, which gave the impression the café got busy. I discovered later that it never got busy. In fact, there were never more than one or two people in the place at the same time. On the kitchen wall, a neon Coke sign buzzed inharmoniously along with a persistent fly. A gallery of Elvis posters and Italian flags draped the walls. These were mingled with faded advertising signs from the '50s that promoted products that were no longer on the market. They, like everything else, were coated with a yellow membrane of grease that was sticky to touch. Nursing my head, one ad caught my eye. It was for Bex Headache Powders. The copy ran: 'Don't be vexed with pain, drink Bex again!'

The cheesy illustration showed a young, post-war couple with white-toothed smiles, about to down a glass of foul-tasting Bex Powders. It was so far removed from reality it was an insult to the intelligence. It was one, big hilarious headache. The ad business must have been a cakewalk in Julian's day, I thought. People were so gullible. I limped outside.

A panorama of red sand and blinding light stabbed at my pupils. It could have been a café on Mars for all I knew. The landscape was utterly alien. I walked back inside. The screen door slapped behind me. I smelt mould and stale cigarettes.

'What's your name again, my fren?' he asked.

'Gordon. What's yours?'

'Akmed Joseph Allam. But people call me "Joe",' he said, wiping his sausage-like fingers on a Hawaiian shirt. (A shirt not intended to be seen without safety goggles.) He shook my hand and nearly crushed it.

'Akmed Joseph Allam?' I said.

'My father was Christian. My mother was Muslim.'

'That must have been confusing at times.'

'Yes, at Easter my mother insisted my father wear a veil.'

'Are you from Israel or Lebanon or something?'

He removed the sunglasses, 'I'm no stinking Jew. If that's what you mean.' He walked back into the kitchen.

'I kind of gathered that. What have you got against Jews, anyway, man?' I asked gingerly. 'The most creative, funny people I know are Jewish. They're fine people, you know.'

'I'm from Palestine,' he growled, dissecting a piece of fatty bacon with a meat cleaver. 'Need I say more, my fren?'

I went to say something but looked at the cleaver and thought better of it. I was too tired and sore to be strangled again by a crazed Arab. I sipped the coffee while 'Viva Las Goebbels' cooked breakfast. I looked around the café again.

'What a shit hole,' I mumbled.

'Sorry?'

'I said is that a pizza oven?'

'Yes, my fren!'

'Do you sell a lot of pizzas around here?'

'Yes! How many people in the desert can get pizza from a real Italian?'

'They think you're Italian? You're an Arab.'

'It's good for business,' he winked.

'Can't they hear your accent?'

'You're from the city, my fren. Around here, if you're dark, have accent, speak with your hands a lot and say "*Mama Mia*!" occasionally, you're Italian.'

'I see.'

'How's the Italian coffee?' he asked.

'Tastes like Nescafé,' I said flatly.

'That's right, my fren! You know your coffee.' He started cooking. He was whistling something that was either 'Love Me Tender' or Bach's *Fugue in D Minor*.

'You must really like Elvis,' I yelled over the hiss of the grill.

'The King? Best there ever was, best there ever will be.'

'If you say so.'

'You musician, aren't you?'

'How did you know that?'

He passed me Chuck's music. 'I found this in your car. You travel light, my fren.'

'I do. So where am I, the desert?'

'Yep.'

'How long have you lived out here?'

'Too long, my fren. Too long.'

Through a concerto of scraping, tossing eggs, smoking cigarettes, banging pots and singing intolerably, he gave me sketchy details about arriving in Coober Pedy twenty years ago to fossick for opal. He was a lazy prospector, but good at poker. He won the café in a card game. Having worked as a cook in the old country, he saw it as a chance to leave the Coober and send his liver on a vacation. He saw it as temporary at the time. Twenty years on, it was still temporary.

He waddled over and dumped a breakfast in front of me that would have sustained an African village. A small cow that he called a T-bone steak, two lamb chops, four eggs, six rashers of bacon, toast and a sausage that stretched across the plate like a felled tree. I studied the shiny repast.

'Does this come with an instruction book?' I asked, lifting the sausage.

Joe pulled a stool from behind the counter, spread his vast arse across it, and started eating his equally enormous serve with gusto.

'I see you're into health food, man.'

'Yes, I am!' he said, beaming, with a mouthful of bacon. 'Eat, my fren. Eat! Flying Doctor say you need your strength.'

I picked at the food. My head hurt. My bones ached. I had been half-strangled by a mad Arab who thought I was a Jew and he was an Italian. Apart from that I felt fine. My face throbbed with each mouthful. I blew my nose on a napkin and clots of blood were deposited in it.

'Where's the bathroom, Joe?'

He thumbed out back with a mouthful of toast.

Looking into the scaly mirror, I noticed with horror that I had two black eyes, lacerations (that were neatly stitched) and a broken nose. I felt worse for looking at myself, actually. I dried my hands on some paper towel and stumbled out to resume my meal in quiet disbelief.

'I've seen worse,' Joe said, sucking on a T-bone.

'I didn't think I was driving that fast.'

'Oh, you were drivin fast, my fren. I see where car left highway and where bluddy thing end up.'

I dipped the toast into a runny egg that could well have been my brain.

'You just bluddy lucky a big semi wasn't comin. Cause you would'a bin smeared all over windscreen.'

I was startled by the long scream of airbrakes. An enormous truck squatted in front of the café. It let out a sigh of air as the driver climbed down from the cabin.

'Like that bluddy thing, for example,' he said, jumping up and pulling out some pre-prepared sandwiches and stale-looking pastries from a box. A tattooed man, with a chest that resembled a Fiat Bambino, opened the flyscreen door. He looked hot and flustered.

'Giza Coke, wilya, Joe? I'm sweatin bullets in that flammin cab. And a large pizza to go. I'm drivin right through tonight.' He turned to me. 'Struth, who belted the crap owda *you*?'

'A rather mean kangaroo, apparently.'

'Ya wanna pick on someone yown size, mate, like a possum or somthin.' The driver seemed pleased with his comment, laughing at his own humour.

'Thanks for the advice.'

Joe handed the sweating driver a buxom bottle of Coke. The driver downed it in one guzzle, spilling a little down his chin and onto his faded blue singlet.

'Giz another, Joe?' The driver looked at me again and twisted his face. 'Zat *your* car I saw bout half a moil down the hoiway, matey?'

'Probably.'

'Shit . . . and you walked away from that?'

'It's a talent. I only wish I could teach it.'

The driver shook his head again, firing missiles of sweat across the counter, 'Hit a roo?'

'Guess so.'

'Reckon ya might'a nodded off at the wheel?'

'I can't remember, I was asleep at the time.' Nursing the headache, I hoped the anthropoid would get the message and leave me alone.

'Where ya from, mate?' He opened a packet of sandwiches and took a crocodile-like bite. Joe orbited the pizza dough.

'Sydney.'

'Had an uncle from Sydney once,' he said through the mouthful of sandwich.

'Small world.'

'Hope those pants are wash'n'wear,' he said through the sandwich.

'Hmmm?'

'Said, I hope those pants are wash'n'wear cause there ain't a dry-cleaner round ere for over two hundred moil. That blood'll wash out, though. Matey, believe me, I'm a bloke who knows owda get blood outta clothes.'

'Lady Macbeth could use your card.'

'You buedy.' He gave me a grimy business card. 'Nice sheila, is she? I like big tits. Now tell her to call next week.' Joe eventually handed the driver the pizza. 'Listen, I'll see ya later. Ow much do I owe ya, Joe?'

'$24.95, my fren.'

The driver paid and looked askance at Joe. He looked at me and then again at Joe. Joe looked at me.

'Aren't ya forgettin somethin?' the driver asked.

Joe looked at me and then at the driver.

'I mean, I did orda a Hound Dog with extra anchovies . . .'

Joe's eyes lit up. In a flash, he hit a switch from behind the counter and the curtains shrouded the café in darkness. A mirror ball stutteringly descended from the ceiling as chips of light whirlpooled around, transforming the café into an aquarium of coloured light. Music blared from hidden speakers, startling me, as Joe ran back to the kitchen. He emerged, clutching a squealing microphone, and through a bog of echo, sang 'You ain't nothin but a Hound Dog'. Which sounded something like: 'You ant nutin borer howndoor'. The singing was so out of tune that at one stage it sounded like he was reciting Tennyson whilst being tortured with an electric cattleprod. However, the dancing was quite good – if it was, in fact, a tango. But somehow I was convinced it wasn't. The only way to describe it is to imagine someone trying to dance who had one leg five inches shorter than the other and a stone in the shoe of the good leg. As a kind of finale, Joe slid along the café on one knee, jumping up and finishing with a karate kick. Upon which, he fell over and tore the ass out of his shiny, pearl-coloured jumpsuit.

Clutching his arse, he crawled behind the counter and hit a switch, returning the café to its original decrepit state. He emerged smiling, pleased with the impromptu soirée. The driver looked at me. I looked at him, mouth agape.

Suddenly, the driver started a slow clap and shook his head. 'That was fucken spectacular. You should be in showbiz, Joe. Fair dinkum.'

Joe beamed. 'I think I might of missed a note in the second verse.'

The driver walked out. We followed him. Me, mouth still agape.

'You're a fucken legend, Joe!' the driver hollered, taking off in a train of rust-coloured dust, honking his air horn like a teenager.

Joe turned to me, 'Well, what did you think?'

'Eh . . . I've never seen anything quite like it. It's . . . eh . . . truly unique.'

Joe seemed pleased. We walked back inside.

'Nice fella, Johnny,' he said. 'You wouldn't want to fight him, though.'

'I'll keep that in mind.'

'Bit a bloke's ear off at the pub once.'

'That can happen when you run out of pretzels.'

Joe nodded, packing away the stale pastries.

'Where is this pub?' I asked, aborting another attempt at the coronary-on-a-plate that was Joe's 'breakfast special'.

'Down road, off highway. It's called "The Globe". I take you some time.'

'Yeah, I could do with a drink.'

'You like to drink, my fren?'

'I like to drink, *my fren*,' I said.

He drew a watermelon smile. 'I can see we are going to be good frens.'

I took a painful breath and grimaced. It was difficult to expand my bruised ribs. So I tried to take shallow chest breaths (not an easy thing to do for a professional singer). I stared at him for a few minutes. His face, with its assorted pock marks and scars, looked like a large potato that someone had tossed aside because it was too tedious to peel.

'Listen . . . thanks for everything, I mean, pulling me out of the car and letting me stay here . . . feeding me . . . strangling me and looking at my dick.'

'Forget it, my fren. I wasn't going to drive past and leave you, was I?

'What if I had a bumper sticker that read "Honk if you're Moses"?'

Joe exploded with laughter, 'Another coffee?'

'Thanks.'

As he poured the coffee, I noticed that after years in the sun his green tattoos were smudgy, nondescript ink pads.

'Always have plenty coffee handy,' he said.

'Why?'

'Keeps truck drivers awake.'

'Always handy when driving a road-train at a hundred k's an hour.'

He peeked at me from under his caterpillar eyebrows, 'You should talk, my fren.'

'Fair call.'

'So who's this Jenny?' he asked unexpectedly.

'What do you mean?'

Joe lit a cigarette, blowing smoke through a terrain of nostril-hair. 'I heard you say her name a few time in your slip, my fren.'

'Just someone I want to forget, man.'

'I understand.'

I got up and peeked through the grimy windows again. The edges of low-lying dunes blurred in the heat. They looked like a rippling breakwater. Joe cleared up the dishes, cigarette dangling from rubbery lips, ash flaking off in all directions.

'What's the name of this town anyway, man?'

'Venice,' he said.

'Venice?'

'Venice.'

I squinted through the window. 'I see it's low tide, then.'

'Venice, Sous Australia, my fren.'

'You work here alone?' I asked.

'Yeah, keeps me out of pub.'

'The Globe, right?'

'The Globe,' he nodded. 'You play poker?'

'I play Snap. Is that the same thing?'

'Exactly.'

I spotted an old jukebox in the corner. 'Wow, is that an original

Wurlitzer? Where did you get *that*?' I reviewed the musical selection.

'It was here when I took over the place. Ahhh, bluddy thing hasn't worked for donkey's years.'

I peered through a quilt of dust and read the play-list.

'Man, you got yourself one hell of a hip selection here. Christ, I didn't even know some of these records existed.'

He hung his head. 'No Elvis, though.'

'We can get some.'

'Great idea.'

I curled my lip and threw out my hip, 'Thankya very murch.'

⌒

Over the next few days, weeks and months I came to know all about Joe and grew to like him a lot. He was a lonely sort of a person. Although always jolly, there seemed to be a sadness that belied his breezy persona. Joe spoke very little of his life back in the Middle East. He'd given up many dreams. He chided himself many times for giving up his lifelong ambition to dance with the Royal Ballet in London when they told him at the audition that he'd have to lose seventy kilos and actually learn to dance.

Joe was also the strongest person I'd ever met. He could actually rip a phone book in half. Sometimes in a card game, he would rip the remaining halves into quarters or even into eighths in a kind of drunken stupor. Needless to say, a small wager often accompanied this demonstration of strength. It was often a last-ditch fundraising effort by Joe if he'd lost his chips to someone who was a little sharper than he took them for.

The café itself stood thirty-odd feet back from the road and had parking off to the side. There was no parking area as such. If Joe parked his rusting Valiant Safari on one side of the café, that became the car park for the day. Things were pretty casual in the outback.

Perched on the corroded iron roof of the building was a crackling neon sign that read: 'The Cosmopolitan Café'. Over the years, people had thrown stones at the glowing epitaph so it actually read: 'mop'.

I suppose to describe Joe's place as a 'café' was somewhat generous. It was more of a roadside diner-cum-pizzeria, where truck drivers doped on speed, caffeine tablets and various other heart-thumping concoctions paused for a coffee and donut before careering into some poor bastard in a Mazda.

When the café was quiet, which was most of the time, Joe would lean over the bar and read a week-old paper, or play solitaire, or, if he could find someone foolish enough, play poker.

A few months after I arrived, a truck driver lost a lot of money to Joe and refused to pay. Each fortnight, in the dead of night, the cocky driver would scream past, honking his horn, giving Joe the finger. (It was a kind of highlight for me. Very funny, actually. Joe would be fuming and swearing at him.) The café stood on the edge of a long secluded highway. So, in the still of the night, you could hear a truck coming from Hobart. One night, Joe heard the semi tearing up the highway. I saw him saunter out the back and return with a long, spiked piece of steel. He walked outside and placed the sinister artefact across the highway, then strolled back inside, casually poured himself a coffee and continued reading the paper. As usual, the driver screamed past, honking his horn and bellowing the usual collection of expletives at the café. Suddenly, I heard the tyres blow. They sounded like the short burst of a machine gun. Joe took to the driver with a baseball bat. He was still swinging at the poor guy with me in the unenviable John-Wayne-meets-Julian-Clary position of bull riding his back and pulling his hair to stop. Suffice to say, Joe got his money, word got around, and very few people played cards with Joe again (including yours truly).

⌒

But I'll never forget that first night in Venice (that I was conscious).

I remember the crisp desert air. I remember watching the stars tunnel through the night sky. I'll never forget the moonlight dolefully painting the desert in ivory tones.

After a while, I felt at home in the desert. It felt right. I was the prodigal, the penitent, cast into oblivion. I felt as though I had run away from nothing to nowhere – and found it.

'LIFE'S THE THING THAT HAPPENS WHILE YOU'RE WASHING PANS'*

'*YOU* ARE BLOODY BARRED!' a raspy voice barked from behind the bar.

Joe placed a leopard-skin brothel-creeper shoe on the brass foot rail of the bar. 'Mr Max, I've brought you new customer,' Joe replied with oily politeness.

The little stout man became very red in the face. I'd never seen a face so red. It could well have been buffed with sandpaper.

'I don't fuckin care if you've brought me Dolly Parton's bigger-titted sister! You're bloody *barred*, ya mad eye-tie bastard.' His face now the colour of beetroot. This made the sunspots on his head look like ink blots. I now realised why Joe had taken so long to buy me that drink at The Globe. He pressed on with a Jehovah's Witness smile.

'Mr Max, may I present Gordon . . . eh . . . ?'

'Shoesmith,' I said.

'Shoesmith,' Joe hissed.

The ruddy little man puffed his bulky chest, which looked exceedingly out of proportion to his small round head and tiny ears,

* John Lennon's butler

and reached across the bar. 'Max Parsons, pleased to know ya. Now, fuck off. You can come back later without that mad wog bastard,' he said, shaking my hand with deceptive strength and almost cracking my knuckles.

'Nice to meet you, too.' I reclaimed what was left of my career.

Joe placed a sweaty palm on the barman's shoulder.

'Mr Max, I apologise bout other night but, look, I bring you a new customer.' The publican brushed off Joe's hand as if removing bird shit.

'You stayin in town, mate?' asked the barman.

'Yeah, I've been staying at the café.'

He sighed. 'All right, listen wog, no more poker with anyone in this flamin pub. Oright?' he said, poking a stubby finger in Joe's leviathan chest.

'Okay, Mr Max, okay. You come down road, I give you free pizza, any time. On the house, my fren.'

'I wouldn't eat in that fuckin greasy café a yours if Elle MacPherson was ya new topless waitress. Now, just bloody behave yourself – and no cards, no blues!' he said through gritted teeth, strangling some beer out of a bar towel.

Joe grinned from ear to ear. 'Okay, okay, Mr Max, you the boss, my fren.'

'And, another thing. I'm not ya bloody friend!'

Suddenly I heard a blood-curdling scream that made me jump. 'What the fuck was that?'

Max gave a throaty chuckle. 'Oh, that's just Charlie.' He tossed his head toward a battered cage that incarcerated a sulfur-crested cockatoo. 'Say hello, Charlie.' The milky parrot screeched an aspirin-coated greeting.

'What you have, my fren?' Joe asked.

'Oh . . . um . . . I'll have a Depth Charge, thanks.'

'Two Depth Charges, Mr Max.'

'What the fuck's that?' Max snapped.

Joe shrugged his bulky shoulders and turned to me.

'Well, it's a schooner of beer with a shot glass. Now, in the shot glass, you pour a finger of schnapps. Okay, now you drop the shot glass in the beer . . . you know . . . like a depth charge . . . so when you finish the beer, you hit the spirit. Now, it's important to add the shot just when –'

'Listen. I got beer, and if you want somethin a little classy, I can give ya beer with a paper umbrella in it left over from Chook's farewell.'

I looked around and casually studied the patrons. It was a typical outback pub. The sour smell of beer. The nasal drone of a transistor radio. The staccato butting of a blowfly against a window. A pall of cigarette smoke. The inexorable squeak of a ceiling fan. The unaccompanied belching of a fat man in a soiled baseball cap in the corner. Down the end of the bar I noticed an old Koori perched in front of a glass of spirits. He wore a moth-eaten Akubra hat, which sprouted a red-tipped, black feather.

'What's *he* drinking then?' I asked.

'*He* is drinkin cheap rum.'

'Would you recommend it?'

'That depends. If you need to strip the paint off ya back fence, I'd highly recommend it. But to drink? No.'

'How about two beers?' I said.

'Smart man.' He dropped the overflowing schooners on the bar and sneered down a broken nose at Joe. '$5.60 . . . NO SLATE!'

Joe begrudgingly paid the sum.

Max poured himself a midi. 'So how did ya get here?' He pulled up a stool from behind the bar and peered under a wad of scar tissue. 'I don't see no car.'

'My valet is having it cleaned.'

'You been in a fight or somethin? Look like ya been beaten up by a pack'a wild Abos.'

I'd almost forgotten about the accident. I touched my face. 'Oh,

I came off the highway trying to avoid a kangaroo.'

'That was you, was it? I heard about that. You a bloody Greenie or somethin?'

'Why do you ask that?'

Joe interjected. 'Because if you from round here, you don't avoid roo, you just run over the busted.'

'Not worth riskin your bloody life for. A roo. Is it? Just one less to shoot,' Max said.

'I didn't care about the kangaroo . . . it's just . . .'

'Thinks he'd run over bluddy Abo,' Joe roared.

Max narrowed his eyes. 'Nod off at the wheel, did ya?'

I looked down the end of the bar at the old Koori.

Max noticed and laughed.

'Oh, don't worry about old Sunfly. He's as blind as a bloody bandicoot and deaf as fuckin post. Aren't ya, mate?' Max yelled in kindergarten tones across the bar. The old man slowly turned and stared at me with milky eyes.

'So, didja think ya killed an Abo, Gordon?' Max said, wiping a glass.

'Well . . .'

'Not too many left round these parts. Poor bastards. Plenty at the Coober, though,' he said.

'Coober Pedy?'

'Yeah, poor devils. They lie on the street drinkin metho and beg for spare change all day. Bloody disgrace.'

'That's terrible.'

'So thought ya hit one, didja?' he persisted.

'Well . . . I thought I'd –'

Joe interjected. 'Only kangaroo, Mr Max. I found a dead one next to car.'

'You pulled him out didja, Joe?' Max asked, looking into my bruised face.

'Yep.' Joe turned to me. 'Same again, my fren?'

'Oh, okay,' I spluttered, gulping down the beer. I'd hardly had a chance to drink the first one.

'Same again, Mr Max.'

Max pulled two more beers. 'So whadya reckon about the desert country? Like it?'

'I do. At first I couldn't wait to get out of here, but now . . . I don't know . . . I like it. It's peaceful. You know, I've never seen the stars so clearly. Quite beautiful.'

'You an astronomer or somethin?'

'No. Just an aesthete.'

'Bullshit. You don't look fit enough for lawn bowls!'

Joe waved a fleshy arm around the bar. 'And what you think of Globe, my little fren?'

'It's hot,' I replied, fanning myself with a handful of coasters. 'Don't you have air-conditioning, Max?'

'Too pricey. As you can see, rush hour's just a blur'a people.'

I sipped the beer and nodded.

'Ahh, here's half of the rush hour, now,' Max added flatly.

'Oh, Jesus,' Joe mumbled into a glass.

I felt a moist palm on my tender shoulder. I winced.

'New parishioner have we, Landlord?' the clergyman said in stuffy tones.

'Seems that way, Rev,' said Max.

He sat at the bar and outstretched a moist hand. 'Reverend Samuel Jebediah Fruit. How do you do?'

I shook it. 'Gordon Shoesmith,' I replied, furtively wiping my hand on my trousers.

'Glass of water thanks, Landlord,' he said, tugging at his steaming dog-collar. Max handed him a suspicious-looking wine-glass of water. He was dressed strangely for a minister, in his black bib and dog-collar, frayed shorts and white canvas tennis shoes with no socks.

'What religion are you, my son?' he asked.

'Um . . . The Church of Our Lady of the Self-Flagellation.'

'Baptist, eh? Well, that won't matter around here. All God's children are welcome in our parish.'

'Where's the church?' I asked.

'Just down the street.'

I pulled a face. 'That old ruin?'

The holy man stood up in his white Dunlops and raised his glass.

'A toast to St Jude's of Venice!' he called across the bar. His boozy breath made my eyes water. A couple of dozing drinkers raised their sloping glasses.

'But it's just a ruin. I mean, there's no roof or anything.'

'Closer to our Lord, my son. Closer to our Lord.'

'What if it rains?'

Max and Joe looked at each other. They exploded with laughter.

The holy man nodded. 'You know, Gordon, we never even thought of that. Good suggestion! We must start a St Jude's Roof Fund,' he said, with wide-eyed enthusiasm.

Max shook his head and wiped an ashtray. 'Yeah, with all the rain round ere, why don't we build an eighteen-hole golf course. I'll get the "Shark" on the blower and we'll hold the fuckin Australian Open.'

'Who needs money when there's faith, Max. Jesus once said: "Render to Nero what belongs to Nero, and render to God what belongs to God."'

'Caesar,' I said.

'Eh?'

'You know, as in the salad.'

He screwed up his face, 'Sorry, Gordon?' He twisted his hand, making a veiled boozing gesture to Max.

'I think you mean "Render to Caesar what is Caesar's",' I said. 'Nero wasn't around for that part of the gig.'

'What? Oh, yes, I must have been thinking about the Old Testament.'

I looked sideways at Joe. Joe rolled his eyes and shook his head. (Suddenly I felt like I was one of those absurd Irish characters in a Beckett play.) Later that day Max told me all about the curious Reverend Fruit.

⌢

The 'Rev', as the locals referred to him, came to Venice when he was forced to leave his parish in the leafy suburb of Toorak because he had one eye on the 'sauce' and one eye on the deacon's rather portly wife (he liked them 'full-figured' apparently). Sober, the Reverend Fruit was quite charming, but after sucking on the communion wine all afternoon the charm got a bit too 'cuddly' for some. I suppose he was just like most horny old blokes after a few clarets, but unfortunately, it wasn't in the job description.

In the end, his sermons became a little racy. When the sermon entitled 'How the Virgin Mary eventually shagged Joseph' was slurred from the pulpit, the Archbishop was called. Fruit narrowly kept his job and apparently toned it down for a while until he found his hands 'divinely' attached to Mrs Perkins' rather plump behind. He was finally asked to leave.

However, it wasn't so easy to get rid of the wily Reverend Fruit. Being the cloistered party animal that he was, he knew of other clergymen with even *less* of a grip on the Ten Commandments than himself. Therefore, he was prepared to spill the consecrated beans if they didn't find him another parish. In the end, the cunning Bishop found him one.

⌢

The pub was streaked in peach sunlight. I noticed the yellowing photos of boxing matches among greening trophies that lined the back wall. Behind the bar was a collection of beer cans from all parts of the world. It was a veritable shrine to beer. I counted over two hundred different brands. Apparently Max asked tourists, who stumbled across the pub, to send a sample of their native beverage when they got home. Above the bar on the far wall hung a nicotine-brown sign with a crude caricature reading: 'Politicians and Poofters: Free bungy-jumping, no strings attached.'

With the aid of my dear friends Mr V and Mr B, I started to relax – the blessed amber nectar. Fruit eventually left and I sat at the bar, chatting with Max and Joe for hours. I liked Max. He was a straight shooter. Joe, on the other hand, tended to be more circumspect, but I liked him nonetheless. Max whispered to me to watch Joe as he was as 'cunning as a rat with a gold tooth'. Max and Joe had a testy relationship at the best of times. I must say though, it was a breath of fresh air to meet people who weren't afraid to be themselves for a change. City people were never like that. There was always an agenda. It was simply 'like it or lump it' with the likes of Max Parsons and Joe Allam. In the space of one hot afternoon, Max and Joe had revealed more about their dreams, loves and political credos than any of my city friends would have in a lifetime. It was from the heart. No bullshit. No coffee shop agendas. No point-scoring. I did my best to pepper the conversation with humorous anecdotes and stories – beer being a wonderful lubricant for the mechanics of conversation – and had one of the best afternoons of my life. You felt you could trust these people with your soul.

I discovered that Max and his brother had inherited the antiquated hotel from their father. His brother was killed in Vietnam. Max gave away a promising boxing career to stay and run the family business and help his father who was dying of cancer. Max seemed a tad bitter towards his old man for bequeathing him the boozy legacy. At times, he saw it as an easy living. Other times a curse.

Max was married at one time and had a son. He said his son had moved away some years ago. They apparently had some kind of falling out. He had never heard from him since. As a result, his wife

Shirley walked out six months later. He received the divorce papers from some 'fast-talking lawyer from the city' and a forty-year marriage was ended with the stroke of a Bic pen. It was obvious that many issues in his life still caused Max great pain and he welcomed a sympathetic ear to talk them over. He felt easy talking to me for some reason. He said it was a welcome change from the usual slurring philosophies.

Several years ago a truck driver bumped into a young soldier in the city, who asked about the owner of The Globe when he saw a bumper sticker with the pub's name on it. From the photo, the driver said it was Max's son Tony. But Max thought the driver was trying to get himself unbarred after being involved in a brawl in the pub a couple of months earlier. Out of curiosity, Max called army personnel and asked if they had anyone in service by the name of 'Tony Parsons', but no luck. He wasn't sure what he would have said to him anyway, he told me.

Max pointed to an old photograph behind the bar. 'That's Tony there,' he said.

'So, he followed in his father's footsteps, he was a boxer, too?' I asked.

'Yeah, he was no Les Darcy, but he had a big heart. Never say die, that was Tony.'

'I guess you miss him.'

The little man became red in the face. His eyes grew moist.

'Same again?' he choked.

'Can I ask you a question, Max?

'Shoot.'

'Why is the town called "Venice"? I mean, I don't see any gondolas.'

Max pulled a fresh beer and proceeded to tell me, in great detail I might add, the bittersweet history of the town.

On a dry, dusty day in June 1879, an Italian explorer by the name of Salvatore Garibaldi rested his men at a spot about sixty kilometres north of where the transcontinental railway now dissects the burning heart of the continent. Although the region seemed to be the most godforsaken place on earth, Garibaldi was convinced that this was the place to begin his search for the fabled Inland Sea. With this discovery, he would etch his name in the history books and, moreover, build a township in his name and profit by his enterprise. No one quite knows why the intrepid Italian was so optimistic about the area or what he saw in the flat, lifeless plains that faded into infinity in every direction.

Despite the inhospitable surroundings, many Aborigines inhabited the area. Perhaps this influenced Garibaldi and his quest. In the middle of the night, he would hear them performing their corroborees and secret ceremonies. He would drift in and out of dream to the distant drone of the didgeridoos, accompanied by men singing haunting melodies in hypnotic rhythms. At these strange rituals the tribesmen would smear their naked bodies with white ochre, don black feathers and sing and dance. They drew patterns of great fish and mysterious sea creatures in the sand. This convinced Garibaldi that the Inland Sea was nearby.

Unlike other tribes in South Australia who were left destitute and displaced by colonial rule, these men were a magnificent and proud people. Garibaldi noted in his journal: 'They most certainly were noble-looking and handsome men. Endowed with the qualities of wonderful patience and powerful endurance.'

Eventually, the explorer became friendly with the local tribe. With their strange cave paintings and rituals of the sea, he was convinced that they would lead him to his objective. The tribe taught the Italian how to survive in the desert. On occasion, they would spear a wallaby and invite him to share it with them. Meanwhile, his men were undertaking the arduous task of sinking wells to find water. To build a township, and launch exploration and open up the inland, they needed water.

Christmas Day was depressing in the scorching heat. He invited the tribe to share the measly Christmas dinner he and his men had set aside for the festive occasion. In crude sign language, he spoke to the elders of the tribe about his desperate search for water. They didn't quite understand why the whitefella wanted to find such a large quantity of water, or what the ramifications would be for their people if a large underground well were to be found, but they prayed to the spirits of the Dreamtime to help Garibaldi in his foolhardy quest. Astonishingly, the next day, he struck water. Not fresh enough for humans to drink, but water that could support sheep, cattle and horses.

It must have been a strange sight for the Aborigines to observe the white men singing and dancing jigs around a little hole in the desert. After all, given the saline content, you couldn't really drink the water. And what was a sheep or a cow to a desert-dwelling Aborigine?

A triumphant Garibaldi returned to Adelaide with his intrepid dream on the verge of becoming a reality. The eccentric Italian pioneer was seen buying rounds of drinks at the Adelaide Hotel, painting pictures of his dream for the new land, and chastising those who doubted and ridiculed him. From the new town, the Inland Sea would soon be found.

Armed with additional men and a fresh injection of finance from his rich patrons in Italy, he returned to the well a few months later to bolster the walls with a timber frame. As the men started to reinforce the well forty-two metres down, the top part of the well started collapsing in on them. When they finally dug the sand back out, they found the well was virtually dry. It appeared that, in his overwhelming optimism and self-confidence, Garibaldi had failed to gauge the well's capacity. The well held no more than a few buckets at most. A soak.

A shattered Garibaldi dropped to his knees beside the well and looked pleadingly at the sky. His rich fertile dream had turned to wet sand and rock in the space of minutes. Still on his knees, the little Italian wiped salty tears from his tired eyes and gazed into the infinite cyclorama of orange. He thought of home. The lush hillsides of Florence. The busy streets of Milan. The Venetian Opera House with its golden roof. His pretty wife and smiling children. Suddenly, something caught his eye. On the edge of the horizon stood a young Aboriginal boy. The boy handed the defeated explorer a long black feather and whispered in his ear. The Italian held it in the wind and slowly wiped the remaining tears from his bloodshot eyes. He looked up. The boy was gone. A brokenhearted Garibaldi began the long, hot, depressing trek back to Adelaide and eventually home to Florence, never to return again. As a parting shot, he acerbically named the area 'Venice'.

☺

Joe and I stumbled out of the pub quite 'smiley'. Being a spirit man, I wasn't used to drinking so much beer. I felt like a tyre that had been filled with too much air. We sat on the verandah for a while in silence. Joe was good like that. He didn't feel the compulsion to putty the conversational gaps with small talk. I remember staring into the horizon. Sunset. I watched the flaming red ball gradually sink into the earth. Red drained from the sky. Evening. The heavens blanketed the earth in purple darkness – as if tucking in a sleeping child. I heard the metronome of the crickets. I listened to the random note of a desert owl. I watched Venus winking at me from the horizon.

'Come on, my fren, we cut keep customer waitin,' he slurred.

Joe and I fell into the car. We snaked back to the café. Emus, startled by the growling engine, bolted in all directions like madmen released from an asylum.

As stars surfaced, I reflected on Max's story about his wife and son. It made me think about Jenny. A wave of despair dumped over me. I had no pills. This was going to be the toughest few months of my life.

'I don't suppose you've got any Scotch back at the café?' I sulked.

Joe winked and touched his chest. 'Now I know why I like you, my fren. You a man ufta my own hut.'

ALAS, THAT WAS THE WINTER OF MY DISCOUNT TENT

I'D BEEN LIVING in the back of the café for over three months by then. Mainly earning my keep washing dishes and doing odd jobs around the café and the pub. With me a bad sleeper and Joe a chronic snorer, sleep became a distant memory. I can't explain just how bad Joe's snoring was, except to say it would rattle the cutlery and bring flakes of paint down from the ceiling. In the end I had to start lashing things down.

As the toxins from years of medication made their lingering journey out of my body, stomach cramps, acute anxiety attacks and little sleep made those early months a living hell. I was crippled with uncontrollable bouts of the shakes on most days. This was particularly noticeable to the locals if I was serving them a cup of coffee or a pizza while Joe was down at The Globe competing in the Cirrhosis Event at the Liver Olympics. The locals would often ask: 'You and Joe get on the piss again larse night? You're fair dinkum shakin like a fuckin leaf!'

It wasn't long before I'd had enough of sleeping in the back of the café – my clothes smelling of pizza, my hair stinking of cigarette smoke, the bedsprings of the camp bed carving ugly motifs in my back, and Joe snoring in three languages. So, even though it was winter, I slept outside in an old army tent that Max had lent me. Joe kindly offered me his own room, but I declined. Max had also offered to put me up, but the pub was too noisy.

Joe's own room wasn't much chop anyway. It was on the bad side of shithouse. He didn't care. Joe was usually so pissed most of the time that he could sleep standing up.

His room stunk of BO and stale cigarette smoke. It was sparsely furnished. A pole hammered between two walls he called a 'wardrobe'. There was a broken chair and a sagging double bed peppered with cigarette burns. (Many a time I had to run in and throw a bucket of water over him before he set himself – and me! – on fire.) The walls were a gallery of busty centrefolds (you know, the type of 'models' for whom elephantiasis is a desirable affliction). I used to ask him why girls with tits as big as beanbags turned him on. But he couldn't explain it. And I was only making conversation, anyway. I had my own problems.

Anxiety.

Seems like such an impotent word when trying to describe the sort of agony I was going through each night when I first arrived in Venice.

Anxiety.

A word, like so many others in the modern vocabulary that has had its original definition watered down over the years. You know, people say things like, 'I'm feeling anxious about the job interview today'. Or 'I'm feeling anxious about meeting your parents next week'. With this illness, the word 'terror' would seem more apt. Sheer gut-wrenching terror. It was a two-hundred-metre dash through the bowels of Hell.

Anxiety.

Its cruelty is beyond belief. It knows no compassion, as it deftly pinpoints your deepest fears and darkest horrors. It then meticulously isolates those terrors and throws you headfirst into them with the sensitivity of a serial killer who's had his car blocked in.

Anxiety.

If this crippling disorder were to manifest itself in the form of a physical illness, it would be too hideous to look at. Weeping sores, broken bones, gaping head wounds and copious amounts of thick, dark blood. Tragically for those afflicted, it's a hidden illness. People say things to you like: 'Be positive – Smile more.' You feel like replying: 'Oh, is that what I've been doing wrong all these years? I know! I'll put on this fake nose and glasses and look into the mirror when I'm crying and spewing at three o'clock in the morning.'

Anxiety.

Sleep is your only escape from the waking nightmare. If I could only get to sleep, you tell yourself. Sleep. Sleep. Sleep. But anyone who has experienced chronic anxiety attacks will tell you: you can't sleep because the adrenaline is keeping you awake. So, you lie there half the goddamn night. Shaking. A river of sweat. Voices screaming inside your head. For an hour's sleep, you offer your soul at bargain prices, but no one's buying. Anything for sleep. Anything. Anyone. Eventually you collapse from sheer exhaustion. Only to wake up the following day. Knowing that it will be calling for you again, at sunset.

Anxiety.

It's true, pills took the pain away, but it was a fool's paradise. It merely tucked the horror away in a little pocket of your mind while you sprinted from the carnage. This meant it became stronger, while you became weaker.

Eventually, I was backed into a corner. So I laughed in its face with my chest exposed screaming 'FUCKING KILL ME'. But that would be too easy. Too quick. Too merciful. Ultimately, I decided to fight it. Scratch its eyes out. Tear its face off. Kick its lungs in. It was the illness or me. It took time. It was a thousand five-minute rounds with Lucifer. The battle forever loomed. Each night, you frantically donned the armour. The prize: your sanity. With each bare-knuckled fight I weakened the neurological infidel. It wasn't long before I had my foot on its throat. Life began to change.

⌢

If an attack petered out early, I would feel euphoric and wildly philosophical (violent mood swings are a by-product of the illness, the shrinks will tell you). In the wee hours, I would wander aimlessly through the desert – keeping sight of the glowing beacon that was the café's neon sign – and absorb the emptiness of it into my willing soul. I would completely surrender to it. These would be the hours when my battered and bruised muse would most often call. I'd wander the desert for hours. Thinking. Listening. Playing music inside my head. Searching my soul for answers. Do I go to New York? Do I return to the quotidian world of advertising? Am I still in love with Jenny? Am I able to carry on? As I ambled down mammoth dunes like great Atlantic rollers, I would hear the wind whistle a sour tune. It was almost as if it had something pressing to say. Telling me to be strong. Be brave. The answers were near.

As the months ticked over, I became remarkably adept at blocking out any thoughts of my life back in Sydney – and the people who would be somewhat concerned by my sudden disappearance. I assumed that Jenny would soon start her life with Finius and forget me. But I worried about my uncle and aunt and my sister fretting about me. I asked a driver hauling pigs to Western Australia to mail a note to them from Perth. In it I told them I was all right. And I was getting on a plane to New York.

So those early months dragged on with brain-numbing tedium. With plum-coloured eyes, I would saunter around the café with the lethargy that is born only of sleepless nights of sheer terror. Sometimes I read the paper. Or an old magazine. I couldn't tell you what was in them five minutes after I put them down. Often I helped Joe with the cooking. I recall picking up a blackened piece of the Jailhouse Rock (aptly named) Ham and Pineapple Supreme.

'These pizzas are overcooked, Joe. What do you have the oven set to?'

'West.'

'There's your problem right there. Try south.'

'Okay, my fren.'

'What kind of tomato paste do you use?'

'Tomato *paste*? You mean tomato *sauce*.'

'Hmmm.'

I discovered the Palestinians make great kebabs, but lousy pizzas. Years of working in the pizza business at least taught me how to make a decent pizza. Business improved. (In other words, people actually ordered food.) Joe was happy.

I was keen to get the old jukebox going again. It became a kind of crusade of mine for a while. I found the original records intact, and in the end, after much tinkering, it just needed a little rewiring to bypass a scorched fuse box.

One day, I was tinkering with it as usual.

'Why not you forget that busted of a thing. It's fucked, my fren. Some prick pour beer down it one night and bluddy thing never work again.'

'I could fix it easily if I had a manual.'

'Why? Does he know how to fix them?'

'I think it might be the wiring,' I said, holding a screw in my lips.

'Forget it, my fren. It's had it.'

'You *do* realise it's an original Wurlitzer?'

'Wurlitzer? That's a song by The King.'

'What?'

'You know, "*Wurlitzer, one for the money, two for the show . . .*".'

I shook my head. 'Actually, I think I might know what the trouble –'

Suddenly, Sinatra's voice leapt out, '*Come fly with me . . .*'

Joe shook a pumpkin fist, 'You little beauty!'

'It was just the fuse box,' I replied like I knew what I was doing.

'I thought the bluddy thing was cactus.'

'Listen Joey, now that I've got the jukebox working, how about we lose the transistor radio?'

'I need it for the races.'

'I forgot.' I didn't forget.

'Bluddy shame there's only those boring old records and no Elvis. I guess I'll have to sing more to make up for it.'

The blood drained from my face.

'Look Joe, we'll find some Elvis and bung it in the machine, it shouldn't be too hard,' I said a little too quickly.

'All his best tunes!'

'Were there any?'

'Of course!'

Joe danced a little jig. This made his body ripple like jelly and plates fall from the shelves. He stopped. 'Hang on. Where we buy them from? My records all melted when it hit 50 in the late '80s. There's no record store out here, my fren.'

'Oh, right . . . um . . . we'll get one of the drivers to bring some vinyl from Adelaide, on his way through or something. Who can we trust to give the cash to?'

'Um. Nobody.'

'Surely there must –'

'Maybe I ask Barry! Yeah, he owe me a favour that Barry.'

'Barry it is!'

I cleaned the disks and punched some numbers into the old contraption. I gestured grandly towards the jukebox, 'The Cosmopolitan Café cordially presents an afternoon of fine music, Mr Allam.'

'Thank you, Mr Shoesmith.'

'My pleasure, Mr Allam.'

The music of Tommy Dorsey filled the café.

That afternoon, over a bottle of oily tequila, we chatted. Joe started to talk about Las Vegas again. He had this dream of moving there and becoming a professional Elvis impersonator. He talked about his obsession *ad nauseam*. I'd catch him leaning against the pizza oven, sweating in currents, quietly talking to himself and announcing under his breath: 'The Las Vagas Hilton proudly presents . . . *da da da da* . . .' He'd then wiggle his great undulating arse as he mumbled the intro, 'Joseph Allam as The King . . .'

He had the act all planned out. (Right down to the last painful detail.) Sometimes he'd make me be the announcer. He'd perform the whole show to an imaginary audience. (Complete with three encores.)

Sometimes he'd hold karaoke nights and Max and others would come down to get pissed and have a singalong. Max loved a singalong. Reminded him of Christmas with the family, he used to say. I never sang. I told him I just played the piano and couldn't sing. It was Joe's big moment and I didn't want to upstage him. Reverend Fruit was always good for a religious song and usually ended up getting the words wrong. We'd laugh like drains. Then he'd get quite silly. Sometimes, he'd take all his clothes off and streak through the café in nothing but his dog-collar. This would completely crack us up. Max laughed so hard once that a tear ran down his leg. Then the lights would dim. The mirror ball would plunge into the room. Joe's intro music would build to a crescendo. I'd make the announcement.

'*Da da da* Ladies and gentleman – and members of the clergy . . . *da da da* . . . the Venetian Hilton proudly presents . . . Mr Joseph . . . *da da da* . . . Allam – The Palestinian Hound Dog! . . .'

Joe would explode into the main room of the café and perform the entire act – complete with five costume changes. Everyone loved it. They were all tone-deaf and completely rat-arsed by that stage. There he'd be, in a full-length diamanté jumpsuit, singing 'Viva Las Vegas' in a tone only intelligible to dingos and low-flying aircraft – and dancing across the café like Martha Graham with MS – with everyone screaming for more.

Quite often, when he was down, Joe actually thought he was Elvis. I mean, *really* thought he was Elvis. He'd talk about missing Priscilla. And how difficult it was filming *Blue Hawaii*. On those dark days, it was hard for him to distinguish fantasy from fact. Sometimes I had to point out that Elvis wasn't actually born in the Middle East. He would always be on at me whether I thought he looked like 'The King'. I told him that he *did* resemble Elvis just before he died. He seemed pleased with this.

⌢

Joe had no doubt whatsoever that he could make it as an Elvis impersonator in America – despite the competition. To let him down gently, I told Joe that I had read somewhere that there are so many Elvis impersonators in America that, by the year 2020, one in every seven Americans will be an Elvis impersonator. And that, in fact, they were having the White House decked out in red velvet even as we speak. However, he was excited by this. He would simply stand out from the crowd of would-be Kings. It was tough. I never had the heart to tell Joe that he looked about as much like Elvis as Elvis looked like a sweaty, middle-aged Palestinian pizza chef. Tell me why people who are fat, over forty, and look nothing like Elvis, think they look like Elvis. And why do they always portray him in his obese, burgerama, rhinestone-studded jumpsuit period?

I often wondered about Joe. I would sit in the café thinking about him. His life. His dreams. His childhood. What was Joe like as a boy growing up in Palestine? He must have had someone who loved him once. Someone who watched over him, perhaps playing on a little rug on the stone floor of his house in the West Bank. A mother? A father? A wife? Someone. If his mother and father were dead, and there *was* an afterlife, how would they feel about their son's lonely existence now? Living alone in the café at the end of the earth? If we do in fact learn lessons from life in order to continue the journey, what were Joe's lessons? What was he learning? Perhaps we all have some sort of bumbling guardian angel, haplessly clutching a torch before us and guiding us through the dark passages of our lives. If we *do* have a guardian angel, I was convinced Joe's had died from heat exhaustion on the outskirts of the desert. I had never met anyone more completely alone.

As the record in the jukebox crackled to a finish, the flyscreen door slapped open. A sweaty, wizened man in a safari suit hobbled in and ordered a cup of tea. I was starting to get to know most of the locals at that stage, but had not met this man before. He had been in Adelaide on business. He greeted me with a crooked smile that gave the impression he was trying to smell a fart from over his shoulder.

He wasn't tall. He wasn't short. He was about five foot eight, but in the heat, four foot three. He spoke in whispers. As if trying to conserve air with each phrase. His conversation was wrapped in little coughs and short panting breaths.

'Look at this, Joseph!' he said. He pulled out a large pink potato. 'A first-class McCormack Red.'

Joe feigned interest.

'Boot look [*gag*] at this! Pseudomonas Solanacearum.'

Joe shrugged, fisting some pizza dough.

'It got a bloody parasite. Aye, very dangerous that.'

Bartholomew Squales was passionate about potatoes. The humble spud was his life's work. He grew up on a potato farm in Yorkshire. The family spent many hours around the table talking about potatoes. As a boy he even made stamped pictures with them and hung them in his room. For years he had been trying to grow potatoes in the desert, without success. He was always trying new methods.

Bart seemed curious about me. He'd heard about me in the pub and had been discreetly making inquiries about me via Max and the others. He offered a damp palm.

'I don't believe we've [*cough*] met, lad,' he said in a weighty Northern English accent – the sort of accent you couldn't remove with Dettol and a wire brush.

'Gordon Shoesmith,' I said, unobtrusively wiping my soggy hand on my trouser leg. It was hard not to stare at his ill-fitting wig. It listed in the heat like an injured animal.

'Squales. Bartholomew Squales.' (Joe later told me that the locals simply called him 'Pommy Bart', 'Postman Pat', 'Squeals', or simply 'The Rug'.)

'Nice to meet you.'

Squales placed a malodourous Turkish cigarette in a nicotine-stained holder. He lit it. A band of sweat glinted above his lip as he smiled. He peered around a pointy nose.

'Where did you [*cough*] say you coom from again, lad?'

'Around.'

'I ear it's a nice place that – "Around".'

I nodded and wiped a table with a greasy cloth.

'Ow [*cough*] did ye get ere, lad? I don't see a motor.'

'Mine's the wreck on the side of the highway.' The Saab was now a rusting shell.

Squales seemed relieved somehow. 'Oh, is that your motor?' Ash fell on his jacket. He didn't remove it. I had an overwhelming desire to blow it off.

'Yeah, I rolled off the highway a few months ago. Gee . . . has it been that long already, Joe?'

'Yes, my fren,' Joe said.

'Where ye lodgin then?' he asked.

'Here.'

'In this hovel?' he whispered.

'Well, not exactly. Joe snores like Darth Vader with adenoids. No, I sleep in a tent out back.'

'Must be cold?'

'Cold? Look at this.' I showed him my tongue which had a spoon stuck to it.

Joe started humming 'Love Me Tender' as he kneaded the dough with his fat fists.

Squales flashed his crooked dentures. 'Where was it again ye said ye coom from, lad?'

'I didn't.'

'Oh, quite right. Quite right.'

He stubbed out his cigarette. He made this look like a strenuous exercise.

'[*Cough cough*] Not everydare we get a yung lad from city round ere. Lot of people in this town are [*cough*] worried about [*gag*] people from the city. Activists, like.'

'Why?' I asked.

'Native title. Land rights.'

'What land rights?'

He pointed to the desert, 'Out there.'

'Are there any Aborigines out there?'

'One.'

'Sunfly?'

'No.'

Joe brought some tea.

With some effort, the old man opened a tiny, wooden box and, with the tepid tea, swallowed a handful of brightly coloured pills. He pointed to the medication, 'Angina, emphysema, diabetes, arthritis, gout –'

'Jesus, what don't you have?' I said cleaning a table with a rag that smelt like cabbage.

'Not a lot, lad.' He sipped his tea. 'Looking for a better place to stay?' he asked.

'Sure.' I sat down with him.

'You look like a lad that can [*cough*] keep his mouth shut . . . am I right?' He winked, dentures gleaming.

'Sure.'

'Coom outside and we'll ave a quiet chat. You play the piano. Is that right?'

I followed him outside and immediately the heat hit us like a truckload of hot towels. I started sweating instantly. I swatted at a pepper mill of flies. Squales seemed untroubled by them. So many flies landed on his face that at one stage I thought he had slipped on a balaclava. He spoke in panting breaths as we walked into the desert.

'Bout thirty year ago or so [*cough*] I used to be the stationmaster for this town.'

'Stationmaster? I don't see any station.'

'Oh, it's still [*catching his breath*] there. Bout a fifteen-minute walk that ware.' He gestured weakly toward the open desert – I felt he almost needed help to raise his arm.

'Well, why is the town not built around the station then?'

'It was, lad. But with all the prospecting around ere over the years, the ground was too unstable for the line so they moved it.' He spat an ugly piece of phlegm. It made a sizzling noise as it hit the sand. It looked like a snail without its shell.

'So how did you become the stationmaster then?'

'Interesting story, lad.'

As we walked into the duckling-coloured horizon, he told me of his life in the town. (Max filled in the rest for me later over a couple of beers.)

Squales arrived in the desert in the early '50s to work at Woomera (taken from the Aboriginal word for 'spear-thrower') – the British, post-war, secret rocket project.

When the British finally realised that Ian Fleming novels were actually based on fiction, and that James Bond was a 55-year-old clerk with a plastic hip in the foreign office in Clapham, they discarded their delusions of grandeur. Woomera was abandoned. Squales remained in the general area to run the station and then the local post office of the nearby town of Venice. The deserted site, equipped with its monolithic launching towers and antiquated control rooms, stands today as an eerie mausoleum to the final days of the Empire.

By the late '60s, with the demise of Woomera, the rail link was abandoned. However, it seemed someone forgot to tell the computer in the State Rail office. Therefore, the stationmaster, one Bartholomew Squales, received a fortnightly income for thirty odd years for a job he no longer did. So, when anyone from the city arrived in the town, Squales would become extremely agitated.

Squales was an officious individual. As the postmaster, he felt it was his business to know everybody's business. He secretly opened everybody's mail.

Squales was never short of a dollar either. His extra income supposedly hailed from a large potato farm down south. He had quite a collection of potatoes on display in the back of the Post Office. If you weren't careful, he'd trap you and talk about them for hours.

Squales was notorious for investing in harebrained ideas. Sadly, he insisted on wearing most of them on his head. (He had a different coloured wig for each season of the year. His spring wig looked exactly like a bird's nest.)

Other ideas were money-making schemes that never failed to turn sour. He was forever in someone's ear at The Globe about some 'dead-cert' he could put them into for a few 'lazy shillings'. Locals became wary. People had been burned. Especially after the petrol-fuelled vacuum cleaners fiasco. Needless to say, Squales was short on friends in the town.

Having heard a rumour that some geologist was arriving (he initially thought it was me) and needed to use the old rail link to freight samples from the area to the city, Squales now rather badly needed somebody to live at the station house. If the station was abandoned, and the man reported back to State Rail, Squales could be looking at a five-year vertical suntan.

Squales and I struck a deal. For a few 'quiet shillings', as he put it, I would live there rent-free. If any inquiring geologists sniffed around, I would pretend to be Squales – the stationmaster of Venice. I wasn't entirely convinced of the plan but was sick of living in the tent. So I agreed to have a look at the old hut anyway – after all, I wasn't exactly waiting around to have drinks with Cameron Diaz that afternoon.

The heat was intolerable as we tramped through the desert. It seemed alarmingly difficult for Squales to muster the energy to put one leg in front of the other. The journey took much longer than necessary with the old man shuffling in the sand.

'How far did you say this place was again?' I asked.

'Only over that [*cough*] ill there.'

I squinted into the blurring haze. Just at that moment, Squales stopped and clutched my shoulder. He was having a coughing fit. The old man's body shuddered with each bone-rattling hack. It echoed through the desert. I thought he was going to pop his cloggs on the spot. I was imagining having to lug the old geezer back to the café on my own. After a while, he seemed to recover. We continued walking as if nothing had happened.

'You sure you can actually walk this far without the aid of a respirator?'

He kind of smiled and grunted, wiping his foaming mouth with a hanky.

We walked in silence for a while as the old man paced himself with concentrated breath. The incessant flies buzzed around us like a troupe of Chinese dancers.

'Moost give up the fags one day,' he wheezed, desperately sucking in air.

'Might be a good idea.'

'Oh well, I've had a good life. A man's got to go soom tarm, lad.'

'Some time soon, I'd imagine. I wouldn't start reading *Finnegan's Wake*.'

In the fuzzy distance, I saw an old shack perched on an orange-rust piece of railway track.

'Well, what do you think, lad?' Squales said in an excited wheeze.

'It looks like a shit hole,' I replied, with my usual tact.

'Never joodge a [*cough*] book by its cover, lad.'

'If that was a book, it'd be titled: *Great Shit Holes of the World*.'

'Needs a bit of spit and polish, mind.'

'Spit and polish? If you spat on it, it'd fall over.'

Squales grunted and wheezed as he climbed onto the hot platform. It must have been painful for the old man. Carl Lewis would have found it tough going breathing that day. The air was thick with heat. It was like sticking your mouth over the end of a hair dryer set on 'Afro'.

'What's that shed to the side?' I asked, feigning enthusiasm.

'The bog.'

'Septic?'

'No, joost a bloody great ole in grownd. Piss in there, and they ear it splash in Peking.'

'So that's why they call it the *Yellow* River.'

'Has it got power?'

'The station house?'

'No, that.' I pointed to his wig. He frowned.

'Of course it has. Straight from town.'

'All the mod cons, eh?'

'Absolutely.'

'Water?'

'Eh . . . that's the rain tank at the back.'

'Rain? What rain?'

'Water truck, if needed.'

'Keep the number handy.' I opened the door. A battalion of rodents squealed onto the baking platform. 'FUCK!' I danced around the irate vermin. Squales laughed.

'Oh, don't let a [*cough cough cough*] coople of little mice put you off, lad.'

'A couple of little mice? And I suppose *The Birds* was a nature film?'

We walked in. I found it impossible to breathe in the nutmeg-coloured dust so I wondered how the old man was coping. He was okay. He stood in the corner, cross-eyed and turning blue.

'When was the last time you were here, for Christ's sake?' I asked.

Squales spluttered in the dust for a while before answering. (For about a week.) After a few minutes the dust began to settle. 'Oh, soom tarm ago [*cough cough cough*] . . . soom tarm ago . . . [*splutter splutter*] . . . about . . .' It was obvious he wouldn't finish the sentence without the aid of an iron lung, so I walked around the single-roomed shack (that Squales had euphemistically referred to as 'open-planning') as he spluttered.

The cottage had a musty smell. Like blue-vein cheese. Amid Squales's gasping breaths, I could hear the random, ticking footsteps of a bird walking on the tin roof. Above the mangled brass bed hung a flattering portrait of a young Queen Elizabeth. The kind I recall singing 'God Save You' to at sweaty school assemblies. One of the walls was draped with a moth-eaten Union Jack. This concealed a snaking crack that ran from floor to ceiling. Chipped Wedgwood plates painted with train motifs dotted the mantelpiece. They served as weights for pennants from dull northern English cities that dangled in autumn colours. In the centre of the room was an enormous lever which changed a track somewhere along the line. It sat anchored to the dirty wooden floor. It transformed the room into a giant metronome. I walked over to the kitchen bench and flicked through some browning newspapers. They were from the '70s and were strewn across the lime-green laminated kitchen table as if someone had vacated the cottage the same day as reading them. 'Nixon to resign' one read. 'Oil crisis worsens', another read. I walked over and sat on the bed. It made a thwang as it sagged beneath my weight. A cloud of dust mushroomed above.

Squales could tell that I was less than impressed. Yet something in the corner caught my eye. Something covered with a mould-dotted sheet. It was a familiar shape. Squales drew a torpid smile. He removed the sheet like a magician. It was a piano.

Lifting the lid, I played a clumsy note. The action of the old instrument was a little wobbly but the tone was true. I dusted off the brand name: Steinway. My heart leapt with secret joy (not wishing to give away too much to the enterprising Squales).

'Okay, you got yourself a deal.' I shook Squales's hand, which at this stage was like a mop.

'Champion,' he wheezed.

I reclaimed my sodden hand and nodded. 'You know, I think I'm going to like it here, Mr Squales.'

'Excellent . . . [*cough*] excellent. Remember, lad. Moom's the word,' he said, tapping his pointy nose.

I tapped my bruised nose in reply (forgetting it was still a little tender from the accident), 'No problem'.

We both walked out into the hot sun. I felt it sear the back of my neck. It was like your mother ironing a crease out of your collar while you were still wearing your shirt.

Squales handed me a rusty key.

'By the way. What happened to the last tenant?' I asked, as he walked off the platform.

'Oh, e left in a hurray.'

'Why?'

Squales didn't answer the question. He just kept walking in the direction of the café. 'Oh, one thing lad,' he yelled. 'When a [*gasp*] train cooms through, pull that lever to the right.'

'Okay, so every time a train comes through, pull that lever.'

'Good, lad,' he shouted, spitting out a rogue fly.

I looked down the line and hollered, 'What time was the last train through?' I heard my voice trailing off into the desert.

'Three-thirty.'

'Right.' I checked my watch.

'Three-thirty, November the 17th, 1975!' the old man yelled with a tobacco laugh. I watched him shuffle off and liquefy into the burning horizon.

A CUP OF COFFEE AND A DANISH TO GO

I CAN SEE IT', she said.

'Where?' the other said, with a sleepy scowl.

'Just up ahead.'

'Does it look like they sell petrol, yes?'

'Yes.'

She painted her lips with pale lipstick. The sun had cracked them and they were stinging with salty sweat. The punishing morning heat was not helping. They pulled up in a cloud of pumpkin-coloured dust. I walked out in nothing but a pair of Levis. It was hot. My chest was shiny with sweat. It was certainly a stinker of a day. I pumped some leaded into the car for them and that's when I noticed. The blonde, who I guessed was in her late twenties, was staring at me. Her grey eyes fixed on me with that weary gaze that they all have after driving through the same unbroken scene for hours on end. I'd met backpackers before. They all had that dirty laundry smell about them. But as the blonde stepped out of the car, she smelled of jasmine. She was wearing tight shorts, a singlet and a pair of those Homy-ped sandals that they seem to prefer. The other was a blonde who had dyed her hair cherry red. They had the usual backpacker this-is-the-last-sunshine-of-my-life tan about them. These girls made Whoopi Goldberg look pale.

The blonde looked hungrily at my chest and at my nipples that were brown, like chocolate drops. I politely reciprocated. (Her chest was much nicer to look at.) It had been a long drive for them: the windscreen was caked with orange mud. She stretched and rolled her broad shoulders and thick neck. She was the kind of girl mothers euphemistically describe as 'big-boned' and guys in pubs describe as 'built like a brick shithouse'. Her white singlet strained to contain two leviathan breasts, although the imagination is apt to expand things – no, goddamn it, they were *huge*. The singlet had two ink-blot-shaped sweat stains on them. I opened the hood and checked the oil. We never had any oil – pizza yes, oil, no. But this made them feel secure – like I knew something about cars and they wouldn't break down in the middle of nowhere.

'He peeked at my breasts again,' the blonde whispered.

'Kirsten, if I had a crown for all the men that stared at your breasts, I'd be staying at the Hyatt Coolum instead of in a room of snoring, sweaty girls at the Kalgoorlie Youth Hostel,' Cherry Hair said in a grumpy mumble.

Her ass looked great in those khaki shorts, I thought. Although, after staring at Mount Palestine that was Joe's great hairy ass for the last couple of months, Roseanne Arnold's butt would seem a tad petite.

'That's $35 bucks.' (In the desert, you never ask: 'How much would you like?' It's not like someone says: 'Oh, just five dollars worth, thanks.') You just fill it to the brim and ask if they have a jerry can, too.

The blonde handed me some cash, 'My name's Kirsten and this is Ingrid.'

'Hi, I'm Gordon.' I offered an oil-stained hand. 'Your friend looks tired. She doing all the driving?'

Kirsten nodded.

'You sell coffee, yes?' Ingrid asked through heavy eyes.

'Sure.'

'We've got to be in Kalgoorlie tonight,' Kirsten said.

'Looks like your friend could do with a couple of hours sleep.'

Ingrid nodded and smiled through mulberry eyes. 'Ya, um . . . yes, I could.'

'You can park around back and sleep for a while if you like,' I said, twisting the rusting petrol cap back on. It shrieked tight. They discussed it.

'Ya, that would be kind, thank you.' There he goes, looking at my tits again, Kirsten thought.

I wonder if she saw me looking at her breasts? I thought.

Ingrid drove around the back. The motor coughed to a stop and she must have fallen asleep because I didn't see her again. Kirsten and I walked inside. It wasn't much cooler.

'Are you from Denmark?' I asked, pouring her a cup of coffee.

Her thick, plasticine lips broke into a drowsy smile, 'How did you know?'

'Oh, when I lived in the city I was a professional jazz musician, the ears pick up the accent.'

(This had nothing to do with the two hundred and fifty Scandinavian badges wallpapered across the car, culminating with the 'Honk, if you're Danish' sticker on the bumper.)

'Not a lot of jazz clubs in the desert, yes?' she said.

'You've noticed.'

'This your place?'

'No, I just work here. The owner's at the pub.'

She wiped some sweat from her forehead with a napkin. 'How do you stand this heat?'

'When it gets too hot, I just grab my surfboard and run for the beach.'

'There's no beach out here.'

'I wondered why I was getting tired.'

She smiled, painting on some lip gloss, hoping I'd notice her ample lips.

I returned with some ice cubes in a glass and some Cokes. She iced her stinging lips, with little moans of pleasure. I felt a fire in my pants.

'Hmm, this feels faboolous.'

'Big lips are a curse in the outback,' I said.

'So are big tits, I've noticed.'

I turned red.

Shit, I shouldn't have said that, she thought. Ingrid always says that the English are prudish when it comes right down to it. (To the Scandinavian, the Australian is merely an Englishman with a suntan and thongs.) 'Er . . . I joke, yes?'

I roared with nervous laughter.

'So tell me. What's it like to live in a desert?' she asked.

'Different.'

'How so?'

I opened a can of Coke. 'Oh, I don't know, people are different out here.'

'But it must be lonely. Do you have a girlfriend?' she asked, out of the blue.

'That would mean you'd have to find a girl. There aren't a lot of girls out here. Sorry if I ogled you when you hopped out. It's just . . .'

'No, I liked it,' she said politely.

'I'm sure you're quite sick of it.'

'It depends on who's doing the ogling, yes?'

I smiled.

She slouched in the chair and looked me slowly up and down. 'Besides, I might have been doing a bit of ogling myself, yes?'

'Be my guest. Everything in this catalogue's on sale.'

She raised a bushy eyebrow. 'Do you have a girl in the city?'

'Yes, well . . . no. Did have. Not any more. She ran off with another musician.'

'Is that why you live here? Running away?'

I smiled and downed some Coke. I burped without opening my mouth which made my eyes water.

'It's so hot.' She pulled at her singlet, revealing a ravine of cleavage. 'Let's have a swim, yes?' she said.

'Yeah, right. Like where?'

'The lagoon. We cooled off in that . . . eh . . . howdoyoucallit . . . billabong.'

'What billabong?'

'Back down the highway, yes?'

'You're kidding. There's a billabong around here?'

'Ya, I'm serious. It's ten minutes off the highway. I show you but eh . . .' She shook her head, gripping an imaginary steering wheel. 'I can't drive.'

'We'll take my car.' (Suddenly, Joe's car became my car.)

'Hey. Why not? I'll leave a note on the windscreen for Ingrid.'

⌢

As we chatted over the throaty gurgle of the engine, I discovered that this was Kirsten's big global adventure before starting a Master's degree in Biology at Copenhagen University. It had always been a dream of hers to visit the outback since seeing a documentary on Australia on television. I made attempts at witty conversation, but all I thought about was getting into her pants to be honest. In hindsight, I think I saw her as a way of putting Jenny behind me. Perhaps I wanted to get back at her for Finius. Perhaps I just craved the touch of another human being. Perhaps I was just horny. Yes, I think that was it. I was horny. (It had been a while.)

We reached the billabong in a plume of dust. Slender, inky shadows of a desert oak stretched across the turbid water. Parrots loitered on its branches, tentatively. We sat and stared into the tranquil pond. It was wonderful. I watched a jaffa-coloured yabbie skip across the water. It left a chain of rings across the surface.

I tore off my Levis and belly-flopped into the tepid pool – my underpants sagging in the water. It felt deliciously refreshing. I splashed it against my sunburned face. I felt my feet sink into the sloppy mud. That too felt therapeutic. I tasted it. It was brackish.

You couldn't really drink it. I must have splashed about in my own world for about twenty minutes, completely forgetting about my Scandinavian guest. She sat on the copper-coloured bank and watched my toddler-like movements in the water. I waved to her like a schoolboy. It made me think of Jenny and the time she used to drag me down to Bronte Beach. With her alabaster-white skin, she'd umbrella herself from the sun like Queen Victoria while I'd dive into the water like James Bond.

I waved at Kirsten to come in. She stood, and slowly peeled off her sweat-soaked singlet. She carefully unhitched her bra – which resembled a small hammock – and her enormous tan-lined breasts sprung out, almost heaving with a sigh of relief. Then she peeled off her shorts. In white briefs, made diaphanous by the water, she waded in. (It was then that I discovered she was not a natural blonde.) Her breasts floated to the surface like oil drums. She paddled around for a while before hopping out. She lay resting on her elbows on the sticky bank, catching some more rays. (She obviously thought she needed more tanning. A crematorium perhaps?) Her beacon-like breasts drooped to the side. She crossed her caramel legs and stared at me. They glinted in the sunlight like hot toffee. Now, I had a real problem. A problem that is unique to pimply-faced teenagers and most men not taking Viagra. I was in the water in my sopping underpants with an erection that would present a danger to light aircraft. After an age, she looked at me, wondering what the hell I was doing. The invitation was obvious. I stood there pretending to feel the water ripple against my arms.

Why won't he come out of the water and screw me? she asked herself. What more do I have to do? Paint a sign on my tits saying: 'Welcome aboard'?

I had to do something. It was either spend the rest of my life in the pond like a kind of horny Toulouse-Lautrec or walk out and face the music. Even the thought of Joe in a G-string and pink lipstick didn't deflate my turgid friend that periscoped below the surface. There was no other course of action. I had to walk out of the water with the hard-on to end all hard-ons. I'll be matter of fact about it. She's hip. She's Scandinavian. I'm sure she realises that the desert is a lonely place, I thought. It's natural. I shuffled to the bank with my head/s held high. Her nipples turned to pebbles.

She smiled at me, spreading her legs.

Before I knew what I was doing, I found myself on top of her, chewing her nipples. She threw her legs in the air. They're looking fat, she thought for moment.

This girl's an animal, I thought. She's tearing at my underwear.

This guy's an animal, she thought. He's tearing at my underwear.

With her panties thrown over her shoulder, mine dangling from a branch, she fanned her legs wide. Her tongue wrestling with my tonsils. I rolled off her.

'What? Don't stop. Fuck me, yes?' she panted.

I sighed, 'I can't.'

'The girl?'

'The girl.'

She let out a big sigh. We lay looking into the cobalt sky for a while. She finally leaned over and kissed me on the forehead. She took my hand and placed it in her sodden crotch. 'Please, yes?'

I rubbed her. She moaned like a wounded animal. I heard her buttocks slapping against the mud. Her breasts shimmied. I felt her plunge her nails into my chest. Her hands then found their way down to my belly, and before long she was milking me like a cow. I whispered a 'no' but she let out a long 'shhhh'. It was hard to argue with her logic. Finally, as a coarse duet we let out a long note. A flock of budgerigars suddenly became a green cloud against the sky.

⌒

I waved to her as the twilight bled from the sky. The desert looked like one of those Lloyd Rees landscapes painted just before he died – when his eyesight was fading and he saw things in hazy pastels. She blew me a kiss from the passenger window. Thinking it was for him, Joe blew a kiss back. I waved to her and winked. Joe realised. He spoke through a fake smile, waving at the van. 'Did you root her, my fren?' he said.

'No.'

'You not poof are you?'

'No. I'm not poof, Joe.'

THE POLICEMAN IN BOTTLE-GREEN THONGS

∾

I GUZZLED AN ICY BEER. It was ludicrously hot that afternoon. The pub, with its usual bouquet of beer swill, urinal vapours and cigarette smoke, stung my eyes in the heat. Even the parrot looked hot. I listened to the incessant buzzing of the transistor radio. At low volume it sounded like a blowfly trapped in a milk bottle. I felt depressed.

Feeling sorry for myself, I struck my usual abandoned pose: crinkled brow, hand on forehead, staring out into the desert. By that stage I'd weaned myself down to about thirteen neglected attitudes and forlorn postures a week.

Trying to look as Jean-Paul Belmondo as hell, I let out a sigh. I followed it towards the ceiling only to see it be torn apart by the fan. I thought of Jenny. Incessantly. I tried to push her out of my mind but found it hard. Thinking about her screwing Finius was like a knife in my stomach. I tried not to picture it. I felt confused. Was I still in love with her despite what had happened? I was tough at first. All talk. But now my heart felt a pang at the thought of her soft lips. The nape of her neck that was evocative of a Boldini portrait. Those sea-green eyes. I took another gulp of the amber fluid. Then I thought bitterly of her – the way you do to lessen the pain. Her father. Her snobby friends. Her middle-class values. I screwed up my face and swigged some beer.

'Don't even bloody think about em,' a voice barked from behind the bar.

'Think about what, Max?'

'Women. You see "that look" a lot round ere. Get to know it pretty well.'

'All right, give me another beer and help me forget again.'

'Works for me!'

Max obligingly poured another frothy glass, 'Put it on the eye-tie's slate?'

'Yep.'

'You just make sure that bastard pays me or none of yuse will drink here,' he smiled menacingly.

'Don't worry Max, I know when the big fella's cashed up,' I winked.

'Good man.'

Sunfly perched over his rum in stony silence. I sipped my beer and continued torturing myself thinking about Jenny in the sack with Finius.

A lofty man walked into the bar wearing an Akubra hat. I turned the colour of sour milk. It was a policeman. (I had discovered – via Squales – that Jenny had reported me missing and I planned to stay that way.)

The big man chatted easily with a couple of drinkers in the corner as I hovered nervously over my schooner.

Max noticed my unease. He leaned in. His breath smelt of chicken chips. 'Don't worry about Dave. He's all right, Dave is.'

Suddenly the towering policeman strode up to the bar. Max threw out a scabrous hand.

'Well, if it isn't the copper with the whopper!' (The policeman apparently renowned in the trouser department.) 'How ya been keepin, Dave?'

'Oh, fair to middley, Maxy, fair to middley. G'day Sunfly,' he hollered down the bar.

The eerie old man tipped his moth-eaten hat, then continued to sip his rum.

'We ain't seen ya for a while, whacha been up to, old son?' Max asked.

'Oh, we had a bit of trouble with the Abos at the Coober,' he said in a slow drawl.

Sunfly cocked an ear.

'Yeah, what kinda trouble?' Max asked, cleaning a glass.

'Ar, just the usual. Yer know, they get on the piss and smash up the joint. Then the miners wanna bash em. And somewhere in the bloody middle is a cupla cranky coppers.'

Max poured the lawman a glass of beer without asking, 'Okay now, though?'

'Cheers. Yeah. For now.'

I never saw a policeman dressed so strangely. He wore the ubiquitous Akubra hat. A khaki shirt. Khaki shorts. And on his blackened feet, a pair of bottle-green thongs. I sneaked a glance at the policeman's barge-like feet. He noticed.

'Too hot fer shoes,' the policeman smiled.

'Um . . . oh . . . yeah.' I took a sheepish swig of beer.

'Don't always wear em.'

'Huh?'

'You know, thongs. But, if I've got'a lazy day on and I'm doin a lot of drivin, I wear em. Too bloody hot fer boots in this heat.'

'Mmmm.' I nodded, not wanting to be dragged into conversation with the cheery constable. The policeman shot out a leathery hand that resembled a baseball mitt that had been left in the sun for a year. 'Dave Rodgers.'

I shook his hand. I had never shaken a policeman's hand before. I remained quiet. He was waiting for me to say something.

Max enthusiastically butted in, 'This is Gordon, Dave.'

'G'day Gordon. I don't believe I've seen yer round ere before? Would I be right?'

'You'd be right.' I was praying he wouldn't ask too many questions. I had a sudden flash of me being dragged back to Jenny in handcuffs, with Finius in my dressing-gown laughing at me.

'Gordon's our new resident. He's from the city,' Max said, trying to start a conversation. He poured himself a small beer – much to the irritation of one Gordon B. Shoesmith.

The policeman took the lead. 'I'm from the city meself originally,' the man boomed.

There was an awkward silence.

'How long have you been doing this?' I begrudgingly asked.

'Oh, years. I can remember when I first come to the outback. Remember that Max? I was stationed at Winoonah.'

Max nodded, with a mouthful of chips.

'The room they give me was a bloody dog kennel. Tiny. In the mornin it faced the sun. By Christ, it was hot in there! I felt like a chicken in a bloody oven. I lodged that many transfers to go back to Adelaide,' he chuckled to himself, 'but in the end I kinda got used to it. Jeeze,' he said, shaking pearls of sweat from his forehead, 'it was tough at first. With the isolation and that typa thing.'

'Are you the policeman for this town?' I asked, trying not to appear too standoffish.

Max and the policeman belly-laughed. 'Gordon, Dave's beat is about twenty-four thousand square miles!'

'You're kidding? But that's . . . about the size of Ireland, isn't it?'

'Is it?' grunted the policeman.

'Do you cover all that in a car?' I asked.

'Yeah, well, a four-wheel drive, actually. I guess I do an average of about two to three thousand k's a month across the joint. I camp out a cupla nights a week under the stars. Winter's bit cool. Summer's oright. The mozzies annoy yer but.'

Max ducked to the cellar to change a keg. I was left alone with the lawman.

'How do you find your way around out there?'

'Just follow the old nose.'

'Sounds dangerous.'

'Nearly died out there recently,' he said, gesturing towards the desert. 'Thought I was done for. If it wasn't for –' The big lawman stopped mid sentence, chuckled to himself, and downed some beer.

'Huh? You were going to say something.'

'Oh, yer'll think I'm round the bloody twist if I tell yer,' he said in a drawling tone.

'Try me.'

He took a gulp of beer. He reflected as he methodically rolled a fat cigarette. A tuft of tobacco poked out like a general's moustache. He smiled, thinking. Finally, he spoke in a low voice, 'It's funny, I've never told anyone this story.'

He ran his pink tongue along the edge of the paper, gave it a final roll, lit it, and blew the sentence out with the smoke. 'I guess it would have been . . . oooh a good two years ago now.' He looked out into the desert. The horizon undulating in the heat.

'I was called out to a remote campsite in the desert where a cupla German backpackers had stumbled across a corpse. Not far from ere.' He puffed the handmade fag.

'When I got there, the tourists were a bit shaken. Yer can tell. I talked to em for a bit. Asked the usual questions. I could see the body in the distance. Flies buzzing around it and that. They'd thrown a sleeping bag over it. I told em to make a cuppa tea and relax. Told em to wait by their vehicle. They had one of them bloody whatchamacallits. You know, kombivan things that all them mob have.'

'Ah! The ubiquitous kombivan. The backpackers' rollerskate,' I smiled.

'Yeah, great if yer touring the fucken Alps, but heapsa shit if yer travellin the desert. I can't tell yer how many times I've found em broken down or bogged out here. The engines, the suspension, all built in Germany over thirty year ago, for cold weather, that typa thing.'

'Right. So you were saying . . .'

'It was an eerie day. We'd had a lota hot days with no wind. The desert was very still. So I walk over to the deceased. It was the Jap tourist who had gone missing bout a week before. We'd been expecting him to turn up sooner or later. Three or four people die like that in the desert each year. Their car breaks down. They wander off instead of staying put where we can find em once they're reported missing. People forget that in older cars they have a week's wortha water in their radiator alone. Anyway, this bloke had wandered from a campsite in the middle of the night – probably looking for a place to have a crap, that typa thing, and disappeared. Just another drinker . . .'

I shot a quizzical look at the lawman.

'Oh . . . that's what we call em. Yer know, cause they wander around the joint and die lookin for a drink,' he said with the good old Australian sense of irony. 'Shook me up a bit, though.'

'Seeing a corpse would shake anyone up, I'd imagine.'

'No . . . no, it wasn't that. I seen heapsa bodies before. I'd seen em when I was stationed in the city. Yer know, we'd fish em outa the river. Or find em in some back alley. Drug addicts, that typa thing,' he said in a quiet drawl.

'Sure.'

'But, this was different. The dogs had been at him.'

'Corgies?'

'Nar, dingoes.'

'Oh, of course.'

'Yeah. Ripped his intestine out. Bloody long thing the human intestine. Well, that was bad enough but –' The policeman stopped and shook his head. He started to roll another cigarette.

'But what?' I said, taking a careful sip of beer. (It was so sweaty in the pub that the glass would sometimes slip out of your hands if you weren't careful.)

'Well, it sounds kinda strange now, but when I looked closely at his body, there were all these sort of weird drawings on im.'

'Like samurai tattoos?'

'Oh, no. These were Abo drawings.' He lit the handmade cigarette and thought for a moment. 'Water . . . waves, that typa thing. The ocean. I could be wrong, but that's what it looked like to me. The sea. Gave me the fucken creeps, I'll tell yer. I asked the Krauts if they knew anything about it. They said no. Anyway, they seemed as spooked by it as I was.'

'So what did you do?'

'Well, I go to call base. Guess what? The radio's cooked.'

'Shit.'

'My thoughts exactly. So I couldn't just leave him there. I held me nose and threw im in the back of the Landrover and took off. Jeeze, he ponged. Started to make me feel a bit crook, actually. Then suddenly BANG. The fanbelt snapped – the bastard! Scared shit out of me actually,' he laughed to himself. 'It made a terrific old noise. And yer know with Fuji in the back there and those weird drawings and that, I was little spooked, I don't mind tellin yer.'

'So what did you do?'

'Nothin I could do. I didn't bring no spare with me. Blokes in the know, bush blokes, keep a packet of pantyhose handy.'

'Why?'

'Use it as a fanbelt.'

'Sure, but how do they explain the stilettos?'

'So, like a silly bastard I kept bloody drivin, while the car kept overheating. Kept toppin up the radiator with me spare water, forgettin that I might want to drink some of the bloody stuff!'

'Shit!'

'My thoughts again. It wasn't like me to do silly stuff like that. Anyway, I just drove like a mad bastard till the incvitable happened.'

'What was that?'

'I blew up the engine.'

'So what did you do, then?'

'Shit meself.'

'I see we share the same bowel functions.'

'Right! Well, hours and hours I waited. I was desperate for a drink, I'll tell yer that much. I was as dry as a dead dingo's donger. I waited by the car all day but nothing – I was on a very remote road. Then I really shit meself. I remembered that I'd told base that I might call in on a few sheep stations on me way back. Mick, a mate of mine, runs one of em and he doesn't see many folk out there. He usually forces a few beers down me neck and we end up getting on the piss for a few days. It would take them at least a week to start to miss me round the joint. The next day I started to really fucken panic. I was that thirsty I could have drunk me own piss.'

'Cancel my invite to your next wine-tasting.'

'Then I thought about Fuji in the backa the car. The dogs at im. Those weird drawings. It was terrible, so I started to panic a bit.'

'Anyone would.'

He leaned into me. I smelt his nicotined face. 'Yer won't believe this, but to be honest, the thing that worried me the most,' he chuckled to himself, 'was what the boys back at base would say. They'd piss emselves laughing. Experienced bush copper like me, goes out to pick up a "drinker", then becomes one. Oh, they'd love that all right. They'd dine out on that little one for years.' He took a slug of beer and shook his head. 'It's funny, but that's what worried me the most: the humiliation. Does that surprise yer?'

'Not really.' I clasped my hands behind my head and leaned back in my chair. Unfortunately, I was sitting on a bar stool. I got up off the floor.

'Why?' he asked. 'Cigarette?'

'Thanks.'

I rolled a withered cigarette, spilling half of its contents onto the floor. I lit it and took a hard drag. Forgetting I didn't smoke, I coughed for a while – till about August. I put the horrid thing out.

'An acquired taste, rollies. Don't like tailor's meself. Anyway, why doesn't it surprise yer that I was more worried about what the boys back at the base would say than dina thirst in the desert like a silly prick?'

'They say the number one fear in life is public speaking. Death comes as a poor second, I'm afraid.'

'I don't get it. I wasn't out there to give a speech or nuthin.'

'No, you don't follow me. People don't really fear public speaking per se, they fear embarrassment more than death. Odd. Isn't it?'

'Yeah right.'

'So what happened?'

'I did something yer should never do.'

'Sing "Feelings" in the style of Liza Minnelli?'

'No, I wandered off.'

'Shit.'

'Yer got it again.' The lofty lawman shook his head. 'Silly prick I was. Shoulda known betta. See, I was that thirsty. I started to feel delirious. Me head started spinning. All I could think about was fucken water! Water, water, water. I wandered off into the desert looking for it. Good place to look, don't yer reckon? In about twenty minutes I was completely lost. It don't take long out there. I was wandering the desert for about two days without water, they reckon. By the end of the week, I'd come to the end of the line. I was dead but me brain wouldn't admit it.'

'So what was it like?' I asked.

'Well, sounds weird but . . . I thought I was under the ocean. Walkin on the seabed. Big fish swimmin round me. Hallucinating, that typa thing. I think I was actually losin me marbles. It happens, you know. That's the first stage. Anyway, I remember struggling up this big sand dune. Like a fucken mountain, it was. The bloody thing musta been a good fifty metres high. Ever seen one?'

'No.'

'Big red bastards. Like tryna walk up a tidal wave of sand. As yer climb it, it almost swallows you up to yer waist. Bout half way up, I was buggered. I was that bloody tired. I just wanted to sleep. Couldn't go on. The sun was burnin like a blowtorch on me face. I could see meself buried in the bastard and no one finding me. Nearly started to cry, I don't mind tellin yer. Thought about me Mum – never seein her again – her not knowing what happened to me, that typa thing. Got a bit silly. Anyway, I looked up an there he was.'

'Who?'

'The Spook.'

'Who *is* this Spook? I've heard his name mentioned before.'

'Oh, yer don't know about im yet? He's a mad Abo kid that lives out in the desert. Lives on snakes and lizards and shit. The rest he just steals from town. Had all the spears and whatnot. I remember his hair. Wild as buggery. And his eyes, like a madman. Anyway, where on earth he come from I couldn't tell yer. Well, he just stood there like fucken Moses on the mountain. And there's me, half-buried in sand just lookin up at im, helpless as a kitten. Well, the Spook – strong for a little bloke – digs me out of the sand and helps me down the dune.'

Suddenly he leaned over the bar and called to Max. 'Two more, thanks Maxy.'

Max arrived, sweating, with two frothy beers. 'VB's off for a minute. West End okay, boys?'

We nodded and Max returned to the cellar. The policeman licked his chapped lips and handed me a frost-covered glass.

'Thanks, that's very decent of you,' I said. 'Anyway, you were just about to die of thirst,' I smiled.

The policeman guzzled the beer. He noticed himself and laughed.

'Yeah, makes me thirsty just thinkin about it. Anyway, so the Spook dragged me along for a while. The whole time he says nothing to me. We must have walked for fucken miles. Then he sees this withered-looking tree – a desert oak, I found out later. With a sharp stone he makes a hole in the tree. Then he placed me under the tree, and lo and behold, water starts to trickle outa the bastard. Just like tappin a bloody keg! I found out later that the desert oak stores water in its trunk and roots. Lets the top half of the tree sorta die off and stores the water in the lower parts of the tree in order to survive. The Abos have used em for thousands of years. Well, you can imagine, I drunk like a fucken mad man. As soon as I had a drink I started to feel a little better. Let me tell yer, water never tasted so good! I started to pull meself together a bit and took a good look at im as he plugged up the tree with a little sap for next time – very respectful of the environment, the Abos. Always thinking about the next bloke to use it. Anyway, I had a good look at the kid. I'd been tryin to talk with him for years. It was funny meetin im like this.

'He was lean and slim. But fit and powerful. He had them ceremonial scars on his body. Great welts, like someone had flogged him with a peasa hot wire. I tried talkin to him, but he said nuthin. He just gazed into the distance – like I wasn't even there. We just sat there under the tree. Then after about ten minutes of complete silence he took three fingers and placed them in the sand and made little patterns. Looked like animal tracks, that typa thing.'

The policeman dipped his brown fingers in his beer and simulated some crude tracks on the bar. 'He goes, he goes: "Follow these tracks and yer'll find yer way out. Come back into the sandy country again and I'll kill yer." Then he just walked off into the desert. I saw the tracks and realised they were dog tracks. Dingoes. Followed em. They led me to Mick's place.'

'Who's Mick?'

'Oh, he's that bloke I was tellin yer about earlier. You know, the one with the sheep station.'

'Gotcha.'

'So when I see the sheep station, I realise that the Spook knew the dogs would lead me to sheep sooner or later because the dingoes hunt the bastards. Well, when I saw Mick's place I was so relieved, I musta passed out. When I came to, Mick told me he knew I was lost and was out lookin for me in the Cessna.'

'How did he know you were lost?'

'Well yer not goin to believe this.'

'Try me.'

'One of the blackfella's that works for Mick told im I was lost.'

'How did he know?'

'Said the Spook come to im in a dream.'

I looked askance at the sweating copper.

'I know. Sounds crazy. Well, Mick thought so too. Thought this Abo had been on the piss again, as he likes a drink this Abo. So Mick's blackfella went back to work and said nuthin more about it. Well this kinda spooked Mick a bit and he thought he'd better radio base and check.' He stole a glance at Sunfly and lowered his voice. 'Apparently they reckon blackfellas are telepathic and speak to each other through dreams and shit. Have yer heard that before?'

'Yes, but I think it's bullshit,' I said quietly.

'So do I.'

'Anyway, go on.'

'So Mick checked. Base said they had been tryin to call me on the radio. They wanted to know how Mick knew I was missin.' He leaned in. 'I spose they thought I was on the piss with him. Having a lend of em, that typa thing. Mick told em that he was sorta expectin me and when I didn't turn up, started to worry. Mick didn't want to sound crazy, tellin em some Abo's had a fucken dream.' He paused, drank the remnants of his beer and ordered two more.

'Wow, that's certainly an amazing story,' I said. 'Oh, my shout!'

'Cheers! Oh, it don't end there, old mate. Remember Fuji in the back seat? The deceased?'

'Oh yeah. What happened?'

'They eventually took him to the city for a post-mortem. Cupla weeks later I get this phone call – it's the quack doin the post-mortem. He starts askin me all these weird questions. Did I draw them pictures on his body? Did I try to give him a drink? That typa thing. Very strange. As if I'd give him a fucken drink when he was dead with half his intestine dragged across the desert! Silly prick. I thought it was a bit strange after I put the phone down. So I ordered a copy of the inquest.

'It didn't come for months – fucken typical red tape – so I forgot all about it. Well, one night I had a cuppa coffee with that mad Italian who runs the café out on the old highway. Do yer know the bloke I mean? Thinks he's Elvis Presley,' he chuckled.

'Vaguely,' I said with a wry smile.

'I'd been in town doin the rounds for the day so I popped in for a coffee. Had a long drive in fronna me. Musta been about . . . oooh . . . ten-thirty at night, I s'pose. Well, I was pickin through some mail and I look out the window. There's the Spook. Standin on a dune. It was a full moon and I could see im there plain as day. Just starin at me. I didn't try chasin im that night because every time I do he just scarpers off into the desert like a bandicoot. Just wanted to clear a few things up. Thank him, really. That's all. Nuthin more.'

The bronzed policeman continued with the same drawling sense of urgency, yet his voice grew more intimate. 'So, I'm in the café, I don't worry about the Spook, he's as mad as a hatter anyway, but it's a bit creepy all the same: him starin at me from the dunes but I keep drinkin me coffee. I read some papers for a bit and then I look out the window. He's still there, just fucken starin at me in the moonlight – like a man possessed. Then, with a long spear, he starts drawin in the sand. I go out to talk to the bloke. And he's gone. But he's left behind all these tribal drawings. The same kind that I found on the deceased. Water. Waves. Sea creatures. That typa thing.

'I'm back inside drinkin me coffee when in my pile of mail I come across the coroner's report. I rip open the envelope and read it. All looks pretty normal, I thought. Then I come to the cause of death.' He paused.

'Well, obviously he died of dehydration,' I suggested.

'That's what I thought. But when I read it, I was stunned. I couldn't believe me eyes. I tell yer, the hairs on the back of me neck could have pierced me shirt.'

'I don't understand. What was the cause of death?'

'Death by drowning.'

SHOTGUN AND SAGGING UNDERPANTS

∽

WITH A CLINK, I dropped a coin into the jukebox. The record crackled as Peggy Lee filled the café with doleful tones. A pizza hissed in the oven. I smelt the weedy perfume of oregano. I sat at the front table, chin resting on my wrists. Through the window, I watched a moth dancing under the lamppost that drooped over the highway. I watched it hurtling itself against the light. Endlessly. Violently. With no question of resignation. With each violent impact, micro-particles of flesh exploded around the creature with stellar forces. What a stupid insect, I thought. What kind of creature would bash the life out of itself for no apparent reason? I studied some lyrics I'd been writing on the back of a meal docket. It was stained with black tears of Worcestershire sauce.

Standing still on an empty beach,
I wrestle with thoughts and with dreams out of reach,
ghosts from the past laugh and shout,
so unkind,
and twist and convulse within the depths of my mind,
as blue fades to red,
and day kisses night,
spectres and demons glove up to fight,
I weather the storm,

the beacon shines bright,
taking on water,
at midnight.

Dawn caresses,
my lids open wide,
I salvage the wreck that's adrift with the tide,
I swim to the shore,
and look seaward at last,
as the flotsam and jetsam of years drift on past,
and the spillage of pain,
that's awash on the reef,
strikes me with fear,
beyond all belief,
I stand on the beach,
awaiting in fright,
till the carnage again,
at midnight.

I watched the moth hurtle itself against the light for the final time before plummeting to its death. Joe farted from behind the counter. Why is it that people lift up one leg to fart? Do they think the fart will become trapped somehow and they will spontaneously combust? Between his feet and his flatulence, I decided it was a good time to get some air.

The night was crisp. Standing under an umbrella of stars, I picked up the fallen insect to study it. What is a moth but a butterfly with a penchant for beige? I thought. I placed it on the palm of my hand and blew it off. Looking up I picked out a lean silhouette on the horizon. A shaving of moon lingered behind it. The silhouette watched me. I heard the flyscreen door squawk open behind me.

Joe stood in the doorway, watching the eerie figure creep down the dune. I heard the flyscreen again as Joe went back inside.

I stood uncomfortably. Crickets screamed like a stadium of soccer hooligans. I felt the night air cut into my face.

It was him. The kid they called the 'Spook'. He *did* look wild. He wore a pair of frayed jeans with no shoes. Although bare-chested, a tattered lumber jacket quilted his bony frame. This gave the impression of a stray dog in a coat that some kind-hearted stranger thought would keep the animal warm. I guessed he was about seventeen or eighteen. His face was polished ebony in the moonlight and his hair blew in the breeze like seaweed. I stood motionless, as the young Koori gently yet purposefully walked down the dune towards me. I heard the screen door again.

BOOM!

I hit the cold sand as the blast of shot whistled over my head. The boy scampered over the dune, rabbit-like.

'WHAT THE FUCK . . .?' I cried, spitting out grains of cold sand.

'I didn't shoot the busted. Just scare him off,' Joe said casually – as if he were firing the noon gun in Hong Kong Harbour. He pointed the weapon to the stars. 'Just in the air, my fren.'

'You scared the living crap out of me, you dopey bastard!'

'You want him to kill you?'

'What makes you think he wants to kill me, man?'

'He's very dangerous this boy. He know no law. He live in desert like a wild dog. If you wander out on your own, he will slit your sthroat.' Joe said, dragging a fat finger across his rippling neck.

'How do you know all this?' I asked.

'Everybody know.' We walked back inside. 'Relax, my fren.'

My heart was pounding sixteen to the bar. I sat at the counter. 'So, what else do you know about this kid?'

Joe poured two oily cups of coffee and backed his spongy ass onto a stool. 'I know plenty bout him. This boy, his family used to live out in the desert till social worker take him away. Locals said the boy not being look ufta properly. Social worker take him when he was a toddler. They give him to some rich white family. Then one day, he left city and come back. But his family had gone.'

'Who told you this?'

'The local walloper. Dave Rodgers. Nice bloke for a copper.'

'So why do people call him the "Spook"?'

'Because he spook people, my fren. You might not sleep one night, get up to make coffee, look out the window and he's staring at you like a total madman.'

'Why does he spook people?'

'Dave say he's angry at whitefellas. Dave say his mother was hysterical when social worker took him away. They send her to mental home. She start to drink. And you know Abos love to drink.'

'Unlike your good self.'

'Right. So ufta awhile she kill herself in the nut-house. After his mother kill herself, his father go bad and shoot a copper. Gets life. Grandfather used to look after him, but he die early this year. So now he's gone completely fucking bonkers. Like his old lady.'

'That's a terrible story.'

'Greed, my fren.'

'What do you mean?'

'They want to get them all off the land. The family was the last traditional owners. Now it's just him.'

'It's the desert. It's worthless!'

'Not to a mining company. People say the desert is full of riches. But believe me, he's got you marked, my fren.'

'Bullshit, I've got nothing against him and he's got nothing against me, man,' I said with the conviction of Cook telling his anxious crew not to worry, the Hawaiians are a peaceful people who give you flower necklaces and play the ukulele.

'Do you want to take the chance?' Joe lit a cigarette and blew a cylinder of smoke through his fat nose.

'This is crazy. I'm off.'

'You better take this with you,' Joe pulled the shotgun from under the counter.

'Are you crazy? What do you propose I do, shoot him like a dog because he happens to walk over to me?'

'Just take the shotgun, my fren. Just point it at him. Look, I even take out the cartridges.'

'Good. I don't want to end up blowing my bloody foot off or something.'

⌒

I walked back to the shack with false bravado. A lemon-peel moon still clung to the evening sky, glowing dully like a vandalised street light. Crickets continued with their grating harmonies as I listened for unfriendly footsteps. In my imagination I heard a thousand Koori warriors creeping behind me. Finally the soft light of the cottage beckoned.

I walked in and bolted the door, jamming a chair up against the knob.

This is not rational, I told myself.

I took the chair away. I jammed it up again. I took it away. I called myself a fuckwit. I walked away. I ran back and jammed it up again. I walked over to the sink and ran my head under the tap. The water was freezing. In an effort to do normal things, I picked at the piano and played a little Jerome Kern. I looked at the clock. One-fifteen. I threw myself on the bed and stared at the plaster-bubbled ceiling – listening for footsteps. Eventually, I fell asleep.

I woke. I squinted at the clock. Three-thirty. I rubbed my eyes and started to unravel my strange dream. I'd recall it in fragments – as you do with dreams. I'd catch glimpses, only to lose them again a moment later. It was like trying to tune-in a community radio station from a speeding train.

I could remember flying. Flying and crashing. Pain. Fear. Desperation. Unfriendly voices. And then nothing. Then I remembered.

I was the moth at the café. I remembered hurtling myself uncontrollably at the light. I remember the sickening blows. I felt pain. I felt my bones shatter and flesh tear from my body. I felt a mixture of desperation and agony. I felt an overwhelming desire to become one with the light. I could remember feeling that the light was the only way out of the darkness and if I could just break through the glass, nirvana would be waiting. But what was the other voice saying? That soft voice. Calling from the desert. What was it saying? Something important. But what?

I got up and put the kettle on. I stood pensively at the window, rubbing my forehead. The blind was drawn, and behind it, the moon pierced the corners. What was the voice saying? It was desperately trying to tell me something. Yes, that was it!

You are the light!

At that moment I pulled the blind. It flapped maniacally around the roller. I saw the boy. His face pressed against the glass. His eyes, flaming coals. I dropped the cup. It shattered on the floor in white splinters. I ran for the shotgun, picked it up and pointed it at the window. He was gone.

I sat shaking uncontrollably. I thought about going outside to speak with him. Reason with him. However, I felt safer in the shack with a gun and four walls, decrepit as they were, around my person. I listened for footsteps, but heard nothing. That didn't surprise me because I remembered how lightly the boy walked before. The adrenaline was pumping. I walked around the room and suddenly caught myself in the mirror. I looked ridiculous in sagging Y-fronts and shotgun ensemble. It wasn't very Harrison Ford. I stopped. What about the boy? What was I going to do? Shoot him because he looked through the window at me? I calmed myself.

'Be rational for fuck's sake, Gordon!' I said out loud, my voice, startling me after the long quiet.

Fifteen minutes later, I gingerly opened the door and walked outside, gun poking into the lavender darkness. The crickets stopped like a hall of noisy schoolboys upon seeing the principal. It was freezing and my least-used appendage shrunk to an unfashionable size. The boy had vanished. I scanned the horizon. Nothing. I saw the wind fizz across the sand.

I circled the shack before going inside and bolting the door. Placing the gun beside the bed, I put my head on the pillow. After a few more wide-eyed hours, I again fell asleep.

The long groan of a crow woke me. Gradually, I opened my heavy eyelids. I saw the sky crimson through the crack in the blind. Snuggled beneath the blankets, I listened to the wind whistle through the old shack, rattling the windows and blowing gravel along the tin roof. I got up and lit the oil heater. It smelt like a burning tyre as it warmed the room. I placed my freezing hands, toast-like, over it in an attempt to bring them back to life. The old heater creaked like the hull of a tanker as it warmed the shack. I splashed my face with water and put the kettle on. After some strong coffee, I felt better. I half-heartedly played a few chords on the piano. But again, I felt I was being watched. I looked out the window. Nothing. With shotgun in hand, I crept outside to scan the horizon. And there he was. His hair whipping in the wind.

'HEY MYSTERY MAN,' I shouted bravely from the safety of my doorway. 'FUCK OFF!'

The boy stood motionless. Around him, sand sprayed along the tops of low-lying dunes.

'I'VE GOT A GUN HERE, MAN, AND I KNOW HOW TO USE IT!'

I looked down to see the butt pointing to the boy. With the slickness of Jerry Lewis on cough medicine, I spun it around. 'WHAT DO YOU WANT? I'VE DONE NOTHING TO YOU, MAN,' I pleaded.

The boy remained silent.

'WHITEFELLA NO MONEY AND NO BOOZE HERE,' I added with redneck logic.

The young man remained silent, anchored to the horizon like a she-oak.

'FUCK OFF!' I finally said.

He walked off.

I went inside. I peered through the window, shotgun cold against my pocked cheek. I collected my thoughts. A lit fuse of sand trailed across the horizon. I heard the tromboning of a camel in the distance. In the end, feeling well and truly spooked, I decided to sleep at the café.

⌒

'Are you cooking that fish soup again, or have you just taken your boots off?' I asked, tossing a pillow and a bag on a table.

'What are you doing here? It's six in bluddy morning?'

I laid the shotgun on the counter. 'I can't seem to get a note on this thing, must be the embouchure.'

'Scared, my fren?'

'Give me a coffee, will you? Why aren't you asleep, anyway?'

'Driver came in ufta you leave. We play some card.'

'Anyone I know?'

'Bobby Jameson, you know that bloke?'

'No, I don't think so.'

'TNT driver.' Joe poured two cups of coffee and lit a drooping cigarette.

'I had a visitor,' I said, doing my best to disguise the tremor in my voice.

'Not –'

'Yeah.'

'Did you shoot the busted?'

'You didn't give me any shells, remember? Anyway, I'm not going to just shoot –'

Suddenly the door creaked. We both looked at each other with wide eyes. Joe grabbed the shotgun. We both watched the handle as it turned in jerks. Joe pulled two ruby-coloured cartridges out of the cash register and placed one in the barrel, dropping the other onto the floor. It rolled under a table, sounding like a ball dropping into a roulette wheel. He cocked the gun, making me jump. When it came down to it, fear turned me into a different person. A killer? The door flung open. My blood turned to ice.

An old man put his hands in the air, 'Mr Chef, do I owe you money?'

Joe and I blew a collective sigh of relief.

'Jimmy, I nearly blew your bluddy brains out, my fren. You scared shit out of us,' Joe said, putting the gun under the counter.

The old man removed a flat cloth cap and shook his head gravely. 'Business must be bad, Mr Chef, eh?'

Joe cracked a tobacco laugh.

I flopped at the counter and rubbed my forehead.

'Sorry, you want coffee, Jimmy?' Joe asked.

'Yes, Mr Chef. Strong! Like Greek coffee.' The old man rubbed his salt-and-pepper three-day growth. He walked to the counter. I noticed he walked as if crouching along a mine shaft. In hushed tones, we relayed the night's events. Joe prepared a fresh pot of coffee.

'He spooked you at the window, eh?' the old man asked.

'Yeah, lucky I was wearing my brown underwear,' I said.

'Mr Chef is right. You shoot. Ask questions later. He's a bladdy marniac.'

'I've never even *held* a gun until this morning.'

Joe pressed a broken nose into the conversation.

'My advice, my fren, is to shoot the busted and ask no question.'

The little Greek got up to use the bathroom. His miner's hunch made him look even shorter than he actually was. I heard the screen door clap behind him. His gurgling piss echoed in the café. It was the longest piss known to man. Even Joe looked sideways at me when we thought he'd finished, but then resumed, as though for an encore.

'Anyway, in the desert, we shoot freaks,' Joe added.

'Don't be ridiculous,' I said.

'Why not?'

'Mr Chef's right. You see theis boy, you shoot him!' Jimmy said, as he crabbed across the room, pulling at his fly. 'He's a crie-zy malaka, eh?'

I had met Jimmy before, but he normally sipped his coffee, played cards with Joe and said little to me. That morning, I found out more about him. Dimitri Poulopoulos had come to Venice when reports filtered around the world of opal in Australia. As most of the original miners gradually drifted across the desert to the more lucrative terra firma of Coober Pedy, Dimitri persisted with his stubborn claim, finding enough gems to keep him digging.

His mine sat halfway between Coober Pedy and Venice. The claim begrudgingly coughed up the odd stone, and from this, he eked out a frugal living. He waxed lyrical about the next strike and what he would do with the money. He planned to go home to his birthplace in Greece and buy the whole island. This was his dream. Max later told me that Jimmy occasionally pulled out breathtaking gems that were supposedly from the mine – although Squales swore they were bought from an Armenian dealer at the Coober.

He hovered over the counter, casting a shadow with his pelican-like nose. 'He a crie-zy theis boy, very dangerous, eh?' he reiterated, tapping his head with a soiled fingernail.

'Yeah? Seems nobody's even talked to him.'

'I've talked to him,' said Dimitri quietly.

Joe and I looked at each other.

'You never told me. When was this, Jimmy?' Joe said, lighting a smoke.

The old man helped himself to a fresh cup of coffee. 'I told you, Mr Chef, remember it was about six month ago.'

'That's right, he come to the mine.'

'Yes, he frighten the bladdy hell out of me.'

'Did he attack you?' I asked.

'No, but –' The door opened. We all jumped. Squales walked in, spluttering, tractor-like, to the counter. 'Drove past and saw [*cough*] ye light on.'

'Coffee?'

'No, but I'd murder a copper tea.'

'Sure, my fren. Hey, any post for me?'

He shuffled over in a pair of carpet slippers. 'Is there [*splutter*] ever?'

Joe scowled and made the tea.

'You're up early,' I said.

'Always am, lad. Best part of the daye.' Squales must have slipped his wig on in the dark because he looked uncannily like a mannequin. 'Ow are ye, lad? Settled in all right?'

'I prefer my villa in Naples.'

'Coom-pared to where ah grew op in Yorkshire, lad, it's a [*cough*] bluedy palace.' He placed a cigarette in his bizarre holder and lit it. Curiously, it seemed to curb his coughing a little.

'Well, it certainly puts the word "shat" into "château",' I said.

'No friendly visitors, then?' Squales asked, touching the tip of his pointy nose.

'No.'

'Good lad. Remember, if anyone cooms sniffin, ye know nout about nout, right?'

'Well, you had one visitor,' Joe smiled.

Squales turned lime, 'Oo was it?'

'Bladdy Spook,' said Jimmy.

'Oh, im.'

'You know him?' I asked.

'Oh, aye. Not the full quid, im.'

'Have you *actually* met him?'

'Nay, and I don't [*splutter*] tend to neither.' A long piece of ash fell on his shirt, and as usual, he didn't seem to mind. 'E's as mad as moostard, that lad. Reckon he's killed many a man ooo's [*cough*] walked them dunes.'

'That wasn't mentioned in your realty brochure,' I snapped.

BEWARE OF GREEKS
BEARING GUILT

I WOKE TO BASS DRUM thuds at the door. I'd seen the wrong end of an Ouzo bottle with Joe and Jimmy the previous evening, so I buried my head in the pillow. The pounding continued. I sat up. My head felt too heavy for my body.

'Okay, okay, I'm coming!'

I opened the door. The air was blue with exhaust. Jimmy leaned against a battered truck. The engine, gurgling and spitting staccato puffs of black smoke, 'You ready, Gordo?'

'Huh?' I rubbed my face.

'What's bin keepin you?'

'A sweaty Arab and two credit cards.'

The old Grecian hopped in the rust-coloured truck and leaned out the window, gesturing wildly, 'Come, we go. We busy day, eh?'

'Oh. Shit.' I suddenly remembered saying something in a drunken stupor about working in the mine one day with Jimmy to see what it was actually like. Again, the old man gestured enthusiastically.

I sighed. What an idiot I was. Dropping my shoulders, I signalled that I'd be out in a minute.

The drive to the old shaft was quite comfortable. I'd compare it to a rodeo ride with a severe case of haemorrhoids. The two of us were thrown around the cab of the '47 Dodge like two corks in a washing machine.

'Do you think your shock absorbers might need replacing, Jimmy?' I asked.

'A bit too bumpy, eh?'

'Not really, but I think I've lost three fillings since we turned onto this road.'

'Not far now, Gordo, not far.' The old man pointed to the horizon.

My face turned olive as my hangover was bludgeoned with the fumes from oily rags on the floor. I could taste the oil in the back of my throat. Over the hooting note of the engine, the old miner filled in the missing pieces of the town's geological history.

As World War I washed over Europe, only a handful of prospectors remained in Venice. Like the tens of thousands of others picking at goldfields across the country, most of them rushed off to defend the 'Empire'. So Venice became a sleeping wasteland once more.

The true believers remained and persisted in their search for the precious metal. One stubborn prospector, Bill O'Shanahan, was blasting through a new shaft when he accidentally uncovered a treasure of a different kind: Opal.

Jimmy explained that, as in the days of the gold rush, Venice was flooded with desperate men. And they were trailed by the usual hustlers, merchants, pimps and snake-oil salesmen who preyed on them. Soon Venice became a concerto of drills and clangs and small explosions. Thousands of men with picks and shovels and dreams and theories came in search of the jewel-encrusted path to heaven on earth. They dug, they drank, they fought, they dreamed, they pulled at their pricks. It was a lawless town where justice was meted out at the end of a knife or a loose stick of dynamite pitched down an open shaft.

Cruelly, the O'Shanahan discovery was the only opal found in the area. However, the strike was not entirely in vain as it alerted people to the fact that opal existed in Australia – and possibly somewhere nearby. Many weary years later they finally discovered the rich deposits that the O'Shanahan fault had alluded to in a place called 'Coober Pedy'. (That's Aboriginal for 'whitefella hole in the ground', my guide and host for the day informed me.) Today, ninety-seven per cent of the world's opals are mined in Coober Pedy, Jimmy boasted, waving his honey-brown hand wildly.

By the time we reached the mine, I was swimming in sweat. Battling the searing heat and 'the dry horrors', I felt as though I'd completed a day's work before I'd even started. The temperature was in the fifties. This made simply breathing and walking an arduous task, let alone toiling beneath the choking earth.

The old man handed me an ill-fitting white hard hat and donned one himself. Mine sat on my head like a plastic fez. I trailed him down the shaft with drooping shoulders – the torchlight from our helmets splashing the walls in drowsy ribbons of light. I was relieved to feel the temperature cool as we made our descent. But it was stuffy and, as you can imagine, not for the claustrophobic.

I guessed we had been walking for about twenty minutes before arriving at the 'new dig'. The journey was much tougher for me than for Jimmy. Being almost a foot taller than the little Greek, I had to stoop to avoid the rotting beams that held the flimsy mine overhead. I didn't feel very secure, but was too tired and sick in the stomach to worry about it.

Once we arrived, I was spent. Fortunately, I didn't have to do much as the old Greek fell into his familiar, lone routine. I found it hard to breathe, so he lit a cigarette. This insured that the little oxygen that was left was soon exhausted. He started a machine that chipped away at the stubborn rock in stuttering bursts. The noise of the contraption was deafening – amplified considerably by my hangover. Dust and dirt were thrown into the air, making it even easier to breathe. I could taste it in my mouth. It was so thick at one stage that if it wasn't for the cherry glow of the old man's fag,

I would have lost sight of him completely. I must admit, I was in awe of his indefatigability. To think that he had worked in these conditions almost every day for the last thirty years was staggering.

After a couple of painful hours, the piercing din of the machinery mercifully stopped. He was pointing to a section of the wall. I shrugged my shoulders in reply. The little man, cigarette dangling from bulbous lips, shone a hand-held torch at it. I squinted through an aquarium of dust. A milky speck sat pitted in the rock. It twinkled in the torchlight like Orion at twilight.

'Look Gordo, look!' the old man shouted excitedly. With a chisel and brush, he chipped around the gem and removed it. He placed it in my hand and drowned it in torchlight.

'The opal, she is a beautiful stone, eh?'

I feigned an impressed look but didn't think I'd win the Oscar. The tiny stone looked dreary in its uncut state.

'So how much [*cough*] would a stone like this be worth?' I asked through the choking dust. I was shouting – although the machinery had stopped.

'Eh . . . to a dealer . . . eh . . . fifteen dollar maybe.'

'Sorry, I can't hear you. That bloody thing's still ringing in my ears. How much did you say?'

'Bout twenty dollar!'

I pretended to be impressed. 'That much?'

'Yes! We find more, eh?'

'Listen, I'm tired. Too much drink last night.' I took an imaginary drink to my lips. I pointed to the roof. 'Let's go up top for a breather.'

'But we just start work.'

'What did you say?' I shouted.

'I say we just start work!' the old man shouted back.

'Um, yeah I know but I'm not used to it like you are,' I choked, waving the dust away. 'You don't know this but [*cough*] I have an allergy that afflicts me on occasion.'

'What is theis allergy?'
'Oh, it's terrible. I've got it right now,' I spluttered.
'You got the asthma?'
'No.'
'What then?'
'It's very common. A lot of people suffer from it. Particularly in the arts.'
'What is it?' the old man asked gravely.
'I'm allergic to hard work.'
'Eh?'
'Yes, as soon as I start to do any kind of physical labour, I break into a sweat and need to lie down. I've had it since birth.'
'That's terrible.'
'Yes. It's been very difficult over the years, but I get by. I've been to numerous doctors and they all give me the same prognosis.'
'What he say, theis doctor?'
'I'm bone idle.'
'Eh . . . you want to stop then?'
'Um, that's the general idea.'
'Hoki doki, we go up top.'

We began the laborious trek back to the surface – me hitting my head a few times along the way for good measure. Jimmy seemed okay about stopping. I think he just wanted some company for the day and to show off his mine. It seemed to take an age to reach the top. I could feel the desert heat pressing in on me as we made our ascent. It was as if someone were slowly turning up the heat in an oven with each exhausting step. Finally, I saw the crack of light that was the entrance. As we reached the opening, I couldn't believe how much I welcomed the desert heat. I breathed as if I'd been held under water by the school bully. We stood beneath the belting sun. It felt luxurious. I started coughing a little. I found some shade to catch my breath and have a drink of water, spluttering like an old lawnmower. I'd swallowed a little sand – Fraser Island, I think.

'Eh... you not so fit for a young fella.'

'You've noticed.'

'You young man, you should be strong, eh?'

'Yes,' I smiled. 'Listen Jimmy, you never did tell me what happened when you met the boy, you know, the one they call the "Spook".'

'Oh, yes. I tell you.'

The old man went to the truck and returned with a thermos of coffee with some kind of booze napping at the bottom. He poured two battered mugs' worth and handed one to me. With his great Grecian nose, he took a Hoover-like sniff.

'Ahhh, that's real coffee, mayte. Not like Mr Chef's coffee. Greek coffee!'

I took a sip.

'Now you feel good, eh?'

'Well...'

'I tell you what happen. Bout six month ago, I was digging late one night. I see a little blue-green speck. Not like the one we find today, eh? Different colour. The colour of money, mayte. That kind of opal I never see in my mine for twenty year. Last time I find a big fault like that,' he clapped his dusty hands, 'a fortune pass through my hand!'

'What do mean?'

'Oh, it's a long story, I no bore you with my life, eh?'

I put my lips to the dented mug, 'Bore me.'

The old man chuckled and stared into his black pond of coffee. 'Okay, well... eh... I come from a little island called Kapros. A beautiful island with white sandy beaches so white she look like the snow, eh? And surrounded by the turquoise sea of the Aegean.

'My house was on a hill that overlook the whole island. Oh, mayte, the water was so clear. From the cliff you would see schools of the sardine move in great shadows.' He waved his hand like a fish.

'Like most people in Kapros, my bratha and me went to sea each day in our little wooden boat for the sardine. We catch him in the long net, you know? Each morning we prepare the net, lay him all out, and set out to sea. Looking back, she was a nice life.' He pointed to the mine's entrance. 'Not like theis, eh? Theis hard work. Dirty work.

'My family bin fishermen on Kapros since Adam was a boy. We would leave for sea before sunrise and be back around midday to take the sardine to market, to sell him. Then, we walk to bay, strip off, and dive around the rock. I can still see our brown bodies glistening in the water,' he smiled. 'We look for eh . . . how you say . . . calamari, eh . . . the squid! We used to catch him and smash him on the rock and get the ink out of him. Then cook him.

'In the evening we would go into the centre of town and drink retsina and sing songs of the sea. Oh, how we would drink! My bratha he play the bouzouki. We would sit in the café and sing. It had a pergola that was covered in grapevines. We would sit outside, drinking and telling lies.' He chuckled. 'The moonlight, she would trickle through those vines, lighting up our brown, smiling faces.' He shook his head and looked down at the red sand. His voice grew soft. 'Dancing, singing, laughing . . .'

'Sounds like a beautiful life, Jim.'

'Yes, mayte, it was a beautiful life. I had a beautiful girl, too. She would sit on my knee those warm nights. I can still feel her smooth legs. We'd sit watching the little boats rocking against the shore, listening to the waves licking the hulls.'

'What was her name?'

'Athena.'

'What was she like?'

The old man lit a Winfield Red and smiled. 'She was beautiful. Dark skin, aqua eyes. Like the Aegean. Like the stone. Like theis, eh?' The old man pulled out of his pocket the most exquisite gem I had ever seen. It caught the sunlight and almost sung.

'They look nice when they clean up, eh?' he said with a twinkle in his eye, recognising my earlier prefabricated enthusiasm.

I pointed down the shaft, 'Is that from down there?'

'Yes, mayte.' He cackled. 'No one bladdy believe me, but yes. I'm an old man. I don't have to prove my mine to nobody. She's full of riches theis mine. Yes, theis I pulled out six month ago.'

'So why did you leave the village?'

'When I was your age, Gris was a very poor country, Gordo. Now things have changed a little. But back then, many young people leave to come to Owstralia to make money and go back to Gris to live like the king! Just like your ancestor came to this country from England or Ireland about a hundred fifty year before, eh? They no think to stay here forever, eh? They make the money to go home to Europe, too.'

'Yes, except many of them came with fancy bracelets.' I made a gesture of hands being cuffed together.

'Oh, that's right! The convict.' He poured some more coffee. 'Hair of dog, eh?' The old salt's eyes sparkled. (My hunch about the 'coffee' was correct. Ouzo.)

'So what happened?'

'When you are a young man in Gris, you had to do your eh . . . how you say,' he pointed a pretend rifle, 'bang bang . . . National Service – the army! But if you had money, you could buy your way out. I wanted to marry Athena, but her fartha wanted her to marry theis man with much money. Not the son of a poor fisherman. If I join the army, he would marry her off. Athena want to eh . . . how you say . . . elope, but that mean we could never return to the island. She say she no care about that, but I say, I am a proud man. I live on the island where my family has lived since Adam was a boy. I had a plan.

'I hear many people find the opal in Owstralia. I decide to try. I sell the fishing boat and pay to get out of National Service. I buy my ticket on the ship and pack my bags. Then I tell her fartha: I will return a rich man and ask your daughter for her hand.

'Well, when I tell Athena I was leaving for Owstralia, she cry for seven day and seven night. On the last day, she very brave and she give me theis.' He opened his shirt and showed me a crude necklace fashioned from hundreds of tiny pink shells. 'She said to me: "On theis necklace hang my tears. When you think of not coming home to me, look at theis necklace and remember my tears."' The old man choked on the last few words. I remained silent.

'We buy theis mine. My brather and me work hard. After only six month of digging, we find the stones. Like theis.' He flashed the opal again. 'But my bladdy bratha, he say okay Dimitri, we find the stone, let's leave. We go home. He hate Owstralia, my bratha. But I say no! Theis is not enough. He say we can buy a small house and our boat back for this stones. I tell him: "I return a king, not a prince. We dig!" He say no and we have a big fight, eh?'

He held up two sinewy, honey-skinned fists. 'Bad, bad fight. No bratha should fight like theis. I throw the stones at him and say: "You are a fool, Alexi! Go home like a dog." So, I continue to dig.' He sighed and shook his head. 'I dig for twenty-five long years,' he said slowly.

'Owstralia was a tough place back then. With tough men. And you work hard for your money. Blady hard work, mayte. Not like now with this new machines, eh?'

'Yeah, now it's easy,' I said, rolling my eyes. 'So what became of your brother?'

The old man cracked a smile, exposing gold-capped molars.

'My bratha, he became a very rich man.'

'Really?'

'Yes. He has a little boat that he takes to the sea to catch the sardine. He has our old cottage on the hill overlooking the sea. He has a beautiful wife. She carries the fish each day in the big basket from the harbour. Then she sells them in the market. And he has beautiful children – oh, and now grandchildren, too!' he added. He pulled out a wrinkled picture from his wallet. The children were barefooted and scruffy with matted hair.

'So in actual fact . . . he's not very rich?' I asked, a little confused.

'Yes, he is very rich,' the old man said softly. 'He became king.'

I wasn't exactly sure of the old man's meaning, but I went on.

'So, what happened to Athena?'

The old man looked at the necklace. A sad smile broke on his thick, loose lips. He looked up at me with glistening eyes. I suddenly realised what he meant. I felt a pang in my heart. 'He married her, didn't he?' I said quietly.

'Yes. He became a very rich man,' he whispered, smiling.

We sat in silence and drank the rest of the coffee. After a while I spoke. 'You never did finish the story about the time you met the boy.'

The old man sipped his coffee before continuing.

'Well, when I see the specks of opal bout six month ago, I thought I'd finally cracked it, eh? It was like before, you know, with my bratha all those years ago, eh? In the light of my torch, the walls sparkled like the Aegean. Oh, what a sight! I worked through the night to work around the gems by hand. Opals fell from the wall as sweetly as words of love.' He held some of the stones in his calloused hand.

'This stones were much more beautiful than the stone my bratha and I found. This were . . . eh . . . how you say . . . spectacular! I had enough to go home to my village, not return a rich man, but enough to go home and retire in style. My mother was dying and I wanted to see her before she went to God. This was my chance. I went up top and lit a fire. I drink! I have a party with myself. The stones, they glistened in the firelight.

'Funny, as I sat by the fire I think about my Athena. I cry. Cry like a little baby. If only I returned to Kapros all those years ago, I say to myself. So I thought, if I find more stones, I return the richest man on the island. I return a king. I buy the whole island. That will show them!

'A few days later I sold them all to a dealer in Coober. Except this one. I buy all new equipment. I dig deeper . . . and deeper but . . .' he chuckled sadly to himself, 'I find nothing.' He hit his forehead with his palm. 'Stupid malaka. I lost the rest on the cards and horses.'

'Is this when you met the Spook?'

'Yes. That night when I cry. I think he hear me. I get drunk and fall asleep. I wake to find the boy standing over me. The bladdy marniac was holding some big black feather.' The old man aped the gesture. 'He wanted me to take it and tell me a story, or something crie-zy like theis. I was drunk. I swore at him.'

'What did he do?'

'He walk off into the desert. I was drunk, but yes, a big black feather.' He tapped the side of his head with a soiled forefinger aggressively. 'He crie-zy, theis boy.'

☾

That night in the café I mulled over the day's events. I thought about going to New York, again. Joe had been paying me some cash of late and it was easy to save in the desert with nowhere to spend your money. I pulled out my air ticket and stared at it: imagining stepping off the plane at JFK; thinking about accommodation; seeing myself playing at all those fabulous clubs like the Blue Note and the Village Gate, the Vanguard and Sweet Basil.

'You want another coffee?' Joe asked lazily, interrupting my third encore with Roy Hargrove.

'I'll wash up first.' I lumbered over to the sink and studied the grimy dishes. They smelled of egg. I had to do my bit. After all, that was the arrangement.

I finished off the last saucepan and sat down at my usual spot at the front window. The husks of dead insects lay in a conga line along the sill. I got up and dropped a coin into the old jukebox. The machine rattled and clicked before the Duke Ellington Orchestra smothered the room with fat trombones. I sat back down. Staring through the glass, I studied the landscape that was smeared with moonlight. I watched the wind pick up the shifting sand and sprinkle it over the desert floor as if making some magical recipe.

I finished the coffee and spat the dregs back into the cup. A foul medicine. Bidding goodnight to Joe, I stumbled into the cold night and trekked back to the station house.

NEVER GO SURFING WITH A SCORPION

∽

I WOKE UP in a soup of sweat that morning. I'd had that dream again. I was the moth, hurtling myself against the light. I could hear the soft voice calling from the desert. Consoling me. I felt confused and dazed. The dream was so real it was palpable.

I sat up. It was going to be another stinker of a day – no doubt in the high forties. This heat took some getting used to. It wasn't a wet, tropical Club Med kind of heat, but a dry, scorching Club Mercury kind of heat. The kind of heat that makes your eyeballs sweat and your balls itch. The kind of heat that sends you a little troppo or makes you wear shorts with long white socks and join the National Party. Yet the desert nights were incredibly cold. You had to bury yourself in scratchy blankets. This left you baking like a spud when the morning sun belted the tin roof of the cottage.

I threw my sodden pyjamas in the corner and squeezed a measured amount of water into the kettle. I spat a pistachio nut of phlegm into the sink and watched it shimmy on the cracked porcelain before it slithered away. Getting dressed, I passed the mirror that stretched along the wardrobe door. Squinting sideways, I looked at the naked body snared in the glass. The body was a stranger to me.

Since my bewildered body had been subjected to enormous greasy meals at the diner instead of my usual spartan cuisine of freshly chopped Valium with a slice of lemon, I had put on a few pounds. The hearty meals, coupled with three swimming pools of beer a week, had fleshed me out and even given me – God forbid – a slight beer belly.

God, Jenny would hardly recognise me. There was something else that was different about me. I looked closer, fogging the glass with briny morning breath.

I was *really* sun-tanned. Now, instead of my usual medicated pallor, I was bronzed and – dare I say it – fit. I'd seen this body on television – in beer commercials. You know: tanned blokes laughing, standing around a barbecue poking sausages with long tongs and winking at each other's wives.

I looked around for some clean underwear. As I had none, it was the dreaded 'Elephant Undies' again. As a joke, Joe had sent away for a pair of novelty underpants for my birthday. They were in the design of an elephant's head. You slipped your penis into the trunk (which made going to the toilet a drag), therefore making the joke complete (hilarious). If I ran out of clean underwear, or if my underwear stood up on its own and started coughing because I hadn't washed for a while, 'Dumbo' snuggled furtively beneath the Levis for the day. Suddenly, I heard a queer noise outside. I stopped to listen for a moment. It sounded like a great rumbling wave. I cocked an ear as the metallic surf drew closer. I walked outside and into the heat, squinting into the distance. Incredulously, I watched the object approach. It was a train.

The whole time I had been camped at the station house I had assumed the line was no longer in operation. Since no loco had supposedly travelled the rusting track since the seventies, I assumed it was inoperable. I recalled Squales intimating something about if a train came through I was to throw a switch or something, but I had thought it was a wind-up.

After a couple of minutes, a centipede of shimmying carriages shrieked to halt at the platform. In crude, handpainted letters the words 'Crocodile Bart's Great Aussie Tours' sprawled across the carriages. As the sooty diesel engine idled, a ribbon of black smoke trailed overhead. A hive of Japanese tourists poked their collective heads out of the windows. I stood with my mouth open and heard Squales's spluttering voice over a squealing loudspeaker: 'One of the desert wonders . . . eh . . . the Elephant Man of Venice.'

At that moment I looked down to discover that I was in fact standing in nothing but the Elephant Undies. To make matters worse, I had the curse of young men who hunch their way to the toilet first thing in the morning. I had the good old 'morning stiffy'. Therefore, the elephant's trunk unceremoniously pointed to Neptune.

'Wave to em, lad . . . wave and smile . . .' he said.

I limply waved, red-faced. Instantly, I was blinded by a firework of camera flashes. Followed by a minuet of clicking and whirring. I shielded my eyes.

'Pull the switch, lad!' Squales shouted through the squealing loudspeaker. 'Pull the fookin switch!'

Blinded by the flashes, I groped back inside and, with Herculean effort, pulled the great lever that pendulumed in the centre of the room. I felt a gentle click down the end of the line. Peeking through the curtain, I saw the train pull away in a sea of black smoke.

With clothes now on, I walked outside. The desert returned to its familiar stillness. I tapped the rippled side of the water tank. I listened to the parched echo. Almost empty. I decided to shower at the café. I'd have to get the water truck in from the Coober again as little green men from Mars would arrive before rain.

I could feel the sun preparing its midday torture session as I straddled the railway track before walking to the café. The heat rising from the desert made the line fishhook in the distance. As I stood in the choking heat, I thought about the origin of the old track. The train must have come from somewhere. Perhaps there's another 'Venice' down the line. Wasn't there a place called 'Hopetown'? I gaped down the palisade of rotten-toothed sleepers that blurred in the heat. I decided to satisfy my curiosity. After all, the diary wasn't exactly full that day. I'd only be sitting around the café trying to sort out my life as Joe farted or hummed 'The Green Green Grass of Home' in the key of Q sharp. Before attempting the expedition, I popped back inside to fetch a canteen of water. The rusting pipes shook and creaked before begrudgingly spitting some orange water into the canteen. I walked down the end of the platform and onto the track to begin my excursion.

After about twenty blistering minutes, I looked back over my shoulder to see the shack as a fuzzy blip on the horizon. Replacement panels of the tin roof flashed silver in the distance. As I kept walking, the landscape changed slightly. The usual stony environs of low-lying sandhills, dry scrub, spinifex and rocky mounds were being transformed into vast, undulating, blood-red dunes. This gave the impression of being cast adrift in a great ocean. A gentle breeze tickled my lashes as I continued.

I must have been walking for about thirty minutes when I saw it. A flash of colour exploding out of the monochrome of baking earth. I squinted at the prism of colour in awe. As I walked towards it, the hues separated, and before me stood a grove of spectacular wild flowers. The colours were breathtaking: Gauguin crimsons, Monet lavenders and luminous Van Gogh yellows. In a suburban backyard the flora would perhaps look prosaic, but pitched against the lifeless, barren landscape the little garden looked like the front window of Tiffanys.

As I scaled the sandhill I found a water hole glistening in the sunlight. Kneeling, I cupped my hands and drew some to my lips. It tasted sweet, not like the brackish water at the billabong. I gazed at the flowers swaying in the breeze and realised I hadn't seen a flower or even a pot plant since arriving in the desert.

I topped up the canteen and took an extravagant drink – spilling a little down my T-shirt. I revelled in the feeling of utter decadence that only water brings to the desert. As I sat, I listened. I listened to that beautiful, luxurious sound. The sound of complete silence.

When you live in a city, there is no escape from sound. A barking dog, a car engine, the growl of a distant jet, all invading the sanctuary of your mind. I simply filled my soul with the sound of complete nothingness.

As I sat watching the wind spray the rust-coloured sand across the desert, the fauna, too, came to life. Smelling the sweet water, I watched a thorny lizard creep along with Jurassic pulchritude. Its stony body swayed and rocked, throwing its tail from side to side. A thorny metronome. Occasionally, it stood transfixed, as if it became invisible to all around it, then continued, convinced it had fooled everyone.

I experienced a new feeling that day as I sat meditatively among the flowers. A feeling of inner peace. Each fragrant sniff seemed to cleanse my musty soul of a lifetime of dark thoughts. I looked around. The little oasis was perched on a small dune and I could see the old rail line in the distance. This gave me a feeling of security. I was terrified of being lost in the desert. So seeing it there was a solace. A rusting umbilical cord.

I felt philosophical that day, musing that amid the bleak emptiness of human existence there was always the essence of life. I felt the garden was saying to me that the spirit will always look for a way to break through the vast plains of pain and sorrow that are an intrinsic part of life's journey. For all of us – me, Joe, Jimmy, Max – there was always a doorway that led to the rest of your life.

Sitting up, I looked around. I felt that someone was watching me. I scanned the horizon and noticed an inky figure in the distance, drifting down a far dune. I suddenly felt like a lamb being stalked by a dingo.

It was the Spook.

Where I sat I could feel a large rock buried beneath me. I drove my hand into the scorching sand to dig it out.

The boy was close now, studying me with a curious look. I could feel the blood and adrenaline charging through my veins, but fear had crippled me momentarily. I couldn't lift the damn rock. It felt like lead in my hand.

The young Koori sat a few feet away on the other side of the garden. He stared into the distance. As if I weren't even there. A faint breeze whistled in my ears as I listened to my heart thump harder and harder against my breastbone. The boy leaned back and let the sun beat against his shiny black face. He looked wild and ferocious, yet possessed that tranquil look of the insane. It was as if he'd glimpsed another universe and treated the current one with indifference. There was something I can only explain as unattainably spiritual in his bearing.

Then the boy sat up and my blood dropped to thirty degrees below. I felt for the rock again.

'Fear turns us into ugly people, doesn't it, mate?' the boy said as he leaned over to smell a flower.

I turned red. He spoke so softly that each word seemed to float on the end of the breeze. It was barely audible even in the still of the desert.

'You . . . you speak English well,' I said, with the tact of Pauline Hanson at an ATSIC meeting.

He scanned the horizon without looking at me. 'Is that a good thing, whitefella?'

'No . . . I mean, I wasn't sure whether –'

'Whether I was a mad blackfella who needed to be shot like a dingo, or whether I was "*civilised*".'

'Oh, I hope you didn't take the fuck-off-or-I'll-shoot-you-thing too seriously. Anyway, where do you live? I mean, where's your home?' I asked, trying to change the subject.

'All around you.'

'But where do you sleep, where's your stuff, man?'

He picked up some sand and scattered it around him. 'Everywhere, mate. My stuff is all around you.'

I shrugged my shoulders, 'Fair enough.'

We sat in silence.

'Why do you spook everyone, man? I mean, why do you spook me late at night? What have I ever done to you?'

He pulled a face. 'Why do you think I spook you? I just like to listen to you play that music.'

'What?'

'That piano.'

'Really?'

'Yeah.'

'Do you like jazz?'

'Is that what you play?'

'Well, that depends on which music critic you read, but, yes.'

'Well, if you play jazz, then I like jazz.'

'Wow. Thanks, man.'

'Are you American?'

'No, I just talk like one sometimes. Makes me feel cool. Pathetic, isn't it?'

The boy laughed, flashing a row of white teeth. 'You're a city boy, aren't you? So, what are you doing in this desert country . . . what's your name?'

'Gordon. What's yours?'

'Johnny. Johnny Wishbone. So why are you here, Gordon?'

'I don't know what I'm doing out here, to be honest. Just drifting. Looking for something, I guess. Don't ask me what.'

'Well, you can let go of that rock. I think you know I'm not going to kill you by now.'

I quickly pulled my hand out of the sand and turned the colour of crushed mulberries. I'd forgotten that little thing about belting him around the head with a rock only minutes earlier.

'Oh, I wasn't sure . . . they said –'

'Whitefellas,' he said, shaking his head. 'You don't understand us, so you want to destroy us.'

'Things *have* changed a little in two hundred years,' I said with student-canteen reasoning.

'Have they really?' he smiled, looking at the tip of the rock sticking out of the sand. 'Whitefellas never change, Gordon.'

He sat meditating in silence, then drew something in the sand with his twig-like finger. I studied it for a moment. It looked like the outline of a crab. He told a story in his queer mixture of long eloquent phrases punctuated by choppy monosyllables. The odd rounded vowel smelled of private schooling to me. It were as if Johnny had been educated at an elite school, but tried to bury it in the idiomatic nasal twang of the outback. The hissing wind gently snatched at the boy's hair as he spoke.

The boy then drew a rippled line beneath it. 'Long ago there was a river that kept the scorpion from the other spirit creatures. Scorpion could not cross the river because Scorpion couldn't swim. One day he saw Frog, who would sometimes cross the river, and asked: "Frog, let me ride on your back to cross the river."

'Frog said: "Do you think I'm a fool, Scorpion? As soon as we get halfway across, you will sting me, and I will die."

'"Why would I do that?" asked Scorpion. "If I do that, I will drown, too."

'Frog went away to think it over. He came back the next day and said to Scorpion: "I will take you across the river because, if you sting me, we will both die and you'll never cross this river."

'Scorpion agreed and Frog allowed Scorpion to jump on his back. They both leapt into the water. About halfway, Frog felt a sharp pain in his back. He turned to see Scorpion stinging him. As they both started to drown, Frog asked: "Why did you do that, Scorpion? Now we will both die."

'Scorpion answered: "I couldn't help myself, it's in my nature."'

I nodded and we sat in silence.

'Is that an ancient story?' I finally asked.

'No, it's from *The Crying Game*. Ever seen it?'

'Eh, yeah.'

'What about the girlfriend with the dick, eh? I never saw that coming.'

And with that, the boy got up, turned to me, gently smiled, and walked off. I blinked at the sun. I refocused. The boy had disappeared over a dune.

⌒

I woke from a disturbing dream. Sticky with sweat, I looked at the clock: two-thirty in the morning. I rubbed my matted hair as I tried to unravel the dream. This time I'd shed the wings of the moth. They lay battered and fissured on the ground. I remember wandering through the desert. Searching. Looking for something that wasn't there. I felt the hot gibber stones brand the flesh of my bare feet. I felt spinifex needles pierce my thighs, stinging, itching. I felt the sun sear the back of my neck as I inexorably tramped, deeper into the maw of the desert. I remember an inner voice telling me to look over a distant dune. And another and yet another. As I climbed each sandy monolith, I tumbled down the other side like a rag doll. Finally, I found the boy – dead. Eyes open, smiling. His body covered in shiny black scorpions. I stood over his body. A stiff breeze blowing against my sunburned cheeks. Then, slowly, the scorpions turned into hundred dollar bills and blew away into the desert.

⌒

Feeling shaky from the dream, I walked to the kitchen and poured myself a finger-glass of rum. I downed the sharp-tasting drink and walked over and started to play a new melody at the piano. I jotted down some lyrics on a scrap of paper. As I doodled, I thought of the day's events. I wondered if the boy could hear me at that moment. I persisted with the embryonic melody. It's hard to compose when you think people are listening. Any composer will tell you. You can't help but play things you think will impress the covert listener. In the end, nothing is achieved. It's only when wading through a junkyard of sounds that you sometimes discover something new. I would never let Jenny listen to me compose. She understood. She called me a prima donna.

I pined for Jenny. The little things. Her throaty laugh. Her determined walk. The twinkle in her eyes when I made her laugh and she tried not to. I recreated in my mind the sticky summer nights when we would catch a ferry to nowhere, just to watch the lights thawing on the harbour.

I looked out the window and into the desert. I thought about her face the last time I saw her. There's nothing more all-consuming than unrequited love. When love is returned, it lacks passion. Why are the coals of desire only stoked by rejection?

Alone, and in the outback, it became painfully clear just how much she meant to me. I knew I would never feel that way about anybody again. She was the great love of my life. My soul mate. I thought about those moments on the harbour and other times when I should have told her how I really felt. I never once told her that I loved her. Missed opportunities. Maybe I'd meet someone else when I got to New York – hard as it was to imagine.

I peered through the window. Moonlight painted the desert in chalky light. I had an unpleasant foreboding that this would be the place I would spend the rest of my life. Would I end up like Joe and the rest of them? Would I ever find the pluck to face my demons and actually get on with my life? Joe and Max and Dimitri had not planned to stay in the desert forever, either.

I pegged a couple of chords on the buzzing piano. Picking up the pencil, I wrote:

There was a time when I knew love,
a time with no regrets,
a time before I drowned myself,
in coffee and cigarettes.

I played a few more notes and some plaintive voicings.

*The hopes I hoped for,
the dreams I dreamed,
are quite funny now it seems,
I never thought I'd end up in this lonely place,
this small café,
this cheap palais,
called 'Broken Dreams'.*

I walked outside. The moon hung like a pearl in the night sky. I thought, again, of Jenny. What she would be doing at that very moment. Would she too be gazing at the same moon? Or would she be downing sake in some trendy Japanese restaurant in Paddington with Finius Thistlehorne?

☾

The moon coloured the rails silver as I tramped towards the desert garden, again. I looked up at the twitching stars. I walked faster. Led by plumes of my fogging breath and three-o'clock-in-the-morning logic, I wanted to talk to the boy again.

Eventually, I saw the faint silhouette on the horizon. Somehow I knew he would be there, waiting. His sculptured face, indigo in the moonlight, split into a luminous smile. He stood motionless as I scrambled up the sandhill. We both sat for a while in silence. Watching the stars.

'Do you know, in our language, the word for "place of spirits" and "place of flowers" is the same?' he said, out of the blue.

'Really?'

The boy nodded, 'Yep. All these flowers are the spirits of my people.'

I remained silent.

The boy spoke in a wide-eyed whisper, 'You can smell their spirit.' He smelled the moonlit flora.

⌒

We sat talking for what seemed a couple of hours as the emerging sun smeared the darkness with rose. I watched a black snake 'S' its way along the sand. All was quiet but for the sound of a wild camel snorting in the distance.

I watched a frill-necked lizard shuffling lugubriously towards us. It reminded me of a drunk who had stuck his head through a Christmas hat. The boy gestured not to move. He then slid down the hill, rubbing dewy sand on his body as he went. He trailed the scaly interloper for a few careful steps, performing a kind of jerky dance. Finally he grabbed it and said something to it in his native tongue, and swiftly broke its neck. He scaled the dune and placed it in front of me like a waiter bringing a bottle of prize-winning shiraz to the table.

'You hungry?' the youth asked.

'Eh . . . I could go a cheeseburger . . . but if its McLizard Burgers, then I think I'm kind'a full.'

'I'm having some, anyway.'

'Good for you.'

The boy prepared a fire with some spinifex and twigs. He used matches to get it started – which I noted, not without disappointment. The boy noticed.

'What did you expect, mate? I spend an hour rubbing two sticks together? I'm too lazy,' he said with a cheeky smile.

After impaling the lizard on a sharp stick, he placed it on the licking flames. After some more conversation, the boy prodded it and tore a blackened leg off the sorry specimen.

'It's good. Try some,' he said through a mouthful of lizard leg.

'I read in Weight Watchers that lizard is loaded with calories.'

'Yeah?'

'Never have them with peanuts, it's deadly.'

'Go on, it won't kill you, whitey.'

It felt awful being called 'whitey'. So I felt obliged. Johnny snapped off another leg and passed it to me. I was green at the thought of having to eat the unfortunate creature who only a while ago was minding its own business, sucking bugs from the desert floor. He handed me the sizzling limb. I pulled a face. 'I'm really a breast man myself.'

'Eh?'

'What I mean is, do you think I could have something that looks a little less like the leg of a lizard and more like a piece of chicken?' I winced. 'Maybe a little meat off its back or something.'

'Sure!' He prodded at the lizard with a blackened stick. He then passed me a handful of stringy flesh.

'Can I have a cracker or something with this?' I took a grimacing bite and chewed with a sour face.

'Tastes like chicken, don't you think?' he said enthusiastically.

I knitted my brow. I chewed a little more. 'Hang on . . .' I chewed some more, 'I know what it tastes like . . . it tastes like . . . um.' I swallowed some, 'Yes, I think I know what it tastes like.'

'What?'

'Shit. It tastes like shit. I've never had the pleasure of eating shit, but if I ever do, I'll know exactly what it'll taste like,' I spat the remaining pieces into the fire, wiping a shoelace of drool from my chin.

'Yeah, it does taste like shit, I spose,' he chuckled. 'But the menu's fairly restricted round here.'

We both laughed.

'Why did you cover yourself in sand before you grabbed our poor little friend over here?' I asked.

'So he can't smell me downwind.'

'Lizards can smell?'

'Very well.'

'Then it's rather fortunate that they don't have to eat each other.'

He smiled, eating his catch.

'And what did you say to him before you gave him the neck massage?'

'I said: "I respect you. Your spirit. For you are a part of this land as much as I am. I will eat you and you shall leave this world but you will soon return",' he added through a mouthful of reptile.

(Yes, that's what I usually say after twelve schooners and a pizza, I thought, but refrained from saying it.) Johnny ate some more of the catch.

I pulled a face, 'Do you believe in all that stuff?'

'Yes, I do, mate.'

'We always seem to be thinking about other worlds and too little of our own, I think.'

'Do you believe in an alternative universe?' he asked.

'I do, but what I want to know is, do they have late-night shopping and can I park there?'

He raised an eyebrow.

'What about you. Do you believe in God?' I asked.

He paused. 'I believe that God is all around me. In that rock, the sand, the moon.'

I grinned, a little cynically.

'The whitefella laughs at our beliefs, but he's prepared to believe in a snake tricking a whitefella into eating an apple, a woman being created from a man's rib, a man parting a great sea with the wave of his hand. Why is that more plausible than a man's spirit being part of the earth around him?'

'Interesting point.'

The boy looked up at the crimson sky and continued softly. 'With these "primitive" beliefs we've managed to maintain and care for this land for more than forty thousand years. Your people, with your "superior" beliefs, have been on this land for only two hundred years and you've practically destroyed it and us along with it.'

I nodded in agreement.

'The fundamental mistake your religion makes is that it assumes we are *humans* having a *spiritual* experience. Whereas we believe that we are *spirituals* having a *human* experience.'

'That's quite profound for someone who lives in the middle of nowhere and eats lizards for breakfast.'

'Do you believe in God, Gordon?'

'No . . . well . . . I believe in right or wrong. I guess I've simply abandoned the creed, but hung on to the morality.'

'I believe there is no right or wrong, just learning. The whitefella will learn to respect the land one day. And us. Perhaps when it's too late. I suppose everyone has something to learn. Eventually.'

'Well, I wonder what I'm learning?'

He looked into my eyes. 'Perhaps you're learning about you. Who you really are. Perhaps you're not drifting out here in this desert after all. Perhaps you've been drifting all your life till this very moment in time. Perhaps this is a door you are to travel through to continue the journey.'

It was as if he had read my mind. 'Do you think so?'

'What do you think, Gordon?' he smiled.

And with a wave, Johnny Wishbone stood, turned and wandered off into the fat sun.

AND GOD SAID UNTO JOB

JOB, SEEKETH NEW WORLDS AND BOLDLY GO WHERE NO MAN HATH GONE BEFORE . . .

∽

IT WAS UNBEARABLY hot that day in The Globe. So hot you needed a twenty-page manual to cope with it. Max had The Globe's state-of-the-art temperature control system in operation: a wheezing table fan behind a tall bowl of ice. Nevertheless, we all greedily soaked up the miserable breeze that it expectorated. In mid conversation you would see someone close his sweating eyelids in ecstasy each time the contraption swung past in a slow, jerking arc.

'Another one, Gordon?' Max asked across the bar, droplets of sweat falling from his nose.

'Yeah, why not. My liver transplant's not until four.'

Max squeezed some nut-coloured liquid into a glass. I gazed out the window. A strange funeral procession crept solemnly up the street. The Reverend Fruit was leading the grim party. He was garbed in his usual ensemble of shorts, white Dunlop tennis shoes, black shirt and dog-collar. He was holding a soft sack and reaching in periodically and throwing handfuls of white feathers over his head. They splayed over the coffin like snow. Six stony-faced pallbearers dressed in white chicken suits carried the casket behind him. They looked hot and tired.

'What the hell's that all about?' I asked Max.

'Oh, that was Old Man Mathews. You know, the "Chicken King". He was born here in Venice. Had a chicken farm down south. Biggest in the State, they reckon. His widow's a bit odd. That was what she wanted for his funeral. Each to their own, I spose.'

Everyone in the pub stood and removed their hats as the feathered cavalcade marched slowly past. Then they sat and continued drinking as if nothing had happened.

I spotted Sunfly nestled in a corner. I wandered over. 'Hot enough for you, Sunfly?'

'Who dat? Dat you Gord?' the old man asked, gaping around with toothpaste eyes.

'Yes. How have you been?'

'Ah, not too bad for an old blackpella wid a crook back and an eye for de lady.'

'They reckon it's going to hit fifty again today!'

'Dat right? Fifty?'

'Yeah, hot enough to fry an egg in your hand, they reckon.'

'Dat right?'

'Yeah. Although, I suggest a pan if you're having people over.' I lowered my voice, 'Listen Sunfly, what do you know about this kid?'

'What kid?'

'You know, the one who lives out there,' I thumbed to the desert. I then rolled my eyes, realising the poor old bugger couldn't see. 'One of your mob . . . you know, Johnny Wishbone.'

'What you want to know for, Gord?' he asked suspiciously.

'I wanted to find out a little more about him. After I met him I –'

'You met Johnny?'

'Yeah, twice.'

He spoke to my shoulder, guessing it was my head. 'How *is* dat boy?' The old man asked as he took a swig of beer to wet his few remaining teeth.

'Fine. What's his story, Sunfly?'

'What you mean?'

'Why does he live out there, in the desert, all alone?'

The old man upturned his glass and emptied the beer down his jowly throat and leaned forward, speaking in rumbling undertones. 'Long time ago, long before your mob de whitepella come ere, dere were de people from de stony lands and people from de sandy lands. Hopetown is in between dose lands.'

'Where *is* Hopetown?'

'Dat's a big township up the rail line. Up in sandy country.'

'What land are you from?'

'Me? I'm from de stony country. Most of our mob lib in de Coober now. No one lib out dere no more. But dat's how we all used to lib, us blackpellas, long time ago. Just out in de desert. He from dat mob who libed in de sandy lands. Deep in de desert. Secret people. Magic people. All de udder blackpellas scared of dem pellas. Dat mob know secret magic. Johnny Wishbone is de last of de sandy people. He lib like we all used to, just hunt and dream. De old ways.'

'Yeah, he seems to just kind of wander around the desert.'

'Be careful. People in this town don't like im. Want to hurt Johnny. Maybe hurt you if you his friend.'

'Why?'

'Dey blame him for all kind of trouble. If you see im, tell im Sunfly say to be berry careful.'

'Sure, sure.'

Sunfly picked up his walking stick and hobbled to the door. He turned to me and tipped a moth-eaten hat with the large, black feather poking out. And with a smile that displayed a selection of dental work that could have been arranged by Jackson Pollock, he said, 'Dat must be de reason you here, Gord. To meet Johnny. He will guide you somewhere. He know magic.' I rolled my eyes. Sunfly walked out into the dusty street. The panting wind making him hold his hat.

'Hey Gordon! Come over here matey and try some of this,' Max barked from behind the bar, spoon in hand.

I looked into the tall pot to see chunks of purple meat bobbing in a turbid pond of brown sauce. 'What is it?'

'Just bloody taste it, will ya?'

'Okay, okay.' I tasted it. It was a very salty stew. 'Yeah, it's okay,' I said, pulling a face at the excess salt.

'Good.' Max brought the steaming spoon to his chapped lips. 'Mmm. Needs a little salt, I think.'

'Yeah, I was thinking that myself.'

Max added a cloud of salt in defiance of his last functioning artery.

'Bit hot for stew today, Max. You should be serving salad or something.'

'Does this look like a fuckin delicatessen to you?'

'No it's just –'

'Next you'll be wantin flamin foccacia.' (He pronounced it *fakosia*.)

'No, it's just –'

'Anyway, it's got salad in it. Look at them potatas. And there's a carrot floatin round somewhere. Parsley and that,' he added.

'Yeah, it's a regular vegetarian's El Dorado.'

'Anyway. Bloody salad. How many people do ya think round ere would want salad?'

'"Five beers and a caesar salad", does sound a little strange, I suppose.'

'Too bloody right.' Max pulled out a dusty blackboard and a piece of chalk and wrote: *Lamb Stew $5.50. Free fuckin salad.*

'Where's the mad Italian today?' Max asked, positioning the sign.

'Oh, he'll come over later, he's got a few dollars on some nag at Birdsville. He's listening to the race on the radio at the caff. You know what he's like.'

'That lunatic would bet on two flies crawling on a turd.'

'So you're familiar with this month's "Chef's Specials".' I paused to feel the fan. 'You know, Max, he'll be dirty on you selling food in the pub – taking his trade away, and all that,' I joked.

Max became red in the face. 'Well, I figure if anyone is stupid enough to eat the greasy shit he sells for food, they'll eat my flamin stew. So I midaswel make a few bob out of it. Anyway, Pommy Bart give me some spuds and Barney give me a lamb yesterday, so I thought I'd make a stew. I cut its throat, kept the legs, and threw the rest in the pot. Can't eat the whole bloody thing meself. It'll go off in this heat. The cool room's chock-a-block with kegs.'

'Very industrious of you.'

'Oh, well, save em going off home for dinner. They might stay and drink a bit longer.'

'Give em a bed and have sex with them occasionally and they never have to leave.'

Max laughed, 'You really remind me of him sometimes . . .'

'Who?'

Max nodded towards the yellowing photo of his son on the wall, fighting in some outback boxing match. 'Him.'

'Why would *I* remind you of him?'

He looked fondly at the photo. 'Oh, just little things you say now and then. He used to say stuff like that. Reckoned all the people round here were drunks and ratbags.'

'Now why on earth would he think that?'

'Yeah, why would he?' he chuckled.

'You never did track him down, did you, Max?'

'No,' he sighed, 'never did. Army had no record of a Tony Parsons. And that's where he went they tell me, the army. Nutha beer?'

'Yeah, thanks.'

Max plopped a foaming glass on the bar. I drank some and wiped my brow with the glass. It felt cool.

'What would you say to him if he walked in the door right now?' I asked.

Max stopped and sat down. He rested his chin on his broken knuckles and pondered. Then he jumped up. His face turned the colour of beetroot. His voice wobbled. 'I'd say, "Tony, if you've changed, you can come back. But if you're still a flamin fairy, then you can piss off right now!"'

'You should write Country 'n' Western songs.'

'I can't change the way I am, Gordon.'

'Well, perhaps you'll have to if you want to move forward with your life.'

'Sounds like a lot of trendy bullshit.'

'Well, ask yourself this. Is your *prejudice* greater than your *love* for him?'

He thought for a while before shaking his head. 'I'm too bloody old ta change. I'm from the old school, Gordon.'

'I thought you said you loved him?'

'I do . . . but I can't cop that poofter stuff. Kissing blokes. Fair dinkum.'

'He's not a serial killer, Max. He's still your son. Sounds like you've got a lot of things to work out.'

He slammed his glass down. '*I've* got things to work out! It's him that's got to work out that fucking blokes is wrong. It's against nature.'

I remained silent.

'Where did Shirley and me go wrong? I know the town's not overflowin with sheilas, but we took im to country dances and that. B&S balls. So he'd meet girls. I even bought im a copy'a *Playboy* once!'

'Now why didn't Quentin Crisp's father think of that.'

He lowered his voice, 'You're not one are you, for fuck's sake?'

'No, although I do enjoy shopping for shoes.'

'Country people are different, Gordon.'

'No, people are the same everywhere. You just have to work out how much you want him in your life.'

The bulky little publican poured himself a fresh glass of beer and let out a long sigh. He thought long and hard about this. It was difficult. It's easy to be sanctimonious. But this was an agonising impasse for him. I was asking him to unravel the very fabric that bound his world together.

I looked around. Apart from the belching sheep farmer and his blowsy wife and a truck driver with a load of squealing pigs out the front who was reading a paper and eating a bowl of the famous stew with free salad, the hotel was relatively quiet. Even the cockatoo was silent, stalking a blowfly that had perilously entered the cage. The muggy silence made it seem an age before Max answered.

'You mean . . . accept him *that way*. As a poofter?' he said in a loud whisper.

'I think the preferred word is "gay" these days.'

He looked to me for support, 'Well . . . I dunno.'

'All I'm saying is think about it, Max.'

'I do love the kid. I really do but . . .' He jumped up. 'Not in *that way* of course.'

'Max, if you tell him you love him, you won't start suddenly wearing stilettos and listening to Judy Garland records.'

Max smiled.

The flyscreen door slapped open and three sweaty men in Akubras walked in, laughing. Sweat made their faces gloss in the white sunlight of the doorway. They ordered a round of beers and took them to a corner table.

'How does your ex feel about it? Have you got in touch?' I asked.

'Yes, but she won't say anything. Shirley says it's up to him if he wants to see me. All the Triplechurches say the same thing.'

'Triplechurch?'

'Oh, that's her maiden name.'

'Unusual.'

'Yeah.' Max poured himself a fresh pint of beer. He was a typical outback publican. He would drink beer all day with the punters – as his father had done – and you would never know he had had a drop. One of the men, tall, square-chinned, in a blue singlet, walked over to the bar with three snow-ringed glasses.

'Three more thanks, Maxy. Those didn't even touch the sides.' He pulled some crumpled notes from his pocket to pay.

'Yeah, she's right, Barney,' Max smiled, nodding him away.

'Yer sure?'

'Yeah, you gave me that lamb yesterday. It's my shout.'

He broke into a smile that could burn your retinas. 'Thanks, Max. Very decent of yer.'

'There go the catering profits,' I said.

'Barney, I don't think you've met our new resident, yet? Gordon Shoesmith, Barney Franklin.' Max opened the hatch to the cellar and left us to talk.

The handsome farmer shot out a brawny hand that was cracked and split and felt like sandpaper. 'Nice ta meet yer,' he drawled.

'So you're the one responsible for that dreadful stew,' I laughed.

'Just gave im the bullets, e's the one who loaded the gun,' he chuckled, blue eyes twinkling like pools.

'Well, we know who won't be eating the stew then,' Max hollered from the cellar.

'I've seen yer at the café. Do yer work for the Italian?' he asked, wiping a slick of sweat from his mouth.

'Well, you could call it work. I just kind of hang out there and eat his food and drink his booze. I sometimes do some work for a few bucks for him – and Max. Helping unload kegs from the beer truck mainly.'

'Are yer looking to make a few bucks, then?' he said quickly.

'I'm always looking.'

'Yer look fit.' (No one had ever actually said I looked 'fit' before. You look *fucked* but never *fit*. In hindsight, this must have added to my agrarian delirium when volunteering to help him fix fences.) 'Ever done any farmin?'

'No, but I've always wanted to see what it was like.'

'Not much ta see, really,' he said.

'Oh, I don't know. There's something so primeval about farming, isn't there?'

'If yer say so,' he smiled. 'Hard way to make a quid, really.'

'What would I have to do?' I asked cautiously, remembering the last time I volunteered to help Jimmy.

'Up to you.' He downed a mouthful of beer. 'I work on me own so I could just use the company, really.'

'Look, don't worry about paying me, I'll just come out to help. I'm interested, anyway. I've never been to a farm. Green pastures and fresh milk, and all that.'

The man grinned into an upturned glass.

'What would you want me to do? I mean, I couldn't shear sheep or anything.' (That I knew to be something resembling manual labour.)

He smiled, 'Wrong tima year fer that. Ever done any fencin?'

'Just at school. I wasn't very good. Always confusing parry and thrust. Lucky I wasn't born in the Middle Ages.'

'Fixin fences, yer goose,' he said with a tobacco chuckle.

'Sounds like hard yakka, as they say around here.'

'Na. Just hold stuff in place while I fix it and that,' he drawled.

Couldn't be too hard, I thought. 'Like holding nails and things?'

'Yer could say that.'

I shrugged my shoulders, 'Okay.'

'I'll pick yer up tomorra bout five.'

'Five, that's a late start.'

The farmer flashed a row of even, white teeth. 'That's five in the mornin, ol mate.'

'Five in the *morning*?' I said, spluttering my beer.

'That's farmin, Gordon.'

'I knew there was a reason I skipped it as a career option. Um . . . er . . . five in the morning you say . . .'

He raised his eyebrows, 'If that's okay?'

'Um . . . that's when I usually go to bed,' I said under my breath. 'Okay, it'll be different, I guess.'

The farmer cracked a watermelon smile. 'Oh, I think it'll be different. See yer in the mornin.' We clinked glasses.

'Ah . . . yeah . . . in the morning. That's that part of the day the sun rises from the east, isn't it?'

The grinning farmer waved me away and sat with his companions, finished his beer and left while I visited the toilet to have a leak.

The stench from the urinal burned my eyes as I pissed on the yellow lolly that floated in a sea of lime. Apparently, the sugary disk was supposed to make the toilet smell nice. That was the theory anyway. By quick calculation, I worked out that it would have to be roughly the size of Christmas Island for this to occur. (I'm told the Dunny Lolly was invented by the same person who invented seatbelts on jumbos.) Quite frankly, it was a relief to wash my hands and walk out.

I sat at the bar waiting for the fan to make its seemingly endless pass and blow some air my way. I watched the cockatoo. It sneered at me. Looking hot and miserable, it listed on its perch – almost at a right angle.

The Reverend Fruit, with a light frost of chicken feathers in his hair, strode in with papal aplomb. 'The usual, thanks Landlord!'

Max slipped behind the bar and returned with some oily-looking water.

'Ahh, young Mr Shoesmith. We didn't see you at church on Sunday.'

'Sorry, I was sacrificing a goat.'

'Presbyterian, eh? Don't let that stop you from coming, we're all God's children,' he boomed. He took a sip of 'water' and tugged at his plastic collar. 'Damn hot today!' he added.

'Too bloody hot,' Max growled.

'Even the poor parrot looks hot,' he said.

'Hot day for a funeral.' I said, sipping my beer.

Max interrupted. 'Hot for a funeral? This is nuthin. Tell Gordon about old Morrie, Rev.'

'Oh, I'd rather not.'

'Garn, it's bloody hilarious.'

'Some other time perhaps,' he said.

Max decided to tell me anyway. 'You see, Morrie was having a crap one day in the dunny here when he had a heart attack. Not the way *I* want to go. Anyway, we had to bury him at the Coober. We had the main procession down the street like today and then we load the coffin into The Flamingo's station wagon.'

'The Flamingo?' I asked.

'Yeah, legs like a canary and a nose like the sharp end of an anvil.'

'So go on . . .'

'Anyway, it was hot. Bloody hot. Not like today. It was a shocker. The Flamingo's drivin the "hearse" and The Flamingo is a real lead foot. So The Bird and The Rev take off and leave us all in a clouda dust. The old Kingswood's got no air-conditioning. Anyway, like I said, it was the hottest day all year. So they're drivin along and what do you reckon happens?'

'The body exploded,' the minister said in a flat voice as though he was trying to forget the whole episode.

'All the build-up of gasses and that,' said Max. 'Boom!'

'I was only new to the town, too. It was quite a shock. Threw up when we reached the crematorium,' said the Rev.

'Tell him about the service.'

'I'd prefer not to.'

'Garn, tell him. Well, anyway, the widow is on her way. And they panic. See, Morrie's spread all over the car. So as not to upset her, they stuff all the bits back in the coffin and continue with the service s'thow nuthins happened. Then, The Rev is doing the eulogy in the chapel at the crematorium and we hear this blood-curdling shriek. It was the widow. One of old Morrie's ears has fallen out of The Rev's pocket and onto the floor. We all knew what had happened. The widow didn't but.'

'Yes, and you didn't have to all break into hysterical fits of laughter,' Fruit said dryly.

'We couldn't bloody help it,' Max said, smothering a laugh. 'You know, Gordon, what it's like when you're not supposed to laugh, but you can't help it. It builds like a volcano. Anyway, the widow runs out screaming, we're all on the floor, pissing ouselves laughing. Tell im what you said, Rev.'

'I'd rather not.'

'Garn, tell him.'

The minister pulled uncomfortably at his plastic collar. 'Ear lies a fine man.'

Max turned blue with laughter. It took him several minutes to compose himself as the clergyman stood stony-faced, sipping his 'water'.

'I'll just water the holy horses.' The clergyman strode off to the toilet. Max was still in hysterics. The minister, tugging his football shorts, sat back at the bar. Max dried his eyes with a bar towel. In an effort to change the subject, the reverend turned to me.

'You know Gordon, you strike me as a young man looking for something. Looking for God, perhaps?'

'Will he answer me if I try and find him?'

The vicar's eyes flashed. 'Yes, my son.'

'Does he have email? I tried him at god.com but got a porno site. Sorry, tell a lie. That was ohgod.com.'

Fruit looked annoyed, 'Do you actually *like* Christians, Gordon?'

'It's the answer for some people. I respect that. I've got no beef against Christians, it's just I'm not crazy about the ones in America who tell you that "Jesus is the King of the Peacemakers" and if you don't agree, they'll blow your head off.'

He upturned an oily glass. 'I'm not crazy about Catholics either.'

'Wasn't it Voltaire who said, "I may disagree with what you have to say, but I shall defend, to the death, your right to say it." Or was that Genghis Khan?'

'Another, Rev?' Max asked.

'Yes, I think I will. Must keep up the fluids in this heat,' he said, blowing high-octane breath across the bar. He climbed up on the bar and raised his glass. Max rolled his eyes.

'Don't forget, you're all God's children – services every Sunday.' The barflies raised their glasses limply. Someone belched.

He resumed his seat feeling satisfied.

'If you don't mind me asking, why do you have the service every Sunday when nobody turns up?' I asked.

He placed a hot palm on my shoulder and smiled, 'Jesus once said: "The wonder of man lies in his ability to believe in the impossible".'

I nodded.

'*Star Trek*,' Max snapped as he walked down the end of the bar.

'What?' I asked.

'Fuckin *Star Trek*. Jesus never said that, Dr flamin Spock said that. *Star Trek IV*. The return of Spock. When Kirk finds him alive on that planet.'

'Was it? I had it down as St Paul. I better scrub that from this week's sermon. Spock, eh?' He turned to me. 'What religion was he, do you think?'

I shrugged my shoulders, 'Vulcan.'

'Buddhist, eh? Smart people, the Buddhists.'

'Beer, Gordon?' Max asked, shaking his head.

'Cheers.'

'Damn! I'll have to go and rewrite the *whole* sermon.' The preacher downed his drink and raced out.

I looked up at the old photos of Max and his son at various boxing fixtures.

Triplechurch. That's an unusual name, I thought to myself.

'Where you goin?' Max asked.

'Need to pop into Rugs 'R' Us for a sec.'

I walked over to the post office. If you thought it was hot *inside*, you should have walked outside. You were engulfed by an invisible sea of heat.

A tinkling bell rang on the back of the door to alert the post master that someone had actually bothered to come in (he mostly handed out letters in the pub). I could hear a horse race being squeezed from a transistor radio in the back room.

'Go . . . go . . . you rotten blighter [*cough*]. Oh, be with you in a moment,' a voice wheezed from the back. The race finished to the tune of paper being torn into tiny pieces. Squales popped his wigless head around the corner.

'Oh, it's you lad [*splutter*] just a minute.'

'I'll come back later if you're busy.'

'No, no, I'm cooming, lad.'

I *really* struggled to keep a straight face as Squales walked in – rug precariously perched on his sweaty scalp like an inverted bird's nest holding a large egg.

'Bloody nag. I knew [*cough*] I shouldn't ave listened to that bloody Italian. What can I do for you, son? Everything all right [*cough*] at the station ouse, I troost? Remember, moom's the word if any nosy people ask.'

'Yeah, yeah. Listen, Bart. Can you do me a favour?'

'Oh, I moost [*cough*] show you this! You'll be very excited.' He raced out the back and returned quickly. 'What do you think that is?'

'A potato.'

'It's the Bismarck.'

'No wonder you people won the battle of the Atlantic. Hitler was a fool!'

'No, no. You [*gag*] don't oonderstand. A Silver-Skin Bismarck. They said I couldn't grow one in the desert. These only grow in Tasmania. They laughed at me when I said I could do it! Laughed in my face.'

'Fools!' I said.

'Aye, fools! That's right, lad.'

'Listen, I need a favour.'

'Yes, lad. What is it?'

'Can you make a phone call for me?'

'Me? Where to?'

'The Army Records Office in Adelaide.'

'Sure. What do ye want me to say, lad?'

'Just ask them if they have any record of an Anthony Triplechurch.'

'All [*cough cough*] right,' he answered suspiciously.

The old man proceeded to make the call, coughing and spluttering his way through most of it. After much talk he put his hand over the receiver and turned to me.

'They won't release [*splutter*] information over the phone. What do you want me to do?'

'Put me on.'

Squales handed me one of those annoying, flimsy, mini-flip phones that someone had given him. The kind where a pimple on your chin disconnects the call and a nostril hair dials Istanbul. Squales listened in on an old Bakelite handset.

'Ahem . . . Hello, is that Army Records? Good. My name's Gordon Shoesmith, from Shoesmith, Bumstead and Ringworm. I'm a solicitor. I'm trying to track down one Anthony Triplechurch. I've been told that he possibly joined the army some years ago,' I spruiked in my best Cranbrook accent. 'Yes, I appreciate you can't release that sort of information over the phone, but I'm in rather a sticky situation. You see, Mr Triplechurch has been bequeathed quite a considerable sum from a deceased relative and if I fail to find him this week, the money's automatically forfeited to the Government in probate. Now let me ask you . . . Sharon is it? Sharon, would you rather see a battling soldier, who's trying to feed his family, receive this handsome legacy, or the Government? I'm sure they'd spend it wisely on a new swimming pool for the Prime Minister's Lodge or something.' I waited anxiously by the phone for a few moments. 'Yes, I have a pen . . . Thank you.' I put the phone down.

'Cheers, Bart.'

'Any tarm lad. I'll see you over [*gag*] there later and perhaps [*splutter*] you'll tell me what you're op to,' he gasped.

'Sure. I'll buy you a beer, and one for your friend,' I said, pointing to the wig. (I couldn't help myself.)

Squales peered at his wig from under his eyebrows and frowned.

I took the slip of paper, folded it into my pocket, and walked over to the pub.

HATS ARE NOT ONLY FOR BALD PEOPLE

WE WERE STANDING on the seabed. Great undulating fingers of spinifex swayed in the current. I wiggled my toes in ochre-coloured sand. Bloated bodies of white farmers floated past in a procession. They looked like a school of dead puffer fish. Some were in nineteenth-century dress. Some carried muskets. Others carried rifles. Women held babies. I gaped at their open faces. I turned to the boy. I tried to speak, bubbles shooting from my mouth. The boy brought his finger to his lips. As if to tell me to remain silent.

'What the fuck . . .!'

It was pitch-black when I woke to the tap at the window.

'Jesus, you frightened the crap out of me,' I said, letting Barney in the door. 'What time is it, man?'

'Five-thirty. Thought I'd give yer a sleep in,' he drawled.

'Thanks, you're all heart.' (As usual, I had forgotten about the job.) 'Coffee?' I asked, stalling, trying to wake up.

Barney looked at his watch. 'Ar, oright then.' The farmer glanced around the dilapidated shack. He was obviously unimpressed. He watched me like a cat, as I tinkered drowsily with the percolator.

Barney had a fascination with people from the Big Smoke, as he called it. People who chose to live on top of each other like cockroaches. People who sardined themselves into trains and buses every day, breathing each other's foul air. To Barney, these people were as alien as little green men from Mars. His land and his sheep were his life's work. His career. His hobby. His art. He thought of little else. He fed those people in the city with their electronic organisers and computer tans. The people who made decisions about *his* welfare and *his* future from behind the mirrored glass of their air-conditioned citadels. He often wondered when they tried on a lamb's-wool sweater in a trendy boutique, if they thought about the sweat and heartache that brought it into being. The droughts. The floods. The foreclosures. He wondered if they ever thought about people like him, with the sun scorching his neck like a blowtorch and flies crawling inside his mouth, as they looked at themselves in the mirror of that boutique. So Barney was always keen to show a city slicker *his* world. *His* universe.

I brewed some coffee and we drank in early morning silence. Crickets chattered between the ticking of the warming oil heater. Barney rolled a cigarette and lit it.

'So why does a bloke like you live out ere?' he asked, tonguing the petal of paper.

'Good a place as any, I suppose,' I yawned.

'Who's that bloke?' he asked, staring at the black-and-white photo sitting on the piano that I had ripped out of a magazine.

'That's John Coltrane,' I said, putting my T-shirt on.

'He a musician?'

'Some people think he's a god. I speak posthumously, of course.'

I looked in the mirror and slapped my haggard face a few times in an effort to wake up. Barney chuckled.

'Yer look a bit rough. Kick on yesterday did yer?'

'Yeah, I'm a bit hung over.'

'Yeah, yer look like shit,' he said with good old Aussie tact.

'No, I always look like shit. The hangover merely gives me an excuse to look like shit.' I finished the coffee.

'Let's hit the road, Gordon! What'a yer say?'

'Okay.' I yawned.

'Yer can change yer mind if yer want, it's oright by me.'

'No, I'm up now. Let us fence!'

Barney had parked a Toyota four-wheel drive out the front. Although it was dark, I could see the fencing gear in the back. Poles, wire, cutters and such. Just seeing it made me feel fatigued. I fell into the car as Barney started the engine. He turned the headlights on.

⌢

We drove south for about an hour in somnolent silence. I watched the sun belly over the dunes, thawing the impotent landscape. Three pink galahs bobbed on a current in the middle distance. They glowed like Chinese lanterns in the emerging sunlight.

We drove into endless horizons over teeth-jarring bulldust holes. There was little sign of life apart from a crazed emu, as always, that ran hysterically in odd directions. As we tore down the gun-barrel roads, the Toyota left a pluming red cloud in its wake. I wound down the window in an effort to wake up. I could taste the dust in the back of my throat.

Although we'd driven for some time, it seemed to me that the landscape had changed little, if at all. The terracotta earth remained a treeless expanse in every direction. I scanned the horizon for greener pastures. I was imagining a scene from the pastoral paintings by Heysen.

'How far to the farm?' I asked drowsily.

'Yer've been driving through it for the last forty minutes.'

I screwed up my face, 'Where are the fences to keep the sheep in and stuff?'

'Don't have any. Too big ter fence, the stock just roam around in bunches, sorta thing. Me partner keeps an eye on em.'

'Oh, that's handy. Just how big is this little farm, then?'

'Oh, bout thirteen thousand square mile, I spose,' his last word jolted by a bulldust hole.

'What, you mean your farm is . . . bigger than . . . Holland?'

'Is it? Not a lot of tulips unfortunately,' he grinned.

I thumbed to the back. 'So, what's all the fencing gear for if there are no fences?'

'Oh, that. I do a bit of fencin on the dog fence to pay the bills.'

'What's the *dog* fence?'

'Yer'll find out shortly.'

After another twenty minutes or so, we reached Barney's single-chimney homestead. There were some crude pens made from rotting timber and the large house chiefly constructed of rusting corrugated iron. A crooked verandah snaked around it. It listed in the wind like a battle-weary soldier.

I got out of the vehicle. My nostrils tingled with the smell of sheep turds and rotting fodder. A yapping blue cattle dog charged me, sniffing at my crotch. (Why do dogs always do that? Do balls *really* smell that good?) Barney let out a whistle that could shatter a glass-bottom boat. The canine raced around and jumped into the handsome farmer's nut-brown arms.

'G'day, Lucky. Did yer miss me, mate?'

I took a look around, the earth puffing in orange clouds at my feet. I gaped at the parched, cracked landscape. Its surface was a spider web of fractures and gaps – some so cavernous I could stick my entire fist in them. The wind whistled in my ears as I walked. The only sound was the iron house creaking in the wind like an old ship. I felt a pang in my heart as I tramped around the dreary station. I felt pained because Barney was so excited to show me. Show me what? This?

My depression deepened as I spotted a few emaciated sheep. They dotted the horizon like puffs of smoke as they struggled against the wind. I picked up a piece of stale earth. It crumbled to dust in my fingers and was siphoned by the wind. Barney noted my disappointment.

'Yeah, bit dry at the moment,' he said, breaking the silence.

'Bit *dry*?'

'Should see it after a dropa rain. Very different. The land's a sea of wild flowers. Yellows. Purples. Crimsons. Quite beautiful, actually.'

'How long since you've had a decent drop of rain, Barney?'

'Oh, April –'

'That long?'

'April 1992.'

'Shit! It hasn't rained since 1992? What do the poor fuckers drink?'

'Bore.'

'What?'

'Beneath yer is the Great Artesian Basin. Covers more than one-fifth of the continent. We sink bores to find worta. Sometimes it takes months to find a new bore –'

'You should meet people in politics.'

'And the worta's not too fresh, neither. Every bit helps but. Come and I'll show yer.'

We walked over to one of the bores. It looked like a small oil rig.

'What's the long trench for?'

'That's to cool it. Yer see, when it comes outa the ground, it's boilin at around ninety degrees. Could cook eggs in it, actually. Anyway, it runs down this trough and cools. So then the stock can drink.'

'And what do they eat?'

'Oh, just bits of mulga and that. They eat anything. Sometimes I throw a bita fodda at em. Fodda's pricey. But they're happy.'

I gazed at the gaunt creatures sheltering their faces from the wind. Yeah, they look fucking delighted, I thought.

Barney kicked the dirt and spoke in a soft drawl. 'Years ago, the land never looked like this, you know. They stuffed it.'

'Who?'

'The settlers. The ones who come ere, you know, from England and Ireland, and that. They all come with a copy of that bloody

Campbell's Soil Culture Manual under their arm, thinkin they had all the answers.'

'I stared blankly.'

'He was a bloke who wrote a book round the turner the century for people farmin dry land. Reckoned he could show folk how to farm arid regions. Show em how to grow crops in the desert and that.'

'Seriously?'

'Yeah. As you can imagine, all the good land was snapped up pretty quickly by the gentry and the pommy bureaucrats. So this typa land was cheap as chips for the battlers in them days. But they couldn't farm it like soil in England or Ireland. So this guy came up with all these new techniques. Me great-grandfather had a copy of it. Problem was, it was all theories and ideas. None of which fucken worked. So they all come out ere, and also to dry parts of America, too, like Montana and that, thinkin they could snap up the land cheap and farm it. Most of em never even seen a plough or a sheep before. Come out from the slums of Europe thinkin they could be farmers and that. Yer can imagine the damage they did. The main problem was they ran too much bloody stock on the joint. They all run more sheep and cattle than the land could sustain. The stock ate everything down to seed level,' he looked around, 'left nuthin but this.' He picked up some dry earth and threw it into the wind. 'We only know *now* that yer can only run a fraction of the sheep on this kinda land compared to what they used to run on the joint. That's why the properties need to be big out ere. But that Campbell told em that small farms were best and even told em they could grow wheat crops and all sorts of shit out here. Madness. Sheer bloody madness. The tragic thing was that the poor pricks sold everything they had in the world to get out ere, only to lose it all because of that flamin book.'

'So your family has been here for a long time, Barney?'

'Since 1896. Me family come from Sheffield in England. In the first gold rush. Jeeze, bit different to Sheffield, this place, I reckon.'

'You could say that,' I said, as a sheep staggered in front of me like a junkie. 'So you live out here all alone?'

'Yeah, since the missus left.'

'How do you cope with all the work on your own?'

'Well, I have a pretty hard-workin partner. He does mosta the work round the joint.'

'Where is this partner?'

'That was im sniffin ya crotch,' he smiled, squinting at the sun.

'And such charming manners.'

He chuckled. 'Yeah. What's more, he doesn't take all the profits.' He looked at the sun again. 'Jeeze, we better get crackin, Gordon. Come on, Lucky.'

He let out another siren-like whistle and we hopped in the car. The dog vaulted in the back, yelping and spinning in circles. The animal's enthusiasm for the impending day's work in the belting sun was slightly more exuberant than my own. I asked myself why I was about to fix fences in the middle of the desert? After all, I'd seen the farm. I was over it, quite frankly.

'Here, yer'll need this,' he said, handing me a wide-brimmed hat.

'Thanks, but I'm not really a hat kind of guy. Some people suit hats, particularly bald people. Bruce Willis, Garth Brooks. Elton John springs to mind –'

'Yer'll be a sunburnt and sick kinda guy without one. It's not a fashion accessory out here, Gordon. It's a necessity. But suit yerself,' he smiled.

The morning sun started to get a little nasty as we sped for the dog fence. I felt it burn my elbow that V'd out the window. We chatted as we ripped along the dusty, sanguine roads that blurred in the heat. Barney talked about life on the land. I talked about life in the city – the conversation punctuated by the usual potholes, stones and dips. I guess we had been motoring along for about an hour as Barney lamented how the country was in such bad shape.

In just two hundred years of European settlement, our ancestors had managed to turn the great southern continent, with its precariously poised ecosystem, into an eroding, desolate wasteland.

'Much longer to go?' I asked.

'See it?' Barney pointed to the object that bridged the entire horizon. The structure seemed to span infinity and, if you didn't know its function, would appear as mysterious as happening upon a sculpture by Christo.

'Yeah, I see it. Big.'

'Biggest fence in the world. Like the bloody Great Wall of China. Runs from the cliffs at the Bight here in South Australia to Jimbour in Queensland.'

'What for?'

'Keeps the dingoes outa the sheep country.'

'They attack sheep?'

'Do they what. They don't always eat em, neither. You could understand if they needed to eat em, but they just rip their guts out and leave em to die. One dog can kill up to eighty sheep a night. Sometimes more. So round the turner the century they started to build a bloody great big fence. Different blokes patrol huge sections of it cross Austraya. They useta patrol it in camels in the old days. Then Model T Fords. And now four-wheel drives. Lot easier in a four-wheel drive than a camel, don't yer reckon?'

'Yes, I'd imagine. So is your farm inside or outside the dog fence?'

'Outside.'

'Oh.'

'Yeah. Lose quite a few sheep too, although I shoot heepsa dogs.'

'Can you bait them?'

'I can, but I don't like leavin baits around. That's how I lost me last dog. Horrible way to die, poison. The missus was devastated when we lost Banjo. Poor mongrel took days to die. In terrible agony. Awful to see. In the end I had to put a bullet in im. Awful.

Awful. I don't bait dingoes no more. Just shoot the bastards, if I can. They're cunning little pricks but.'

'Quite a beautiful dog, the dingo.'

'Yeah, with a bullet in its head. Them bloody do-gooders in the city want to protect em, but they wouldn't think that way if they'd carried a bleating lamb with its intestine dragging behind it like a clothesline.'

'Fair point.'

We reached the fence and then diverted to a bumpy side road that straddled the endless expanse of netting. The fence fascinated me. It was more than a physical barrier, it was also a symbolic barrier that kept white Australia from the secret country – a country it seemed we had not yet come to grips with.

Barney dropped a size 12 R.M. Williams boot on the brake and hopped out. The dog was turning itself inside out, frothing at the mouth as Barney tried to separate a feral cat from the wire netting. The crazed feline hissed and cursed at the farmer like Kate from *The Taming of the Shrew*. He went to the back of the Toyota, pulled out a crowbar and struck it cleanly on the head. It made a dreadful sound. Like someone stamping on a violin. I winced. The dog settled down.

'Bloody things,' Barney said, wiping a berry of blood from his cheek. 'People dump em in the bush thinkin its better than puttin em down. If they only knew how much native wildlife those cats can kill.'

He tossed the carcass over the fence and started the repairs diligently. I'd never seen anyone work so hard. He came over to grab some tools.

As he repaired the fence, he asked me to grab some poles from the back of the ute. Nests of wire lay in the back. The twisted shapes reminded me of the bulls Picasso drew with a single unbroken line. I passed him the poles and the wire.

'Yer feel a bit more awake then?' he asked, giving the Barcoo salute (swatting a fly).

I nodded. In my own pathetic way I helped as best I could –

bumbling my way through as the bearable heat of the morning fused into the unbearable heat of the day. I suspect the work would have gone quicker without me, actually. (But I think Barney enjoyed the company.)

It was hot and exhausting work to say the least. There was no shade. Every metal object was like a hot iron to touch: the tools, the poles, the netting, the wire, even the car.

Stripped to the waist, we repaired holes and propped up netting. Sweat shiny on our brown backs. Barney toiled like Samson in the punishing heat. I stood holding poles and passing him tools. I really admired his work ethic. I mean, let's face it, who was around to check on his workmanship?

Some repairs would take as little as ten minutes, while areas that were seriously damaged, could take over an hour. Wombats were a problem. They were constantly burrowing beneath the netting, creating tunnels for the wily dogs to enter lamb-chop heaven. Some animals, like kangaroos, would simply smash against the fence, bringing down entire sections of netting.

After a few hours, I felt exhausted. Barney could see I was fading fast. I wasn't used to hard work, particularly in the heat of the day. I regretted not taking up the offer of the hat, yet was too embarrassed to ask for it now. My face burned. No one would have seen me in the goddamn hat after all. Sparing me the humiliation of passing out, Barney kindly put the tools down.

'There's a gum tree over that dune. Let's have a break and a bitta lunch.'

'Oh, if you like,' I panted. He may have noticed my sense of relief. Perhaps hugging him and doing a jig gave it away.

We tossed the tools in the back and traversed a low-lying sandhill. We parked under the solitary gum. In its welcome shade we sat eating sandwiches of corned beef and hot English mustard.

'Do you get lonely working on your own, Barney?' I asked through a mouthful of corned beef.

Barney stood up for a moment. He picked up a sheep skull and punted it into the distance through imagined goalposts. He took a swig from a canteen and wiped his dripping chops with the end of his faded blue singlet. 'Yeah, sometimes. Now the missus is gone. Gets harder every year.'

'Was she from around here?'

'No. But she was a country girl, though from greener pastures. She's from the river country, down south. Ever been there?'

'The Murray? No, I can't say that I have. I hear it's beautiful country,' I said, removing a stone from beneath my buttocks.

'Yeah, her parents have a dairy farm. The properties are a lot smaller down there. Nice soil, though. Very forgiving,' he said sitting down.

'What was her name?'

'Nancy,' he smiled.

'How did you meet her?'

'We met at a cattle sale near Adelaide. I was workin as a ringer at the time. Come down for the sale. Any chance to go to the city. I always find the city strange. All them people running around the joint. Makes me feel good about my way of life when I see it.

'When I got to the sale I didn't see her for a couple of days. I eventually saw her feedin some stock. She had a Drizabone coat on, so I couldn't see her figure but she looked beautiful. Pretty face. She was only about twenty back then. She seen me lookin at her too. So eventually she said hello. Those hazel-green eyes. Jeeze. She was a beauty. And the wind blowin through that burgundy hair. And she had them cute little brown, powdery freckles on her nose which, I dunno, made her look friendly and kinda warm. Yeah, I can remember that day real well, mate.'

'How long ago was this, Barney?'

'Oooh, Jeeze, bout eight years ago now, I spose. Wow, has it been eight years?' he said to himself. 'I didn't get the chance to talk to her at the sale. Blokes were hangin round her like bees on a honey pot.

But funny enough, later that afternoon I took a trip down to the beach by meself. Yer don't see the ocean much, livin in the outback, so when I get the chance I always seem to head for the sea.'

'Keneally once wrote that because we originally come from the sea, returning to it is like a spiritual roast lamb dinner.'

'Yeah, right!'

'So go on.'

'Well, it was winter, so the beach was deserted. Too cold to swim. So I took me boots off and just started walkin along the sand. Feel it in me toes and that. Just walked and picked up little shells and stuff. Walked for miles. Didn't see no one. Not a soul. It was pretty overcast, mind you. Not really a beach day.

'Well, after walkin for about an hour, I spotted someone on the beach. Just on the edge of the water. It was the girl from the sale. She was barefoot and she was wearin a beautiful white lamb's-wool jumper and blue jeans. She stared at me. Her hair was tied back, but when she saw me she let it all out and it fell over her shoulders. Well, fair dinkum, it looked like a peasa Chinese silk. Beautiful. Me stomach hit the ground. I just stood there starin at her like a bloody goose, when all of a sudden there's a loud crack. It starts bucketin with rain. Real heavy rain, too. We were gettin soaked and just starin at each other. I didn't know what to do so I just smiled and shrugged me shoulders, then, out of the blue, she burst out laughin. Laughed her silly head off. I ran over and grabbed her hand and we bolted for shelter like a couple of rabbits. We were soaked through, so I drove her back to her motel and well, I'll leave the rest to your imagination.'

'That's a nice story, Barney.'

'It's nice to tell it, actually. Makes me remember it,' he said, volleying a stubborn fly across the sand.

'How long has she been gone?'

Barney cracked a wry smile. 'Coupla years now.' He gazed at the blurring horizon. 'Feels like a hundred.' His voice cracked on the last word. 'Funny, I walked down that beach a month ago, you know. I dunno why. Dunno what I was lookin for. I just found meself in that area by accident on a trip down south. I stopped the car and went for a walk. I was fine till it started to bucket down with rain. Just like that day. Then it hurt, mate. It really bloody hurt. Started cryin. You probably think I'm weak or somethin,' he smiled.

'Not at all, Barney.'

'It just brought back that many memories, mate. It's funny the little things yer can remember. Like the smell of her hair. I couldn't even tell yer what it smelt like, but it's so strong in my mind I can almost smell it now. It's funny how one person can come into yer life and change it forever, isn't it?' he said quietly. 'Yer'd think yer'd be unchangeable and no one could get inside you're soul, but it's not true. It's like you're a dark room just waiting for someone to turn a light on.'

I smiled and nodded. Behind us, a black cockatoo stood apprehensively on the edge of the shade – carefully assessing the two of us out of the corner of its eye. Barney rolled a cigarette, battling the breeze to light it.

'This may seem like a strange question, Barney, but what made her so special?'

Barney took a deep drag. 'That's like asking me to describe the feeling I have when I watch a lamb being born or when I visit the sea. I dunno, I guess she taught me to look at things differently.'

'How? In what way?'

He pondered for a moment. 'Oh, I dunno, Gordon. Not so serious all the time, I spose. It's pretty serious country out here, yer know. Can't make too many mistakes. Yer can forget to smile sometimes. But Nancy, she thought everything was funny. Great sense of humour. She'd watch a sheep fall asleep and fall over and then she'd laugh her silly head off. She was a warm person. Big heart. Just like the first day I met her: it buckets down with rain and she laughs her silly head off.'

Barney's eyes twinkled as they caught the cracks of sunlight that edged through the stirring foliage, 'Every day was fun with her, especially in them early days.'

'Why did she leave, if you don't mind me asking?'

'No, not at all. Probably good to talk about it, I spose. Not too many people are interested enough to listen out here at times. Hey, I'm not boring you, am I?'

'You're not boring me, Barney,' I said softly.

He took off his hat and slowly ran his fingers through his greasy, dark brown hair. 'Why did she leave me?' he chuckled to himself rhetorically. 'I ask myself that question every day. I dunno. I spose she started to change.'

'Change? In what way?'

He took a searching look over the desolate landscape. 'Like I said, Gordon, things get pretty grim out here. After we got married, Dad retired and I took over the station. She got a bit of a shock when she come out ere and first saw it, she told me later. Yer see, her family's farm looked a bit different to mine, yer could say. Yer gotta understand, she come from money. Real money. Dairy money. Her old man raised prize-winnin cattle. Well, when her old man come out to see our property, he was in shock or somethin. Like he didn't know farms existed this far inside. Can yer believe it?' His hands became animated. 'Said we couldn't make it. That we were crazy. That he knew a bloke down south with some land . . . blah, blah, blah. It was humiliatin. He made a point about the fence. He goes: "Especially outside the dog fence." Said the land was too dry for cattle and the dogs would keep attackin the sheep blah blah. Do yer think he wasn't telling me anythin I didn't know? I mean, fair dinkum, me family have been ere for years. Sure, some tough times, but they managed. I had a good life.

'Anyway when her old man said all this that day he come up, I felt lower than a pregnant snake. Humiliated. Well, at that moment

I knew I had found the greatest woman in the world.'

'Why's that?'

His eyes grew liquid. 'Cause she just looked im dead in the eye and said: "Just watch us, Dad! Just you watch us."'

I smiled and nodded.

'She had a lot of spirit, but maybe she wasn't tough enough in the end.'

'Why?'

'Well it's easy to say we'll make it work, but harder in reality, I spose. Nancy was too soft-hearted. Like I said, this is unforgiving country. Only the tough survive out ere. Droughts, floods, disease. Yer have to battle everything in this joint. A dribble of rain comes and yer crack open the bubbly. Yer think, next week the plains will be green, the sheep will be fed.' He clicked his brown fingers. 'Then it stops just like that! Or it'll come down and won't flamin stop like in '92.'

'Flood?'

'Yep. Half the stock drown and yer back to square one. It's as if the country's laughing at yer. Teasing yer. Having a joke at yer expense.' He tossed his smouldering cigarette butt into the wind. 'It's cruel country at times, Gordon. Very cruel country.'

I noticed a strange shadow on the ground and looked up. A hawk circled in silence, suspended on a pocket of warm air. It looked like a jet waiting for permission to land. It had spotted the loafing cockatoo and was patiently waiting for its chance to swoop. We sat in silence for a while, listening to the whistling wind.

'It was that bloody foal that did it in the end. Maybe she'd still be here if we hadn't got that foal. I bet her dad knew what would happen.'

'What happened?' I asked.

He let out a big sigh and hung his head, removing his hat to rub his fingers through his thick hair again. 'It was her birthday. Her dad come up with this foal as a present. It come from racing stock, so it was worth a few bob. It was in beautiful condition when it arrived. Its coat shined like it had been French-polished. We had a few horses and that, but they were pretty rough. Desert horses. They'd never even bent their heads to eat grass. They were just eatin mulga and scrub and that. They looked pretty mangy next to bloody Phar Lap,' he sniggered. 'Well, after about six months out ere, this little foal was a skeleton. Just skin and bones. Poor little bastard. And all the other horses were belting the little bugger. Wouldn't let him eat the mulga and bits of food that were round. He was that thin that in the end all his hair fell out.'

'You're kidding?'

'Nuh. Anyway, Nancy was very upset. She became obsessed with this little foal. Dunno why. We'd had foals before, and that. Anyway, she used to boil barley and vegetable peelings for the little bloke. Fatten him up. He was that thin, yer have no idea. Every little stone or stick seemed to trip im over. Then she'd run out in tears. Trying to help him up. He was too weak to get up imself. In the end, that little foal followed Nancy everywhere. Thought she was his mother, I reckon.

'Anyway, one day I had to do some shearin over the border. We'd been through a very dry patch, so I had to earn a few bucks on the side. Nancy wanted to come with me for the trip. So I had a mate take care of the station. Up in the northwest they had some major floods and we got caught. We were landlocked for six weeks.

'When we finally got back and drove up to the station, Nancy started to get hysterical cause she could see the little foal lying dead on the ground near the house. Chook, me mate, said it died the night before. Just fretted for her, I reckon. After a while, she couldn't go outside in the main paddock without cryin. Said she could hear it whinnying all the time.

'Well, the next six months were tough. Food was scarce. A lot of the stock became diseased and died. I was workin fourteen-hour days. We were goin through a real tough patch. But there's plenty of em out ere. Then one evening, months later, we were havin a cuppa tea and she heard one of the horses whinny. She just got up, said nuthin, and walked out. Drove off and I never seen her again.'

'Did you try to get in contact with her?'

'Oh, of course, but she wouldn't talk to me. Her old man would always pick up the bloody phone.' Barney turned to me, 'Why do yer think she got so worked up over that bloody foal, for Christ sake?'

I watched the hawk slowly circling while I thought of something that would be of some solace to the farmer. 'I don't know,' I finally said. 'The foal came from the same area she did, you say? Maybe in its suffering she saw her own.'

'Do yer think so?'

'Barney, I'm only guessing. Human nature is a fathomless sea. To you it was just another farm animal. To her it was something else. A part of herself, perhaps.'

The farmer turned his face away from me. I suspected he was hiding tears. With his back turned, he dried his eyes. I looked tactfully away. I watched the hawk run out of patience and take off over a dune to find easier prey. The black cockatoo almost seemed to smile, as if it had outwitted the hawk.

An afternoon wind blew up. We walked to the car. Barney turned to me. 'Thanks for coming out today, Gordon.'

'Oh, I wasn't much help, I'm afraid.'

He smiled. 'Oh, I wouldn't say that.'

We drove into the sun in reflective silence. The sky, an upturned glass of mango juice.

SHEEP WITH SORE TESTICLES

JOE WAS IN GOOD spirits that evening. He strutted around the café in his Stetson and Hawaiian shirt, singing and dancing. The shirt was so loud it came with a built-in graphic-equaliser. He was crooning 'Jailhouse Rock' in a malodorous key only intelligible to himself and the five per cent of the population statistically known to be tone-deaf. I gritted my back teeth as the Maestro of the Middle East cracked another high note. The note sounded uncannily like someone dropping a bucket of ball bearings on an alley cat. This state of felicity had been brought about by one questionable horse winning one suspicious race in Birdsville. He'd heard a whisper that a ring-in was being used. After many frantic phone calls – one with me impersonating a vet – a tidy sum was placed on the nose of the nag and it paid handsomely (also for yours truly). As word spread, the odds were dramatically reduced as more and more cash piled up on the suspect filly, alerting the shrewder bookmakers that something was awry. Nevertheless, a win was a win in Joe's book, and this was the start of his new winning streak. (His third in the last six months.)

I nestled myself in my usual spot at the table in the front window, gazing out into the desert. Joe bellowed as he cleaned behind the grill, cigarette dangling from rubbery lips. He shimmied his jellied backside to the song. 'Shoulda herd those knocked-out shail birds sing, less rock. Every body, less rock . . .'

I took a sip of coffee and tried to tune out Radio Aspirin. It was tricky. It was like being at a concert with the Berlin Philharmonic playing the theme from *Neighbours*, completely naked. The singing mercifully stopped. (It was at this point the whole scene became Kafkaesque.) Joe started whistling. He whistled for hours. For his bravura, he whistled 'Love Me Tender' or it could well have been Eric Satie's 'Gymnopedies'.

As usual, I was wrestling with some lyrics. I had almost finished the song, but the last verse was giving me trouble.

Life just seems to pass me by,
as if waiting for a train,
it rushes past the station house,
and hollers out my name.
I wander through the lonely streets,
they're all the same it seems,
they always lead me down to the same old place,
near the bay,
a small café,
called 'Broken Dreams'.

There was a time when I knew love,
a time with no regrets,
a time before I drowned myself,
in coffee and cigarettes,
the hopes I hoped for,
the dreams I dreamed,
are quite funny now it seems,
I never thought I'd end up in this lonely place,
this small café,
this chic palais,
called 'Broken Dreams'.

I looked at it. Where does it go from here? I asked myself. The same place you're going, pal, nowhere, I mouthed to my reflection in the window. I gazed into the middle distance, deep in thought. Mulga dotted the landscape with lavender as the afternoon sun cast blotting shadows across the pebbled red sand. I thought for a while about Barney, and the maudlin account of the breakdown of his marriage. I thought about the rest of the players in the cast of my wandering life. I thought about Julian back in Sin City and his cynical credo of cash. I thought about Chuck. I thought about playing the Blue Note and the Vanguard in New York in the fall and walking through Central Park as the leaves turned to red and gold overhead. However, my thoughts soon drifted to a more familiar province: Jenny. This theme had bordered on the obsessive of late. I couldn't fight it, so I no longer tried. I could see her face, smell her hair, hear the throaty note of her laugh in my mind each night. There was no escape.

Ironically, Jenny had always wanted to visit the outback. I dismissed it saying that if I'd wanted a holiday with flies and yobbos, I'd go to a football match and rub shit in my hair. Peculiar the way life turns out. My goals had changed. Nothing mattered. I hadn't conversed with anyone about anything remotely related to the arts since arriving in this sleepy nook and, quite frankly, felt happier for it. The locals had their own philosophy and their own art. It was called 'survival'. It seemed less pretentious and far more pressing. While it's true that Nietzsche once said that 'only an aesthetic attitude could justify the world', he never had to castrate a sheep with his teeth.

I looked up. It was now evening. The moon flooded the landscape with a viscous silver light. I heard the tortured sound of a dingo baying in the distance. I could see its pointy silhouette on the horizon. It was an unusually gentle evening. The desert wind flirted with the spinifex. And the night air was warm for a change. I spotted Johnny on a small sandhill and gave a gentle wave. He waved back. I was surprised to see him so near the café after Joe had taken a pot shot at him last time he came by this way.

I walked outside. It was unusual that I didn't need a jacket. I'd become so used to the temperature dropping at night that it felt odd. I walked over to the dune where he was standing. Johnny touched my shoulder in greeting. We walked into the desert in silence.

Eventually he spoke in soft whispers, 'Have you had strange dreams?'

'Yes.'

'Me too. We wander through each other's dreaming when the moon is full and the creatures of the desert are still.'

We ambled over a procession of undulating sandhills where he had a campfire burning. It hissed in the darkness. Flames fingered the warm breeze as we sat. Our faces red in the glow of the fire.

'What is it you think you're looking for, Gordon?' he asked.

'I don't know? Answers.'

'First you must find the questions.'

I remained silent. My life suddenly sounded like a giant riddle. I stared into the flames.

'Life is a lot simpler than you think, mate. Like most whitefellas, it's you who make life more complicated than it need be.'

I gazed up at the string bag stuffed with stars that stretched over us. Johnny noticed, looked up and whispered, 'Yes, they all have something to tell you. Each and every one of them. Listen to your heart, Gordon. Listen to it sing when you play your music.'

I sighed. 'I can't play music any more without thinking about it all too intensely. I get stressed. I don't enjoy it. I really need to get to New York, man.'

'Why?'

'To play music.'

A strong gust of wind aroused the flames for a moment. Sparks from the crackling fire shot into the night sky and danced with the stars in a corroboree of fire.

'Your music is not in New York. It's not in London. It's not even in Sydney.'

'Where is it then?'

He touched my chest. 'It's in here, Gordon. Right in here. You don't need to go anywhere to find it. Stop looking for it. And it'll find you.'

I stared into the fire. This sounded even more cryptic.

'See. You've lost the essence of what music is, Gordon.'

'I don't follow.'

'Music is about the heart, mate. Not the head. It's about magic. The fact that these sounds can move you so strongly, that you are willing to give up everything to possess them. That is true magic. Powerful magic. Problem is, you've stopped believing in magic. Lost your sense of wonder.'

I put my hand up in surrender. 'Yes, I don't believe in magic. Like most people, I'm a cynic. I confess.'

The boy smiled and got up and walked over and picked up something from the ground. He came over and handed it to me. I held it to the moonlight. It was a shell – bleached white by the sun over thousands of years.

'Place it against your ear.'

I obliged.

'Can you hear it?'

'Hear what?' I asked, shaking my head.

'The spirit of the sea?'

I chuckled. 'I can hear the acoustic configuration of the shell and the anatomy of my ear canal playing tricks with my senses, if that's what you mean.'

The boy shook his head, 'That's the whitefella's explanation.'

'No, that's science.'

He grinned, his white smile piercing the darkness. 'When you were a little boy, on the beach, didn't your mother tell you that it was the sea?'

I laughed to myself. 'Yes, she did as I remember. It's a long time ago, but yes, she did used to say that.'

The boy's eyes grew wide and shone in the fire like coals. 'That's because there was a time in your life when you believed in magic. A time when the smell of your mother's skin and sound of her voice made you feel safe and warm. A magical time when nothing seemed impossible. A time when every flower had a personality and every tree a name. You see, each little disappointment and failure in life makes us hard and brittle. You become cynical, mate. People stop believing in magic because they're frightened of more disappointment. Then you become negative to other people and their dreams. The cycle continues. You need to start believing in magic again, Gordon.'

I pondered as I poked the fire with a stick, breathing some life into the drowsy flames.

'Do you know why the shell has the spirit of the sea within it?' Johnny asked. 'Because this land was once covered by a great ocean. And the spirit of the sea remains within the shell, because one day the sea will return to this place and the shell knows this because it is its destiny. It waits here for the sea.'

'So what are you saying?'

'I'm saying, what you're looking for is perhaps trying to find you at the same time.'

I sighed. Again, this was a little too enigmatic for me. After a long silence, the softly-spoken youth started to recount a story that his grandfather had told him.

It was the story of a king and a secret tribe, which to this day lives in the tropical clime on the coast of the Arafura Sea. He told me it is beautiful country and that anyone who truly sees it never leaves. It is a magical place. Its shores are lined with casuarina trees. When the ocean breeze stirs their lacy foliage, they make the sound of people whispering. He assured me that if you stand under the trees at midnight you will hear the voices of the Dreamtime telling you the secrets of the earth.

Each day, as they have done for thousands and thousands of years, the men would bravely paddle out in canoes carved from trunks to hunt the torpid green sea turtles. They'd call on the spirits who live in the sea to keep them safe from sharks. On shore, the women would pour a magic elixir made from a local plant into the placid rivers and streams. Then they would simply wait for the plump fish to leap from the tea-coloured waters into their large oval baskets.

I interrupted his story. 'Yes, I've heard about that – a kind of drug that makes the fish jump right out of the water.'

'That's the whitefella's explanation. But the people believe it is the spirit who lives in the plant. The fish jump out of the water because they are frightened of the spirit. Long ago in the Dreamtime, two sisters fought for the love of a young warrior. They grew to hate each other because of their jealousy. One day, one of the sisters saw her reflection in the water and, thinking it was her sister, she tried to kill her and she drowned. The other sister did the same. The spirits of the Dreamtime separated them forever. One became the plant and one became the river fish. That is why the fish jump out of the water when the plant's juices are poured into the river.

'Anyway, this tribe's king was known to be very wise. One day he was lazing in the sun, fishing, when a white man came to the village and asked to see him.

'This man was a big boss fella from far away. He was rich and had fallen in love with the coast straightaway. When the whitefella asked where the king was, he was told by the sea, fishing. The white man mocked: "What kind of king does his own fishing?"

'The whitefella made his way through the shoulder-high grass and the twisting mangroves to the shore. He found the king and sat beside him on the beach. They both stared into the green ocean. He offered the king big money for the land. He wanted to build a place for white people to come and stay for holiday. The king said: "What would I want with your whitefella money?"

'This boss man thought for a while – he was smart, this fella – looked at him fishing, and said: "Because you could buy a big fishing boat."

'"Why would I want a fishing boat when I have a canoe?"'
'"So you could catch more fish."'
'"What would I want with more fish? I can only eat so many."'
'The white man thought for a while and said: "I could help you sell the fish and you could make lots of money."'
'"What would I want with lots of money?" he asked as he baited his fish-bone hook.'
'"You could buy more boats and pay people to catch fish for you."'
'"What for?" the king laughed.'
'"To become a rich man, of course!"'
'"Why would I want to become a rich man?" the king asked the white boss as he cast his line into the silent sea.'
'"Then you'd never have to worry about money! You'd be so rich you could sit on the beach and go fishing all day!"'
'He simply laughed at the white man and said: "You worry about money, I'll worry about fish."'
'The white man smiled, looked out over the sea and quietly nodded. He realised he was a fool. The king never saw him again.'

Gordon nodded. 'I see your point.'

The boy got up and threw sand on the fire and said: 'Gordon, you need to find the feather of the black cockatoo.'

'What . . . why?'

'When you find it, all will become clear to you. You will learn the meaning of life.'

'Um . . . I don't get it . . .'

'Mate, someone is coming. I must go. Be careful not to tell people you have been speaking to me. They'll follow you to try and kill me.'

I was too embarrassed to tell him that I had already told a few people – well, more than a few, actually – and that by now most of the town knew that I met with the Spook regularly. The boy disappeared into the desert like a lizard. As I neared the café, a shadowy figure lurched towards me.

'I was just about to send out bluddy search party for you, my fren. Where you bin?' Joe asked in the moonlight.

'Oh, just over there talking to –' I remembered the boy's entreaty. He looked up. 'Nice night.'

'Very.'

We both walked inside the café as a chorus of crickets started their vocal exercises for the evening. I sat on a stool at the counter. Joe sat across from me on the other side, surreptitiously picking his nose. You know the way people try to make it look as if they are only scratching it. We all know what's going on but everyone's too polite to say anything.

I nodded to his nose. 'You looking for opals up there, Joe?'

'Just scratching it, my fren.'

'Oh.'

'Why you talk to that stupid kid?'

'He's not so stupid, you know.'

'What does he bluddy know, this kid? Live in bluddy desert like a scungy dog,' he said, furtively wiping a seed of snot onto his trousers.

'You'd be surprised. He has an interesting perspective on things.'

'Yeah?'

'A kind of a no-frills philosophy on life, I guess . . . I don't know, I'm still trying to work him out.'

Joe lit a cigarette and some toffee-coloured smoke weaved through a forest of nostril hair.

We talked about our dreams and our lives till the wee hours.

◠

Joe staggered out of bed the next morning. He nursed a heavy head. He lethargically picked up the empty beer bottles and overflowing ashtrays before cleaning up with a sour-smelling rag. He was thinking about his family. About the old country. He thought about his old pals. He thought about the times they used to spend together as wild youths. Driving a stolen car through the hives of white villages to the stony beaches. Floating on their backs in the Dead Sea. Tasting the salt on their lips. Drifting for hours, weightless, in the thick water and talking about their dreams. Their hopes. Their fears. They were a close bunch. Closer than any brothers could be. He wondered where they were now.

Joe played a couple of records on the jukebox before hearing a car growl to a halt in the gravel outside. The screen door chirped open. His jowly jaw dropped to the floor.

'Excuse me. I'm looking for someone. His name is Gordon Shoesmith.'

PART THREE

THE DILEMMA IN HIGH HEELS

'CHRIST, IT'S YOU!' I rubbed bran-like sleep out of my eyes.

Jenny stood uncertain in the doorway.

'Hello,' she said nervously.

I felt a pang in my heart, but put on a brave face. I nonchalantly walked off to the sink.

She walked in and looked around, her pantyhose crackling with static. 'So this has been home for the last twelve months.' She looked very dressed up for the desert. Dressing up for a woman in the desert usually meant changing from shorts and thongs to trackie daks and dress-thongs.

'Yeah. I'm still waiting for the decorators to come in. I'm not sure, I'm thinking marble. What do you think?'

A smile grew on her full lips. They glistened with sweat. I could always make her laugh – even when she didn't want to. It must have been strange seeing me so fit. I usually resembled a corpse with a faint pulse. I don't think she was quite ready for the suntan and muscles. It turned her on. (I could always tell.)

Jenny had put on a couple of pounds – as had I. She was dressed in a clingy silk blouse and tight mini which made her hips and breasts look a little fuller than I'd remembered. It turned me on – which wasn't difficult. I was so sexually deprived at that stage that if someone uttered the word "pumpkin" it was likely to induce an instant orgasm. She leaned over to study something on the mantle which presented me with a view of her fullish backside. She dropped a postcard and picked it up (perhaps on purpose). I saw a flash of white panties. (What is it with guys and the proverbial flash of knickers? I mean, you can go to Bondi and gawk at the most beautiful women in the world wearing nothing but a G-string, zinc cream and a sneer, and think nothing of it, but one stolen peek at the cleaning lady's bloomers and it sends the heart racing. Men. We're pathetic.)

Anyway, what can I tell you except that I got the kind of hard-on that only a man living alone in the desert with a sweaty Arab in a satin jumpsuit could possibly get. I awkwardly covered my pyjamas. She noticed. This was not how I had imagined our reunion would pan out. I would be in a tuxedo at a celebrity cocktail party with a supermodel on my arm, just about to jet off to New York again to play at the Lincoln Centre. My bodyguard would be threatening some poor little paparazzo in the corner. This was not how I wanted to meet her: in a pair of striped pyjamas trying to hide my todger.

My erection grew by the minute. It was like slowly raising the Union Jack at an IRA meeting and being unable to stop it. I stood slightly buckled over, yet trying to look cool. This was difficult. She smiled at my swelling crotch through fat lashes.

'Nice to see your wife can still do it for you.' The mini-skirt, clingy blouse and heels strategy had not been in vain.

'Oh, you've never been a slouch in that department, Mrs Shoesmith.' (She hated being called 'Mrs Shoesmith'. It was a Pyrrhic victory.)

She pulled back a piece of rogue hair from her face that had slipped from behind her ear. An affectation I'd always been enamoured with. She smiled. She sat down on a rickety chair opposite me and crossed her shapely legs. She caught me sneaking a look up her mini. (Sorry, I couldn't help it.)

'How the hell did you find me?' I finally asked, thinking about Margaret Thatcher in a wet T-shirt coyly licking a lollipop – it wasn't working.

'Your credit card.' She wiped some sweat from her long neck. She balanced her sling-back provocatively on the end of her toe – a gesture that told me she felt in control. 'It's hot,' she said, unfastening the top button of her blouse, exposing an ample cleavage. I spotted the black lace seam of her bra beneath her blouse. She leaned, exposing a little more. (The cow!)

'Welcome to the desert,' I said coolly. I wanted her badly.

'Thanks.' She uncrossed her legs. My eyes flashed. Damn!

'Have you come to ask for a divorce?' I said, steam coming from my ears.

She shook her head. 'Shut up, you fool,' she said quietly. Her breathing was getting heavy. I remembered that there was no turning back when her breathing was like that. It was like trying to stop the engine of the *Queen Mary*.

She got up and walked slowly over to me – it took about a week – and shot her hand down the opening of my pyjama pants. I could feel the granite smoothness of her manicured nails. She kissed me, darting her tongue in around my palate and teeth.

Not wanting to bring things to an early finish, she slowly stood up and carefully stepped out of her mini. This took about a month. She peeled off her shiny pantyhose. A nylon membrane floated to the floor. Her legs glistened with beads of sweat. I sat motionless on the edge of the bed, my heart pounding like a wild horse. She stood in front of me and unbuttoned her blouse. This took about a year. Each button revealed more and more cleavage bursting out of her black lacy bra. She remained silent. Her breath heavy. She moved closer to me and slowly removed her panties. This took a decade. She stood with her pubic hair in my face. My nostrils were filled with the briny smell of her arousal.

However, I was a man of principles. I was still angry with her.

Hurt. I tried to talk. This was difficult with my face where it was. Nevertheless, I told her that I was stronger now than I have ever been and that we'd never be together again and that I had not forgiven her, but it came out something like: Oh, God, this is good! Yes, yes, yes! Don't stop!

She straddled me and rocked from side to side, throwing her head back and screaming in ecstasy. I reciprocated in a lower key with complementary bass notes. Our faces transfigured with pleasure. (I'd been twanging the old one-string bass for so long I'd forgotten how good the real thing was!)

She rubbed her dark nipples and pumped violently. She was like a piston. That was all it took for the party to come to an end. My eyes spun back in my head like a slot machine and I exploded.

Although the initial performance was short-lived, I was like a stick of Brighton Rock that day and we made love for hours and hours in the sweltering heat. We didn't say a word to each other the whole time.

⌢

Sunlight writhed through the windows and painted our shiny bodies in autumn colours. I felt Jenny's sweaty buttocks against my thigh as she slept. She woke and stretched like a tabby. I looked at her body that was shiny from sweat.

'You look good,' I said.

'Yeah, put on a couple of pounds, though.'

'I hadn't noticed.'

'Liar.'

I smiled. I looked down at my flaccid penis. It was now in need of a hundred-k service. 'That was good. It's been a while.'

'Me too.'

I shot a quizzical look at her. 'What about lover boy? Finius Hornbag?' (I had worked six months on that one. Quite proud of it.)

'There *is* no lover boy, Gordon,' she replied dryly.

'Well, who was it with his tongue down your throat in the Dugout Bar? The Archbishop of Canterbury?'

'I asked Finius that day to meet me for an interview. He saw you walk in and he suddenly kissed me.'

'What? Well, I didn't see you exactly hitting him over the head with your brolly.'

'He caught me off guard.' She looked away.

'Right.'

'Okay, I liked it. I was flattered. I was depressed. I was . . . I don't know . . . confused. For one stupid moment, I was confused. Have you ever been confused?'

'Constantly. But I'm not playing tonsil hockey with a nineteen-year-old air hostess.'

(Why do guys always talk about air hostesses like they are supermodels? Granted, in the 1960s the stewardess was the zenith of glamour, but, I mean, have you flown lately?)

She ran her hands through her raven hair. 'I'm sorry. It was a weak moment. He just did it to get to you. He's obsessed with you.'

'Me?'

'Has all your CDs.'

'What *are* you talking about?'

'Said you were the biggest influence on his career. The reason he started singing. It was all in the interview. It was more an article about you in the end.'

'Well, how do you like that,' I mumbled.

'That's why I wanted to do the story on him. To help position you.'

'Just tell me this, Jenny. Did you sleep with him?'

'No, I didn't fuck him,' she said through gritted teeth. 'Like I told you, I just flirted with him.'

I remained silent.

'Gordon, I do the same with leads all the time. Some managing director I need to interview. It's the good old high heels, lipstick, miniskirt, let him think he's got a chance – never fails. Two martinis and I've milked him like a big cow.'

I remained silent.

'Oh, don't look so fucking sanctimonious, Gordon. Remember that time you were at the agency Christmas party and that client made that comment about the "Abos deserving everything they got". I saw you look down into your glass and say nothing. Nothing! I remember a time when you would have told the guy that if he kept it up, he'd go blind.'

I rubbed my eyes. (A Freudian slip?)

'So don't come all Father Virtue with me,' she said. 'Now you know. I sometimes use . . .' She gestured to herself like a quiz-show model . . . '"The Package", to get the edge over my male colleagues who play Rugby and golf and sail with their contacts. And you know what? I shouldn't fucking have to.'

'Fair enough.'

Her exquisite shoulders that could have been the inspiration for Botticelli's Venus dropped. 'Sorry Gordon. I've never really told you how it works. But now you know. So does that change things?'

'It wasn't just you and Finius. Sure, that was the icing on the cake, but it was a lot of things that made me leave. But I think you know that.'

'Yes. Julian called me the following day and explained the whole thing. Can you believe he's left advertising?'

'You're kidding?'

'No, he's a full-time painter now. I went to his new show. It's a sell-out.'

'Wow! Hey, have you heard from Brian?'

'Yes, he's dying to get in touch with you. He's become a producer. He's produced the new Monkey Dog album.'

I shrugged.

'Oh, you wouldn't have heard of them. Now he's got all these kids wanting him to produce their records. He's even opened his own studio. He's really happy, Gordon.'

'Did you know Chuck died?'

She looked shocked. 'No. There wasn't anything in the papers.' She lay next to me and held me.

'Does that surprise you? Your people are more interested in writing stories about the Queen Mother's bunion operation than the death of an Australian jazz icon.' I suddenly sounded like an art student.

'Not all of us,' she said, kissing my brown chest.

'No, not all of you,' I agreed.

We lay in each other's arms in silence as the desert wind whistled quietly outside.

⌢

I woke up and untangled myself from her soft arms. I leant over to smell her skin. I remembered that smell. It was the smell of an angel's breath. I made some coffee and I sat on a chair and watched her. I remembered how much I used to enjoy watching her sleep. Watching her eyes dart capriciously beneath her pale lids. Watching the sheet swell with the motion of her breath. She was always so determined. But when she slept, she looked vulnerable. Soft. Like a little girl. The desert was such a hard place. Things of softness were anathema to it.

I threw some pants on and a singlet and walked outside into the cherry-stained twilight. I meditated on the situation. What did she want me to do? Return with her. I hummed 'Embraceable You' as I frisbeed warm gibbers into the distance. She appeared in the doorway, fully dressed. Her hair was dishevelled and the mascara inky on her white face, yet she looked beautiful. Her green eyes lilac in the red light. She had quickly gathered her things, stuffing her pantyhose in her handbag. One of the legs poked out and dangled like a cobweb.

'You could always win me over with Gershwin,' she smiled.

A black parrot glided overhead. We watched its shadow peel across a nearby dune.

'Are you coming with me?' she asked.

I shook my head. 'No,' I said quietly. 'I'm on my way to New York.'

'Most people go via Hawaii.'

'Will you come with me?'

'You know the answer to that one already.' She dropped her bag. 'I love you Gordon, but I won't wait by the fire for you like some character out of a fucking Brontë novel. I'll eventually meet someone and get on with my life.'

Then she did something unexpected. She started crying. I realised, in the whole time I'd known her, I'd never seen her cry. She was always so tough. So guarded. Her shoulders shook as she sobbed noiselessly.

'Please don't cry, Jen,' I said quietly.

We stood in the twilight for a while in silence. 'What are you looking for, Gordon?' she finally sniffed.

I shrugged, 'Answers.'

'When you find them, give me a call, eh?' she said in an unsteady voice.

She placed her tear-soaked lips on mine before walking back to her car at the café.

THE QUEEN OF QUEENS

A DEAFENING SILENCE hung over the desert as she tramped across the red earth and up and over the undulating dunes towards the café – its outline blurred and softened in the searing morning heat. This land certainly was, as they say, 'The Dead Heart'.

Drought had left the landscape with a blowtorch finish. The sun-bleached bones of dead animals littered the parched earth like shipwrecked china. Further south, no grass and little scrub had left the sheep mostly dead or diseased. Aside from the oasis, no wildflowers had grown for over a decade. It was bleak to say the least.

The day was a scorcher – over 50 degrees in the shade (if you could find any) – and as she made notes of her findings, the lead in her pencil bled across the page.

There wasn't even a whisper of a breeze that day. It was funny how the wind suggested life. Perhaps because it originated from another place and brought with it the seed of somewhere else.

The stillness of that day made the whole atmosphere seem even more desolate in its eerie silence. It was like wandering through the belly of a giant dessicated corpse, she thought. If this land is the Dead Heart, then the marrow of life must be water. The sea that had been here millennia before had deserted this land – given up on it. Abandoned it like a bastard child. I wonder if it knows something, she thought.

She kicked the dry red sand with her new R.M. Williams boots. The sun shining off their polished surface like beacons.

'Gawd, this heat is unbearable,' she said out loud, breaking the long quiet.

She touched her flesh. It felt like leather. Humans are supposed to be over seventy per cent water. Perhaps it's the water in us that is our soul. Not the heart. Not the mind. But the water. Water. Water. Water . . . She felt dizzy and collapsed onto the hot earth.

⌢

I walked out into the blanket of hot air. Even though it had been a week since she left, I could still smell Jenny on my skin. It smelt wonderful. I recreated that moment in my mind over and over again. Her smiling face in the doorway. Her soft lips on my neck. Should I have gone with her? I had asked myself a thousand times since she'd left. But I *had* to get to New York. I had planned it every day for the last twelve months. I had enough money to stay for at least six months. Yet in a strange way, I felt that my time in the desert was not yet complete. It was as if the desert still had something pressing to say to me. Something I needed to find out in order to continue my journey.

Squinting at the fat sun, and swatting flies nineteen to the dozen, I saw a body on the ground. I bolted over. It was a woman. She was wearing a khaki shirt and shorts. I removed a bright lemon scarf from around her sunburnt neck. She was still breathing. I picked her up in my arms and ran in stumbling steps to the café. She was tiny – perhaps just over five feet – so was quite light. But nevertheless it was tiring carrying her in the heat.

Fumbling for the keys, I let myself in (Joe was out to it with a hangover as usual). I put her down on the floor and placed a cushion under her head. I pulled the blinds. Shafts of sunlight raced to find a seat. I checked her breathing again. She came around and, in her delirium, mumbled something about her case. I promised I would go back for it in the way you tell people that you will become Barbara Cartland in fishnets for the evening if they will stop vomiting in your car. I put a glass of water to her parched lips. It spilt down her blouse. She looked up at me and mentioned her case, again. I told her I'd run back and grab it if she'd try and drink the water. She nodded. I ran back to find her case. It took me a while. Her Range Rover was hidden behind a sandhill. I returned to find her sitting up at the counter, as Joe crooned 'Love Me Tender' in his 1970s Elvis-style sunglasses, soiled white singlet and boxer shorts. She was laughing at him and clapping as she sipped a cup of coffee. She had a lovely smile. I waited for 'The King' to finish the performance.

'Gordon, meet . . . what was your name again, darling?'

'Ruth,' she said.

'Ruth,' Joe said.

'I see you're alive, then,' I said in panting breaths. 'What happened out there?'

She looked up at me with dark eyes, 'I must have fainted'. She had a thick New York accent. 'Thanks for bringing me here, mayte.' (She pronounced 'mate' the way Americans do when conversing with antipodeans, under the misapprehension that they are being charming.)

'Gordon, Ruth is our guest for awhile. I'm putting her up. She's looking for dirt.'

I screwed up my face, 'Dirt?'

She chuckled, 'Oh my Gawd, Joe. I've been sent here to conduct some tests on the soyal, that's all.'

'Why?'

'A multinational oyal conglomerate is looking into exploring the whole region.'

'But what about the traditional owners – or . . . well . . . owner?' I said.

'I'm told they're negotiating with the natives at the moment.'

(The natives?)

'Gordon, Ruth grew up in Gaza. Can you believe it?' Joe yelled, doing the getting-into-trousers-quickly-dance out back.

'But have you found any minerals out there?' I asked, pouring myself a coffee.

Her tiny hands put down her coffee cup. 'Yes, it looks very promising. I can't understand why it hasn't been explored already.'

'I think they've sent people out here before but they have been scared off.'

'Well, sweetheart, with the money my company is paying me, I won't be scared off by any "Spook".'

'Oh, they've told you about him, then.'

She crossed her tanned legs. 'Joe told me, honey. It takes more than a kid with a spear to frighten this girl. I like a fight. That's probably why they sent me.'

She rubbed her tiny sunburned fingers through her short, spiky, dark brown hair while she peered at Joe getting dressed in the back room. Suddenly her eyes flashed as though she had seen a baseball-sized gold nugget. Joe entered, fastening his belt. Hairy gut drooping over his pants.

'More coffee, my sweet?' Joe asked.

'Why thank you, darling,' I replied.

'Not you. Ruth,' Joe grinned.

'I won't say no,' she laughed, swatting a nagging fly.

'I see you've learnt the Barcoo salute,' I said.

'What's that?' she said, swinging again at the fly.

'That's it. You just did it.'

'You get used to flies around here, Ruth,' added Joe.

'The rain will kill them orf,' she said.

We both roared with laughter.

'It hasn't rained for years, Ruth,' Joe said.

She looked askance at Joe, sipping her coffee. 'Do you know much about meteorology?'

'Yes. I know a lot about it,' he said. Ruth seemed impressed. 'I'm a Virgo who likes creature comforts, crossword puzzles and short brunettes,' he added.

'Hey, you're a hoot, Joey, you know that?' she said with a flirtatious smile.

Joe beamed.

'Long-range forecasting is taken more seriously these days, although people still dismiss it,' she said. 'These forecasters are able to predict the weather years in advance. Sometimes fifty years in advance. Particularly in arid zones such as this one.'

'Are you trying to tell me that it might rain here?' I instantly thought of Barney.

'You betcha. If our calculations are right, rain shouldn't be too far away, that's why I'm here now. Before it happens.'

'Man, I know a couple of people around here that would run up and kiss you on the lips if you told them that.'

'Line em up, honey. Do you know how long it's been? Gawd, being single and over fowrty in Noo Yawrk you've got more chance of meeting the Dali Lama at McDonalds.'

'Really?' Joe said, rubbing the stubble on his chin.

'Oh, sweetheart, my vibrator's got friction marks.'

Joe and I where stunned, then exploded with nervous laughter.

'As you can imagine, long-range forecasting is not an exact science . . . but . . . it looks like it will certainly rain sometime soon,' she added.

'That's fantastic.' I couldn't wait to tell Barney – who'd become quite a chum of late.

'By the way, you don't know a man called Quales do you?'

'No,' I said.

'Oh.'

I turned to the diminutive geologist. 'You don't mean Squales, by any chance?'

'Yeah, the schmuck! He was supposed to meet me out in the desert.'

'Sure. What do you want with him?' I asked, pouring some more coffee.

'I may need to freight some samples back to the city.'

'Yeah? Well, just follow the first road that turns off the highway and you'll find him at the post office . . . or the pub. Actually, try the pub first,' I said, throwing some sugar into the cup.

'Okay!' she smiled. 'By the way, there's a rail line somewhere out here. Do you know where, sweetie?'

'Yes, you could say that,' I said. 'It's just over those dunes. In the direction I was coming from when I found you.'

'Fabulous. Now, where can a girl get a drink around here?' she asked as the coffee percolator sputtered away like a mezzosoprano gargling motor oil. 'This cawfee tastes like crap, Joey.'

'I'll take you, Ruth.' Joe put on a new shirt like a schoolboy getting dressed for the big dance.

Joe and Ruth drove off in a plume of red dust for The Globe. I sat down and meditated on what the curious geologist had told me. Had Johnny Wishbone actually sold the land? It seemed incredible.

The trek back to the station house was endless in the steady midday heat. I paused briefly there to top up the canteen, and then pushed on to the oasis. I wasn't even sure if Johnny would be there – it had been a couple of weeks since we'd last met.

As I traced the rusting track to the desert garden, I spotted a feral camel struggling up a sloppy dune. It looked like a novice on a pair of skis trying to reach the beginners' slope. Strange, I thought. You'd think that after thousands of years of genetic refinement the camel would appear more graceful in its natural habitat than a marionette on heroin. I took a sloppy swig from the canteen and laughed at the maladroit creature in the blurring haze.

I saw the garden in the distance. The heat rose from the desert floor, turning the garden into a carnival of colour. Clambering up the sandhill, I sat amongst the flowers, breathing in the heady aroma made sharper by the heat. Their perfumes hung in the dry air like competing cosmetic counters in a department store. I leaned over to smell a crimson specimen, its shrill fragrance tingling my nostrils. I motioned to pick the exotic Sturt's desert pea. It was beautiful, with its scarlet and black bulbous lips.

'When you remove a spirit from its place of dreaming, you must replace it with another,' a soft voice whispered behind me.

'Jesus! You've got to stop doing that.'

'Doing what?'

'Scaring the shit out of me by creeping out of nowhere.'

He placed his long black hands in his pockets and smiled. 'Walk softly and carry a big stick, they reckon, mate?'

I laughed.

We looked out into the desert. A black streaky cloud stretched along the horizon. It was as if someone had lazily dragged a piece of charcoal across the sky. A slight breeze drifted across the landscape. It felt cool against my sunburned face. The wild flowers embraced it, too, swaying in a collective, graceful movement. Johnny's hair ruffled. It was almost as if he had brought the breeze with him.

'Something's on your mind,' he said.

I nodded, 'There is'.

'What is it?'

'Many things, mostly of the female kind, but firstly tell me this, are you selling the mining rights to this land?'

He screamed with laughter. 'Who told you that?'

'Are you?'

'Not in 20000 years.'

I chuckled. We sat for a while in silence. Feeling the breeze tickle our lashes.

'How old were you when you started playing music?' he asked.

'I don't know. Seven or eight, I guess.'

'Why did you want to play music? Can you remember?'

I thought for a while. That was the good thing about outback people, they're never afraid to let the conversation breathe – to let you think about your answers. In the city, if you haven't answered somebody in one nano-second, they are offering you ginkgo tablets.

'Like I told you, my parents died when I was young and I was brought up by my aunt and uncle. My uncle's passion was music. He used to listen to jazz records, particularly piano players. I guess, that's when I first heard the music.'

'Jazz music?'

'Yeah.'

'This must have meaning in your life beyond what is the obvious.'

'Again, I don't follow.'

'Did this represent something more to you?'

I thought and shook my head.

'Think,' he whispered.

'Well, I don't know ... my uncle used to listen to these jazz records late at night. My aunt would hate the records. Never understood the music. But my uncle would listen to them for hours and hours. He would invite me to listen with him. Listen for things he told me were buried deep within the music. Inner voicings. Counter melodies. Rhythms. Beats. When we listened to the music, I don't know, it was as if we were sharing something. A secret language that was ours. The language of music. Of jazz, I suppose.'

Johnny listened to me with the intensity of a safe-cracker.

'My uncle was very taciturn when I was a kid. A good provider and all that, but a closed book emotionally. He never really made an effort to find out what was lingering inside my heart. I don't know ... perhaps he was scared of what he'd find. With all the dramas and fights with my sister and me and then I was always running away from home. You see, his father walked out on him when he was very young, so he didn't have much of a role model – again, emotionally speaking. I think he just felt his responsibility ended with putting food on the table and taking me to cricket on the weekends. I guess music was a kind of magic we could use to look into each other's hearts at a safe distance. A kind of spiritual telescope, if you like.'

'It's the language of your dreaming, Gordon.'
'How?'
'You try to tap the soul through sound, that is your way.'
'Like soul mining?'
'If you like.'
'What about you? Do you remember much about your family?' I asked.

The boy squinted at the sun. 'No.'

'What can you remember?' I asked.

'Like you, I never knew my *real* parents. The police came out of the blue one day and took me away from my family when I was three years old. I grew up in a middle-class home trying to scrub the black off my face every night. They said my name was Toby Palmer. They were professional hippies, my foster parents. She was a lawyer. He was a surgeon. They sent me to the best schools and bought me nice clothes. I wanted for nothing. But I never saw them. They were always working. I suppose they had good intentions. They were kind people. They were full of ideals and left-wing theories. And they were extremely wealthy. They had everything . . . except children. You see, she couldn't have children, so they thought they'd buy one.

'I'd heard them fighting one night on my tenth birthday. I was lying in bed when I heard him scream at her: "You wanted the little black bastard, you handle it."'

'How old were you when you decided to come home, Johnny?'

'Well, I started to have these dreams when I was about fourteen.'

'Dreams?'

'Yeah. In these dreams, my grandfather was calling me from the desert. I told my foster mother about them. She said I needed to see someone to help me interpret these dreams. So she sent me to a friend who was a Jungian analyst. So I meet this shrink and he asks me: "What is this person saying to you in your dream?"

'I said that he was just calling: "Johnny Wishbone, Johnny

Wishbone, come home. Come home."

'My foster mother went pale. She turned to the doctor with a shocked look on her face: "That's his tribal name. There is no way he could have known that."

'She never stood in my way after that. She knew one day I would return to the desert. Eventually I drifted back to my people. My grandfather was the only one left. He's dead now.'

'Are you glad you returned? Was the dream realised?'

'Yes and no.'

'So why are some dreams realised and others not? Why are some visions right and others wrong?' I asked.

The boy thought a while before he spoke in soft undertones, 'Some people don't read the omens.'

'What do you mean? What omens?'

He was pensive, then said, 'As you walk this way, along the track, have you ever noticed an old ruin in the distance?'

'Yes, I have as a matter of fact.'

'Today, on your return, visit this building.'

'Okay. But what about you? Have you read any omens lately?'

'Yes and they are all bad, mate. Very bad. I must go.' And with a gentle wave, he got up and walked into the desert. I sat amongst the flowers for a while, meditating on what he had said. What would an omen look like if I saw one? I lay in the flowers, staring into the pink sky.

I noticed the sun begin to belly over the dunes. I stumbled down the sandhill and walked back towards the station house. About ten minutes later I spotted the dilapidated sandstone cottage in the distance. I'd seen it before but thought little of it. I trekked across the warm sand and stood before it.

The roof had rotted away from its orbiting verandah. With the strawberry afternoon sun pitched against it, a scaffold of shadows crawled across its crumbling walls. The rotting doorframe crumbled in my fingers as I entered sheepishly. It was an eerie feeling. The cottage floor was a beach of red sand that had elbowed its way inside over the years of exile. Yawning holes in the roof allowed the rich, dusky sunlight to stream in. As I looked around, thick clouds of dust hung in the air with each infringing step. I could hear the wind whistling through the rooms. It made a queer sound – like a child whimpering.

Discarded essentials of nineteenth-century isolation littered the floor. Steel knitting needles, cups without handles, a copper clothespeg, Victorian medicine bottles, cutlery, and rusting tins of bully beef were castaways, half-buried in the sand. I picked up a couple of the green medicine bottles. Some of the remedies made outrageous claims. One offered a cure from just about anything from tuberculosis to typhoid. These were the halcyon days of the snake-oil salesman, when gullible settlers were prepared to believe in anything that had a fancy label stuck to it and tasted like shit. I tossed the miracle cures onto the floor – they pifft in the sand as they fell. I noticed a crumbling, leather-bound book poking out of a small dune. I picked it up and flicked through the browning pages that almost crumbled in my fingers. The ledger was full of florid figures in pale brown ink. It was dated 1910. As I laconically flicked through the brittle pages, it dawned on me that I was reading the final, desperate account book of the previous occupant. Creditors were underlined and frantically crossed out – some with frenzied scribbled notes and tiny question or exclamation marks pitted beside the names.

One creditor by the name of Joshua Smith, simply had the word 'How?' scrawled beside it. Another creditor, Samuel Bates, appeared frequently with larger sums cascading down the columns. The final page seemed to be the most despairing. The handwriting was very erratic, with crazed figures and sums scribbled in the tiny columns to the side, names of creditors double-underlined, with frenzied circles around their names.

I put the ledger down and spotted the tip of another book in the sand. It was a sinister dark green book with a picture of a camel embossed on the front. The inside cover read: '*Campbell's Soil Culture Manual: A complete guide to scientific agriculture as adapted to the semi-arid regions.*'

I slowly thumbed the dog-eared pages and read some underlined passages. I couldn't help thinking that it looked like a prayer book (which was ironic because it was probably more of a prayer book than a genuine agricultural guide). One passage read:

ADVANTAGES OF THE SEMI-ARID REGION
Don't apologise for being a farmer of the semi-arid region. It is not advisable to be boastful beyond that which is easily demonstrated; but at least do not feel that in conducting the business of agriculture in the region where rainfall is small that you are defying nature. It is true that you may be defying the traditions of the past and doing violence to the old accepted theories on agriculture, but you need not concern yourself about these things.

Don't belittle your own state and your farm by bewailing the fact that the rain does not fall as often there as it did on the farm where you spent your boyhood days. There were seemingly some advantages in having rainstorms so often and so great that the waste of serious water was not seriously felt. It may be a nice thing to have more water than you know what to do with. But even this has its drawbacks. Perhaps it is better on the whole not to have so much water. Let us see.

I skipped through the pages and read one of the countless testimonials from the chapter entitled: 'WORLDWIDE FAME OF THIS BOOK'.

Mr Campbell, without irrigation, can make crops grow on hundreds of thousands of square miles of 'desert' that otherwise would be fruitless and flowerless except for the wild growths, sparse and unprofitable, indigenous to such land and climate. In the natural habitat of the cactus, he grows wheat, corn and vegetables. 'Dry farming' has become a phrase of hope.

I tossed the book to the floor. It disappeared into a cloud of dust. I walked into the bedroom. This darkened chamber was empty, except for a crude, handmade desk beneath a window. I stood next to it and looked out over the desolate landscape. A small screwed-up piece of paper on the floor beneath the desk caught my eye. I picked it up, ironed the creases out on the desk and blew away grains of paprika-like sand.

It was a letter dated 14 November 1910. It was addressed to a Mary Blake of Sussex, England. I felt a lump in my throat, as I read the copperplate handwriting that scrolled across the wrinkled page.

Dearest Mary,
I was so delighted to receive another of your letters. I'm sorry I haven't written sooner but we have been terribly busy. I hope this letter finds you well and with Providence smiling upon you.

Things are well for us. We were fortunate to buy this land so inexpensively. Mac is convalescing well and the doctor says he should recover. Tuberculosis is very common in this region but you know my husband, he is a hardy soul.

The homestead is beautiful and the flowers are blooming. I've grown some vegetables and the garden has been a great solace to me. By the way, thank you for the money you sent. It was a relief to receive it and we will endeavour to repay your kindness as soon as it is humanly possible. Mac doesn't know of your generous loan and I would prefer it to stay as such. As you know, Mac is a proud man and would gravely disapprove of your benevolence. Even though it is merely for the short term.

Mary, please don't fret for us. We have moved from wheat to sheep farming. As you know, the price of wool is high at the moment and sheep are legion among the colonies.

In your letters you keep asking me to describe the area and the surrounding countryside. I'm sorry that I have not done so in previous correspondence, dear.

Well, I suppose you'd say the countryside's a lot like our Sussex. With the gentle rolling hills and lush green valleys. At times you feel as though you've never left England. Mary, you would think you are still in Edenbridge. Lovely tranquil ponds surround the homestead and the natives, who are warm and friendly, swim gaily in them during warmer periods of the day. The fields are green and rich and the many sheep we own are fat and healthy. The rivers are–

The letter stopped abruptly. I gazed slowly out the window. The sunset quietly painted the sandhills in magenta and crimson. The bleached skeleton of what looked like a sheep lay prostrate beneath the wine-coloured sky. The desiccated landscape seemed to speak at that moment. But it whispered in raspy undertones. Like a man who had been without water since the dawn of time. A parched and ancient voice that only spoke to those who cared to listen. Was the omen for all of us the desert itself?

I placed the letter neatly on the desk, but a gust of wind snatched it and I watched it flap off into the desert.

⌒

I wandered back to the café later that evening. As I approached I saw Ruth bowed and peering out at the stars. She seemed to notice me and smiled. I waved. She was opening her mouth and pulling silly faces at me. I pulled silly faces back. Elvis's 'I'm All Shook Up' was blaring from the café. As I walked in, I noticed a flotsam of empty whisky bottles and beer cans. I looked over to see Ruth with her panties around her ankles, hands pressed against the glass. Joe was straddling her from behind. When I say from behind, he could well have been in Adelaide as his todger was enormous. I'd never seen one so large. Obviously, either had Ruth. You could have hung the entire team jerseys of the Brisbane Broncos on it and still had room for the socks. Never having stolen a glance at his attenuated pudenda (not even at the urinal – for me its like golf: concentrate on the grip and keep the head down), I now knew how Joe leaned over and cleaned behind the grill without falling over.

Ruth squealed like a saxophone. Her mouth was transfigured from an oval to a wide arc. Her ears lifted so much with her smile that they almost met at the top of her cropped head. Joe, greedily peeling off her dress like a banana, didn't see me walk in, so I walked straight out again – red-faced. She watched me walk away and across the highway. I looked over my shoulder to see her breasts, two pancakes against the window. She stared at me, smiling as the glass fogged with her hot breath.

THE TOWN OF SAND

I LOOKED AROUND the cramped caravan. It had that popcorn smell of dirty laundry and stale sheets. On a wall above the good reverend's brass bed, pictures of the Virgin Mary and various saints were squeezed between 'full-figured' centrefolds. I crouched on a stool as the parson shaved with a long, sardine-like razor. The wind was howling outside and throttling the mobile home at random intervals, making shaving perilous for the beetroot-cheeked preacher.

'I'm glad you popped in to see me, Gordon. About time we had a little chat,' he said, in a current of paint-stripper breath.

The clergyman, quite lucid at that time in the morning, walked over to me with a towel draped around his blood-speckled neck. 'I'm guessing I haven't seen you at church lately, Gordon. Am I right?'

I nodded. (As I had never been to the church, this was a fair guess.)

He patted his foam-mottled face. 'Still looking for the meaning of life?'

'You could say that.'

'Let's face it. What you're looking for is Christianity.'

'Is that right?' The wind blew a grey sheet of newspaper against the window. The headline ran: 'Kylie's new love.'

'Tea?' the minister smiled.

As he made a pot of tea the holy man gathered his thoughts.

I spotted a cardboard sign. It read: 'St Jude's Rectory.'

'Who was St Jude, anyway?' I asked, making conversation.

'The patron Saint of Lost Causes. Saint of the Hopeless.'

I looked at the pub through the dirt-speckled window: a pointillist painting in mud, Pissarro in thongs. 'How appropriate,' I mumbled.

'You don't believe in God, do you Gordon?'

'I don't know. Do I believe in someone with a long beard and a caftan, with a glass of shiraz, leaning over a cloud watching my every move? No. I'm not that fascinating.'

'You're wrong. God is watching you, always.'

'Who are you, his agent?'

'The Bible tells us he's watching.'

'Even when *Life of Brian* is on cable?'

The reverend smiled and warmed the pot with hot water.

'He must be very tall,' I said.

'Who?'

'God.'

'Yes, I suppose he must be.'

'I mean, it must be tricky to have a conversation with him. Perhaps you have to use a can-and-string telephone to speak with him.'

The vicar gave a frowning smile.

'Seriously. What makes your religion so right and . . . say . . . the Muslims so wrong? Or the Hindus? Or the Buddhists, for that matter? I mean, are fifty million Hindus going to hell?'

The minister artfully avoided the question. He spooned a mound of black tea into the pot. 'Faith is the most important thing, Gordon . . . faith.'

'Is that what Christianity is all about? Just believing in something to keep you going. Turning a blind eye to all the crap and suffering around you and declaring it's God's will and be done with it. Didn't Jesus once say that Heaven and Hell are here on earth? Don't you think he was trying to tell us all something? Is blind faith really all you've got for me, Rev?'

'Where would we be without it, Gordon?' he said, pouring the tea from a battered tin pot. 'Think about the days of the plague. When mankind was on the brink of extinction. The Great War. The Depression. Our darkest hours. Without faith we would never have survived. The Church has fed our souls for centuries, Gordon.'

'It's our *artists* who have fed our souls. Our painters. Our composers. Our writers. They've kept us going. They've fed our souls. Not the fire-and-brimstone set. Religion has caused more misery and human suffering than any disease or plague. Look at the Crusades. Look at the Inquisition. Look at the Hindus fighting the Muslims across the Indian subcontinent. The Jews fighting the Muslims over Jerusalem. The Protestants and the Catholics in Northern Ireland. All in the name of faith. Meanwhile, we're all standing around with our hands in our pockets looking for the answers with the Pope reassuring us by saying, "Put your faith in God" from behind the bulletproof glass of his golf buggy. Faith. You can have it, buddy.'

'Mankind has caused his own misery, Gordon. God just happened to hold his hand along the way. Believe me, faith will guide you to the answers you're looking for.'

'Well, if God made us in his own image, why should we feel guilty?'

The Reverend could see himself being painted into a corner. He thought for a while, staring at me, sipping his tea. 'Even Kierkegaard came over to our side in the end.'

I raised my eyebrows. 'You're familiar with Existentialism?'

'Oh, I'm full of surprises, Gordon.' Then, looking me in the eye, he said, 'You know, Gordon, you strike me as a very religious person who doesn't believe in God.'

I smiled. This was probably the most insightful thing the boozy clergyman had said to me during my stay in Venice. I finished my tea and, leaning into the wind, walked over to the pub.

Max handed me a frosty glass of beer.

'Cheers,' I said, spitting sand from my mouth.

'Have you seen that bloody Italian?' he snapped.

'No, what's up?' I said, pretending to know nothing.

'He's only gone and borrid me ute, got half-pissed with that bloody Ruth, and pranged it, that's what's flamin up! Do you know anything about it?' Max scanned my face for any trace of complicity. I shook my head like a schoolboy with a slingshot behind his back.

'Well, the shit's gonna hit the fan with G-forces when he comes in ere, I'll bloody tell ya.'

'Oh, he'll see you right, you know, Joe.'

'Yeah. That's the bloody problem. I know Joe.'

It was a relief to be inside that day. A sandstorm was blowing through the town and throttled the walls and windows at nerve-jarring intervals. It had been blowing for a couple of days now. And it placed everybody on edge. The constant howl of the wind sounded like a perpetual draught caught in the pipes of a cathedral organ. Sunfly stood at the window listening to the storm as if it were a Mahler symphony. The parrot became agitated with the wind, also. It shuffled up and down its perch like an inmate on death row. A couple of burly truck drivers held up the other end of the bar and would undoubtedly be quite rat-arsed by late afternoon. They would probably have to stay the night. The reason for this opportune intoxication was obvious. It was impossible for them to drive in this weather. With the storm raging outside, it was difficult to see four feet in front of you and that was a good part of the reason Joe had returned Max's ute with a large dent in it. (He had hit an emu in the storm. Ruth and I were with him at the time.)

I addressed Max sedately. 'Look, if he did scratch it –'

'Scratch it!' Max's face flushed scarlet. 'Scratch it! You have a fuckin look at it!'

'I mean to say ... if he did ... dent it, it was probably an accident. You can't see the hand in front of your face out there at the moment. Or the face in front of your hand if you are standing behind yourself.'

He leaned over the bar and screwed up his bludgeoned nose. 'Well, what was he fuckin drivin it for?'

'Maybe he needed to pick up some supplies for the café,' I replied sheepishly.

'Thought you knew nuthin about it.'

I dropped my head and buried my face as I sipped my beer. I felt the heavy hand of the law on my shoulder. I turned around.

'Can I have a word in your shell-like?'

'Hey, Dave. What's up? If it's about the ute, you'll have to talk with Joe. It's a small dent, really. I just –'

'No, no, it's not about that.' Even the normally affable Dave was cranky with the wind. 'Jesus, it's hard enough as it is without getting involved in shitty squabbles over a prang. Whatcha drinkin?'

I swiftly swallowed the remnants of my glass. 'Well, seeing as this pub only sells beer, and rum that tastes like the urine of a wino with renal failure, I'll have a beer.'

'Two beers thanks, Maxy.'

'G'day, Dave. I didn't see you come in. Howya been keepin, ya sly bastard?'

The lofty policeman tugged at his shorts, releasing a small coastline of sand onto the floor. 'Oh, not bad fer a copper with a sackful of sand in his undies.'

'Jesus, you been out in this storm, Dave?' asked Max. 'Bit risky.'

'Yeah. Listen, I'll catch up with yer in a minute, Maxy. I just want a word with the young bloke here.'

Max looked concerned. He leaned over the bar, 'Listen, Dave, if it's about the car –'

'No, it's not about the *bloody* car. I'll catch up with yer in a sec, Max.'

He steered me to a quiet corner. I started to feel a little apprehensive. 'This is all rather mysterious, Dave,' I bubbled nervously.

'Not really. How yer been?' he asked, trying to make me feel relaxed. He threw his hat on the table. Fine grains of sand shot across the lacquered surface like chilli powder.

'Fine, fine. How about you?'

'Oh, fair to middley. Fair to middley.'

'Good.'

'Listen, Gordon, I been wantin to have a serious chat with yer for a while. I missed yer last time I was out this way.'

'If it's about the drink-driving thing. There was no way I could get home that night. I mean no one was around at that time of night –'

'Will yer let me finish?' The big lawman paused and sighed. 'It's not about you.' He took a gulp of beer.

'Sorry,' I said, feeling relieved.

'Last time I was hear I was tellin yer about the Spook. I hear yer've got to know him quite well.' He started to roll a cigarette. 'Smoke?'

'No. I'd prefer sticking my lips around the exhaust pipe of a Volkswagen than dragging on one of those things again. Thanks, anyway.'

'A little birdie tells me you know where the Spook lives.'

'Which little birdie told you that? Not a little birdie who wears his nest on his head.'

'Pommy Bart? Nar. Anyway, never mind that. I need to talk to the kid.'

'Dave, every time something happens around here, he gets the blame. A case of beer goes missing. Someone disappears in the desert. Anything that can't be readily explained. He's left holding the can. You know why?'

'Why?' he said apathetically.

'Because it's easy.'

'This time it's serious, Gordon.'

'How serious?'

'I've heard a whisper that someone's tryin to kill im.'

My jaw dropped. 'Wow, so that's what he was trying to tell me!'

'So yer *do* know im?' the local copper asked with a wry smile, blowing a stream of blue smoke over my head.

'I might know him. So who's trying to kill him?'

'I can't tell yer at this stage of the investigation, but a mining consortium is desperate to mine the desert. A geologist has been sent already. By birthright, Johnny is the last tribal owner under the Native Title legislation. If he dies, the land automatically goes back to the Government, which means the mining company can bid for exploration rights, which they'll get, fer sure.'

Someone opened the door and walked in. The raging storm poked its head in and threw sand across the bar like a madman. The force of the wind made it difficult to shut the door, so Max raced over to help close it.

'So with him outa the way, the mining company can get on with it.'

'I see.'

'A mine would bring a helluva lot of business to the area. So just about anyone in Venice would have a motive to knock im orf. Too many people stand to make too much money. Makes me nervous. Talk around the place is that he's finished. I don't want to see that happen.'

'Right,' I said slowly. I was a little stunned. I hung my head, crow-like. 'How can I help?'

'If yer could just tell me where he lives . . .'

I looked up in fright. Sunfly was standing over the towering lawman. He was staring straight at me. Looking right through me with those dead eyes that seemed to peer into the pit of your soul. I squirmed in my seat. Sunfly slowly shook his head – as if telling me to remain quiet.

'That's just it, Dave. I mean, eh . . . he doesn't live anywhere. He just kind of wanders the desert looking for food and stuff. Look, if I could help I –'

'Okay, okay. If yer see him, tell him what I said. That's all.'

Dave moved over to the bar to chat with Max. Sunfly walked out. I finished my beer and followed him out into the storm. I needed to talk with him. Tell him I wouldn't do anything to endanger Johnny.

'Where the bloody hell are you goin in this?' hollered Max.

I didn't answer as I struggled to close the door behind me. I leaned down the street while the storm pushed and cajoled me, dragging me along like a cranky father with a stubborn three-year-old. I spotted Joe's car in the grainy distance. Joe skidded and hopped out.

'DID HE SAY ANYTHING BOUT UTE?' he bellowed over the fizzing wind.

'YES, I TOLD YOU HE WOULD,' I hollered, spitting out sand as I spoke.

'WHAT HE SAY?'

'THAT THE SHIT WILL HIT THE FAN. THE USUAL MAX DIATRIBE.'

'WHAT? I CUT HEAR YOU, MY FREN!'

'HE SAID THE SHIT WILL HIT THE FAN,' I screamed, squinting as the dust blew against my retinas. 'BEST THING IS TO COME CLEAN. DON'T PRETEND IT DIDN'T HAPPEN OR HE'LL GO BALLISTIC.'

'OKAY. WHERE YOU GOING?'

'WHAT?'

He screamed inside my ear, 'WHERE YOU GOING?'

'JESUS, THAT WAS LOUD, MAN. TO SEE SUNFLY. HAVE YOU STILL GOT THAT TOWEL IN THE CAR?'

'YEAH.'

Joe fetched a towel. I wrapped it around my face. I looked like a cross between Lawrence of Arabia and Yasser Arafat on laundry day.

'BE CAREFUL, IT'S BLOWING SHIT ALL OVER THE PLACE!'

'I NOTICED.'

'WHAT?'

'FORGET IT! I'LL SEE YOU BACK AT THE PUB.' I disappeared into a blood-coloured cloud of sand and dust.

It was difficult finding Sunfly. I'd see him momentarily, then lose him again. The wind was now howling around me like a fleet of Boeing 747s. I started to lose my bearings. After about fifteen minutes of brawling elements, I was completely lost. It became so difficult to see that I couldn't even make out the direction I had just come from. The sand covered my tracks behind me like a cleaning lady on speed. The belting storm felt like sandpaper on my face. Nevertheless, I pressed on – deeper into the desert.

I kept seeing him and yelling at him to stop, but he either couldn't hear me or ignored me. I had been walking for about twenty minutes when he finally stopped. Then, suddenly, he came hurtling towards me through the orange clouds of swirling dust. Then I was knocked to the ground. My head hit the earth with a crack. I lost consciousness for a second and came around, to see a startled emu frantically galloping off into the storm.

'STUPID FUCKER!' I screamed.

I got up and rubbed my head. I fell over again. I got up. It throbbed, but I was okay. I took stock of the situation. This was no time to panic, I thought. I needed to stay level-headed. To calm myself I screamed: 'OH, SHIT. I'M GOING TO FUCKING DIE!' Yes, I started to panic. The upshot was that I hadn't been following Sunfly but a goddamn emu! Therefore, I was completely lost, staggering in spirals.

There was no horizon. It was like tramping through a gigantic hourglass. I felt exhausted and wanted to lie down. But I was frightened I would fall asleep. (Someone in the pub had told me about a tourist who fell asleep in a sandstorm and was buried alive!)

So, with sandstorm logic, I marched deeper into the desert. I recalled with a sickly foreboding the policeman's story about being lost in the desert. I really did start to wonder if I would get out alive. The storm could go on blowing for days. No plane could spot you even if one was mad enough to fly. My only hope was finding Johnny. I wrapped the makeshift turban tighter around my head and staggered on.

'JOHNNY! JOHNNY! I NEED YOU. HELP ME, JOHNNY. FOR CHRIST'S SAKE HELP ME!'

I remember scaling voluminous dunes and tumbling down the other side like a wind-up toy. With enormous effort, I'd pick myself up and press on, deeper into the desert. As I traversed towering dunes, wading through thick sand, the wind screamed and howled in my ears. It sounded like the souls of a thousand tortured spirits. I walked for miles. On and on. Deeper and deeper. By an act of providence, I found the rail line. I hoped it would lead me to the station house. It was my only hope. My legs started to cramp up. I felt the lactic acid burn through my skin. In the end, I just wanted to sleep. But I resisted.

The line led me into a kind of valley, straddled by great red, undulating sandhills. I followed. Then there was a rippling plateau, encircled by monolithic dunes. I sat in the middle of the sandy ravine. Heavy of breath, I watched the veins of the dunes trickle like tears as they descended and ascended simultaneously. As the wind screamed obscenities at me, I noticed a crude shape in the powdery distance. I clawed through the curtains of dust and grit to get a closer look at it. I touched it. It was a greening copper crucifix, half-buried in the sand. It must have been a grave of some sort, I guessed. Although, it looked a little ornate for a desert grave.

Suddenly, the wind dropped sharply. It sounded like a tuning orchestra falling silent on cue as the conductor takes the stage. The wind eventually drew to nothing more than a trickle, and gradually became a long, low-pitched note.

I unwrapped my makeshift turban and circled the solitary grave.

'IT'S A GRAVE . . . BUT FOR MANY PEOPLE!' a voice echoed from a tidal-wave-shaped sandbank.

'THANK *CHRIST* YOU TURNED UP!' I cried. 'I never thought I'd see anyone ever again.'

'DANGEROUS TO COME OUT HERE IN A STORM, GORDON. WHY ARE YOU HERE?'

'I THOUGHT I WAS FOLLOWING SUNFLY BUT . . .' Then I saw Sunfly, standing solemnly on a neighbouring dune. His face was covered in white ochre. The wind blew a fine spray of sand off dunes around his legs. I grabbed the listing cross. 'SO WHOSE GRAVE IS IT?' I yelled over the droning wind that now sounded like someone blowing air through a bassoon.

'IT'S THE GRAVE OF THIS TOWN – KOOLOOWONG,' the boy hollered. He drifted down the dune. Sunfly remained motionless. He walked up to me and smiled, 'Your mob called it "Hopetown".'

'This is Hopetown? I don't get it? There's supposed to be a whole town here. Houses, schools, pubs . . . Are people buried in this grave?'

'Only their spirits.'

'I don't understand?'

'Dig around it,' he said mysteriously.

I dug the sand away from its vast metallic base. I discovered a shingled roof holding the cross in place. I was confused.

The boy gave a knowing smile.

'If this isn't a grave, then what the hell is it? A monument?' I asked in a hoarse voice.

'It's a church, mate.'

He pointed. 'Look over that dune and you'll get the picture.'

Clumsily scaling the sandy monolith and peering over its powdery lip, all became clear to me. Barely visible, were the battered rooftops of buried buildings. I noticed the odd chimney that poked out of the sand like the arm of a drowning surfer. I stumbled back down the dune in quiet disbelief. The boy stood at the rusty steeple, leaning against his long spear on one leg with the stillness and grace of a flamingo.

'So what the hell happened here?' I asked.

'They didn't read the omens.'

'What omens?'

'Always look for the omens,' he reiterated. Johnny picked up a handful of sand and let it slowly trickle through his black fingers. It was greedily siphoned by the wind. 'This town is buried. The spirits of our people have reclaimed it. Through time. The whitefella never belonged in the desert. They should never have come. This is magic country. Secret country. A place of dreaming. We've been here since the Dreaming began. Before the spirits became the stars and the sand and the moon.'

I wandered around and then turned to him. 'You mean this whole town is entombed? All of it? Everything . . . buried?'

'Yes. Soon the chimneys, the roofs and even this church will vanish without a trace. Swallowed by the spirits of the Sandy People.'

'How did they allow that to happen? Was it sudden?'

'No, they had time to leave, but were powerless to stop it. Like I said. They didn't read the omens. Too busy building empires to notice what was happening around them. You have to learn to read the omens. See the subtle changes around you. They speak to you. They tell you when it's time to move on. Or time to stay and find food. Or time to prepare for hardship. It's how our people survived for thousands of years, Gordon. These people destroyed our world to build their dream. And for what? Sometimes we have to think about whose dream we destroy as we attempt to build our own.'

The boy picked up a handful of sand and let it trickle into the wind. 'Life is like the desert, Gordon: if you stand still long enough, you'll be swallowed by the sand. You need to leave. Get on with your life, mate.'

The boy looked up at the orange and purple sky. I followed his gaze. I'd never seen the desert sky that colour before. It was an angry colour. The heavens looked as though they'd been torched by a crazed arsonist. Johnny put a hand on my shoulder, 'Come on, I'll lead you back to the town.'

'That could be dangerous. Someone is trying to kill you.'

'I know. Sunfly and I have read the omens.'

I nodded.

'Have you found the black cockatoo feather yet?' he asked.

'No. What does it all mean? I don't understand.'

'When you find it, I will tell you.'

We walked through the desert and into town in silence, the wind howling around us.

A BAD MOOD RISING

'WHAT HAPPENED TO you the other day? Max growled.

'My karma ran over my dogma,' I replied, munching some salt-and-vinegar chips.

'What?' he snapped.

'I went for a stroll.'

'We were wondering what in Christ happened to ya! Then we seen ya led outta the desert by that kid. Joo get lost out there?' he asked as he milked some beige foam from an empty keg.

'Yeah, Johnny saved my life, actually,' I said, wiping the salt from my stinging, chapped lips.

'That his name, is it?'

'Yeah. Johnny. Anyway, he led me back to town and then I decided to skip the pub and head to the café. I was exhausted.'

'He was takin a risk comin into town, wasn't he?'

'Yes, he was well aware of that.'

'Anyway. You! You're lucky to be alive, ya silly prick. Pretty bloody stupid to go out into the desert at any time, but especially when it's like this, ya wanker.' (Nothing implies intimacy among Australians more than verbal abuse.) The wind continued to howl with venom.

'I thought I was following Sunfly. I thought I'd be okay but –'

'*But* you're a silly bastard,' said Max, in parental tones.

Apart from the occasional lull, the dust storm had been blowing for five solid days now. It was impossible to do any work outdoors, so most of the locals and the odd driver huddled in the bar, taking the opportunity to get well and truly plastered. Everybody was on edge. Max tried to cheer things up. It was Christmas. He had a string of green tinsel across the bar and fake snow sprayed around the edges of the windows. He was wearing a set of felt reindeer antlers and a T-shirt saying: 'Smile, it's fucking Christmas!'

Sunfly sat stoically at the bar listening to the oscillating harmonic of the storm. He listened intensely – as if trying to crack a secret code. For some reason I couldn't help staring at him that evening. I wanted to talk to him, but the pub wasn't the place. I had been sighted with the boy and there was bad feeling in Venice as a result of this confirmed association. I was an outsider, from the city, and the earlier paranoia about me had been rekindled. Some even suspected I was a member of the Land Council who had been sent to spy on the town to ensure the surrounding lands remained in tribal hands. People were pretty snaky with me, to tell you the truth. So, like the snivelling coward that I am, it seemed prudent to distance myself from Sunfly that day.

'Beer?' Max asked laconically, antlers drooping at the sides.

'Max, I think I'll try something different.'

Max shot a quizzical look at me.

'I'll have a Venetian Margarita,'

'What the fuck's that?' he snapped.

'It's a schooner of beer, and when you give it to me, you sprinkle salt over a map of Mexico and say: "*Olé*!"'

He placed a foaming beer on the damp beer mat and said in a flat voice, 'Fuckin *Olé*.'

'*Muchos gracias*.' I took a gulp. 'I hear Joe's going to have your ute fixed.'

Max stopped milking the lathering tap. 'No. *I'm* going to have my ute fixed an that bloody wog is gunna pay for it!' Flecks of foam shot from his stubby forefinger with each word.

'Oh, my mistake.' I buried my head in my beer. 'Good to see you're okay about it.'

'Some of the fuckin lemons that live out here, fair dinkum,' he mumbled, shaking his head.

Squales shuffled over to me at the bar. He always looked unwell, but that day he looked positively green. His queer fag-holder held the omnipresent foul-smelling cigarette. The conversation was peppered with the usual caesuras of coughs, splutters and gasps.

'[*Cough*] Hello lad, I ear you went for a stroll the [*splutter*] other day. Very foolish in this inclement weather, wouldn't you say, Max?'

'He knows my thoughts on the matter,' Max growled.

'Why did [*gasp*] you do that, son?' he choked.

'They say it's healthy to walk two hundred miles in delirious circles every morning. You should try it.'

'Really?'

'I had to see someone,' I said, tearing up a coaster into fragments for no reason.

'Who, that lad that [*splutter gasp*] lives out in the desert?'

A brief coughing fit overcame him. When he'd recovered, I said, 'If you don't mind me saying, you don't seem at all well today.'

'All this [*gag*] bluddy doost. Plays havoc with mah chest.'

'I'm glad to hear it's not the two hundred cigarettes a day you smoke.'

'Oooh, it won't be the fags that kill me, lad.'

(He was right in the end. Squales died some years later of a combination of haemorrhoids, in-grown toenails and the inability to actually breathe.)

'I just coom over to let you know that there's a parcel for you at the post office.'

'Does it feel like a T-shirt?'

'Yes,' he wheezed. He knew it was a T-shirt. Squales opened everybody's mail. 'Cheers. I'll drop by later and pick it up.'

'No hurrah, lad. This is the land of plenty of tarm.' The old man sat down in a corner to continue reading a week-old paper and splutter over the sports section.

The T-shirt had arrived just in time. I was worried it wouldn't. It was Joe's Christmas present. Joe was always depressed about his weight. Late at night, he would stand in front of the mirror holding his great bulbous belly, moaning to himself. I said that late in the evening was the wrong time of the day to judge his true size. I said that he was merely bloated after the 25 beers he'd just swallowed that day and that he should look at his stomach in the morning, and not at the end of the day when his belly was distended by booze. So I took a photo of his stomach first thing one morning and had it printed onto a life-size T-shirt so he could wear it in the evenings.

Max scratched a bushy eyebrow. 'If ya don't mind me saying that wife of yours is a cracking sort.'

'Yeah, she *is* a cracking sort. Her arms fell off when we first met.'

'You never told me you were married.'

I put my nose in the air. 'It didn't seem to matter when we were making love in the dunes the other day.'

Max shook his head. 'I wonder about you sometimes, Gordon. Fair dinkum.' He wiped his hands. 'So ya left *her* to live out here with a hairy-arsed Italian. You sure you're not a poof?'

'If dressing up in drag and rooting guys occasionally makes me a poof, then, yes, I'll put my hand up – although I'm not into kinky stuff – yes, I suppose that makes me a poof.'

Max looked shocked.

'It's a joke, Max.'

'Good.'

'Would it be the end of the world if I was, anyway?'

'I'll have no poofter in this pub.'

'Does that rule apply to your own son?'

'Keep ya voice down, will ya?' he whispered. 'Even if it's me own son. I've been thinking about what ya said and it's been good to talk about it, but I've decided: I never want to see the bloke again.'

'You don't really mean that, Max. Your face betrays you.'

'Bullshit. If I see him, this face will tell him to fuck off – immediately.'

I frowned at him and shook my head.

'Joe still with that Ruth?' he asked, quickly changing the subject.

'Yeah, although her job's finished here, she'll be off soon.'

'He'll be lost without her. I've never seen the bloke so happy.'

I nodded.

Ruth and Joe had been living in each other's pockets for weeks now. They held hands everywhere they went. Sometimes, I'd wander over to the café late at night and if I didn't turn on my heels because I could hear them screwing each other stupid, I'd walk in to find them staring into each other's eyes, slow-dancing under the mirror-ball – Joe dressed as Elvis, Ruth dressed as Priscilla– to 'You Can't Say No in Acapulco'.

I walked over and sat on a stool at the front window and sunk a few more soul-numbing beers. I pulled out the photograph of Jenny that I pinched from her bag. I then reflected on the events of the past few weeks. The letter at the ghostly farmhouse. The town entombed by the desert. The boy's pressing entreaty for me to leave Venice. I downed some more beer. I didn't really want to leave. I actually liked living in the town. I was relatively happy, nestled in the little pocket of hopelessness that was the town of Venice. The stillness of the desert. The monastic solitude of the station house. The boozy tranquillity of the pub. The snug of the café. There was no pressure. I made no commitments to anyone or myself. I felt utterly inconsequential – and liked it. The musical ambitions that had given my life such meaning and drive seemed to fade into insignificance. The fragmented melodies and lyrics for my proposed album felt as ephemeral as the dotted rooftops and flagging chimneys of Hopetown. The upshot was that I merely wished to be left alone and forgotten. The booze helped. Jenny had mentioned that my sister was worried, so I wrote to allay her concern. But that was the last contact I ever wanted with my life back in Sydney. I decided to stay in Venice till I had enough money to live in New York for a year.

The elements continued to scorn the town as I sat thinking. The pub was rattling in the wailing wind like an old clipper. You'd see the odd drunk raise his drooping head if a particularly nasty blast shook the windows and rattled glasses on the bar, but most remained intoxicatedly indifferent. Through the snow-in-a-can-encrusted window, I watched a wiry tumbleweed Daytona around the street. I downed another beer, ordered a fresh one and sat back at the window. I gazed out onto the street until I saw Ruth pull up in her four-wheel drive. She struggled, trying to close the driver's door before walking in.

'G'day, Ruthy!' Max yelled from the bar. She gave a little wave and sat beside me.

'Ruth, is everything all right. You look upset,' I said.

She pulled up a stool. Her mascara boot-laced down her cheeks. Her eyes looked red and puffy. 'Oh, this weather! How can you stand it? Anyway, Gordon, I came to say goodbye.'

'I thought you weren't leaving till next week.'

'I've got to go. I can't explain.'

'That's a shame. No doubt you'll miss Joe.'

'Honey, I don't know what I'll miss more. Joe or that twelve-inch dick of his. My Gawd, that thing would need it's own seat in economy.'

I laughed. She was great, Ruth, I'd really miss her. 'Are you and Joe going to keep in touch?'

She flushed to cherry. 'This is my address in Queens, honey. I never mentioned this but my uncle runs a little jazz club. You've heard of the Village Vanguard?'

I jumped in my seat. 'The Village Vanguard? Who hasn't? You never mentioned it before. Are you serious, Ruth?'

'When you make it to Noo Yawk. Look me up. Uncle Abe owes me big time. I'll get you a job there.'

'But, Ruth what about Joe?'

She started crying and kissed me on the cheek and ran out. She drove off never to return to Venice again.

It was always going to be difficult for Ruth to say goodbye to Joe. I often wondered how the big fellow would cope. Was he okay about it? We'd never really talked about it because he was never out of Ruth's company. He *was* getting edgy the last few days before her departure. Or was it the storm? It was hard to tell with Joe. He never discussed his feelings. Ever.

I looked at the address she had scribbled on a meal docket with a blue eyebrow pencil. Was this an omen? Was it now time to leave for New York? Right now? I downed some more beer and pondered. Why was Johnny so adamant that I should leave, anyway? What did it matter to him? Could he see a bad omen for me? And what was the black cockatoo feather all about? What would returning home mean? Home only meant thinking about the failures. The subjugated dreams. The maybes. The what-ifs. The if-onlys. Then I thought of Jenny and how I pined for her. She was the only reason to go back. After realising that Finius was a phantom amour, the dynamic of the situation had changed markedly. I loved her and she still loved me. But she wouldn't live in 'The Big Rotting Apple' as she dubbed it. I pulled out her picture again and sighed. In the other hand I held the address Ruth had given me.

I stared out into the desert. It looked like a rolling sea in a storm. After a few more amber ales, I scribbled some more lyrics on the back of some coasters.

The tide dragged me out with so much pain and emotion,
my heart drifted out to sea,
I'll swim with the rip,
just to float in the ocean,
helplessly . . .

The storm warnings rang across the waves of the ocean,
gulls flew from shore to sea,
but I'll just keep drifting along with the notion,
of you and me . . .

Drifting, drifting, drifting drifting . . .

I placed the coasters in my shirt pocket and pondered. I'd changed a lot since arriving in the outback. Not merely physically, but emotionally. I'd grown up. In the end I discovered that the pills were merely a Band-aid for a wound that had finally had time to heal. Was I strong enough to return to the city? I thought of Manhattan. The surf of traffic. The buzzing coffee shops. The late-night gigs in snappy nightclubs. Was it time to leave? Right now. Just walk out and pack my bags and split?

I looked out into the swirling desert. I looked at the address again. Perhaps, if I didn't leave now, I never would. Joe had only planned a brief and prosperous sojourn when he first arrived. Pluck the opals from the earth, cash in the stones, then it's off to glittering Las Vegas. Find a rich old American lady who is too wealthy to wear her 'real jewels' in public, show her a photo of his twanger, and get hitched. Twenty years later he found himself cooking greasy burgers and singing Elvis's 'Hunk'a Hunk'a Hunk'a Burger Love' in a remote roadside diner. Would Joe ever have the guts to leave? Would I? Sure, the city seemed attractive at times. But I wanted to stay in the outback. Life was simple. I had made genuine friends in the desert, and aside from Jenny I had nothing to return to except disappointment and pills – possibly. What about my career? Was I putting off New York because I was afraid? Of more disappointment? Of failure? When it came right down to it, was I really strong enough to tough it out? Alone in a foreign city? Now I had Ruth there, the wheels were greased. My internal conflicts were suddenly interrupted.

'Problem with Abos izzz they're aaall lazy thfuckin pissss heads. Sin their nature,' an ugly, drunken voice bellowed from across the room.

I ignored the remark. However, the driver made some more offensive remarks (which were of great amusement to himself and his inebriated friends). I looked around to find Max. Max wouldn't tolerate that kind of talk in the pub, particularly in front of Sunfly. He was downstairs changing over that keg. Sunfly remained stoically silent.

It was funny, I hadn't experienced rampant racism in Venice. I'd allow the odd comment from a local slip by unchallenged (which on occasion made me feel ashamed), but I was careful not to be baited. Often that's all it was. I neither defended the remark nor gave it currency, I simply drove over the churlish slur with fresh conversation as if it were road-kill. I guess this was a cop-out in the end.

Tragically, one of the reasons for the lack of naked hostility toward the Kooris of Venice was the fact that there *were* none – bar old Sunfly. Over at Coober Pedy or Alice Springs, it was a different matter. Young Koori kids could be seen wandering around the town with small tins of petrol tied around their necks. A few sniffs and they simply staggered off to their cultural Armageddon. Heartbreaking. The Kooris are so angry at the whites in the Alice, for example, I'd heard, that if you get someone offside, it is not unknown to have the whole tribe coming to find you and beat the living crap out of you in the street.

My uncle once told me that in the early 1970s he was in Alice Springs for a conference. He was drinking in a pub and recalled a toothless Aboriginal woman storming into the bar. She was drunk – yelling and cursing. A local policeman stood up and smashed her head against the wall several times and then threw her into the street like a mangy dog. My uncle said the most disturbing thing was that the locals in the pub hardly raised an eyebrow. They continued guzzling beer as if it were a regular event. Did my uncle take a stand? He simply said that was life in the outback. He felt it wasn't up to him to tell them how to live their lives when he drove a yellow Volvo around his cosy, milk-bread suburb of Sydney. And what had I done to right the wrongs of the past for that matter?

As I continued drinking, the man's comments became quite nasty. I had a sickly foreboding that things were turning bad. Very bad. I looked around for Max. He was nowhere to be seen. Sunfly drank at the bar – guarded but composed. I told myself that as soon as Max came up from the cellar, he would throw the troglodyte and his cronies out into the storm. The drunken truck driver and his friends giggled and hissed – half-heartedly urging the leader to keep his voice down. Why is it that people are under the misapprehension that rudeness is somehow synonymous with wit?

After a while the disparaging comments were not enough for the portly driver. It wasn't long before he oafishly disentangled himself from his seat, almost knocking over a friend's beer, and sauntered over to Sunfly. He had the rolling gait of a sailor. He wore a chequered shirt with no sleeves. He had no neck and the cauliflower ears of a Rugby forward. He stood behind the old Koori and removed the old man's moth-eaten hat. Sunfly remained motionless.

'Yeah, they like thfuckin drinkin. Like aaa drink, old man?' he guffawed. He poured his glass over Sunfly and staggered off. I jumped from my seat, stormed over to the man, punched him in the mouth, and threw him out – in my imagination of course (I also spoke in the voice of Clint Eastwood). In reality, I hid my face. As usual, I didn't want to get involved. I sat drinking my beer while the old man stood, dripping, in humiliating silence. Not being able to stand his Gandhi-like stance at the bar, I finally walked over and wiped his head with the bar towel. I whispered, 'They'll be gone soon, Sunfly. Max will be up in a sec and toss them out.'

'Oh, you his thfuckin boyfriend, mate?'

I ignored the comment. The man staggered over to me. 'They're all piss heads. Now it's sthhofficial...ha ha ha!' He looked around at his friends, swaying, as if on an imaginary surfboard.

'You being an expert on the subject of drunken slobs,' I replied. (Beer makes you say the funniest things, doesn't it?)

Sunfly turned to me, 'Keep quiet, boy.'

The drunken man looked confused and screwed up his bloated plum-coloured face an inch away from mine and breathed a foul odour. 'Wascha say, mate?'

I felt frightened but unable to control my tongue as usual. Making an excuse to leave, Squales cowered out the door behind me.

'Nothing.'

'You wanna smackina mouth, pal?'

'Not particularly.'

He raised his fist.

I stood my ground. 'I wouldn't do that. I've got a knife.' There was a hush around the room.

'Hear that fellas? He's got a thfuckin knife. Let's see it then.'

'It's at home in the cutlery drawer,' I said.

He obviously had a sense of humour because he decked me. Lucky for me I managed to break the fall with my face. I quickly got up and head-butted him on the bridge of his crimson nose. I felt it crumple, egg-like. Blood Jackson-Pollocked over my white T-shirt.

Now this sounds quite macho, doesn't it? And perhaps I should end the chapter right here. But what really happened was that I jumped up as he lent over (he was surprised to see me go down so easily after what he thought was merely a tap on the chin) and I busted his nose. Panicking, I threw a left hook and, as he was drunk, he fell slowly to the floor. It was like pushing over a piece of Stonehenge. Now, this was a really stupid thing to do. I mean, *really* stupid. The driver's friends instantly leapt from the table and I was left to fight them off – peppering them with limp combinations and wild aeroplane swings. The parrot began a siren of blood-curdling screeches. (A sound familiar to the landlord.) Max bolted up the cellar stairs – three at a time – just as someone hit me over the head with a chair.

'WHAT THE FUCK!' Max yelled, as he hurled a keg across the room at the driver who hit me with the chair. He ducked and it went through the front window. Dust and sand blew furiously into the hotel. 'SHIT,' I heard him say.

Max straddled the bar with the agility of an Olympic gymnast. One of the men threw a stool at Max, knocking him to the floor. Suddenly, I felt a sharp pain at the back of my head. Someone's beer glass. I staggered for a moment with my hands in the air, trying to protect my face from further blows that were coming from all directions. I then fell over. The men began to kick me in the ribs and face.

One of the locals got up (finally!) in an attempt to stop the melee now that the cavalry, in the form of Max Parsons, had arrived on the scene.

Max got to his feet. His face was the colour of beetroot that had been soaked in red wine and then painted with purple paint. The men cowered. Max had a nasty reputation for violence. Although small, he never lost a fight in his pub. Max picked up the stool and belted it over the head of the driver with the jagged beer glass in his hand. The man collapsed like sack. Max threw a blurring propeller of deft, stinging punches at the other two, forcing them out into the windy street. He knocked one unconscious and the other one he grabbed by the neck and smashed his head several times against the door as if cracking open a coconut (or so I was informed later). The bloodied driver staggered to his feet and dragged his unconscious friend to safety.

'And if I EVER catch you in this bar again, I'LL RIP YOUR FUCKIN HEARTS OUT!' Max screamed.

He marched back inside and threw a bucket of icy water over the driver who he had knocked unconscious with the stool. 'And YOU should learn to keep that big fuckin moutha yours shut, Gary. NOW

GET THE FUCK OUT! You're barred. Go on. On ya fuckin bike, arsehole.'

Max dragged the delirious provocateur by the testicles (yes, the testicles) into the street. The whole bar winced and crossed their legs in a collective movement.

'MERRY FUCKIN CHRISTMAS, GARY!'

The wind was almost ripping the door off its hinges. Sunfly walked over and calmly closed it. Max quickly rigged up a tarpaulin over the window. Some people helped. It flapped in staccato bursts as they secured it. After it was secured, the pub returned to the usual low drone of mumbles. Max walked over to Sunfly.

'Did he pour a beer over you again, mate?'

'You mean he's done this kind of thing *before*?' I asked still recovering on the floor.

'It's Gary's fuckin party trick,' he said, helping me to my feet. 'Last time he did it, I gave him a spanking and barred him, but he eventually apologised to Sunfly and me and everything was sweet.' He put a hand on the old Koori's shoulder. 'He even bought ya a bottle of that Wild Turkey, didn't he, mate? Nice drop, too.' The old man nodded as he dried his white hair. 'But this time he's gone too bloody far. He's bloody barred for life. Some blokes just get nasty when they drink, Gordon. There's three types of drunk: the sleepy drunk – he just nods off at the bar. The happy drunk – he goes round tellin everyone that he loves em. Then there's the nasty drunk – that's Gary.'

'What kind of drunk am I, then?'

'A fuckin stupid drunk,' he snapped. 'Why pick a blue with Gary? Why didn't you just come down and get me? I deal with Gary and his ratbag mates all the time.'

I wiped the sticky, jam-like blood from my face. 'I don't really know,' I said drowsily.

'Hey, you didn't tell me you've done a bit of boxing.' Max sounded enthusiastic.

'You never asked.'

'Pretty ordinary, who taught you to fight like that?'

'Sydney University. I boxed skeleton-weight for a couple of years.'

'Were you any good?' he asked, picking up the stool as though nothing had happened.

'I had sixteen fights. All ended in a knockout.'

'Yeah?' He was quite impressed.

'Yeah, I was knocked out sixteen times. Actually, seventeen, if you count the time I got knocked out, came to, and got knocked out again in the next round.'

(Boxing was one of my psychiatrist's alternative drug-free therapies. Something about 'channelling internal anger' – you know, 'releasing the animal within'. Sadly, that animal within turned out to be a ferret with a nosebleed.)

Max giggled hysterically over my pugilistic failures. This seemed to relieve the tension. The whole pub breathed a collective sigh of relief. Then Max interrupted the slurring conversations of the remaining drinkers.

'And what about *you* buncha pathetic arseholes? Just sittin there on ya fat arses while a bloke's havin six parts of crap beaten outa him!' He shook his head. 'Fair fuckin dinkum, I dunno.' He pulled out a bottle of 'medicinal' brandy from under the bar that he was keeping for Christmas and poured a generous glass for Sunfly, me and himself.

He addressed the other drinkers. 'And don't think you assholes are getting any of this top brandy neither.' He took a slug of golden spirit. 'Gordon, I can't for the life of me understand why you'd pick a blue with Gary? That bloke'd punch portholes in ya, sober.'

'Alcohol is a cruel conjurer, Max. Let's face it, where would karaoke be without alcohol?' The brandy stung my bleeding lips. Holding the shot glass to the light, I studied the treacle-looking liquid. 'Yes, it makes me forget that I'm really a coward, until there's no turning back. Give me enough booze and I'll run through Tiananmen Square naked, in nothing but a Chairman Mao mask singing "Tanks for the Memories".'

Max looked into my face like a parent scanning their child for drugs. 'You okay?'

'Um . . . yeah.' I felt a warm feeling at the back of my head. I rubbed it and looked at my hand. It was black with blood.

'You sure you're right, son?'

'I think I'm going to –' I crashed to the floor.

He ran around and felt my head. 'Shit, he's losing blood at the rate of fuckin knots. Better get the doctor in. Mick, grab a lighter and light them kero torches on the runway.'

'You can't ask him to fly out in this,' the farmer said.

I came around briefly. Max turned red and fired off orders like a sergeant-major 'Don't fuckin argue. Eel bloody die if we don't.' He ran to the phone. 'Shit, the phone's dead. Quick, Col, drive up to the café and see if the Italian's phone's working. Just hang in there, mate,' he said to me in shaky tones, 'Don't die on us, Gordon. We'll get the doc out to fix that thick scone of yours. What blood type are ya?'

'Wha . . . ?'

'You know, what's ya blood type?'

'Um . . . er . . .'

'Wake up, Gordon.' Max slapped my face. It hurt. 'What type is it?'

'O . . . um . . . O . . . Positive . . . I think . . . yes . . .'

I passed out.

⌒

As I drifted in and out of consciousness, I heard Sunfly humming an eerie melody. I heard car tyres skid out front. I felt the wind blow grit across my face as the door slapped open. I remember lying on the floor with my head under a lumpy cushion when I heard a familiar voice.

'Jus wait till I catch those busteds. I beat shit out of them, my fren.'

'They won't be back here in a hurry, Joe,' Max whispered.

'I'll find them. Don't worry, my fren. I catch up with vermin like this,' Joe hissed.

I felt nauseous. I threw up over myself. I tried to clean it up but passed out.

'Don't worry son, we'll fix it up,' I heard an unfamiliar voice say.

'Has he lost lot of blood?' Joe asked.

'Too much,' replied Max gravely. 'It'll be touch'n'go. Yep, touch and go.'

As I slipped in and out consciousness, I felt a damp bar towel crudely wrapped around my skull. I remember feeling weak, and the room looking dark and foreboding. I remember seeing Johnny in my mind, waving to me from the dunes, Jenny kissing me on the forehead and Chuck scatting 'It Was Just One of Those Things'.

'He's here!' rasped Sunfly.

'Thank fuckin Christ,' Max trembled. 'Joe, feel his pulse.'

A minute later, I heard the erratic, nasal drone of a Cessna. It was circling the town, finding it perilous to land in the gale-force winds. It buzzed the town several times before landing, sounding like a flying lawnmower.

'Must be mad coming out in weather like this,' I heard a voice mumble from the other end of the room.

'I heard the Cessna. What's happened? Is he all right?' asked Reverend Fruit in startled tones. In some rambling, boozy drivel he started to pray. I remember him mumbling something about 'Keep thy lambs wormed'? (Fruit never failed to turn malapropism into an art form.)

The sound of the engine drew closer and then stopped. Minutes later, I heard a genteel voice say, 'Good god! What happened here?'

I tried to look up. Through fuzzy vision, I saw him. It was Santa. Had I been a good boy?

A MAN WITH A CLAUS

I LISTENED TO BILLIE HOLIDAY crackle out of the jukebox as she sang Jimmy van Heusen's 'Darn that Dream' in that wailing voice of hers. I listened to the jagged melody and fragile lyrics. It was cleverly composed, I thought, the angst-ridden melody never quite coming to terms with itself. The refrain wheeled in my thumping head as I drifted in and out of reality.

'Joe?' I slurred.

'Oh, you're with us now are you?' the polished voice boomed from the next room.

It was a voice unfamiliar to me. It wasn't the usual bevy of nasal tones and choppy sentences that was the outback brogue. This voice was fluid, with rich tones and long open vowels, gift-wrapped in carefully clipped consonants. I thought of Shakespeare for some reason. I staggered out into the room. The café was completely smashed up. It was as though a herd of camels had been locked inside and had panicked, trying to get out.

I looked around, trying to focus. I was unsteady on my feet. I felt a familiar feeling, I felt out of it.

Sitting at the counter, was a man dressed in a red Santa suit. His fake beard flopped on a table nearby.

'What on earth happened to the place?' I asked, rubbing my head. I felt a long row of stitches beneath my palm.

'I don't know. Looks as though someone's rather smashed the place up,' he said.

'Yeah, where's Joe, eh . . . the owner?'

'Gone. He made me this rather tasty hamburger before leaving, though. Nice of him to make this for me – on the house, so to speak.' Kriss Kringle took a large bite of the burger de jour and fastidiously wiped the grease from his pointy chin with a napkin.

'I'll ask you that tomorrow when you're shitting through the eye of a needle. Speaking of which, are you the seamstress?' I said, feeling the stitches, again.

'Oh, you mean . . . yes.'

'Anyway, aren't you supposed to be climbing through chimneys and having sex with elves about this moment?'

'Oh, the outfit,' he giggled. 'At this time of the year I deliver presents to children on outback stations. That is, when someone hasn't been beaten half to death. Weather Station said the storm was blowing over. I was waiting for a lull when I got the call to come here.'

I wandered over to the percolator and drowsily poured myself a cup of coffee. I let out a big sigh. 'Did Joe, the owner, say where he was going?'

'He said he had some people he needed to catch up with urgently.'

'Ruth?'

'He mentioned someone by the name of "Gary the Bastard".'

'Jesus. Oh, well. Can't say he doesn't deserve it,' I mumbled. I felt the side of my mouth and wiggled a loose tooth. 'You're not a dentist too, are you?'

'I do just about anything in these parts.' He shone a pencil torch into my swollen mouth and fingered my teeth. 'Is this the tooth?'

'Arum. Parkinson. Falcon. Arkansas.'

'You feeling okay, now?'

'Arafat.'

'Sure.'

I gave a little gentle wave and nodded. Seemed easier than speaking with a torch down my throat. Apart from my throbbing face, cracked ribs, bruised torso and broken nose (again), I was feeling dandy.

'You'd lost a lot of blood, but once we plugged you up and gave you a top up, you were okay.'

'You don't service Valiants as well, do you?'

The doctor gave a high-pitched giggle. 'Simon Winthrop.' The medico outstretched a soft hand. 'Gordon, isn't it?'

'Yes. Gordon Shoesmith.'

'You don't seem to be from these parts, Gordon. Would I be right?'

'You'd be right. I arrived from the city about a year ago,' I wheezed. 'The night life was so electric and the people so charming, I couldn't leave.' I rubbed my blue cheek.

'I thought I'd recognised you. Rolled your car about a year ago. I flew in to patch you up, if I recall.'

'That's right. You're English, aren't you?'

'Yes, but don't hold it against me,' the physician chortled.

'Whereabouts in the UK?'

'I'm from London. Grew up in Surrey, though. Moved to London after university. I studied at Exeter.'

'Exeter?'

'Yes, if you don't make Oxford or Cambridge, you get Exeter. Came out here to join the Royal Flying Doctor Service.'

(Why does it sound so offensive when British people use the word 'Royal' when referring to Australian institutions? I mean, if the Queen Mum gets thrush, does one of the Flying Doctors traverse the globe in a Cessna with a tub of yogurt?)

'Why'd you leave London to work out here?'

'Oh, I don't know . . . thought I needed a bit of adventure,' he laughed. 'I'd say I rather got that tonight. Didn't think I'd make it, quite frankly. Said a prayer before the landing. The ruddy runway was full of potholes. I asked them to fix that last time. Bit shaken really.'

'Whisky?' I pulled a bottle from behind the counter.

'Cheers. I think I need one.'

'I can't believe you came out in the storm,' I said, filling a cup.

'Either can I,' he said, downing some Scotch, and pulling a face.

'Well, I'll give you this, you're a brave man – or a very stupid one.'

'The latter I'd surmise.'

'Flying a piss-fart little aeroplane through a dust storm *is* pretty mad,' I said. 'Thanks, I owe you one. If you ever need a piano player for your wedding, I'll charge you just over normal rates.'

'Cheers. I say, you're pretty high in the old stupid stakes yourself. How on earth did you end up in a fight with those men?'

'It's a gift.'

'Fighting. Is this a regular thing?'

'No. I'm quite the snivelling coward, actually. Booze, does strange things to you,' I mused.

'I know the feeling. One half of your brain hoodwinks the other half into believing it has limitless potential. A seemingly bottomless pit of courage. Once you've committed yourself, it's too late.'

'Like flying a Cessna in a sandstorm?'

He smiled and chuckled. 'Two glasses of Nurse Parker's Christmas punch and I was in the cockpit like Tom Cruise in *Top Gun*.'

I chuckled.

'I must say, I didn't think it would be as terrifying up there tonight as it was,' he said.

'Pretty frightening, eh?'

'Pretty frightening,' he echoed.

'Wasn't it Oscar Wilde who said: "A brave man is someone who merely lacks imagination"?'

'Sounds like his sort of quote.'

'So does: "Sodomy is bloody fantastic". But it didn't seem appropriate.'

'So what happened tonight?' the physician asked, as he rummaged through his Christmas sack. He removed a soft black bag and pulled out some bottles of medication.

'I was in the wrong place at the wrong time. That's all.' I poured some more whisky. 'Basically, those buffoons were looking to blow off a little steam and I got in the way. That's all. Everyone's going stir-crazy with this dust storm.'

'Yes, I'm not risking going up again. I'll stay at the pub for a few days till it blows over.'

'Don't hold your breath.'

'Here, take these.' The medic placed some chalky pills on the table.

'What are they?'

'Pain-killers. For your head. You'll have a sore skull for a few days. You're not feeling it now because of the morphine, but –'

My heart dropped. '*Please* tell me you haven't shot me up with morphine.'

'I'm afraid I have. Why?'

I sighed. I wondered why I felt so good. I panicked for a moment. What if the anxiety attacks come back in the aftermath of the morphine? Would I be back on the pills again? A tide of opium quickly washed away the panic. 'Never mind. It feels good. Thanks.'

'You needed it.'

'Got any aspirin? I can see I'll need it for later.'

'Sure.' He reached into a wrinkled, black bag.

I stared at the Yuletide medico for a moment. He had a bad skin for life in the desert country. His English-rose complexion was a sunburned canvas of little cuts and sores and crops of pimples. He looked more like a country veterinarian ready to pull a tapeworm from a cow's arse than a qualified surgeon who had graduated from a high-ranking English university, I thought.

'Coffee?' I asked as I glanced at the clock. It was one-thirty in the morning. I poured the doctor a cup and dropped some Scotch into it.

'Cheers.'

Barney walked in. 'Jesus, I heard yer got a touch up, but I didn't think it would be this bad. Did they smash the joint up, too?'

'No, but it looks like someone did. Barney, meet Santa – AKA Simon Winthrop. Barney runs a property a little south of here.'

The doctor threw out a limp hand. 'Pleasure to meet you, Barney.' Barney shook his hand, almost dislocating the physician's shoulder.

'Simon's the Flying Doctor.'

'You replaced the old Red Baron, dinya?'

'Sebastian? Yes. He retired last year.'

'It must be an exciting job, being a Flying Doctor,' I said.

'It's a little different to casualty at St Bartholomew's in London.'

'I'd say so. You must have seen some pretty strange things out here.'

'You *wouldn't* believe me if I told you.'

'Try me. What's the strangest thing you've seen out here?' I made Barney an Irish coffee with a Belfast twist. (A cup of Scotch with a splash of coffee in it. Then you jump from foot to foot, with your hands fixed to your hips.)

'Well, I'd have to say the strangest case I was ever called out to was a case concerning a young Aboriginal chap who was ill in prison.'

'Oh, really?'

'Yes, we call on outback prisons occasionally. I received the call late one evening. The warden called me in. I'd only been in the outback for a few months when it happened.'

'What happened?'

The Englishman wriggled in his seat as he prepared his thoughts. 'Well . . . as I said, I was asked to treat this Aboriginal man in his early twenties who was dying.'

'Of what?'

'That was the problem. Nobody could work out exactly what he was dying *from*. There were no visible signs of anything actually wrong with him . . . yet my prognosis was that he would die soon. When I arrived, his pulse was weak and he was fading fast. We ran tests. Nothing. I'd never seen anything like it. I pleaded with the warden to let me fly him to the nearest hospital, which was quite a distance away. He agreed. When we arrived, the chief surgeon couldn't find anything wrong with him either. X-rays, blood tests, CAT scans, the works. Nothing. Yet this boy was dying. We were all baffled. When he came to briefly, I asked him if he knew what was the cause of this mysterious illness and he told me – through a translator – that he was being "sung".'

'What does that mean?' Barney asked.

'Well, it means that someone from another tribe was "singing" him to death.'

He turned to me. 'Have you heard about this phenomenon before?'

'Yes, but only at Barry Manilow concerts. Go on.'

The doctor drank some coffee. 'You see, this chap had run off with a young woman from another tribe. Therefore, he had subsequently incurred the wrath of the elders. So it had been decreed that he would be "sung". I felt that my only hope was to seek out the clan and ask them to grant this man some sort of tribal clemency and allow him to live.'

Barney pulled a face. 'Doc, don't tell me yer believe he was actually being sung to death.'

'No, of course not. I'm a man of medicine. Of science. Of cause and effect. I was convinced that the illness was psychosomatic. I thought that if I told the chap that the tribe forgave him, he would perhaps recover. It was the only solution I could come up with in the end.

'Anyway, this tribe lived in the remote mountain ranges of the Kimberleys. It was Thursday when I located their camp. They were nestled in caves in some jagged ranges. It took an age to find a place to land. I ultimately found a flat valley and managed a bumpy landing. It was the most inhospitable region I had ever come across. Food certainly must have been scarce.

'After being greeted by a swarm of excited children, I was brought into camp. However, many of the children were ill. And the adults were suffering from all sorts of diseases. Many were in fact blind. It was quite shocking. A multitude of ailments needed urgent treatment: trachoma, ear and chest infections, diabetes, syphilis. Illnesses that are, by western standards, fairly easy to treat. I was quite taken aback, really. I mean, this was the twentieth century after all.'

'Trachoma. That's what Sunfly has, isn't it?' I interrupted.

'The old chap in the pub? No, he has glaucoma.'

'So what happened?' Barney asked, rolling a cigarette.

'I spent the day treating the children and several of the adults. By the evening, I was quite exhausted. Finally, I was led to the tribal elder. Funny, I was so taken aback by their poor standard of health that I'd almost forgotten my original mission. They seated me in a dark cave lit by a small fire. I can remember strange drawings of ghostly faces lining the wall of the cave. They flickered in the firelight, bringing them to life. Human skulls sat in crevices, like an audience of dignitaries at the opera. It was quite eerie, actually. I thought I was alone in the grotto until I heard a wheezing voice call out of the darkness. I jumped out of my skin. Then I saw him. He was a very old man. In his nineties, easily. As black as pitch. All I could really see were two eyes, twinkling at me in the darkness. He spoke in his own language. A young girl entered with a bowed head. She could speak a little English and interpreted for us. One or two of the other older members of the tribe crept in obsequiously. They sat behind her.

'"What brings a whitefella doctor this far into the desert?" he asked through the girl.

'"I have come to ask you to stop the singing of Tommy Kookaburra."

'"He has broken the laws of this tribe and must die," was the reply.

'I thought for a while and said nothing. We all sat in silence. I listened to the ticking of the fire, while the others nervously waited for me to speak. I thought about the prisoner and his love for the girl and the extraordinary risk he must have taken by incurring the ire of the clan. I finally spoke.

'"Only *true* love risks everything. Even death."

'A hush echoed through the cave. It was as if I'd blasphemed in the presence of a saint. The old man leaned into the light of the fire. A slow smile grew on his wrinkled, sapient face.

'"This is true. This is true," the girl relayed.

'With the help of some of the others, the wizened man stood. He raised his twig-like arms. "The singing of Tommy Kookaburra will stop," he commanded.

'I told him I'd return with whitefella medicine to heal the tribe, but he declined the offer. He told me he possessed all the magic needed to heal the ailing tribe. I thought about it for a while and respectfully said: "Trachoma, ear and chest infections, diabetes, syphilis, these are whitefella sickness. Your people never suffered from this sickness before my people – the Englishmen – came to your land. You let me treat the whitefella sickness, you treat the blackfella sickness."

'After careful thought, he smiled. He said, through the girl: "You are a very wise man." Then he gave me a long black feather.'

'Did it have a red tip?' I asked.

'Yes, how on earth did you know?'

'Don't worry. Did he tell you what it meant?' I asked anxiously.

'No.'

'So what happened, doc?' Barney interjected.

'Well, I looked at my watch. It was exactly six-fifteen. Soon it would be dark and difficult to follow the track out of the ranges and then get in the air, so I left some medicine and took off the following morning. I returned with a small medical team some weeks after that.'

'What happened to the guy in prison?' Barney asked, stubbing out his cigarette.

'Well, when I arrived at the prison hospital I was hoping the poor chap would still be alive to relay the good news about the spiritual reprieve. I returned to find him up and about. He ran over and excitedly shook my hand and thanked me over and over again. His lady friend was there at the hospital and she kissed me. I must say, she was the most beautiful girl I'd ever seen. She looked like an Egyptian goddess. I'd be tempted to risk it myself,' he chuckled. 'They told me that Tommy had made a complete recovery. I suspected it was psychosomatic all along, but the speed of his recovery rather caught me off guard.'

'Why?' I asked.

'Well, how did he know my expedition had been successful? I asked myself. I finally deduced that word must have travelled via the infamous bush telegraph. That's how most news travels in the outback. Someone tells someone who tells someone else.'

Barney nodded with a smile.

'Anyway, as I was leaving, just out of curiosity, I glanced at his sheet. It read: "Blood pressure and heartbeat: normal. Patient has gained complete consciousness and has requested food." Then I glanced at the time of this recovery. And do you know what it read?' he asked open-mouthed, eyes as large as moons.

I shook my head.

'Fourteen minutes past six, Thursday evening.'

THE SCORPION STRIKES

I SAT BOLT UPRIGHT IN BED. I'd had another nightmare. I had that potato smell of sweat. With trembling hands, I reached for the pain-killers. As I groped the rustling foil packets, I could hear a queer, unfamiliar sound outside: a pounding rumble that sounded like a team of tennis players serving aces at the tin roof. Ignoring it, I reviewed the latest offering from the unrelenting playhouse of my subconscious. Although the dreams would vary, lately they seemed always to end in the same way: the boy dead, with hundreds of the crab-like insects crawling over his black torso. The intensity of the dreams was remarkable. Apart from the disturbing dreams of my childhood, and the frenzied nightmares I'd had when I first arrived in Venice without my pills, I'd never experienced anything quite like these. These adventures into the surreal were jarringly different from anything I'd experienced previously. It was like Magritte meets Salvador Dali at an acid party. It seemed more real than reality. Was Descartes right? Is there a dual universe, after all? And is it discovered through dreams?

As I sat unravelling the nightmare, the noise continued to peck at the roof of the cottage. Starting to get my head together, I listened to the rumbling clamour more intently. What is that sound? Probably a dust storm throwing gravel and stones against the shack. I listened. I'd never heard this sound in the desert before, yet it seemed vaguely familiar. A comforting sound. A sound from my past. As I lay back on the damp sheets, I looked up at the rotting ceiling. The beating sound against the roof showered me with a light frost of paint. I stared at it with sleepy reasoning.

I got up. I noted a faint smell in the air. A moist scent that I had not smelled since . . . it was almost like . . . it just couldn't be possible! I raced to the window.

Rain.

In fact, it was a downpour. The dripping rain spaghettied against the glass. I walked outside and stood in it for about five incredulous minutes, shaking my head, looking up at the grey sky. Feeling it in my mouth. In my eyelashes. Tasting its sweetness. I took myself inside and then over to the mirror. Dripping, I took my pyjama shirt off. I looked at the bruising around my swollen body that had changed hues daily – from purple to yellow to blue to brown. I got dried and dressed. I sat on the bed. My stomach groaned. I needed to pee. I found an old blanket to cover myself in order to make a dash for the outside toilet (umbrellas being as rare as inside toilets in the desert country). I covered my head and opened the door. I jumped back in fright. Standing at the door, in the deluge, were Sunfly and Simon (someone had given him a pair of shorts and they looked slightly absurd with the knee-high Santa boots). I was surprised to see Simon. The sandstorm had finally blown over and he was due to fly out that morning.

'What are you guys doing here? Come in out of the rain!' (It felt strange saying that.)

'We need your help,' the medico pleaded.

'What's happened?' I shouted over the rain.

'The old man says he's hurt,' said Simon. 'Your friend, Johnny Wishbone.'

'He came to see you? Into town?' I asked quickly, urging Sunfly to come inside, then realising he couldn't see my sleepy gesticulations.

'He come to me in a dream. We must pind im,' the old man said gravely.

I screwed up my face. 'In a dream? Sunfly, you may not have

noticed this, but it's pissing down at the moment.'

'Need your help, Gord.'

'What makes you think I can help you find him?'

'Come, Gord.'

'Oh, Christ.'

I ran inside while they waited on the doorstep. I emerged from the old railway cottage in two odd shoes and an old paint-splattered trench coat that I had found at the café and wore home one chilly evening.

We marched through the wet, tandoori-smeared clay to the desert garden. It was the only place I knew to look. The tepid rain pelted us with heavy drops. As we walked, I fired questions at Sunfly, which he tried to answer. He confessed that he knew Johnny better than he'd first let on. It turned out that he knew the boy's grandfather quite well in the old days. They were trackers for the South Australian police force before Sunfly lost his sight to glaucoma. He spoke about the tribe and the boy's family. As we straddled pockets of water, I noticed that Sunfly, sans walking stick, walked tentatively. He clutched my arm in the slippery mud with surprising strength. He told us that the rain had washed away the tracks he used to follow to find his way around. He felt disorientated. He said he'd usually feel a kind of path, smooth underfoot and he would follow it. If he felt the gibbers press into his feet, he knew he was off course. He could always determine east or west by the direction of the sun against his face. It was that simple. Without the sun, and without the tracks, he was, in fact, blind.

It was slow-going with Sunfly. The journey took twice as long with him shuffling at my arm. On the way I pointed out the old cottage to him. Sunfly said that he had never been inside the cottage because it was haunted by lost souls – whitefella souls. The rain stopped for a while. A soggy hawk flew overhead to beat the next downpour. Visibly stressed, Sunfly was uncharacteristically talkative. He spoke of Hopetown, kindly filling in a few details about the town's ephemeral history.

He said he grew up there and it was once a grand town. It was intended to be the granary for South Australia, after explorers discovered the Great Artesian Basin and decreed the arid zone open to farmers. Despite the warnings from the local tribe, the remote hamlet was built too close to the dunes and was subsequently entombed by them. He even vaguely pointed to its direction (which I couldn't confirm either way). He said he could ascertain its direction because hawks always flew to Hopetown to hunt parrots that bathed and drank at a waterhole behind the town. I looked up. Leaden clouds hung heavy in the purple sky as we continued to trail the meandering line through the desert.

We finally arrived at the sandhill that encircled the desert garden. The flowers seemed to sing Puccini arias to the welcome soak. And there he was, sitting cross-legged among the flowers. He looked fine. I felt a slight irritation with Sunfly for panicking me unnecessarily.

'Glad to see you're okay, I've brought an old friend of yours with me,' I yelled, struggling up the sloppy sandhill. The boy sat motionless, in the lotus position, staring over the soggy desert.

'Crazy old man was worried about you!' I burbled, feeling suddenly ill at ease.

Sunfly hollered from the line. 'No good, Gordo. Dat little blackpella in de place of his dreaming.'

I nudged Johnny on the shoulder. He fell over onto his side. He had been beaten unconscious.

Trembling, I appealed to Simon for help. Seal-like, he bolted up the dune, boots flopping like flippers. Calmly, he felt Johnny's pulse. 'He's still alive,' he said in a relaxed tone.

'HELP HIM! Please, do something!' I screamed.

'We need a kadaitja man, now. Spirit man,' Sunfly shouted from the sandhill.

Simon fell into the medical ritual of checking various parts of his patient's body. Sunfly clambered over to us, sedately picked up a handful of mud, groped for the body, and smeared it over the boy's chest. Then he sketched ancient symbols on his wet torso. The drawings looked like waves and ancient sea creatures. He stood up and gazed blindly over the desert, listening to the whistling wind.

Rain dribbled from the sky. Thick clouds smacked together and let out an enormous crack of thunder that reverberated across the sodden plains. I jumped. White light flickered at the edges of the horizon. Sunfly stood over Johnny, singing in a tortured whining voice. Then Simon and I, stumbling and lurching through the sticky sand, carried Johnny back to the café. While Simon bundled Johnny into the Cessna to whisk him off to hospital, I made a crackled staccato statement to our man in blue, Dave, over the Cessna's radio.

In a state of shock, I stumbled back to the station house. It smelled musty. I got out of my wet clothes and, standing in my damp underwear, made a cup of tea. Timpani rumbles of thunder sounded in the distance. I sipped stewed tea and thought. I felt bad about Johnny. Very bad. The people who had attacked him had probably trailed him after he led me out of the sandstorm.

A tidal wave of despair washed over me. Rain started to snare-drum on the tin roof echoing the hollow emptiness I now felt. I'd almost started to believe Johnny possessed some kind of secret magic. A magic that could keep us all safe. In the end he was just a confused kid who lived in the desert. He didn't have the answers or possess the secret knowledge. It was all bullshit.

I felt cynicism creeping back into my soul that afternoon – like in the old days. I suddenly felt like the protagonist in an existentialist novel. Meandering through life like an unfeeling android. I vomited.

I walked over to the sink and washed the yellow vomit from my T-shirt. I felt sorry for myself. For Johnny. For Sunfly. I had never thought too much about the indigenous people of this country before I fled the city. They were the forgotten people. Australia's secret country. Being honest with myself, my concern for their struggle was as meaningful as the Che Guevara poster on the back of my door when I was at the Conservatorium. It was cool and radical and guaranteed to get you laid if you were lucky enough to talk a uni student into your bedroom. Like most young white Australians at that time, I was more concerned with the black struggle in South Africa than the black struggle on my own doorstep. I even had friends who picked coffee in Nicaragua in support of the socialist struggle against the US imperialists. At home and at school we learnt more about the Holocaust than the genocide of my fellow countrymen. It wasn't until now, with it rubbed in my face like a puppy who had pissed on the carpet, that its profound and tragic significance truly struck me.

Now in my thirties, I had graduated from being a pseudo-socialist to a full card-carrying member of the Complete and Utter Selfish Bastard Party. I seldom read the newspaper because 'I found it depressing' and my commitment to the exposition of social injustice never took precedence over my commitment to wriggling out of it. I suddenly felt angry with myself for these new-found allegiances of conscience. After all, I had come to the desert to escape internal conflict and ethical responsibility.

I snatched the pills that Simon had given me. It irritated me that Simon was so matter-of-fact about Johnny lying there half dead.

I guillotined the pills finely with a razor blade, dissolved them in a glass of Scotch, and downed the foul mixture. As the medicated booze started to take effect I felt my heart slow and the muscles in and around my neck slacken. I threw myself onto my squeaking bed. I felt exhausted. My eyelids felt as though they were made of stone. I closed them for a second.

⌒

Someone knocked at the door. I drowsily answered it. It was

Johnny. He led me outside and into the desert. I was stumbling along the burning red sand. Then I saw it. The black cockatoo. It was gigantic. It was the size of a Boeing 747. I found myself chasing it. Johnny trailed me, watching in silence. The parrot's great shadow oozed across an unfathomable plain of scorching red sand and glistening gibbers. I was desperate to hold the great bird. To drag it into my soul. To touch the magical feathers and be catapulted into nirvana. A plum-coloured sky arched overhead. Suddenly I was a moth, flying, ricocheting off the dunes like a dodgem car as I tried to reach the bird. Dexter Gordon was blowing an echoing version of 'I'm a Fool to Want You' on a windswept dune. I could hear Dex's drooling tone crackle with saliva and breath as it echoed across the desert. I felt the music burrowing into the meandering crevices of my skull. Dexter soloed as the great bird hovered overhead, shrouding him in inky shadow. I watched the parrot grow smaller in the sky. Till it disappeared. Up. Up. Up into heaven. My splintered wings fell from my body. Like a discarded angel. I was human again.

I heard a voice behind me. I turned around. It was a little boy. Tears dribbled down the toddler's face as he glared at me with hateful, dark eyes. He reminded me of the little boy I'd seen in photos of myself when my mother was alive. He was babbling at me in a high-pitched voice. Screwing up his mouth. Crying. Snot and tears glazing his red face.

I walked over to him. I gently kissed him on the forehead. His crying spluttered to a stop. A slow smile crept across his face. He ran off, skipping into the desert. Singing.

☙

I woke, shaking and sweating. I cried. And cried. And cried. Eventually, rubbing my eyes that were like two pieces of puffed corn, I fell back to sleep.

BEES OF A FEATHER

∽

I SCRIBBLED THE REMAINING lyrics of the song while rain played nocturnes on the tin roof of the café. I'd spent a couple of lazy hours reflecting on the events of the past year in the desert. Johnny had died in hospital. They never did find out who did it. It wasn't just one person, Dave said. He said it must have been about three or four. Three or four people who I probably drank with at the wake at the pub. The funeral was awful. The crematorium was a sweaty, three-hour drive from Venice and Sunfly, Dave, Barney, Joe, Max, the Rev and I were the only ones there. Johnny had no family. I wrote to his adopted parents in Sydney, but they wrote back saying they were unable to come as they were attending a conference on 'spiritual healing'. Reverend Fruit said some nice words for a change – quite moving, actually. As the coffin went through the little red velvet curtains, Sunfly sang in that soft, whiny drone of his. And then it was over, leaving me feeling numb.

⌒

The lights on the Christmas tree winked at me from the counter. I continued sipping some gluey black coffee. With the rain, the café had that mossy smell of damp. I was packed and ready to leave. I looked at the airline ticket. Checked the spelling on the name. I looked at Ruth's address. I folded them neatly in my pocket. Yes, it was time. Moving on would mean facing up to the unfulfilled dreams and desires of my life. It would be trite to say: to face the music, but it was a somewhat apt analogy. I had run away from my music, my feelings, my fears for the past year. Leaving the outback meant coming to terms with them all again. But I felt stronger. I would cope.

I gazed out the window. Rainfall in the desert is such an incongruous event. Peering through the rain-streaked window was like looking into one of those kitsch, water-filled paperweights where, when shaken, snow falls on a plastic beach in Hawaii. I reviewed the smudgy handwriting that scrawled across the napkin. I had begun the song when I arrived in Venice. Now it was complete. It was stained with a chain of coffee-cup rings that looked like an Olympic symbol for the disabled games. I downed some more coffee and read the lyrics, mouthing the words.

*Life just seems to pass me by,
as if waiting for a train,
it rushes past the station house,
and hollers out my name,
I wander down the lonely streets,
they're all the same it seems,
they always seem to lead me to the same old place,
near the bay,
a small café,
called 'Broken Dreams'.*

*There was a time when I knew love,
a time with no regrets,
a time before I drowned myself,
in coffee and cigarettes,
the hopes I hoped for,
the dreams I dreamed,
are quite funny now it seems,
I never thought I'd end up in this lonely place,*

this old café,
this cheap palais,
called 'Broken Dreams'.

Once I opened the door,
to my lonely heart,
you simply walked right in,
and lit the flame,
under the spell of amour,
I simply fell apart,
it seemed our love affair,
was not the same.

But memories fade like dying orchids,
and weeds just take their place,
and the lines of grief and grey of sadness,
in time become your face,
I wander through this lonely life,
like a moon who's lost its beams,
like a soul who slipped,
and fell from heaven,
to find his way,
to a cheap café,
called 'Broken Dreams'.

I folded the napkin and placed it in my pocket. I stared at Joe. Joe looked despondent that afternoon. I discovered it was *Joe* who had smashed up the café. Apparently, Ruth finally came clean and told him she was Jewish. To be frank, I thought Joe knew. The fact that she was Ruth Lieberwitz from Queens; her father was a kosher butcher; she went to school at Mount Sinai College for Young Ladies, and would often start sentences with 'Old Rabbi Bernstein always used to say . . .' should have given her away. But while Joe suspected, he had been too afraid to come out and ask her. Things had gone too far. He was in love with her the minute he clapped eyes on her. And she him. So they both avoided the subject. I suppose Ruth felt she had to mention it in the end. After all, Joe was a fanatical anti-Semite. It could be tricky at parties and bar mitzvahs. She left Joe a fifteen-page letter, pleading with him to forget the past and come and live with her. She eventually wanted to go back with him to Jerusalem. Start a new life. He asked me, sniggering cynically, if an Arab and a Jew living in Palestine wasn't the craziest idea that I'd ever heard. I told him I thought the idea was beautiful. We talked about it for hours, but in the end, he tore up the letter and stormed off to the pub.

☙

Joe, hot palms under his chin, gazed out the café window from the counter. I followed suit. We both sat staring into the soggy desert in silence. I wasn't sure how Joe felt about my leaving. We hadn't really talked about it except briefly when Joe gave me the Valiant. (He had bought a Land Rover in Coober Pedy after getting used to driving Ruth's.) I plucked a coin from the register and dropped it into the jukebox. Peggy Lee singing 'Street of Dreams' crackled out of the old machine and into the crevices of the café.

'I spose we should be happy bout rain,' Joe muttered to himself.

'Poor old Barney was jumping for joy – for about *five* minutes. Now it's a flood. Poor bastard. Sheep are drowning, roads washed away . . . life's cruel out here, isn't it, Joe?'

Joe lit a cigarette. 'Yeah, I feel sorry for the farmers. But life's cruel for us all, my fren.' As the brown smoke elbowed its way through the gaps in his teeth, he said, 'That missus of yours is a lovely lady.'

'Yes, she is.'

'You should go back to her and make baby, my fren.'

'I'm not good with kids. *I've* got to grow up first.'

Staring into the desert, and without looking at me, he said, 'I had a kid once.' He blew out some smoke with a sigh. 'Beautiful wife, too.'

I put down my cup with a clink. 'You're kidding? You've never mentioned this before. Where are they now? What happened to them?'

⌢

That day, Joe pulled out photos and scratchy slides and old super-8 home movies. I saw his wife and child. I saw his house. His car. His old neighbourhood. I saw the cedar-lined park where he used to take his daughter. It was funny seeing him so young and so thin!

After a bit of gentle prodding, Joe revisited the ordeal of his final days in Palestine. We talked for a couple of hours, me mostly listening in stunned silence.

His wife's name was Yvette. She wasn't Palestinian, but Lebanese. She was a nurse who came to Palestine to work in a nearby hospital. Joe had met her when he needed a cut stitched above his eye. To impress the young nurse, he sang 'Love Me Tender' as Elvis. It made her laugh so much that she had a pain in her stomach. Out of embarrassment, he laughed too. A man who can laugh at himself is a good man, she told him, and they started to see each other regularly.

They fell hopelessly in love. She became pregnant and they married. It was a modest ceremony in a tiny stone church in Jerusalem. (She too was Christian.) For their honeymoon, they rented a wooden sailboat and drifted in the Dead Sea for a week, getting to know the other's hopes and dreams as never before.

They eventually settled into everyday life. Joe, working as an entertainer on tour, found it difficult to be away from Yvette and the baby for long periods. He eventually abandoned show biz, and found a job as a chef in Gaza. This is where he learned to 'cook so well'.

A few years later, the doors of hell swung open. The Israelis entered the city. After the Israeli occupation, the town was completely sealed. It was tricky to get out. The occupying force was ferreting out suspected terrorists and collaborators with the savoir faire of the Gestapo on amphetamines. Joe decided to get his family out. The plan was to drive north through Tel Aviv and across the border into Southern Lebanon to start a new life.

Joe and Yvette planned the exodus down to the last detail. Joe had a fake Lebanese passport. If necessary, the silver-tongued Joe would bribe the border guards and drive through Israel to Lebanon where Yvette had family waiting. As soon as they got to Lebanon, they would be okay. In hindsight, it was a decision born of panic. He really had little to fear from the Israelis at the time, but could see the situation deteriorating. Also, many of his friends had fled and he felt it was safer for his young family to be out of the West Bank and in the relative safety of Beirut, the 'Paris of the Middle East', as it was then known.

He would have preferred to move away from the Middle East entirely, but it wasn't that easy. Months prior to the hostilities, Joe had applied for visas to the USA, but found it a slow and arduous process. It seemed every man in Palestine would have gladly given his left testicle to immigrate to 'the land of the free' at the time of the occupation. So, like everyone else, Joe was put on a long waiting list.

After obtaining fake papers and successfully negotiating several Israeli checkpoints, he tentatively drove through a hostile Jerusalem. Although things had calmed slightly, he did have Palestinian plates on the car, so there were times when people spat and threw rocks at the vehicle as he passed. His three-year-old daughter was terrified. To comfort the child, Joe and Yvette sang little Arabic nursery rhymes.

They felt quietly confident as they watched the last of Tel Aviv disappear behind them. As they motored through the fawn-coloured, meandering countryside of northern Israel, Joe and his wife plotted and planned their new life together with wide-eyed enthusiasm. As they sped towards the border they could see the purple and yellow mountains of Southern Lebanon in the distance.

They reached the final checkpoint. Joe felt a knot the size of a bowling ball in his stomach as two pimply soldiers hovered zealously at the boom gate. They looked like children with toy guns, he told me. The tyres squelched to a halt on the gravel. Joe fumbled in his top pocket for their passports and limbered his tongue for the final spiel. The young soldiers asked them for their papers in SS tones.

The adolescent guard, with a moustache that could have been easily removed with a piece of dry toast, spoke in an unsteady, pubescent voice. For fun, the other youth shoved the tip of his M15 up Yvette's nostril and then perversely in her mouth. She bore this bravely.

Joe coolly reassured the young soldiers that everything was in order and that they should relax. He offered them an American cigarette. They greedily snatched the packet. So he gave them a carton. It wasn't long before Joe had the guards laughing and Yvette breathed a sigh of relief. As tensions eased, the guards walked back to their pillbox to call their base and confirm Joe's story (something about medical supplies).

After much discussion, the pimply guards returned to inform Joe that he could not pass and that he would have to return to police headquarters in Jerusalem immediately.

Joe rested his head on the wheel. Sunny Lebanon stood three tantalising metres away. They only had to make it across the border. The soldiers' jurisdiction ended on this side and they would not enter Southern Lebanon (not at that time) to retrieve him. Then he noticed Yvette's family, miniatures at the end of the highway. Her brother waved a flat cloth cap. Joe looked across the plains. The mountains seemed to almost beckon him forth. A trembling Yvette could see what her husband was thinking. In an urgent whisper she mouthed: 'NO!'

Joe could hear the guards chattering on the radio as he deliberated with panicky logic. He banged his fat fist against the steering wheel. They had come so far, he thought. It wasn't fair! Suddenly another car pulled up behind him and the young soldiers wandered over to speak with the new driver. He flipped a coin in the air and called 'Heads'.

He looked at his trembling wife and daughter. He watched Yvette's brother nervously pacing in the distance. Then he gazed at the new life that lay metres in front of them all. A life of security and peace. A life without the fear of soldiers dragging you from your bed in the middle of the night. A life without the fear of police stopping you in the street and holding you on trumped-up charges. He looked at his wife and child again. He looked at the mountains. He looked at the coin that had landed neatly on the dash: Heads.

He dropped his foot on the accelerator and floored it – turning the plywood boom gate into splinters. He looked at the cloud of hazelnut dust in the rear-view mirror. He could faintly hear the soldiers screaming at him to stop and turn back. They sounded like boys in a schoolyard.

Joe drove like a drag racer. He was now in Lebanon. He'd made it through the final checkpoint. The skies seemed bluer and sun shone brighter. Almost instantly. Yvette's family grew larger in the windscreen. He could see their worried faces urging him forward.

The soldiers, not being sticklers about international law, sprayed the car with machine-gun fire. Joe frantically looked over his shoulder and back to the road in front of him. Aside from spider webs of cracked glass in the back, everything seemed okay. The vehicle tore along the highway without impediment. Yvette clutched Joe's hand and smiled. He kissed her. They drove on to the new life that awaited them. Joe laughed uproariously, mocking the guards. Then he sang. He sang loudly over the gunfire. But when he got to the huddle of relatives waiting on the other side, his wife and daughter were slumped and their blood was pooling.

Life in Lebanon was depressing. Naturally, Joe blamed his own recklessness for his family's death. It hung heavy around him. Everything seemed to remind him of them. Other Palestinian families had escaped to Southern Lebanon. Every child's laugh or mother's call was a knife in his gut. He needed to escape – this time it was his own pangs of conscience that made him a refugee.

Someone had told him that while it was a painstaking process to emigrate to the USA, there *was* a western country that would take him without question. A country that – so long as you weren't black or Asian and could be bothered to fill in the forms – would accept you. In fact, it would pay the bulk of your passage as an added incentive.

When he arrived at the Embassy, he had to be shown on the map where this 'golden land of opportunity' exactly was. A dishevelled bureaucrat in a polyester beige suit, with a lattice of broken capillaries across his face, spun a globe and enthusiastically pointed to this blessed continent of desperados. He flashed a yellow smile and said: 'No worries.' It was far enough, Joe thought. Far away enough to run from the pain. And he liked what the Australian official had said. No worries. This would become his new mantra.

When he landed in Perth in the 1970s, he couldn't get over the contrast with Gaza. At home the streets had been rivers of sweating flesh. But Australia was a vacuum. So quiet. So still. In Gaza there had always been noise. The nasal chant of a Muslim cleric at sunset. The aviary hum of the market sellers. The punctuation mark of a distant gun shot. This emptiness was a new sensation. A few months later he found himself in the opal fields of Coober Pedy. Being a lazy prospector, he found little opal but was good at cards and won the café in a tight game of poker. This much I already knew.

Joe finished the tale and slowly pulled a tiny Arabic coin out of his pocket. He placed it on the table.

'Is that the coin you flipped?' I asked.

He nodded.

He got up, walked over to the window and stared at the jacaranda-coloured clouds that streaked across the pink sky. He stood behind me and blew a swirl of copper smoke at the window. With a sigh, he then walked into his room and threw himself on the bed and smoked cigarettes, staring at the ceiling – shoelaces of tears across his face.

⌢

The screen door violined open and a tough-looking backpacker in muddied army boots stomped up to the counter. His hair was shortly cropped and he wore a faded combat jacket. He had a badly broken nose and a collection of pink scars around his checkerboard eyebrows. He was wringing wet. His clothes and pack dripped onto the linoleum floor. The stranger smiled and, in a deep country voice, asked me for a cup of coffee.

'Just passing through?' I asked, pouring the coffee.

'I'm headed to The Globe Hotel.'

'Know your way there?'

'Yeah. I know it,' he said, drying his hair with some paper napkins. 'Though it's been quite a while.' He downed the dregs of the coffee. 'Thanks.'

As he opened his wallet to pay, his I.D. flashed. It read: 'Lt Anthony Tripplechurch.'

'Does a guy called Max still run the place?' he asked.

'Yeah, I believe he does.'

'Right. Say hello to the "Italian" for me.'

'I will. Good luck,' I said knowingly.

'Thanks, I'll need it.'

He stepped out into the soggy afternoon light. Through the glass he mouthed the words 'Merry Christmas'.

I picked up a broom and swept up the mud he had brought in with him. It was the last time I would sweep the floor of the café.

I thought about Joe. Cruel how life was so short for those trying to hold on to something, yet so terribly long for those trying to let go.

⌢

The soldier tramped down the muddy main street of Venice. Artfully negotiating the carrot-juice puddles. As he walked past the post office and up the street, he passed the ruined church with the crazy priest in a Jesus T-shirt, shorts and thongs, delivering a sermon to a drunken man and his itching dog. His arms, a sonata of gestures.

At last he saw it. It was just as he pictured it in his mind. With its biscuit-yellow sandstone walls and rusting tin roof that flecked in the wind like red snow. He stood outside for a while, plucking up the courage to enter. He stepped onto the verandah. He stood at the door. A urethral smell seeped under it. Strangely, it was a comforting smell. A smell from his childhood. He listened to the low drone of slurring voices behind the door. He took a deep breath and entered the smoke-filled room.

He looked around. Familiar faces. He saw the balding postman (now, miraculously with hair) mumbling to himself and quietly getting drunk in a corner. The old Aborigine, sipping rum and listening to the wind. A couple of farmers drowning their sorrows with the usual talk of selling up and leaving, and a crusty, little red-faced barman weeping and throwing his fleshy arms around him.

⌢

I said my goodbyes to Joe. I gave him some stuff. My coat, my wok, some books he'd never read. We stood in the doorway of the café. The sky glowed lilac through the clouds.

'Good luck in New York, my fren. Send me postcard,' he said in an unsteady voice.

'I'm not going to New York, Joe. I'm going home. To Sydney.'

'You're joking? Why?'

I paused and looked out into the desert. It looked clean. Like it had almost been freshly polished for my departure. I felt the wind tickling my lashes.

Overlooking the desert, I spoke. 'What if we're all interconnected in some way? I used to lie in the wildflowers for hours with Johnny. He used to talk about bees a lot. He used to say that for the honeybee, the honey is everything. You see, the bee thinks its sole purpose in life is to find honey and build the hive. But inadvertently, it cross-pollinates the flowers. Nature has its own grand plan that's beyond the bee's comprehension.' I turned to him. 'What if we're like bees, Joe?'

'What do you mean?' he said. 'Then what's *our* true purpose?'

'Love. Just to love, Joe.'

I put the ticket – now made out in his name – and Ruth's address in his hand before throwing my slim belongings in the boot. I saw him staring at it, open-mouthed. As I drove, I watched Joe grow smaller in the rear-view mirror.

⌢

I called in on Sunfly to say farewell. He lived in a rusting blue shipping container on a hill that overlooked a vast saltpan. The makeshift house had a fluorescent blue tarpaulin stretched over poles at the front as a kind of crude verandah. I found him sitting outside on the little cushioned oil drums that served as seats. The tarp sagged under a pond of water over his head.

'Dat you, Gord?'

'Yes, I'm leaving. I came to say goodbye.'

He nodded, sagely.

'Thanks for everything, Sunfly.'

'You going to New York?'

'No. Home. To Sydney.'

'You giving up music?'

'No. Not at all. I've tried that but it won't give me up, it seems,' I chuckled. 'No, I'm going home to find out what music means, again. To get in touch with the magic that first drew me to it. It seems I've lost it somewhere along the way.' I kicked the muddied earth. 'If I've learned anything from Johnny, it's to live in the moment. I've always lived in the past: my childhood. Or the future: trying to "make it". I've never lived in the now. From this moment on, Sunfly, I'm going to live every precious moment of my life in the present. In the now. Like Johnny did. You see, Johnny led me to the answers that were staring me in the face. I've been looking for truth. The one truth in my life is my love for Jenny.'

He nodded and smiled. 'Johnny say, if you go home, gib you dis.' He went inside and returned with a long black feather. He handed it to me like a jeweller handling a priceless diamond necklace.

'What does it mean? I *have* to know.'

That was when Sunfly told me the ancient story of the black cockatoo feather.

⌒

In the Dreamtime, a man called Pijarra left his family and tribe in search of the prized black cockatoo feather. With this sacred feather, he would obtain wisdom. And with this wisdom, the meaning of life.

Pijarra spent his whole life in search of this feather. He would wander the desert each day and each night and he would pray to the spirits of the Dreamtime to help him in his quest. He abandoned his wife and family and friends. Many years passed. His children grew up and his wife became old and bitter.

One day he saw his reflection in a billabong. He touched his face. He saw that he was an old man. Tired and weary, he started to cry. He suddenly realised his life had passed him by. He said to the spirits: 'I have given up my whole life to search for the feather of the black cockatoo. Now I am an old man. I am giving up my search to return to my family and enjoy every precious moment I have left with them.'

At that moment, a great shadow fell over his frail body. He looked up at the sky to see a black cockatoo hovering above him. It circled slowly and mysteriously. As he gazed up at the great bird, a long, black feather slowly drifted down to earth at his feet. He picked it up. He had found wisdom.

⌒

I looked at the jet-black feather on the dash. I then gazed out the window as the desert streamed past in a sea of colour. A veritable galaxy of wild flowers covered the landscape after the life-giving soak. Tiny fragments of colour were scattered amongst the sand. Jewels. The wind cajoled and teased them as they collectively swayed in the breeze to their own magical caprice.